THE WITCH AND THE WATCHER

BOOK 2

Laura Detering

ISBN: 978-1-7351404-3-8 (ebook)
ISBN: 978-1-7351404-2-1 (paperback)
LCCN:2021391347

Interior Formatting: Evenstar Books
Book cover Designer: Moor Books Design
Editor: Erin Darling

Second printing edition 2024.

Visit the author's website at lauradetering.com

For Maya and Zoey
Thank you for being my reason
You both inspire and drive me daily
I love you times infinity and beyond

Contents

Part I: Illinois

Chapter 1 - Valentine's Gram ... 1
Chapter 2 - 1, 2, 3 Jump! ... 19
Chapter 3 - Like a Candle ... 32
Chapter 4 - Thundernation! ... 42
Chapter 5 - Flowers for All ... 54
Chapter 6 - A, B, C-Ya ... 73
Chapter 7 - Pizza ... 89
Chapter 8 - History Lesson ... 100
Chapter 9 - Let Me Show You ... 111

Part II: Cristes

Chapter 10 - Nicholas: The Day I Met *Her* ... 127
Chapter 11 - Mara: The Dark Mood ... 132
Chapter 12 - Nicholas: Above Water ... 134
Chapter 13 - Mara: Into the Woods ... 144
Chapter 14 - Nicholas: Our Cave ... 148
Chapter 15 - Nicholas: Mine ... 159
Chapter 16 - Nicholas: The Apprentice ... 174
Chapter 17 - Nicholas: Azure Summit ... 188
Chapter 18 - Nicholas: They Found Us ... 195
Chapter 19 - Nicholas: Six Weeks Later ... 202
Chapter 20 - Mara: Not "No" ... 211
Chapter 21 - Nicholas: Argentang Your Way to My Heart ... 213

Chapter 22 - Nicholas: Final Rehearsal   227

Chapter 23 - Mara: Carnival   233

Chapter 24 - Nicholas: Roaring Like a Lion   240

Chapter 25 - Nicholas: Aftermath   252

Chapter 26 - Nicholas: I'm Sorry   262

Chapter 27 - Mara: Promise Ring   268

Chapter 28 - Mara: Broken Promises Make   276
             for Broken Magic

Chapter 29 - Mara: Full of Surprises   286

Chapter 30 - Mara: Fall of Mara   297

Chapter 31 - Nicholas: Something Dark   303

Chapter 32 - Nicholas: Secrets   314

Chapter 33 - Nicholas: Public Humiliation   320

Part III: Back to the Present

Chapter 34 - Time   343

Chapter 35 - Wow, What a Coincidence   349

Chapter 36 - Power Rangers Sans Costume   356

Chapter 37 - Mortal Kombat   363

Chapter 38 - Blindsided   374

Chapter 39 - Spring Showcase   383

Chapter 40 - The Coward   391

Chapter 41 - A Good Drama   399

Chapter 42 - I Can't Leave   406

Chapter 43 - Taken   410

Chapter 44 - Time to Wake Up   416

Chapter 45 - Honeycomb   426

Chapter 46 - I'll Kill Him   434

Chapter 47 - Hammock Dunes   441

Chapter 48 - 'Til Death Do Us Part   457

Chapter 49 - It's So Hard to Say Goodbye   470

Chapter 50 - No Sleeping Theory   480

Chapter 51 - Pizza, Pizza   495

Chapter 52 - Big Girls Don't Cry   502

Acknowledgments

About the Author

Pronunciation Guide

Abishai: *Ah-beh-shy*

Abaddon: *Aa-bad-din*

Arbolias: *Are-bow-lee-us*

Berrouet: *Bear-roo-et*

Cristes Aventus: *Crease-tis Uh-ven-tis*

Eira: *i- Rah*

Ellasyn: *Ella-sin*

Hellebore Niger: *Hel-leh-bore Ny-jur*

Mara: *Mar-uh*

Melchior: *Mel-key-or*

Melohym: *May-low-him*

Nicholas Klaus: *Knee-ko-lus Clow-ss*

Pas de deux: *Paa-Duh-Dur*

Steelee: *Steal-lee*

Tasi: *Tah-See*

Tevo: *Tay-vo*

Part I

ILLINOIS

Valentine's Gram

ICK'S ABSENCE WAS A HEAVY WEIGHT upon our shoulders. Six weeks. It'd been six weeks since he left to collect and deliver Christmas roses to Cristes. He was only supposed to be gone for a few days.

Though I didn't know Nick well, I couldn't help but be worried about him. He had told me trips to the realm of Cristes were difficult, but he'd also assured me that he had successfully done it many times before. Selfishly, I also feared what would happen to us.

A witch wanted me dead. She wanted Will to exact her revenge and become queen of Cristes. Will and I had only recently learned we were Watchers and yet we knew virtually nothing about our gifts or how to wield them. If she attacked me again, whether in person or my dreams, how would I stop her? Will and I needed Nick, and I was desperate to start training.

Naturally, like in a game of telephone, no one at school had the correct story regarding how I was attacked after the winter formal. Well, no one except for my closest friends and Justin. Weeks on end filled with awkward glances and intrusive stares were enough to make my blood boil.

One sophomore girl, Heather something, became the first and only victim of my roiling frustration in the last week of January. As I walked down the hall, her eyes were like an owl's as they stared at me, wide and unblinking. She'd been talking to her friends, acting as if she knew me and the true details of the assault that nearly succeeded in killing me if Alex hadn't come in at the last second and saved me. Heather either didn't realize it or didn't care that I'd overheard her.

"Is there something you'd like to say to me?" I boomed.

"N-n-no," she stammered, her eyes darting as she realized there was a small audience beyond the safety of her friends.

"Perhaps I have something in my teeth or toilet paper on my shoe?" I sneered, turning slowly for emphasis. "I mean, you have been staring at me since I turned the corner." She shook her head.

My conscience got the better of me as the red flushing her cheeks and water pricking at the corners of her eyes finally registered. I decided to address the crowd instead of singling her out again.

"Listen, whatever happened after the dance is the business of those involved, no one else's! It was an accident and no one's fault. So, everyone needs to quit staring at me all the time like I'm some circus act. You aren't invisible; I can hear you, you know. This ends now!" I stormed toward my next class at the very end of the hall. Will had been observing me as he waited in the cove of a nearby classroom door.

"Don't start with me," I cautioned as he caught up to me.

"Wouldn't dream of it. I'm proud of you for sticking up for yourself, though I do feel a little bad for that blonde girl."

I sighed. "I said don't start."

Will shrugged and began walking with me to class.

"Ugh, you're so annoying sometimes!" I said, as waves of the guilt he was feeling hit me.

He chuckled as I turned and ran to catch up with Heather. When I tapped her shoulder, she jumped back and my stomach knotted with my own guilt.

"Heather, right? I wanted to apologize for yelling at you. Granted, everyone staring all the time and talking about you as if you aren't standing right there is not fun—" Will cleared his throat and intentionally sent me ripples of calm that coaxed my nerves. "But still. That's no excuse to berate you like that, let alone in front of others."

"Thank you," Heather breathed.

It's not only about me, though. It bothers me to hear Justin's name get dragged through the mud. He's still my friend and a good guy. "Could you help me with something?"

"Sure," she whispered.

"Could you make sure people know that Justin was also a victim like me? That he and I are still friends?" She nodded.

The staring stopped...for a week. However, thanks to Coach R. calling me out in dance for wearing jewelry, it started back up again. Now, everyone couldn't help but notice the rather extravagant friendship ring on my right ring finger.

When Will first gave it to me, I embarrassed myself by assuming he was proposing. In my defense, it did look a lot like an engagement ring. But I hated attention, so when those questioning stares inevitably fixated on the hexagonal opal, I'd have to restrain myself from yanking it off and stashing it in my backpack. I'd made a promise to Will, though, one where I had committed to wearing it as a symbol of our unshakeable friendship.

But in the wake of my near-death experience, I found myself making another promise— to not care so much about others' opinions, and to stay true to what my heart wanted. I knew I loved Will, and admitting that to myself was freeing. So, I kept the ring on and held my head high, relishing in the confusion among the people who once knew me as the "Miss Independent" Liddy Erickson.

As I walked toward the cafeteria, my eyes scanned all the colorful paper heart decorations, which meant Valentine's Day was right around the corner. Thanks to the student council's push to sell Valentine's Day grams in support of the athletic department, hundreds of hearts were plastered over almost every inch of available wall space all around the school. Most of the signs were cheesy, especially the one that transformed the mirror in the girls' bathroom into a button and read, "You're cute as a button."

I first began loathing the Hallmark holiday back in middle school. The awkwardness of boys trying to woo their "girlfriends" of only a few days or weeks, their voices and hands shaky, made me cringe.

I remember one boy, Kirk, with beads of sweat on his upper lip, practically throwing a teddy bear at a bewildered Ashley before mumbling something and running off to his class. I'm sure all the boys wasted their meager savings or allowances on meaningless trinkets procured from the drugstore. After all, attempting to live up to those Kay Jewelers or 1-800-Flowers commercials can't be easy.

I thought middle school gift exchanges were bad, but high school blew them out of the water. The small teddy bears or boxes of candy were replaced with wild displays— a competition to see who could profess their love the best. Bouquets of balloons; two-dozen dyed roses; song dedications during morning announcements; graffitiing each other's cars with liquid chalk; long, graphic make-out sessions in between classes... *Barf.* I never understood the need to publicly show someone love simply because some made-up holiday expects me to.

Sara believes I hate Valentine's Day because of a public incident with my freshman-year boyfriend, Ryland. He'd gotten me a ginormous, red case of conversation hearts, which he fumbled while handing to me. Hundreds of hearts spilled all over the hallway. My cheeks burned, and as I dropped down to pick them up, Ryland joked about my butterfingers to the many students staring and laughing, then hightailed it to class. Luckily Sara was there to help me. I shuddered at the memory as I walked past the attendance office.

I entered the busy commons, my attention snagged by two folding tables positioned to the left of the cafeteria's entrance. Taped to the tables were signs that proclaimed "*V-Day Grams: $1*" in pink and red bubble letters. Alex sat there, his gaze locked on me, which seemed to annoy Jackie, who appeared to be in the middle of a conversation with him.

"Hey, Liddy! Come over here," he yelled across the foyer, beckoning me with his pointer finger.

Jackie rolled her eyes as I approached. Alex stood and winked at me, his mischievous grin following suit. Before winter formal, I would've recoiled at his blatant flirting. However, my opinion of Alex, though he was still arrogant much of the time, improved considerably after he saved my life. He had changed that night for the better; he no longer made crude, chauvinistic comments about me or my body. His flirting, I realized, was harmless.

Alex, in my opinion, was becoming a gentleman, though I doubted Jackie felt the same in this moment given he was completely ignoring her. I turned a blind eye to Jackie's scowl and, when she finally acknowledged me, I offered her a sincere smile before returning my focus to Alex. Mara's attack had taught me life was too short to hold grudges.

"Hey, Alex."

"'Sup, Lid? Buy a Valentine's Day gram and support our athletic department?" He leaned over the table, pulled me into a hug, and gestured to the stacks of paper hearts sorted by color. "Our new water polo team could use the help."

Jackie gagged. "We don't need *her* support."

"Every little bit helps," Alex responded, not bothering to look at her, a saccharine sweetness coating his words.

"As if she even has anyone to give one to."

Except for my closest friends, no one knew that Will and I were officially a couple. This provided an excellent excuse to avoid any PDA. My cheeks heated.

Alex's eyes flashed to Jackie and she cowered ever so slightly. "Liddy has plenty of people who love her. In fact, I think she has received the most hearts so far—" the deep line between his brows smoothed out and he smiled— "And I'm sure she has plenty of people in her life that she cares for. Of course, it could also just be a gesture of friendship."

On the first day back from winter break, I slipped a small envelope into Alex's bag during our first-period history class, along with a few rolls of fruit-flavored *Life Savers* attached.

> *Alex,*
> *Words will never be enough to share how truly thankful I am for your act of bravery.*
> *You truly are a wonderful friend and a life saver.*
> *Xoxo*
> *-Liddy*

I smiled absently at him, and his eyes flickered in surprise. When his eyebrows lifted and the corners of his mouth quirked, I cleared my throat, snapping myself out of memory lane.

"Could you please hand me four yellow hearts?"

"Ah, the color of friendship," Alex said, sounding a bit dejected.

I took a pen from the small bucket on the table and jotted anonymous notes to my chicas— Dani, Pree, and Sara. I debated taking the last one home to drop off at Justin's house. He had to finish out his final semester of high school at home with a school-appointed tutor. I'd mustered the courage once, with Will at my side, and tried to visit him after "the incident," but Mrs. Lindor had said he wasn't seeing anyone. I felt terrible for him, but didn't want to pressure him into seeing me. That evil witch, Mara, deserved all the punishment, not him.

Justin had taken this especially hard; it didn't help that his baseball scholarship to UIUC was in jeopardy. I couldn't blame him one bit for wanting to lay low. Mara nearly destroyed his life. What if sending him a heart would only remind him of everything that went wrong?

"Can I trade this for a purple one?"

Alex observed me, his chin resting on his closed fist. His brow lifted, and without saying a word, he handed me the heart clasped between his pointer and middle finger. Ignoring Jackie's soured face, I angled my body away from Alex, cupping my hand over the heart as I wrote.

Dear Alex,

Thank you again for saving my life. A purple heart for a true hero. Happy Valentine's Day. May someone remarkable capture your heart.

Your friend, Liddy

"Where do these go?" I asked after folding the hearts in half.

Alex gestured to the three boxes in front of him. "Depends on what you want attached to your hearts when we deliver them tomorrow. You can choose a carnation, a blow pop, or a small bag of conversation hearts."

I blanched at the conversation hearts and considered the remaining options, freezing when Dani's distinctive laugh and Pree's prominent voice drifted from around the corner. I shoved all the hearts into the slit of the flower box and tossed a five-dollar bill at Alex before my friends could see what I was doing. I dashed to our table in the back of the lunchroom, praying they hadn't seen me.

While waiting for my friends to get through the lunch line, my thoughts drifted to Will. He had charmed his guidance counselor into changing his lunch period so he could be with me and the chicas. However, he wasn't going to make it to lunch today. He'd volunteered to help his physics teacher with a lecture on the dynamics of surfing. I was bummed, but at least we had English class together, which was right after lunch.

Every minute we were apart grew harder to endure. I blamed this whole "being a Watcher" business for that. *You're an independent woman,* I reminded myself. *You can go a few hours without seeing your boyfriend.* I shook my head. Now that I had someone to share Valentine's Day with, though — a real relationship — I couldn't deny my dislike for the holiday had started to thaw. I wanted to show Will my love, and I'd been brainstorming ways to do so over the past few weeks, even roping Nolan into helping me.

Will and I were cautious about not showing any PDA at school. Being so close to him, but having to fight the strong pull our bodies created when near each other, was agonizing. Any time we sat next to each other in a class, Will would slip his hand under the desk and rest it on my thigh, just above my knee. In answer, my body would move my foot to rest against his. Small things, really, but they took the edge off.

We were taking significant strides to heed Nick's warning, limiting ourselves when together, careful to avoid anything that could spark our dormant Watcher powers. Pree assisted in keeping our secrets, and even helped to distract Will and me when she could.

Sara was the first to join me at the table.

"Anything special planned Sunday for Valentine's Day?" I asked her.

"Yes!" She perked up. "I'm so stoked it's on a weekend this year. Matt and I are celebrating Saturday night. That way we'll both have a later curfew."

"What do you need a later curfew for?" I teased, glancing up from my sandwich in time to see her flush.

"Shush your mouth." Sara playfully swatted at my hand.

"Whatcha girls whispering about?" Dani asked, plopping down next to Sara.

"Nothing." Sara averted her eyes down to her tray.

Pree squeezed in next to me. "What'd I miss?"

"Nothing." I waved a hand. "Just discussing Valentine's Day."

"Ugh, don't get me started." Dani groaned.

Ever since winter formal, we all suspected that Dani started crushing on Alex. I only hoped he returned those feelings.

"What?" Dani demanded.

The rest of us giggled. None of us were any good at hiding what we were thinking.

"Chillax, Dani," Sara said patting her hand. "You're allowed to be excited for Valentine's Day."

Pree snorted. "Easy for you to say; you have someone to share it with."

"We all have people to share it with," I said. "Why can't it be about showing love in general, not only to who you're dating? I consider all of you my Valentines."

"Liddy...always showing us the silver lining." Dani rolled her eyes playfully.

"Yep! It's all in your mindset," I chirped.

"I'm sure William will be thrilled to know he's just your friend," Sara teased.

"How's that going, by the way?" Dani asked, a hint of trepidation in her voice.

I hadn't let my friends know why we weren't open about our relationship at school, but I knew I'd owe them an explanation soon.

Leaning toward Dani, I whispered, "We're great. Better than ever."

"OK, good," she responded. "I was a little nervous to ask. You guys barely act like you're dating."

Pree choked on her Snapple, and I flashed her a pleading look. Only she knew that outside of school, Will and I were inseparable, and that we could light up a room like the Bat-signal whenever we got close.

"Sorry, wr—wrong p—pipe," she coughed.

Dani eyed Pree, then turned her focus back to me. "Seriously, Lid. Why are you and Will so secretive?"

"Because I've had enough drama to last me a lifetime. Also, Will and I are shy; we like our privacy."

"Doesn't it bother you?" she pressed.

I frowned. "Doesn't what bother me?"

"How all these girls are constantly vying for his attention, going to absurd lengths to try and get even a glance? Maybe they'd calm down if they knew he was officially off the market."

I laughed. "No, Dani. It doesn't bother me. I trust him."

"Yah, but I wouldn't trust *them*," she muttered.

"I guess Dani does have a point," Sara chimed in as she peeled her orange. "I mean, look what happened with Jackie when she and Will weren't even dating."

"Yeah, seriously. Liddy's wardrobe and body took a lot of hits from Jackie and her Double Dee cronies," Pree added.

We finished lunch and my stomach did a little flip. In a few short minutes, I'd be seeing Will again. Just in time, too, as the empty void of withdrawal was killing my otherwise good mood.

I got to class first and sighed when he slid into the seat next to me and his knee rested against mine. That briefest touch filled me up and would last me the rest of the school day, though I was still glad I'd see him in dance and after school. The final bell of the day was what I couldn't wait for. It signaled the end of separation torture and the start of when we could be truly us; two teens in love who didn't have to worry about alarming the people around us. Poor Pree was still acclimating to it.

Will cleared his throat, his lips twitching, and pushed a folded-up note to me.

Careful with your thoughts. Your eyes are giving you away.

My eyes bugged in alarm. Will stifled a laugh and swiped the note back to his side of the table. A minute later, it was back in front of me.

I can't wait until school is out, either.

My stomach flipped and my face heated. Although Will was not a mind reader, he could definitely sense and sometimes even experience what I was feeling, and vice versa. The same was true for me regarding his emotions and thoughts. Ever since I used the Christmas rose Nick gave me at the hospital, things had remained heightened between us. We didn't dare touch the rest of the period.

Dance class was another challenge.

"Will and Liddy, my office please," Coach R. called to us after assigning small groups to the rest of the ensemble.

We hustled to her office while the rest of the team began working on a shaping exercise.

Coach R. waved us over to her desk. "Close the door, please."

Will shut it behind us.

"The spring showcase is roughly ten weeks away," she continued. "After-school rehearsals won't begin for another two weeks; however, it's time you both started working on your duet."

Will and I had landed the coveted role, usually reserved for seniors, after an impromptu dance we performed in front of the ensemble on his first day back at WHS.

"Many students want to choreograph for this show, and their pieces are strong," Coach R. went on. "So, there won't be a slot allotted to your piece in the rehearsal lineup. You will have to do a majority of your rehearsals in class and on your own time."

I breathed a huge sigh of relief. Rehearsals were something Will and I had been dreading, trying to figure out how we could dance together without giving away our secret.

"That's no problem, Coach R.," I said. "Will and I can find time to work on the duet outside of school."

"Oh, Liddy, you guys are the best. I appreciate your

willingness, but I insist on giving you class time."

My heart sank, but Will shook his head. "You don't need to do that. We'd be happy to spend weekends on it. I wouldn't want to miss class time."

Coach R. waved a hand. "Don't be silly! We have an empty rec room above the pool, a few doors down the back hallway, that I've already arranged for you to use." Panic seized my chest. Will crossed his arms and brushed his elbow against my shoulder. Calming waves rippled through me; my heart slowed, and the tension in my neck eased. "You both can check out a boombox and head over there now."

Will grabbed the silver boombox and we hightailed it to the rec room. A damp, chlorine-infused smell hit my nostrils. The rectangular room was the perfect shape and size for a studio. On the right were a line of windows that overlooked the pool. I peeked out and saw Alex in the water. He waved and I waved back.

"Well, these windows are going to be a problem," I sighed.

Will looked at them thoughtfully. "They shouldn't be *too* big of a problem; at least they all have blinds. I'm more concerned about the possible mold hidden under this old carpet." His nose crinkled.

I laughed. "I remember coming here for a birthday party one year when I was a kid. We swam for hours and then came up here to eat and open presents."

On the far end was a mini-arcade with an electronic Dual Shot Basketball game. There was also a small kitchen with a vending machine and soda dispenser. I sat on the 1970s couch and sank down at least a foot. Will plopped down next to me, leveling us out.

"So," he began, "how do we want to try and do this? We won't be able to hide it in front of an audience."

"I know. I wish Nick was here. I'm sure he'd be able to help us."

Will's jaw twitched. "I'm sure he's fine. He'll be back any day now."

"I know, but what if—?"

"There is no what if," Will cut me off, an edge sharpening his voice. I dropped my gaze. "I'm sorry. I did not mean to snap at you." He sighed. "I have to believe he's coming back; for Charlie's sake."

I felt a flash of Will's fear. I reached over and squeezed his hand. "I get it. He'll be back. Both of them will."

He nodded. "Want to hit the sledding hill today? Check in on Nick's place?"

"Of course." I smiled. "Haven't missed a day yet."

Will stood and offered his hand to me. "Help me close these blinds."

I started working on the white metal blinds on the opposite side. I'd just finished the last one when Will wrapped his arms around me. Speaking into my neck, he said, "We still have another thirty minutes before class ends. Do you think that's enough time to share a kiss and let the light of our gifting fade?"

"I don't know," I breathed. "But let's not risk it quite yet." Will groaned and reluctantly let go. "We can time it later, when we're alone." I winked at him.

"I love that plan!"

I laughed. "Of course you do. In the meantime, let's start figuring out what song we want to choreograph the piece to."

We sat at the bar stools in the kitchen area.

"I've been thinking a lot about that. Have you heard of the song *I'll back you up?*"

"I have." I tried not to let shock morph my face.

"Why do you look so surprised?" Will laughed.

"Because it's the exact song I was thinking of!"

"Seriously? I can't help but picture us performing to that song."

I smiled. "Well, now that we have our music chosen, what are we going to do with the last twenty-five minutes of class?"

"We can start walking through some movements. I'll bring the CD tomorrow." Will stood and moved to a space free of furniture.

"Will, I'm not sure that's a good idea."

"We'll be fine." His eyes sparkled, and he laughed. "This is all a bit ridiculous, and yet, it's our reality."

"I know, right?" I laughed too. "I look forward to the day when we don't have to worry about this."

We lasted barely five minutes before we were glowing. I slumped to the floor, exasperated. I watched Will pace as if cooling down from a hard workout when an idea struck me.

"Will, what if we don't touch while we dance?"

"How would that even..." But Will stopped mid-sentence, inspiration dawning on his face. "That could work for a lot of the dance. Not all of it, of course, but you're a genius!"

"I try." Giggles bubbled from me; I had maybe solved our problem. I turned the radio on to *Q101*.

"We could spend the first minute or so separated from each other, telling our story through dance about how we found each other again," Will suggested.

"I think we need to show us together first, like for

about thirty seconds, and then separate before coming back together again. It would make it more authentic and thus more impactful."

"But that means..."

"Yes, I know. We can choreograph the touching parts outside of school. Once we have the routine down, maybe our bodies will be too distracted by the music and so used to the rehearsal steps they won't..."

"Light us up like a thousand spotlights," Will finished for me.

"Exactly."

Will and I laughed as we played with movements. Every time our bodies came close, our pulses surged, and an invisible but tangible current hummed between us. After fifteen minutes, we were out of breath for reasons other than physical exertion. Even though our eyes had kindled, we'd successfully danced.

"I think we've had enough for the first day." Will panted.

"But we still have five minutes." My chest was rising and falling in rhythm with his.

"Let's take a minute to cool down. If we walk slowly enough, we'll get back to the studio and check in the boombox right before dismissal."

After changing out, Will met me outside the locker room, and we walked to the parking lot hand in hand.

"Meet you at Nick's?" I suggested when we reached our cars parked next to each other.

"Actually, do you want to leave a car here and drive over together? I miss getting that extra time with you," Will admitted.

I walked over to the passenger side door of my red

Oldsmobile, a Christmas present from Will's family. I gripped the handle, opened it, and said, "After you, darling."

Will threw his head back and laughed.

1, 2, 3 Jump!

I PARKED IN THE DESERTED SOUTH END of the parking lot. I reached into my back seat for my boots, but Will cupped my elbow.

"Not so fast, my love. What was it you said earlier, something about timing us?"

"I was waiting for you to make a move," I teased.

A flirtatious grin played on his delicious lips. "How rude of me to keep my princess waiting."

I couldn't resist. All the pent-up anticipation that grew heavier as the day wore on came rushing out. In one swift motion, I slid my seat back, maneuvered from behind the steering wheel, and flung myself at Will. His eyes widened, and he bit his lip.

"Oh no! Did I hurt you?"

Will shook his head. His eyes bore into mine as he laid his seat back, bringing me down with him. Fire roared through me, and before I could completely burst, I kissed him deeply. Finally, when my lips began to go numb, I pulled away.

"Try not to make your princess wait so long next time," I said breathlessly.

Will chuckled. "If this is the end result, she may find herself waiting more often," he teased, his hands still gripping my hips.

I checked my watch. "Let's track how long it takes us to return to a brightness level humans can't detect." Will ogled me. "What?" I asked, suddenly self-conscious.

"I'll never get used to how beautiful you look all flushed and radiant. When you shine so bright, I almost cannot bear it." He kissed me again, so soft and tender, I melted against him.

I sighed. "OK, now the timer really starts."

We left our bags in the back seat, changed into our boots, and trudged our way to the sledding hill. We'd had tons of snowfall over the past few weeks, thanks to the lake effect.

Getting into Nick's gate became second nature to us now; we simply imagined ourselves opening it, then pushed on the right spot. Nick had mentioned that it was bewitched, so only those with Watcher blood could enter, thanks to their inherent magic.

We reached the gate, and a chill prickled through my blood.

"Will!"

He had sensed it, too, and was already pushing hard on the cool steel, but it wouldn't budge.

"What the heck?" He threw his whole weight into it, but

nothing happened. I clasped my hand over his, and together we pressed the spot. I closed my eyes and imagined it opening. With a muffled click, the gate swung open.

"We will talk about what *that* was later," Will said. "This doesn't feel right. Something's happened. Stay behind me."

"As if!" I took off down the tunnel. The faint glow of Nick's living room stopped me in my tracks. Will slammed into me, and I had to catch myself on the wall.

"What's wrong?" He grabbed my shoulders and turned me around to face him, his eyes aglow with concern.

"Mara. She's happy about...something. That can't be a good sign."

Will let go and calmed his breathing. "Let's get in there. Something tells me Nick needs our help."

We ran until we entered the domed sitting room. We hustled from room to room, calling out to Nick.

"Looking for something?" Mara's voice taunted.

Will's anger had my hair bristling before I even registered the intense emerald green of his eyes.

"Don't answer her," I warned.

Will cracked his knuckles. "We need to go into Arbolias." Not-so-distant flashbacks clouded my vision. I closed my eyes, trying to force away the image of a lifeless Will at the base of the Arbolias tree.

I shuddered. "No, we can't. Nick said not to go in there."

"He's not in any other room, is he? What if he's stuck in there?" Will pointed to the room that held the massive tree and glowing envelopes. "He may need our help."

I pressed my fingers to my temples. "Give me a second to think."

"What happened to Nicholas?" Mara's voice trilled. She

almost sounded concerned, which had to be my imagination. This chick wasn't the compassionate type.

A deep, muffled groan broke the eerie silence. "Will, tell me you heard that." But he was already on high alert, peering up at the ceiling.

"What are you looking—?" I saw it before the last word exited my lips. Normally the swirled, thatched ceiling was ornamented with an off-centered opening inlaid with stained-glass; it sparkled with the depiction of the night sky as northern lights danced across it. But now, the thick, frosted glass was blank and obscured by a curled shadow.

I searched the walls for a switch or button but came up empty.

"Liddy, come here. Let me hoist you up. I think the latch to open this is in the ceiling."

Anxiety flooded my system, and I gaped at Will. *Why do I have to be so self-conscious about my weight?* Nick might be trapped, and here I was fretting about Will lifting me.

"What's wrong? Come on. We need to see what's up there!"

"If I'm too heavy, drop me, and we'll try furniture."

"You're kidding me, right?" Will ran a hand down his face.

I shook away my self-deprecating thoughts, and strode over to him.

"See that notch next to the small curve of the shadow?" Will squinted, pointing to the ceiling. "The one with the faint light glinting through the knot?"

"Yes! It looks like it could be a keyhole."

"Exactly." Will squatted and clasped his hands together to form a footrest. "Ready when you are, Princess."

Another groan sounded from above. I rolled my neck and shook out each leg individually, mentally preparing.

Will sighed. "I don't think we have time for a full warmup right now." His expression softened. "Trust me. I won't drop you. Think of this as practice for our duet."

"Fine, I'm ready," I lied, placing my left foot in his hands.

"On the count of three, you're going to push off the floor with your right foot."

"On three, or after three?" I asked, clutching his shoulders, trying not to shake.

He smirked, exuding extra confidence, his attempt to reassure me. "After. Here we go, one... two... three... jump!"

I was up in a flash and as promised, Will was a solid foundation. If Jackie knew Will's strength as a stunt base, I'm sure she'd have worked overtime to recruit him for the cheerleading squad.

"Can you reach it?"

"Yes," I squeaked. I shouldn't have looked down. I squeezed my eyes shut and imagined myself opening the latch. But nothing happened.

"What's wrong? Is it not working?"

"Give me a second, please."

Nick's voice, weak and ragged, echoed in my mind, startling me; I wobbled, nearly losing my balance.

"Easy now. I've got you," Will said.

Again, Nick croaked, "Lock your eyes on the knot, and don't break your focus."

I did as instructed, and a warming sensation built behind my eyes.

"Good girl. Now, be patient," Nick wheezed. "You'll know

when the time is right to use your gift to open the latch."

"I've got about a minute left before I have to put you down," Will called to me, but I didn't respond. I was concentrating on the blood vessels behind my eyes that started to swell and spark. My vision hyper-zoomed, like a Sony full-frame camera, on the flickering spot in the latch, so that it was the only thing in my frame of view. And then, I had a sudden urge to release the built pressure.

When my vision normalized, the latch was opened. I pushed against an uneven pane in the ceiling, but it wouldn't budge.

"Nick, can you hear me?" I yelled. "You are going to need to move over."

No answer.

"Liddy, I promised I wouldn't drop you, but I'm starting to lose my grip. Come down now," Will cautioned.

"Just one more sec!" I pleaded.

Again, I followed the instructions Nick had seemingly communicated telepathically; or, at least, I thought that's what he was doing. Thanks to the frosted glass, I could barely make out the outline of his body, but I lasered in on him. The back of my eyes burned again, and I was able to zero in on the inner mechanisms of the latch; the pressure mounted, then I released.

Nick and Will both groaned, and down I went. Luckily, Will was able to cushion my fall.

"Are you OK?" he asked.

"Yes, I'm fine." I sat up, brushing my hair off my face. I stretched my right leg out and turned my left foot inward to work out the ankle. *Geesh, his grip is firm.*

"That was close!" Will exclaimed. "I asked you to trust me, and I would have felt terrible if something happened to you. What *was* all that up there? That trick with your gift?" His eyes danced.

"Later," I breathed. "We need to figure out how to help Nick down."

As if on cue, the room shook with the sounds of wood splintering and ice cracking. I had no time to move as the large glass pane collapsed, and Nick rolled out. It all seemed to happen in slow motion. His body, heavy and clumsy, slid and landed with a hard *thud*. A loud crack filled my ears, and I screamed.

Stars pricked at the corners of my eyes as inky black stains seeped into the edges of my consciousness. Something brushed my cheek before I plunged into darkness.

I awoke on the red velvet settee, spots swimming in my vision. Blinking away the blurriness, I found Nick slouched in the soft leather armchair, his head resting on his fist and nestled into the wing of the chair. Though he sat near the fire, he was covered with a sherpa-lined blanket. I started to sit up, but my right leg was stiff and unnaturally heavy as I tried to shift it.

"Owww," I moaned. Will, exiting the kitchen with a silver tray, rushed over to me. He set the salver on the coffee table, then peeled back the crocheted blanket that covered my legs. My jeans were torn open, exposing my mangled ankle, tucked between two crimson towels.

"Dang it. My parents are never going to let me out of the

house again," I muttered, dropping my head back onto the couch.

"I tried to wake Nick to do whatever it was he did in the hospital that healed you, but he's too weak. After I carried you to the couch, I had to carry him to the chair."

"How long have I been out?"

"About an hour." Will glanced down at his watch, grimacing. "There's no way you can walk out of here, and I'm going to need to take you to a hospital."

I tried to move again, but every inch of movement sent a sharp, searing pain through me, like I was being stabbed by a hot poker.

Will winced, and I knew some of my suffering registered in his body. "Could you not do that? It's nearly impossible to take care of you when I can feel the same things you do."

"Sorry." I exhaled, leaned my head back, and closed my eyes. Will worked to replace the wet towels on my foot with fresh ones full of ice.

"No hospital or doctors," I firmly stated.

Will pursed his lips, scrutinizing me with narrowed eyes. "Liddy, I really—"

"No," I repeated. "I've had enough hospital visits to last a lifetime, thank-you-very-much."

Will shot me an exasperated look. "OK, well, then what's your plan?"

I puffed out a breath, strands of my hair flying off my face. "Give me a second to think."

The last thing I wanted was to scare my parents with another call from a medical professional informing them I'd been hurt. However, I realized I was in bad shape, and there was no way I'd be able to walk out of here. Heck, even the thought of Will carrying me, his movements jostling my body on the trek to the car, made me squirm.

An idea struck me. "Will!"

He started. "What is it?"

"I figured out a plan to get me home without having to go to the hospital."

"OK, shoot."

"You know how I opened that tiny latch in the ceiling before Nick fell through?"

Will looked at me through narrowed eyes. "Absolutely not."

Humph. "I haven't even told you what I'm thinking yet."

"Yeah, but I can feel your uneasiness mixed with reckless abandon, and that never ends well."

"Oh, hush. It'll be great. Are you ready to listen?"

"Do I have a choice?" Will smirked.

"Fine. I'll do it myself," I huffed. I did my best to shift positions without causing myself any further torment. I closed my eyes and, inhaling deeply, recalled Nick's directions on how to use my gifting.

"Stop!" Will yelled, ripping me out of my meditative state.

"What is your problem?" I snapped.

"You can't! I mean...we don't know what using your gifting on yourself will do." Will's fear thrummed through me.

I sighed. "Right now, this is our only option. We need to take care of Nick and get home without raising suspicion."

"Let me try, then. You've got to be in pain, and I don't want you sapping any more of your energy."

"OK," I relented and leaned my head back against the pillow.

Will sat massaging his forehead. "I don't know what I'm

doing. You are going to have to walk me through it."

I patted his hand. "Lock your eyes on my ankle and don't break your focus." Will obeyed and set his gaze. "Now, when you experience a warming sensation, keep thinking about fixing my ankle, letting the pressure build."

I could sense the electric charge sparking from his body, but just as quickly as it came, it fizzled.

"Dang it!" Will glowered.

"It's OK. We'll try again."

"What if I do it wrong and make it worse?"

"I trust you. This will work, I know it. I just did it."

"That was unlocking a hidden latch in the ceiling, and look how that turned out," he joked, but his voice quivered.

"Hey, I think it was pretty good for my first time," I teased, jutting out my bottom lip. Will leaned over and softly pressed his lips to mine. When he broke away, I hooked the back of his neck and pulled him back down for another kiss. I kept him there until more of my pain ebbed away and his body relaxed.

He rested his forehead against mine. "When it comes to you, I don't like taking chances."

I smiled. "You've got this. I think you'll be surprised how natural it feels."

"How did you know what to do? First at the front gate, then again with the latch?"

I shrugged. "I followed my gut at the door; I figured combining our giftings would naturally make us stronger.

With the latch, well... Nick helped me with that."

Will blinked. "Come again?"

"I heard Nick giving me directions, telepathically. Crazy, right?"

"Maybe a little." Will sat up and again focused on my

ankle.

"That's good, Will. Patience. Imagine what my ankle would look like healed. You'll know when it's time to use your gifting."

Minutes later, the entire room was glowing emerald, and then it faded. Will remained rooted to his spot on the edge of the coffee table. I glanced down at my foot. Though the bruising didn't look much better, my ankle now sat in its normal position.

"You did it!" I cheered.

Will grunted. "It looks the same."

"When Nick came to the hospital to heal me, I slept for a long while after; only then did I look remarkably better. It still took some time to fully heal."

"I guess." Will sounded defeated.

I attempted to swing my legs over the couch. "Here, I'll show you."

"Wait! Not so fast. Let me take a look." Will moved to the edge of the couch, his back to me, and gingerly placed one hand on my heel and the other on the top of my foot. I sighed at his touch, and he glanced over his shoulder, his eyes twinkling.

"I'm going to try moving your ankle. Tell me immediately if the pain is too much." As careful as handling a newborn baby, Will rotated my foot in the smallest of circles. It glided smoothly over the ankle bone, which had been previously bent like the hook of a wire hanger.

"How was that?" He asked.

"I didn't feel a thing." I replied, smiling in relief at this revelation.

"Good. Can I try again?"

"Of course."

His hands warmed as he continued to move my foot, gradually enlarging the circle. "And now?"

"A little tight, but not painful," I responded sheepishly, enjoying his touch.

Will laughed. "I'm going to let go so we can get a real sense of what it feels like when you move it." He removed his hands.

"It feels fine; I promise. I'm going to try to walk on it." Swinging my legs over the side, I wiggled my toes in the rug before pushing off the couch to stand.

Will was already at my side, offering his arm. I took one step, but it was obvious that, though my ankle didn't appear to be broken anymore, I wasn't able to put my full weight on it. I winced and squeezed Will's arm.

"On second thought, I'm going to sit back down." I plopped onto the arm of the settee.

Will looked stricken, his face pale and jaw clenched. "I must not have done it right."

"Are you kidding me? Will, my ankle is no longer crooked. I can move it and stand! You were fantastic! In fact, I haven't properly thanked you." I gave him my most flirtatious smile.

I pulled him onto the couch, then slid off the armrest and onto his lap. "Now who's the one who doesn't give themselves nearly enough credit?"

Will chuckled in response. I cupped his cheeks and, achingly slow, moved in for a kiss, savoring the sparks in his eyes. Right before our lips met, we heard a low groan.

"Nick," Will and I said in unison. Will stood and helped me hop over to Nick.

Nick greeted us by opening one eye. "I'd prefer it if

you two would cease doing that, especially in the company of others," he murmured. My cheeks flushed, but Will just smirked at me.

"Nick, are you OK?" I asked. "Where have you been?"

Nick's eyes fluttered but remained closed. His head fell to his shoulder, his breathing labored. "William," he croaked out.

"Yes?" Will kneeled down next to Nick.

"In my office..." Nick flinched. "In my office, you will find a golden—" he grunted, a bead of sweat on his brow— "star. Press the center...and use it to call your uncle. His assistance is needed."

Like a Candle

"**W**HAT DO YOU MEAN, MY UNCLE?" Will's face was scrunched in sheer perplexion.

"Abishai. I need him. Now would be tremendous." Nick's eyes rolled back as his head slumped over.

"Nick? Nick!" I yelled, but he didn't stir. Placing my cheek near his mouth, I sighed in relief when his breath brushed my skin.

Will stood stock-still, staring at the fire, the crease between his brows deepening.

"Will?" A plethora of emotions roiled off him.

"Lid, do you understand what he said? My uncle. Shai knows...about all of this. He knows!" Will threw his hands in the air. I rested my hand on his shoulder, but he whirled away. I stumbled, but he caught me, righting me as if I were an afterthought, and then continued to pace. "Why wouldn't he tell me who I was? Why not be there for me through all of this? Why the charade?"

Nick's breath hitched and my attention diverted to him. "Will, we can ask your uncle when he arrives. But we need to get him here, now."

Will crossed the room in just four strides. My eyes followed him until his tall, muscular frame disappeared behind the wooden door. I heaved a long sigh, calming my nerves as well as the intense emotions I'd absorbed from Will. Nick coughed and I inspected his face. His lips were powder white, and small cracks were sealed with dried blood. *When was the last time he had water?*

I knew Will would be back any moment, but I suddenly couldn't wait another minute to fetch Nick some water. I scanned the room, but even though the kitchen was close, I wasn't confident enough to hop all the way there and back by myself. A glint off the pewter tray Will had left on the ottoman caught my eye. I staggered over to it and found some small ice chips wrapped in the towels that had hugged my ankle. *Thank goodness the ice didn't actually touch my foot.* Gathering up the towel, I made my way back to Nick as Will reentered the room.

"You shouldn't be walking around." Will beelined it to me.

"I'm fine." I opened the towel and picked out a few ice chips. "Hold his chin for a sec, please." Will placed one hand behind Nick's head, lifting it gently. With his thumb, he guided Nick's mouth open. I slipped the melting pieces into his mouth, Will closing it right after. Nick's Adam's apple bobbed ever so slightly as he swallowed.

"Could you please fill a cup with some more ice?" Will said nothing as he hurried back into the kitchen. A moment later, I heard a loud pounding and a drawer slam shut. When he returned, I took the cup filled with crushed ice and a spoon from his hands, and continued to hydrate Nick. Will sat on the couch, his elbows on his knees, hands fisted together under his chin, staring at the floor. I tried to extend some reassuring vibes his way, but they didn't rouse him. I fed Nick a few more spoonfuls of crushed ice before hobbling over to Will.

I lightly massaged his ear lobe. "How did the call with your uncle go?"

A cool breeze stirred, blowing my hair into my face. I turned to see Shai stand from a crouched position directly under the glass pane where Nick had fallen from, and stride into the living room. Not a single hair was out of place, but his features were contorted with concern. His eyes darted to Will and me before he hastened to Nick's side.

"Uncle," Will said, but Shai did not answer. "Uncle," Will tried again, his voice louder. Shai still had his back turned to us, not acknowledging his nephew. "*Abishai!*" Will yelled, springing to his feet.

Shai whirled, his eyes ablaze, the same green as Will's. I stared nervously at the pair of them.

"William," Shai said, sounding both exhausted and annoyed. "What could you possibly need at this moment that is more important than saving a man who is slowly dying?"

I blanched. "Dying? Nick's dying? Are you able to help him?"

Shai's eyes flitted to mine. "Yes, but I can't have distractions while I tend to him. Could one of you grab me the tincture in the opalescent bottle from Nick's medicine cabinet?"

Will stalled. The chaos of his emotions practically slammed into me. Using the couch as support, I staggered around it and hopped toward the bathroom.

"Lydia, what happened to you?" Shai hurried to my side, seconds ahead of Will.

"I've got her," Will said coolly, his narrowed gaze on his uncle. Shai released my arm and stepped back, raising his hands in surrender. Will gingerly placed me on Nick's bed and disappeared into the bathroom. A moment later, he returned with a small glass bottle, no larger than the size of a perfume sample vial.

"Hold this, please." He placed the tincture in the palm of my hand. I closed my fist around it, and Will scooped me up. Before I could protest, we were on our way back to the living room, and then I was back on the couch. Will delivered the tincture to an expectant Shai.

Shai thanked him and twisted the bottle's top. Will didn't speak, but his body language had loads to say. He stood as still as a statue, his arms crossed over his chest, and his jaw was pulsing so hard, I was nervous he'd crack a tooth.

"I cannot work with you breathing down my neck, William," Shai groused. "Kindly return to the sofa while I administer my work, and then I will tend to Lydia." Shai again spoke without looking at Will.

"Are you serious? You can't dismiss me like this," Will complained.

"I assure you I am dead serious, as Nick will be if you do not control your emotions and have a seat."

Will scoffed and stomped back to the couch. He was usually so calm; it was hard for me to see him like this. I realized this was what he must experience whenever I let my emotions best me. I decided to try and distract Will, the same way he always helped me.

"Will," I whispered, feigning embarrassment. He either didn't hear me or was too distracted by his own thoughts. "Will," I tried again, a little more loudly as I touched his arm, wanting him to feel my emotional plea for him to look at me.

He blinked and faced me. I cupped his cheek, then slid my hand to the back of his neck, drawing his ear close to my mouth. "Do you mind helping me to the bathroom?" I pulled away and dropped my gaze. I totally did need to use the bathroom, but more so, I wanted to get Will away from his uncle.

Again, Will scooped me up and carried me all the way to the bathroom.

"I'll only be a sec."

Will rubbed the back of his neck. "Do you, uh, need any help in there?"

"Gosh, no! I mean, thank you for offering, but I can manage." I shut the door.

I purposely took my time. When I could stall no longer, I turned the gold handle of the faucet and washed my hands, the soap's scent of wassail permeating the air.

"All finished," I said cheerily, trying to lighten the mood as I opened the door.

Will bent to pick me up, but I hopped back. He looked at

me quizzically. "Don't bring me back in there just yet. Can we sit on the bed?"

I could sense Will struggling. "Liddy, as much as I would love to kiss you, I don't think now is the time to..."

I giggled and his cheeks turned pink. "No silly, I meant sit, literally, so we can talk."

Will ran a hand through his hair. "Sorry, I'm a little on edge."

"So, I've noticed." I smiled and tilted my head coyly. Will locked me in a bear hug, easily lifting me off the floor and onto the bed. "So, what are you going to say to your uncle when he is done with Nick?"

"I'm not sure. I was hoping he'd initiate, but it doesn't seem like he is going to." Will sighed.

"Well, his answer may be complicated. Are you sure you're ready to hear it tonight?"

"I probably shouldn't talk to him when I am so dang mad at him, but I truly want to know. Why wasn't he there for me? Helping me walk through this? This whole learning-that-we-aren't-exactly-human was a lot to take, and I was by myself for the first few months of it."

"I totally get it. I'd be mad, confused, even hurt as well." I took his hand and entwined my fingers in his. "I'm here with you, however you want me to be. I'll support your decision, however you want to approach this. If you'd like to speak to him privately, you can take me home."

"No. You are part of this, too." Will brushed my knuckles with his thumb.

I leaned in to kiss him, but before our lips touched, a bright sea-green colored light flashed from the living room.

"Should we go out there?" I asked.

"I think if I go out there, I may punch him in the face. I need another five minutes to cool down."

"Well, while we wait, do you mind massaging my ankle?"

Concern etched his face as he reached for my leg and brought it to his lap. I laid back on a pillow. My few minutes of bliss were interrupted by another bright light, and Nick crying out. Both our heads snapped to the open door.

"William! I need you in here, now!" Shai yelled.

Will moved to pick me up, but I waved him off. "Go, go!"

He darted out of the room, and I hobbled after him. I reached the doorway as Will landed at Nick's side. Nick continued to cry out and arch out of his chair. I feared he would snap his spine.

"Hold him down!" Shai ordered, his body aglow in pinks and greens.

Will and I seemed to light up a room whenever we used our gifting, but Shai was different. He contained the light within inches of his skin and directed small rivers of it from himself into Nick.

Will didn't ask questions and held Nick down.

I finally made it to the armrest of the red sofa. "What's happening?" I asked as fear continued to grip me. Seeing someone in this much pain was extremely distressing.

"His body is fighting the healing. His organs were practically frozen solid." More ripples of light shot from Shai. Nick convulsed, and I watched a bead of sweat trickle down Shai's forehead.

"Come on old man, don't give up on me now!" Shai bellowed, pressing his hands over Nick's heart. Will struggled to hold Nick still. Shai closed his eyes and muttered under his breath. I couldn't make out any of the words, but his lips were moving a mile a minute. The power within Shai pulsated, but he remained resolute. Will gawked, awestruck watching his uncle.

Nick began to glow from various points, all places where his major organs were. A single strand, the size of a cable wire, branched out from each until they were all connected. Like the wick of a candle, light flamed to life, and every inch of Nick was glowing. He cried out, then went still.

"Will!" I screamed as Shai swayed, his eyes rolling back in his head. Will caught him, and eased him to the couch.

"William," Shai rasped. "Can you please retrieve a few Christmas roses from outside?"

Will nodded tersely and bolted from the living room. My eyes zipped to Shai as he leaned his head back on the couch.

"I can sense you staring at me, Ms. Lydia," he commented, his eyes closed.

Embarrassed, I immediately cast my gaze to Nick, who now slept peacefully in his chair. It was my turn to feel someone's eyes on me, and when I glanced at Shai, he was indeed staring. We said nothing to each other, though Shai seemed like he was daring me to talk first.

Will came back with three bright and sparkling Christmas roses in his hand. "Here you go, *Uncle*," he gritted out.

"Excellent. All good choices. Mature and at their highest potency." Shai brought one up to his nose and inhaled deeply.

I hadn't realized his skin had been so ashen until the magic of the rose brought his natural color back.

Shai lifted his head. "Nick wouldn't happen to have any

food in his house, would he? Particularly oranges, or any cookies he may have baked? It greatly helps to replenish Watchers after they've depleted themselves, but any food will do."

"Actually," I chimed in, "We've been bringing fresh groceries every few days since Christmas in case Nick returned."

Shai scowled. I moved to get off the couch to grab him something to eat, but squawked in pain.

Immediately, Will was at my side, helping me sit. "I've got it, Princess." He whisked off to the kitchen. Poor Will, he'd been running around frantically for hours taking care of everyone.

"So, it seems as if Nick has been divulging more than he ought to be," Shai remarked once Will was out of earshot.

"How so?" I asked, annoyed. "I actually think he's been quite vague, except for what he shared with us on Christmas Eve, but even that was minimal."

"We'll see about that," Shai scoffed, shaking his head. "You always seem to find yourself in some sort of trouble. How'd you hurt your foot?"

I resented his tone. "Nick fell from the ceiling directly onto it, but don't worry. Will healed it."

He scrutinized my injury as he inhaled another rose. "That's healed?" He twisted his lips to the side, and I couldn't help but feel like he was mocking me.

This was only the second time I had met Will's Uncle Shai, but tonight he seemed like an entirely different person. *Rude!* "For your information, Will did a great job, especially considering it was his first time, and he did it completely on his own, working on pure instinct. Before, my foot was completely bent into an L-shape. At least now it doesn't hurt, unless I try to walk on it."

Shai considered my words, raised his brows, then nodded in appreciation. "My apologies. I had assumed Nick had already trained him in healing already."

"*Hmph*. Well, you know what they say about people who assume things," I sneered, then slapped my hand over my mouth. "I'm sorry, I didn't mean..."

Shai smiled. "I deserved it. Nick is the one I am angry with. If I wasn't so drained, I would offer to further heal your ankle. May I at least have a look at it?"

"I'm fine, really. I don't want to be a bother."

"No such thing." He adjusted his torso and hips and I propped my leg up on the sofa. Shai held my foot gingerly as he examined it, rotating my ankle clockwise and counterclockwise, up and down. He held my ankle with one hand and, with the other, placed pressure on the bottom of my foot. I hissed.

"Ah, I think you still have a small fracture or two. I can show William how to fix that." Shai set my foot down. "On second thought—" he frowned and laid his head back— "that would take too long. I do not have the energy nor do I wish for him to experiment on you right now. I shall have him take you to my home; Nolan can help you."

My mouth dropped as Will walked in carrying a red tray.

"What? Nolan is a Watcher, too?"

Shai massaged his forehead. "Yes, he is."

Thundernation!

"I CAN'T BELIEVE THIS! Why did no one say anything to me? Did you really think it was best for me to figure this all out on my own?"

"Things are...complicated," Shai sighed.

Nick spoke softly, almost too quiet to hear. "Please, tell them already. It's not your fault, but they need to hear it."

"Nicholas, please. We've been over this," Shai groused.

"I do not...think you-have...a-choice at-this point," he panted.

"Tell us what?" I asked.

"Do you have any idea how much this whole thing has sucked?" Will raged as he paced behind the couch. "Transitioning into a Watcher, learning I'm not human, utterly alone..." He trailed off. "Wait, this means my parents...

they have to be Watchers, too." Will's voice dropped, his brows knitting together. "But they've never shown any sort of gifting abilities, and they've never once said anything to me."

"You're right," I chimed in. "Does that mean, my parents and brother... They have to be too, right?"

Shai looked up, first glancing at Will, then at me. He braced his elbows on his knees, and rested his head on his forearms. "I'm sorry, but I'm not ready to share everything with you yet."

"Too bad. Liddy and I are having a hard time figuring out how to conceal our giftings at school, not to mention Mara almost killed Liddy less than two months ago!" A large vein in Will's neck popped as he shouted.

"I understand you are angry—" Shai paused and clenched his teeth. "However, you cannot yell at me. In Cristes, we treat our elders with respect, especially royalty."

"I don't give a crap!" Will's eyes sparked.

Shai staggered to his feet, his eyes wincing with each deliberate movement. It pained him to stand, but stand he did. Shai met Will's gaze, and his body flickered to life. Icy blue power ignited his eyes and every vein of his body, melting into the whole of his skin. "I said, stand down, William. Do not make me disarm you. It isn't pleasant, and it would take you days to recover."

"You wouldn't dare!" Will snarled.

"Will," I spoke, but he didn't respond. "Will!" I said more forcefully. When he finally turned his attention to me, I pleaded, "Take me home."

"You can't be serious." Will glowered.

It was the first time he'd looked at me like that. My

stomach plummeted. I'd wondered when we'd have our first big fight as a couple, and I cringed, wondering if tonight was it.

"I'm serious. My ankle is bothering me more than I thought. I need to go home...take a bath, and some Advil. Plus, I'm starving."

Shai nodded. "I think that is very wise, although I must request you visit Nolan instead of putting poison in your body. I can make sure he has dinner ready for you along with a bath."

"So, what, you're never going to tell me?" Will spat. "Or do we have to wait for more ambiguity from Nick, which is basically figuring it out on our own?"

"Thundernation, Abishai! They are sitting ducks at this point. *You* need to inform them. They need to train—" Nick began coughing violently. Shai opened his hand, revealing the remaining Christmas rose Will had picked. Nick seized Shai's wrist. "Please, cousin. It is time." Nick's eyes held a pain deeper than any physical wounds could inflict.

"Cousin?" Will's voice cracked.

Shai sighed deeply and placed his hand on Nick's shoulder. "Nick is my cousin, and thus, is your family as well." Will opened his mouth to interrupt, but Shai held his hand up and shook his head. "Let me finish. I need to stay here a few days to nurse Nick back to health while I recover as well. We should assemble in my library on Sunday. All of us. Nick and I will explain everything then."

Will began to protest, but I propped myself up on the couch cushion and grasped his forearm, hoping he could sense the gist of my thoughts. *Please, don't push your uncle.*

He's agreed to talk to us, to finally give us some answers.

We should leave so we don't jeopardize Nick.

Will's eyes widened for a brief moment before his brow furrowed. "Let's go."

"Great, it is settled." Shai clapped his hands together. "I will notify Lydia's parents, apologize for our tardiness in calling, and inform them we insisted she stay for dinner. I will also apprise them of her ankle, and explain she got carried away in an enthralling game of charades."

Will bent down, and I wrapped my arms around his neck, tucking my head into the crook of his shoulder as he carried me from Nick's home. The usual warming sensation my body experienced when touching him was absent, replaced with cool steel. I tried my best to send as many happy vibes to him as possible, but the invisible wall Will placed between us stopped them before they could fully slip past the surface of his skin. *This is new.* I tried again, but this time I sent him my thoughts regarding our earlier kiss.

Will's jaw twitched, and he stopped a few yards short of my red Oldsmobile. "Please stop. I want to be mad right now." He bent his head to look at me. "I'm totally not mad at you. You were only trying to help back there. But I'm definitely pissed off at my uncle, Nolan, my parents... All I've ever known is a lie." He trekked the remaining steps to the car and placed me into the front seat. "So, if you don't mind, I need some time to simmer. I *need* to be mad."

"I understand." I caressed his cheek and pressed play on the Blues Traveler CD.

Hook had just finished playing when Will turned off the car. He kneeled before my open door and had me cling to his back. We approached the front door where Nolan greeted us as usual.

"Good evening, Lord William, Madam Lydia."

"Hi, Nolan," I said sweetly, trying to make up for Will's foul mood.

"Where do you want her?" Will asked, inclining his chin at me and ignoring all pleasantries.

Nolan didn't blanch, as if he'd expected this reaction. "In the apothecary room. There are no windows there." Nolan did an about-face and strode through the spacious atrium. "This way, Lord William."

Nolan led us past the kitchen and through a door that led to the back staircase, the route to Will's room. But instead of going upstairs, Nolan pressed his hand on the floral wallpaper. A hidden door swung inward, and a light switched on. Nolan padded down the carpeted stairs.

Will must have been exhausted from carrying me everywhere all afternoon, but he didn't complain once, his body showing no signs of fatigue. My inner doubts about my body had quieted down, as I grew more and more comfortable with him carrying me.

We'd only descended about ten stairs when we approached a landing. Nolan opened a door and Will carried me through the slightly arched frame into a warm, humid, medium-sized room. The room resembled a high-end athletic training facility. On one of the wood-paneled walls were hundreds of dark amber, opalescent, and blue glass tincture bottles, all labeled. In the corner on a tabletop sat a miniature greenhouse, and inside was a small bed of Christmas roses.

Will and I stood in the doorway, gaping.

"So, you truly didn't know this was here?" I whispered to him. He shook his head as he continued to take in the room, landing on what looked like a table of elements, but specific to the Christmas rose.

"Please, set Madam Lydia here." Nolan gestured to the white table in the middle of the room that looked a lot like a massage table.

Will set me down gently and fetched himself a chair, placing it at my side.

"Roll up your pant leg, please, and remove your sock," Nolan instructed me with quiet assertiveness. I did as asked. He examined my foot and ankle.

"Who did the first pass of healing?" He looked up at us.

Will's hand, which had been holding mine, suddenly grew hot and clammy. "I did," he croaked out.

Nolan smiled at him. "I must say, you did a marvelous job. And, Lord Abishai did a marvelous job walking you through it."

"Actually, Will did it on his own," I chimed in.

Nolan's eyes twinkled, and he grinned even wider. "I wish I could say I am surprised. Healing is probably the first of the many giftings that will come naturally to you. I would love to walk you through more advanced techniques right now, but I am on strict orders to heal her foot quickly and feed you dinner."

Will rolled his eyes. "Whatever," he mumbled.

If Nolan heard him, he pretended not to notice Will's persnicketiness. Nolan straightened himself and walked over to the wall of tinctures, selecting a blue glass bottle. He then went to a silver mini fridge and retrieved what looked like a frostbitten pink scarf. He returned to us and stood near my injured foot.

"Lord William, do you mind standing opposite me?" Will begrudgingly let go of my hand. "Madam Lydia, I am afraid the first pass did not heal as deeply as it needed to. It may be a little uncomfortable, but nothing you can't handle. May I proceed?"

A sudden rush of anxiety coursed up my neck, but I pushed it down. Will was already eyeing me.

"I think I should stand by Liddy," he said nervously.

"I'll be fine. Of course, Nolan. Please proceed and...thank you."

"My pleasure." Nolan grinned. He handed Will the bottle and pink wrap. Nolan placed his hands on either side of my ankle. "Lydia, what's your favorite color?"

His question caught me off guard. "Umm, purple. Why do you..." A blinding light and a loud *crack* reverberated throughout my body. Little bursts of light, like my own fireworks show, popped and sparkled in my vision, and I swayed.

Instantly, Nolan was next to my head with a dropper in his hand, and placed three drops of a honey-like liquid in my mouth. "Swallow please," the butler— *or should I call him healer now?*— instructed. I was instantly righted. He dipped the dropper into the blue bottle Will shakily held in his hands. Nolan took the wrap from Will and placed a few drops of opal-colored liquid on it. Within seconds, my foot was neatly wrapped.

"You will still be a little sore for the next few days, but it should be well enough to place some weight on it," Nolan said.

"You will need to come by every day for a new wrap. It would go faster if you soaked in the silverbell spa. You are welcome to it any time." He extended his hand toward a large, silver basin in the room.

"Thank you. So does this mean I can't shower tonight?"

"You can wrap it in a plastic bag and leave it hanging out of the bath," Nolan instructed.

"Like a cast?" Will asked.

"Exactly." Nolan nodded. He turned to me. "Cane or crutches?"

"Excuse me?" I asked.

"To use for the next few days to help you stay off of your ankle."

"Oh. Um, crutches, I guess."

Nolan proceeded to open a tall cabinet and pulled out a set of crutches, handing them to me. *Well, these are going to suck in the hallways at school.*

"And where would you prefer to take your dinner tonight?"

"My room," Will responded.

"I'm not sure about the tight staircase," I said, somewhat panicky.

A smile stretched Will's cheeks. "I could give you a piggyback ride."

I laughed. "No way. You've done enough carrying me around today. Do you have a family room?"

"Yes, we do," Nolan said. "It is down a little ways from the library. I will set you up in there." He shook his head regretfully. "I've been saying we need an elevator put in, but Lord Abishai didn't want to draw attention to this area of the home. I can carry you up the stairs if you are in need of assistance. It is of no consequence to me."

"I will obviously be carrying her." Will scoffed.

I swung my legs over the edge of the table and slid off, landing with most of my weight on my good foot. I took one careful step on my injured foot and to my surprise, it truly was much better.

"I can totally do it!" I squealed.

Nolan smiled. "I am a skilled healer, Madam, but please don't go messing up my work." He smirked and pushed his glasses up on the bridge of his nose. "Even though it feels better, it is still fragile. Please hold on to William, or use one of your crutches on your way upstairs."

"Will do," I said, still marveling at my fixed ankle.

Nolan rushed ahead of us to the mouth of the staircase. "I will meet you both in the family room. Dinner should be ready in about ten minutes."

I let Will escort me up the stairs, but was relieved to regain my independence once we reached the large, echoing hallway just outside the kitchen. We were silent as we made our way through the atrium, other than the *clop-thud, clop-thud* of my crutches against the marble floor. I plopped down on the leather couch, and rested my foot on the matching ottoman while Will explored the room as if he'd never seen it.

I watched him try to play it cool after the day we had, but I could tell he was stressed. His shoulders sat slightly higher than they normally did, he couldn't sit still, and his eyes were still glowing the same dark green they'd turned when Nick first asked for Shai's help.

We didn't wait long before Nolan rolled his service cart into the room. He removed the lid of his stainless-steel serving basin and filled up bowls with piping hot soup. He lifted two more tray tops, revealing a large salad and bowls of sliced fruit.

"Please leave everything on the tray when you are done. I will clean up later." Nolan ducked out, the slinking sounds of heavy, velvet drapes closing accompanied his exit.

Will took my tray and placed it on the ottoman in front of me, but said nothing.

"Thank you. Do you mind if I turn on the TV?" Will shook his head and I grabbed the remote, clicking through channel after channel until I stopped on *Friends*. Ten minutes passed without either of us saying a word, a definite first for us. I kept stealing glances at him. He barely touched his food, his jaw rigid.

I scooted down the couch, positioning myself behind where Will sat on the floor and laid my hands on his shoulders. When he didn't protest, I began to massage away the tension, believing I was offering the same healing he'd so often bestowed upon me, which was a lot. Apparently, I was a magnet for injuries.

Will sighed and rolled his neck, relaxing into my touch. I scooched a little closer. "I know you said you wanted to be mad, but is it OK if we talk about something else?"

"Of course, Lid. I didn't mean to make you feel like you couldn't talk to me at all."

"So, Sunday is Valentine's Day." Will tensed, and my fingers responded by working his muscles more deeply. "I realize we have to meet here now instead, and—"

"Liddy, I totally forgot!" Will whipped his head around.

"We can change the meeting to another day."

"Don't be silly. We totally have to meet with your uncle. But, are you doing anything Saturday?"

"Yeah, I am." He pulled a face. "With you, of course!" He laughed, finally acting like his normal self.

I slapped his shoulder. "I promised Sara I'd help her set up for her date with Matt, but I'm free after."

Will turned his body around and rested his forearms on my thighs. "Can I help? Many hands make light work."

I was suddenly hyper-aware of how close he was to me, and I blushed.

"Oh man, what has you blushing my favorite shade of pink?" Will asked, squeezing my thigh.

I made a sound somewhere between a scream and a laugh. He knew I was super ticklish. "Stop, don't do that!"

"Then tell me." He readied his hand as if he were going to squeeze again.

"I know you know."

"Yeah, but I want to know if what *you* think I know is what I know."

I rolled my eyes at him. "Well, you're cute, we're alone, and you're *very* close to me."

Will beamed then cleared his throat. "OK, so after you help Sara, what would you like to do for Valentine's Day?"

"This." I said simply.

"What exactly is *this*?"

"Me and you time. Alone. No one bothering us, not having to be careful about who sees us."

"I like the sound of that." He stood and climbed onto the couch, stretching out and resting his head on my thigh.

I smiled and stroked his hair as I returned my gaze to

the TV. My life had been flipped, turned upside down the moment he walked back into my life. A few months ago, I was wholeheartedly against relationships for fear of them holding me back. I couldn't wait to graduate, go off to college, and start working toward my career and my adult future.

Now, everything was uncertain. Everything, that is, except one thing. Will would be a part of my future, however long that future may be. Sure, Mara had been quiet since the afterparty at Joey's, but I was no longer so naive as to think she had given up. Not after seeing the state Nick returned to us in.

I checked the time. "Will, I have to go."

He sat up. "Five more minutes?"

"I think I can spare that." I anticipated him laying his head back down, but instead, he swung his body around and shifted me so my body was in front of his. Wrapping his arms around me, he slowly laid us down until we were snuggled on the couch, my back to his chest. Will's thumb slipped just under the hem of my shirt and I let out a small gasp at the tickling sensation.

"Hey, don't get any ideas," I cautioned half-heartedly. Oh, how I would have loved to be trained enough to control my giftings at this moment.

"I wouldn't dream of it. Well, that's not entirely true." Will kissed my neck. "But, uh, after nearly losing you, I'm sticking with the warning Nick gave us, no matter how vague. Nothing could tempt me enough to risk losing you."

I turned my head in his direction. "I love you," I breathed.

"I love you more."

Flowers for All

THAT NIGHT, I MANAGED TO DRIVE HOME without my ankle giving me any trouble. I came through the front door to find my parents snuggled on the couch, engrossed in their Thursday night TV marathon— *3rd Rock From the Sun*, followed by *Frasier*. I leaned up against the door jamb studying Mom and Dad for a moment. I had never once noticed anything about them that wasn't utterly human.

When I announced my presence, Mom and Dad barely batted an eyelash. Shai must have squelched any angst they might have had about my ankle because they never asked about it. They invited me to sit and watch *Frasier* with them, but I opted to take a bath and go right to sleep. As much as I had tried to remain calm for Will's sake, I was having a hard time with all of this. *Three days,* I repeated to myself. I would finally have some answers in three days.

The next morning zipped by.

"Lydia!" Mom called from downstairs.

"Yeah, Mom?" I yelled over the banister.

"You're not going to get to school early if you don't leave now."

"Crud!" I had taken extra care getting ready and hadn't paid enough attention to the clock. Even though Valentine's Day wasn't until Sunday, the grams were being handed out at school today, and I wanted to look nice for the festivities.

I grabbed my backpack from my chair and flew down the stairs. Mom was standing there holding my coat and already had my Mary Janes out of the shoe bin.

"Thanks, Mom." I slid into my black peacoat, pulling my hair out from under it.

"Aren't you gorgeous," Mom gushed.

"Thanks." I smiled, gave her a hug, and hurried out the door.

I picked up Pree first.

"Hey girl, hey," Pree mumbled as she opened the passenger side door.

"What's up?" I responded cheerfully. "Happy Valentine's Day."

"Speak for yourself," Pree scoffed. "There is nothing happy about this day. You used to feel the same before you landed the catch of a lifetime."

"Valentine's Day isn't only about your significant other; it's about celebrating all the people you care about," I encouraged. "Take me, for example. I love you, and today I'm taking the opportunity to make sure you know that."

"Girl, you're creeping me out. Don't do me any favors by making up crap for me. Where is this Pollyanna attitude coming from anyway?"

I shrugged in reply.

"Whatever, I wore all black for the occasion." Pree unzipped her charcoal coat to show me her outfit, and I laughed.

We arrived at Sara's house, and she and Dani came outside through the garage. Pree and I both got out of the car and flipped our seats down so they could climb in the back.

"Happy Valentine's Day!" Sara sang from the back seat.

"Oh man, not you too," Pree groaned.

"Ugh, I second that," Dani huffed. "You two used to think a lot more like we do before your prince charmings came along"

Sara laughed. "OK, but you gals will change your mind once 'Mr. Right' shows up."

"Probably not." Dani rolled her eyes.

"So, anyone have plans?" Pree asked.

I caught Sara's glance in the mirror.

"Matt and I are doing dinner and a movie," she replied. No one but me appeared to hear the waver in her voice, indicating she'd fibbed.

"And you, Liddy? Are you and Will finally gonna have some PDA to speak of?" Dani waggled her brows.

"Get your head out of the gutter, chica." I laughed. "May I remind you, I'm not planning on having sex until marriage. Will respects that."

"There are other things you can do besides sex," Dani teased.

"Thanks," I replied. "I sat next to you in Mr. Walters' health class, remember?"

We both laughed out loud at the memory of Mr. Walters and how he made the class yell *penis* and *vagina* over ten times each on the first day, to help us get our giggles out.

"Seriously, though," I went on. "Will and I are going to hang at his house, watch a movie, and order takeout."

"We all think it's cool you're waiting, but bring your chastity belt just in case," Sara chimed in, and we all laughed as I pulled into one of the student parking spots.

We walked through the back doors of the school together. To my surprise, Will was right there waiting for me. It was a little early and the halls had not yet filled with students. He carried three bouquets of deep purple roses in one hand, his other hand tucked behind his back.

"Good morning, ladies," Will greeted.

"Morning, Will," Pree muttered, eyeing the flowers.

"These are for all of you." Will handed each of my friends their own bouquet.

"For me?" Pree squealed. "Thanks, Will!" She gave him a massive hug.

"You're welcome." He grinned from ear to ear as Pree jostled him side to side a few times before letting go.

"That was uh, very nice of you," Dani said, her eyes practically twinkling with excitement. "Thank you."

"Come on, girls. Let's let these two have a moment." Sara took her flowers and linked elbows with Dani. "I love them, Will," she said over her shoulder as the three of them walked off.

"These, my beautiful, are for you." Will handed me a set of

lilac and baby pink peonies. Upon closer inspection, a couple of Christmas roses were dispersed throughout.

"They're so lovely. How did you know these were my favorite?"

"I pay attention," he said, his lips tickling my ear.

"Be serious." I laughed.

"Honest." He held a hand over his heart. "One of the cool perks when I'm with you, let's say in the mall, is that I receive a little 'notification' every time something makes you happy."

"Ah, so you have something most dudes with a girlfriend wishes he had."

"And what is that?"

"The ability to read a woman's mind."

A slow, teasing grin slid on his face. "I will deny that all day. I can't read your mind."

"But you do get help from our powers. Some might say that is cheating," I taunted, opening my locker and reaching for my history book.

"I didn't cheat," Will said, leaning his firm body against the locker next to mine. "I still have to be paying close attention, plus tastes can change in different seasons of life."

"I was only teasing you. I'm thankful for such a wonderful boyfriend like you."

I peered around in haste. When I saw the coast was clear, I stood on my tiptoes and gave Will a soft, lingering kiss on his cheek. I pulled back in time to catch the green embers of his eyes flicker to life, dim, then extinguish as I sighed in admiration.

"I have something for you, but you'll receive your other gift tomorrow," I said coyly.

"I thought we said no gifts?" Will protested.

"Oh, like the flowers you recently handed out? Please, this is no big deal, I promise. The other one is homemade." I reached into my backpack and held out the thin rectangle I wrapped in red paper for Will.

He took the present from me and opened it. "'The Princess Bride'!"

On the front of the DVD, I'd attached a Post-It note: *As you wish. Always, Liddy.* Will smiled and kissed my cheek. He locked eyes with mine and his grin widened.

"I'm glad you like it." I said. "We can watch it tomorrow night."

We walked toward Sara's locker but pivoted when we saw Matt handing her a large brown bear holding a heart-shaped box of chocolates. She wrapped her arms around him, and they began making out.

We ended up at Pree's locker, where Dani stood scowling at Sara and Matt.

"Quit staring." I swatted Dani's arm.

"Not that easy. They need to get a room," Dani said, shaking her head.

Alex came walking from the hall adjacent to Pree's locker.

"Happy V-Day everyone," he said, holding up his pointer and middle finger in a "v" shape.

"Yeah, whatever," Dani mumbled.

"I see you've dressed for the holiday, Pree." Alex gestured to her outfit.

"Don't start, Alex," Pree snapped.

"Whoa, whoa! I'm just trying to lighten the mood." Alex held up his hands in mock defense. "Anyway, I'm off to student council to help finish sorting all the grams. They'll be delivered in fourth period." He took a few steps past us but stopped short. Turning his head, he inspected Dani and said, "You look extra beautiful today." He continued down the hall, disappearing into the crowd of students.

"Ummm, did anyone else *hear that*?" I asked.

"So obvious—" Pree rolled her eyes— "I've been telling her for weeks that Alex has a thing for her, but she doesn't believe me."

"No, he doesn't. Alex is a player. He's trying to be cute," Dani insisted.

"Alex has definitely changed a lot," I offered.

"Whatever." Dani scoffed. "Let's go to class."

"Should someone break up the vacuum cleaners? I think their suction settings are stuck at 'on'," Pree joked, jabbing a thumb at Sara and Matt before bending over in laughter at her own observation.

"Nah, let's let the warning bell do its job," Will said, laughing along with Pree. Their laughter was contagious, and I couldn't help but join in. Even Dani cracked a smile.

The first three periods whizzed by. I strode into fourth, excited for my friends to receive their Valentine's Day grams, hoping they would help brighten Pree and Dani's day. About fifteen minutes into class, someone knocked on Mr. Dunbar's door, and in walked Alex and a few freshman student council members. They each held a cardboard box.

"Eyes up here, please," Mr. Dunbar called out. "You still have a test next week."

They set their boxes down on the back table and began sorting through all the grams. I shifted my attention back to my math teacher.

Alex stood by my desk and leaned down to place a small stack of different colored hearts on my desk. Before he moved on to the next student, he whispered, "Thank you for the heart. You don't need to keep thanking me. I only did what anyone else would have done." He stood up fully, winked at me, and continued down the rows.

After class, I was the first one in the commons area, my coat on, waiting for everyone else for lunch. Will and Pree were the first to show up.

"Aww, girl, thanks so much for the gram!" Pree squealed.

I hugged her. "How'd you know?"

"Please, your fabulous handwriting is *so* recognizable."

Sara came rounding the corner with her bear under one arm. Dani was next to Sara and kept punching the bear's head as it slumped against her shoulder. I turned my head to hide my laugh.

"Sorry we're late," Dani said, jerking a thumb toward Sara. "Mrs. Berenstain over here had to wait for the hallway to clear before she was able to walk through."

"Isn't Matt the best?" Sara swooned before kissing his cheek. She stepped toward us, but Matt snatched her hand and stole another long kiss.

"*Ahem!*' Pree cleared her throat. "We're leaving. If you don't come now, it's Wild Cat Shack for you!"

Since we were upperclassmen now, and had the privilege to eat off campus, none of us wanted to settle for cafeteria food, no matter how yummy the Shack's cookies were.

"Coming!" Sara sang, her face flushed, running to catch up with us as we were halfway to the exit doors. "Isn't Matt the best?" she swooned again.

"Yeah, you said that already," Pree pointed out.

"Oh Pree, don't be such a hater," Sara said nonchalantly as she skipped ahead.

Will shook his head, laughing as he opened the trunk of his Wagoneer. Sara shoved her bear in there and jumped into the back seat. We took off and Will turned left out of the parking lot.

"Uh, Earth to Will! Panera is the other way," Dani said.

"I know," he answered, a smirk lifting the corner of his mouth.

"I'm confused," Pree said.

Will grabbed my hand but kept his eyes on the road. A few minutes later, I knew exactly where we were going.

Will pressed the clicker on his visor, and the black iron gate slowly opened. Trees lined the long drive and an expansive lawn at least a mile wide encircled the mansion. A thick forest loomed in the distance as far as the eye could see.

"Are we at a museum?" Sara asked as she craned her neck.

"No, silly!" Pree laughed. "This is Will's house!"

I looked back at Dani, shocked she hadn't said anything, and instantly knew why. Her chin was practically to her chest.

Before Will even rang the bell, Nolan stood in the entryway holding the door open.

"Hey, Nolan," I said.

"Good afternoon, Madam Lydia, Lord William, and guests. Please come in." Nolan closed the door behind us and offered to take our coats. He hung them on the coat rack and asked us to follow him.

Will and I had walked about ten paces before we realized

the rest of the group was still in the front entryway.

"One second, Nolan." Will immediately stopped and waited for the others.

We exchanged knowing smiles as we took in the girls' astonished reactions to the house. I had nearly forgotten how overwhelming and impressive Will's home was the first time I saw it. In fact, I was still getting used to it, and I'd been here over fifty times.

I caught Nolan smiling at them. He cleared his throat, "*Ahem.* The dining room is this way, ladies."

Pree came right over to us, but Sara and Dani took baby steps as their heads swiveled around.

"Nolan, please escort Pree. Liddy and I will bring the other two." Will and I chuckled and met up with Sara and Dani. We linked arms and led them to the dining room.

I'd walked past this ornate room numerous times, but Will and I had never actually eaten in it. Normally, the dining room was simple, with rich textiles and materials in cream, ivory, white, and natural wood that all seamlessly blended together.

Today, red and pink rose petals were sprinkled over a magenta tablecloth covering the sixteen-person table. Pink, red, and white origami hearts dangled from two chandeliers centered over the dining table that Nolan had set for all five of us. Silver plates and goblets were set out and light pink, heart-shaped cloth napkins decorated the plates.

"Liddy told me how you all used to hate Valentine's Day. I thought I might help change that." Will ran a hand through his hair.

"If you don't marry this boy, I volunteer," Dani chortled

directly across from me. I nearly choked on the water I had sipped from the crystal glass. Will gave my hand a reassuring squeeze.

"Nobody's getting married any time soon, I hope," Pree interjected, giving Sara the side eye.

Sara glanced at my ring for a brief moment, and I blushed. "There's something so appealing about getting married young," she said. "You don't have too much excess baggage from past failed relationships. Your heart is fuller; no pieces missing that stay with others."

I couldn't help but assume her comments were directed at me.

Dani gaped at her. I leaned back as Nolan laid a plate before me and removed the silver domed cover.

"You've lost your mind," Pree said incredulously.

"I'm not saying *I'm* getting married." Sara pressed a hand to her chest. "I'm simply saying, I can understand the appeal."

"Thank goodness." Pree leaned back into her chair. "My mom is practically marrying me off already; it's so barbaric. I want to live my life before I settle down."

Sara leaned forward. "Such a tainted viewpoint. Who says you give up your life when you get married? If you marry your best friend, why can't you do life together? I mean, hopefully you are marrying someone who supports your hopes and dreams, and you at least share some common hobbies and interests."

"Tainted viewpoint?" Pree shot back.

Sara huffed. "Yes, tainted. Arranged marriages are not the same as choosing for yourself."

"Hey, can we please quit the marriage squabble and let...

Nolan, right?" Dani turned to face him, and he nodded. He had come around the table with his cart and had been waiting patiently. "And let Mr. Nolan serve this amazing lunch he prepared for us?" she finished.

Sara and Pree shifted in their seats. "Sorry," they mumbled in unison.

I stared at the pink candlestick as liquid wax pooled beneath the flame. I ate in silence for a few moments, watching the wax slide down the smooth tapered body and drip onto the mirror it rested on.

Will spoke first, pulling my attention to him. "So, besides our differing and valid viewpoints on marriage, I say we 'cheers' to friendship." He held up his silver goblet.

"I agree!" I said a little too enthusiastically, glad for the change in subject. Everyone grabbed their ornate cups. "Does everyone want to go around and say something?" My friends all quickly avoided my gaze.

"I'll say something," Will chimed in. "I'm thankful my Liddy has such amazing friends, and for how you all befriended me so quickly. Thanks for making me feel at home."

"I'll drink to that," Sara said. We all clinked our glasses and took a sip.

"Holy Cow! What in the name of all the sweet heavens is this glorious concoction?" Dani blurted.

It tasted a little like punch, but there were flavors in the pink, frothy liquid I could not place. I smiled. *This has to be a Cristes specialty.*

Will laughed. "I have no clue. I've never had it before." He took another swig.

"I shall call it *Hawaiian Sunset*," Dani announced.

The rest of lunch went smoothly. We all ate our broccoli cheddar soup and cobb salad and the girls continued to fuss over the spread Nolan had made for them.

"I'm afraid the time has come for you all to be returning to school, if you wish to not be late for your next classes," Nolan announced as Pree tilted her head back in an effort to consume every last drop of Hawaiian Sunset.

Dani, who had already gotten out of her chair to stretch, rushed over to Nolan and swung her arms around his middle in a tight bear hug. "Thank you, thank you, thank you!" she squeaked. "That was the best food I've had like...ever!" She skipped off toward the foyer. The rest of us looked at each other and shrugged our shoulders. We'd never seen Dani so happy.

Pree and Sara walked ahead of Will and me. Nolan held his arm out, momentarily delaying us.

He turned to us and, in a hushed voice, said, "I put a little something in each of your drinks which should help you both with the glowing problem in dance class. The effects will only last a couple of hours. You won't feel much different, but your giftings will be dampened and you should still take precautions." He glanced at the door and in a rush, he added, "Please don't tell your uncle. This is a one-time gift."

He turned on his heel and reached the coat rack before Pree and Sara arrived there.

"I'm not sure if I should be thankful for his help or creeped out by his admission to spiking our drinks."

Will laughed. "I think we should be thankful, definitely thankful. Dance is a constant stressor nowadays."

Normally we would be racing to class due to having to

wait in lines and for our food when eating out. But thanks to Will's surprise, we were back at school with a few minutes to spare.

When Will and I walked into the dance studio, Coach R. sent us straight to the back pool room. As promised, Will had brought the CD *Remember Two Things*.

"Should we give it a try?" I asked him.

"I don't see why not. Let's play with some movements for the opening phrases, the ones where we are together."

Nolan was true to his word. For the first time, we were able to dance freely, our eyes flickering, but the flame was kept at bay. We had choreographed three sets of eight when my ankle started to bite a little.

"I need to take a short break." I hobbled to the poorly supported couch.

"Your ankle?"

"Yeah. That reminds me; I need a new wrap from Nolan tonight."

Will gingerly lifted my foot and placed his hands on either side of my ankle. The pain barely ebbed.

"Used to it already, I see." Will's brow furrowed.

"Used to what?"

"My healing touch." He smirked playfully.

"As if! Remember what Nolan said? Our giftings would be diminished for a few hours."

"Oh, yeah. Well...bummer. Maybe you should stay off your ankle for the rest of class. We can work on choreography in my pool this weekend to keep weight off of it."

"No. I don't want Nolan's concoction to go to waste. I only need a few minutes to rest. Can I talk to you about what happened yesterday?" I asked hesitantly.

Will dropped his chin. "If you want to."

"So, last night when I got home, I watched my parents for a little while. I kept trying to recall a time when they may have let their Watcher giftings slip and show."

"Were you able to?"

"Not in the least."

"How odd." Will frowned. "Are you sure?"

"I'm pretty observant, and I think I know my own parents," I said a little saltily.

"I'm sorry, Liddy. I didn't mean to offend you. What about your brother, Mickey?"

I bit my bottom lip, taking a moment to consider him before speaking. "He may have a gift, if you consider being able to always avoid consequences one."

Will chuckled. "He is a good kid for the most part."

"I do remember your mom, though. I can remember the first time I met her on the day you all moved in. Her eyes glowed like a lightning bug, only greener, but by the time she got to me, they were normal. I always thought I'd imagined it."

"I can recall a few instances where my parents used a small part of their magic, but after Charlie, even with my memories back, I haven't seen nor do I remember anything." Will's gaze grew distant.

"Do you miss them?" I asked.

"My parents?" Will's voice softened. "Yes. A lot, actually."

I rested my hand on his arm. "I'd love to see them again."

"I'm sure they'd love to see you too, Liddy." Will brightened. "Hey, why don't you come down with me to

Florida over spring break?"

"Really? I would love that! But, I don't think my parents would approve." I sighed. "Two dating teenagers, alone together."

"We wouldn't be alone. We would be staying at my parent's house. You'd have your own room. Plus, we aren't going to be..." Will ran his hand through his hair and bit his bottom lip.

I flushed. "Oh, I know, but they don't understand why we really aren't, *you* know?"

"Liddy, even if Charlie and Cristes weren't on the line, we wouldn't," Will said firmly.

I was taken aback for a second.

"I respect your views on waiting until marriage," he continued. "I wouldn't want to tempt that. Plus—" he ran a hand through his hair again— "I feel the same way."

My heart melted. Most teens my age did not share my beliefs, which was fine. They normally didn't give me a hard time about it, either. But my ex hadn't been as cool about it.

"What?" Will asked, peering at my face. "I find it annoying how my little notification system is too dampened to clue me in on what you're thinking."

"I expected a different reaction, is all. What if Cristes wasn't on the line and I changed my mind?"

Will's eyes bugged and he rubbed the back of his neck. "I, uh, do wish to remain celibate until marriage. I... I would be open to discussion later on if that is a deal-breaker."

"No, not a deal-breaker. I just wish I felt like I had more of a choice."

Will studied me for a long moment. "I understand. I will

do what I can to make sure you— both of us —make the big, important choices. We deserve that much."

"Thank you for understanding." I smiled gratefully at him. "Can I ask one more thing?"

"Of course."

"Can I kiss you now? I'd love to experience you with Nolan's little gift."

Will grinned. "You never have to ask to kiss me."

"Should we close the blinds just in case?"

He laughed. "I'm telling you, we are fine, but if it makes you feel better, you close the blinds and I'll lock the doors."

We met back on the couch. An adrenaline surge like the first time we kissed coursed through me. What if I wasn't a skilled kisser without my gifting? What if Will didn't like me without our Watcher connection?

"Are you alright?" Will asked, concern etched in his face.

"I'm nervous."

"About what?"

"About kissing you." I wrung my hands and dropped my gaze.

"You're going to have to help me follow your train of thought. We've kissed before...a lot." Will smirked at me. "Yeah, but we had heightened Watcher powers. Now that they've been dampened, what if...what if I'm not a good kisser?"

"You're kidding, right? Liddy, you are a fantastic kisser. Believe me. You know, sitting and fretting is only going to make you more anxious. We'll take it slow, OK?"

"OK." I turned to face him.

I leaned in, and his lips met mine— soft, but confident.

He pulled away slightly to look me in the eye, but I closed the gap quickly. I pressed my lips more firmly to his, and his mouth opened in response.

He was right. The kissing part was the same, minus the magnets and lights. I leaned more into the kiss, allowing my body to relax into his. His tongue responded, intensifying the lazy circles he had been making. I groaned slightly, then pulled away, somewhat embarrassed.

"What?" Will breathed, his chest heaving.

"Sorry," I whispered. "I didn't mean to..."

"To what? Show me you were enjoying yourself?" Will's eyes flickered. He leaned in and ran his lips against the base of my ear. Chills ran down my entire body. "Please, never stop" —he kissed my neck—"letting me"—he kissed my jaw—"know because your pleasure brings me pleasure."

His lips were on mine again, more urgent than before. I deepened the kiss, clinging to him with the intention of fully letting myself enjoy this moment. As soon as I let inhibition go, I felt a crack somewhere deep within my body, and I gasped. It didn't hurt, but I pulled away from Will, clutching my chest.

"Oh, no, Liddy. Look." He held up my hand, and my veins were glowing. I gaped at him. "Yep, your eyes are bright as well."

"Yours, too." I breathed heavily. "I guess we pushed it a little too far."

"Don't panic. We still have twenty minutes for this to calm down. I brought a deck of cards. Want to play Spit or War?"

"Yes, please. I could definitely use the distraction."

We played cards for ten minutes before Will's eyes were

back to normal. The light in my veins had retracted enough to the point where the human eye couldn't detect it, and Will reported my eyes had gone back to their usual violet.

"See, we're fine," Will assured me. "Shall we dance?"

"No!" I cried. "And risk glowing again? But I am sad we let Nolan's help go to waste."

"I wouldn't say we wasted it." Will smirked and I flung a card at him.

"That's not what I meant."

"We have plenty of time to choreograph this duet." Will shrugged one shoulder. "I bet we'll have the whole beginning set this weekend. You'll see."

"Starting tomorrow?" I pressed.

"Starting tonight," Will amended.

A, B, C-Ya

WILL AND I WALKED TO THE PARKING LOT, Pree and Dani trailing behind us. Dani didn't have to work for the first time in forever, and Pree's debate practice was canceled. Will gave me a hug, pecked my cheek, and walked away.

"Thank you," Dani said, resting her hand on my arm to still me.

"For the gram? You're welcome. It was nothing."

"Well, yes, for that, but also for not torturing Pree and me with public make-out sessions."

"Weren't you giving Liddy a hard time about *no* PDA at lunch yesterday?" Pree joked.

"This is an A and B conversation, Pree. C yourself out."

"All right, ladies. Simmer down," I said as we got into

my car, Dani claiming the front seat. I started the engine and pulled out of the parking lot. "Did anyone receive any more hearts today?"

"Actually, I did." Dani sounded somewhat embarrassed.

"What color was it?" I asked excitedly.

"Red."

"I bet I can guess who it was from," Pree chimed in.

"Shush." Dani giggled. "It was from..."

"You're killing me, Smalls," I complained at her dramatic pause.

"Alex, it was from Alex!"

"I told you! Didn't I say he had a thing for you?" Pree gloated.

"Liddy, do you really think he's changed?" Dani asked in earnest.

"Definitely. But he's still Alex, if that makes sense."

"Totally, but like a new and improved version?" Dani asked.

"Exactly."

I turned into Dani's neighborhood. After watching her walk safely inside her house, I reversed out of the driveway and headed home.

"I mean, I'm happy for Dani, but I hate being the only single one," Pree lamented quietly.

I didn't really know how to respond, although I empathized with how she was feeling.

"You will always be included."

"Thanks, Liddy. But it's not fun being the third wheel. Anyway, are we going to Nick's? I realized after lunch we didn't arrange who was going to check on his place today."

Crud, I chastised myself, realizing I hadn't clued her in on all the events of yesterday. She deserved to know. "Are you able to come to my house for a little bit?"

She whipped her head, her attention sharp and focused on me. "For sure," she chirped. "To hang out, or did something happen?"

"What makes you think that?" I asked, doing my best to sound innocent.

"I remember you and Will went there yesterday, and today is the first day we haven't made plans to check in on Nick."

"You're very observant." I smiled.

"Something happened yesterday and I'm *just* finding out?" Pree's voice was pitched to hysterics.

"I'm so sorry! It was not intentional. Let me explain." I recapped the story, skipping my makeout sesh with Will in the car.

I pulled into my driveway and parked behind my mom's van. Pree and I grabbed snacks from the kitchen, said hello to Mom, and retreated to my room. I placed a towel under the door while Pree turned on my CD player to help cover our voices from any snooping.

"So let me get this straight; Will freaking healed your ankle?"

"Uh-huh," I said between bites of apple.

"Let me see it."

I pulled up my pant leg, removed my sock, and wiggled my toes in front of her. All that remained of my injury was green and yellow bruising under the skin.

"And Will's uncle *and* his butler are Watchers, too? I

thought Will said he was all alone in this? You, too, by the way." Pree took a sip of her water, but promptly sprayed it all over me. "So, does that mean your parents—"

"Ugh! Thanks for that." I wiped my face.

"Sorry!" She shrugged her shoulders and offered me an apologetic smile.

"To answer your question, no...well, I'm not sure actually. I've never noticed anything abnormal about them, or my brother. I can, however, recall one time with Will's mom."

"Why would Nick make all of this a secret?" Pree wondered. "Why would Nolan and Mr. Jamison not say anything?"

I leaned forward in my seat. "Exactly. Will hasn't been too keen on talking much about it, and I've been trying to be patient in waiting for the answers myself; answers supposedly coming on Sunday from both Nick and Shai." I groaned. "I didn't mention anything to you because I ignored everything so I wouldn't lose my mind waiting for Sunday."

"Remind me, why Sunday and not sooner?" Pree frowned.

"Because Shai said so; something about needing time to heal Nick as well as restoring himself after." I shrugged. "My guess is he needed time before talking to me and Will."

Her lips twisted. "Do you think I can come? Maybe I can help."

"I'll ask. Shai didn't seem too keen on talking to Will and me to begin with," I admitted, adding, "Nick had to practically beg him to talk to us. I'm not naive. I know there's something more considerable that neither of them wants to tell us."

"Bigger than that witch, Mara?"

I sighed. "I have no idea."

"Speaking of which, she's been too quiet. It's making me

very nervous," Pree said.

My stomach dropped. Unconsciously, I placed a hand at my throat where, not too long ago, Mara had used one of my best friends to try to kill me.

"I'm so sorry, Liddy! I did not mean to bring up such horrid memories for you!"

"No worries, Pree. Anyway, now you have all the info."

"Do you promise to talk to me Sunday night and clue me in?" she asked.

"I can't promise I'll be able to call you that evening, but I do promise to fill you in as soon as I can."

"Fair enough."

Pree and I got to hang out for about another hour before I walked her halfway to her house.

"How is your duet coming along, by the way?" she asked sincerely. "I mean, you guys already have a hard enough time keeping your magical lights under wraps. I can't imagine what's going on with dance. Thank goodness Coach R. gave you guys your own isolated room to rehearse in."

"I know, right? Will and I have timed ourselves. It takes anywhere from ten to thirty minutes for our light to dim enough to go unnoticed by the human eye," I explained. However, we can't risk it. We really haven't been able to practice much except for today. Nolan slipped something in our drink to help us."

Pree shuddered. "Soooort of creepy."

"Right? That's what I said to Will."

"Well, did it work?" Pree asked.

"Yes, very well actually."

"So, doesn't that solve your problem? You can just take

that stuff every day."

"Actually," I sighed, "Nolan said it was a one-time gift." Pree tilted her head to the side. With her face scrunched and lips pouted, I practically saw the wheels turning in her mind.

"Wear gloves," she stated, like this was the most obvious conclusion. "Then you won't actually be touching. And..." she nodded to herself, "wear a blindfold." I opened my mouth to interject and ask if she'd lost her dang mind, but she rambled on. "I personally would choose a lighter mesh material so you can still see. That way when your eyes do that—" she gestured vaguely at her face— "thing they do, the light will be dulled."

"Pree, you're a genius!" I nearly toppled her over with a hug.

"Easy killer!" Pree laughed. "I know I'm a genius, but you don't need to rough me up over it."

I laughed, too. "Sorry, Pree."

"Glad I could help. Oh! One other thing," she added, her eyes sparkling. "What if I came to help you during dance class? That way, if something were to happen, I could be the buffer."

"Again, another fantabulous idea." I grinned at her. "I'm so blessed and lucky to have you, Pree."

She jabbed a finger at me. "And don't you ever forget it."

When we reached the halfway point, we separated and I turned around to head back home. Pree and I both waved goodbye when we reached our driveways.

After dinner with my parents, I ran up to my room one last time to triple-check my duffle bag and make sure I hadn't missed any spots while shaving. This would be the first time Will would be seeing me in a swimsuit since we were kids.

"Lydia," Mom called to me from the bottom of the stairs.

I approached the railing. "Yeah, Mom?"

"What time do you think you'll be home?"

"By curfew. Why, what's up?"

Mom was leaning against the door jamb of the dining room, picking at her nails. "Nothing much. Any chance you're free to hang out this weekend? Maybe watch one of our romantic comedy favorites?"

"I'm so sorry, Mom. I would love to, but it's Valentine's Day weekend."

"Isn't Valentine's Day only on Sunday?"

"Yes, but I promised Sara I would help her tomorrow, and after, Will and I are celebrating Valentine's Day because on Sunday, his uncle made plans for all of us to do something together."

Mom's face dropped, and guilt seized me.

"How about next weekend?"

Her face perked up and she smiled. "That sounds wonderful, Lydia. Have fun and be safe."

I arrived at Will's a little after six-thirty.

"Good evening, Madam Lydia. Prince William is already at the pool. If you need to change, there is a small locker room in the cabana. Follow me."

Nolan led me down the main corridor in which the atrium was visible. Instead of going straight through the kitchen, we turned right down a narrow hallway and then left down another hall. As we came closer to a lone door at the end of a short hallway, the faint scent of chlorine roused memories of the summers I'd spent working at the Aquatic Center.

Nolan stopped and turned to face me. "The pool area is right through this door. There's an intercom near the locker room. Please ring me if you need anything. I have stocked the kitchenette area with plenty of snacks and drinks."

I smiled at him. "Is there anything you don't think of, Nolan?"

It was the first time I had seen him almost blush. He gave me a slight bow and proceeded back the way we came.

I walked through the door and found Will lounging in the hot tub.

"Welcome, gorgeous. Are you ready to start dancing, or should I say 'water dancing?'"

The mere sight of him – his defined torso and shoulders, beads of water trickling down his sculpted body – caught me off guard, and my breath hitched.

"I'll need a few minutes," I squeaked. "I need to change into my swimsuit. I didn't realize we'd start in the pool."

"No problem," Will said. "I want to make sure we get our choreography to a place where you are comfortable. Less stress means more fun."

Heat flooded my cheeks. He knew me so well. I walked around the far end of the pool, and past a hot tub that trickled over the pool's edge like a mini waterfall. The water in the pool changed colors every few seconds, lazily melting from violet to green to blue and back to violet.

I entered the changing room, which resembled a miniature guesthouse complete with a sofa, TV, and bathroom. The cabana's walls were built high for privacy, but there was no ceiling.

I undressed and placed my unmentionables back in my bag, hung my jeans and sweatshirt on the door's hook, and shimmied into my metallic purple bikini. Giving myself a final once-over in the vanity mirror, I adjusted the small bow on the bra top, then turned to make sure the boy shorts covered all of my cheeks.

"Liddy, are you alright in there?" Will asked from directly behind the door.

"Yes, I'll only be a sec." I took a deep breath to steady myself. *Confidence Liddy, confidence. He loves you and you love him, and that's all that matters. You are more than a body. You are strong and healthy, and your body deserves your respect because it does so much for you.* I let out the long breath I'd been holding and opened the door.

Will turned around slowly and his eyes met mine.

"You're beautiful," he whispered. Instantly, his eyes were aflame and he looked away, rubbing the back of his neck. His shoulders rose and fell with each breath, and I experienced part of the mini-storm brewing within him.

"Sh-shall we start?" he stammered.

I nodded.

"You're going to love the water... A perfect eighty-four degrees."

"Sounds good. I'm used to the freezing water at the water park, though the private pools I subbed at were tolerable."

We walked over to the shallow end of the pool and slowly made our way down the steps. I paused before the water hit my navel, but Will dove the rest of the way in and popped his head out at the pool's midpoint.

"Come on, I told you the water's perfect. Don't you trust me?"

As if he were daring me, I dove in from the last step, swimming right past him and emerging at the end by the waterfall.

"You're right! It is amazing." I giggled. "Why haven't we

swum here before?"

Will shrugged. "I guess I never viewed swimming as a winter activity."

"But you thought this was a great space to rehearse dancing?" I teased.

"Definitely..." Will ducked his head under the water, emerging strikingly close to my face... "Especially lifts."

My stomach tightened, and I averted my gaze.

"Something wrong?" He lifted my chin so I'd have to look at him. "You acted like this at Nick's as well. Are you afraid of heights or something?"

He would know if I were lying. "No... I've never done any lifts," I admitted with a half-truth.

He smiled, and I was newly determined to not let my past hang-ups interfere with my present relationship.

"I've done quite a few." He winked. "On my dance team in Florida, I was in many Adagio dances so I'm very confident in my lifting abilities. Let's start with some of the trickier ones in the pool."

"If you insist." I grimaced.

"Have you ever wanted to try the *Dirty Dancing* lift?"

My eyes nearly popped out of my head. "You can do that one?"

"Yes, I can," Will said confidently. "As long as the partners trust each other."

Trust wasn't my problem. I fully trusted Will, but I couldn't silence the echoes of my past tormentors. *Fatty, fugly, curvygrl82*...taunts that resurfaced in my mind.

I followed Will to the center of the pool. My hands trembled at the idea of him lifting my full bodyweight above his head. While I knew he was strong, very strong, I still worried about hurting him.

"OK, stand in front of me...good." Will positioned the heels of his hands on either side of the front of my hip bones. "Now on the count of three, you are going to fully jump up and out as much as you can." I nodded in understanding. "Then you will need to put your arms out to your sides and tighten your core for balance."

"Got it," I said, trying my best to keep my emotions in check.

"Here we go. One...two..."

"Wait, wait," I took a step back. "I'm not ready."

"I promise this will be fun! You have nothing to fear." Will placed his hands back at my hips and he wore a crooked grin. "You can't get hurt in the pool."

I bit my lip. "You're right. Let's do this."

"Alright, one...two...three!" Will squatted to shift my weight beneath him and stood swiftly, helping to thrust me toward the sky. I was up and managed to hold my posture perfectly. I was also keenly aware of his hands pressing into my hip bones, along with the nearly imperceptible quivering of his arms. I broke my focus as I tried to see his face, to read if I was too much for him.

"No, no, no!" Will cried out, and down we went. He immediately popped up out of the water, smoothing his hair back. "Liddy, you're incredible! None of my previous partners have ever gotten up that quickly and held it! Let's try again."

"I think I need a break," I said, swimming toward the stairs.

"What?" Will's brow crinkled. "We literally just got

started." He swam over to me and placed his hand on my shoulder, but I shrugged it off. His lips creased. "Did I do something? Did I hurt you?"

"No, you've been great."

Will pulled me to him, moving us into deeper water, and I draped my arms around his neck. Being in the water made it easy and natural for me to wrap my legs around his waist, and he used his arms to propel himself a few inches to the wall. He said nothing, but I knew he must have felt how uneasy I was.

I sighed. "I'm not a fan of lifts because..."

"Because...?" Will prodded, nuzzling his nose against mine.

I hid my face in his neck. "Because I'm too heavy. I'm not super slim like my sisters, Sara, Jackie, or most other girls my age."

"So? Everyone is different. Why are you comparing your stunning beauty to them?"

"I never used to, but I was bullied if you remember. And, well, I guess I haven't fully gotten over it. Believe me, I'm trying."

"I hate how some ignorant kids have hurt you this much, and have completely distorted how you view your own perfect body."

"It doesn't help that coming into my Watcher giftings over the summer has really changed my body as well. I'm still getting used to..." I trailed off.

"Getting used to..." Will encouraged me once again.

"All of this," I said dramatically, pulling away from him. But Will reeled me back.

"I'm not a mind reader. You are going to have to be more specific."

"My body. All of it. The new height, the curves— they're hard to get used to."

Will didn't say anything but brought his lips to mine in a sweet, gentle kiss. He pulled a few millimeters away to whisper in my ear. His hands brushed the outer sides of my hips, then he grabbed them.

"These," he said. "I love these. In fact, they drive me wild." His hands trailed up to my waist, and we both shuddered. "Your skin is so soft and beautiful." He seized my waist and pulled me even closer to him. His fingers ghosted up my back, stopping at my bikini top's clasp. Leaving his hands where they were, he pulled away enough for me to register that we had both ignited like the Fourth of July.

The adrenaline pumping through my body had my stomach doing flips and I was no longer self-conscious. Yes, I knew I still needed to work on loving myself for me, but in this moment, I knew exactly how Will felt about me. He wanted me; his eyes flicking to my chest and back to my face fueled him. Over and over in my mind, I practically begged him to unhook the clasps.

With gusto, he pulled me against him and our lips met with passion, his hands possessively holding me.

"Do it," I breathed. "I want you to, please."

Will kissed me harder and I practically smashed him up against the wall. Slowly, his hands began to work the clasps of my bikini top. *Pop.* One of the three hooks came undone. *Pop,* the second followed suit, and then...nothing. Will froze, his eyes squeezed shut in utter agony as he fought his urges. He moved down the wall, leaving me to tread water.

"Don't stop," I pleaded.

"We can't." Will looked away and held the wall with his

left hand, his back tense and showcasing every outline of each individual muscle. I came up from behind him, draped my arm over his shoulder and splayed my hand on his chest. When I nibbled his ear, a hungry growl escaped his lips and he lit up green. He whipped around so quickly, I would have missed it if it weren't for the waves rocking about us. He kissed me, but almost as soon as he started, he pulled away again.

"I said no!" He ripped his hands through his hair. "We can't do this!"

Pain stabbed my heart. I clutched my chest against the sudden ache as my heart deflated and sank to the bottom of my rib cage. I refastened the clasps at the back of my neck and rushed to the ladder, climbing as quickly as I dared.

"Wait! You misunderstand!" Will yelled after me. He caught up with me before I escaped into the dressing room.

I furiously tried to blink back the tears that threatened to expose how hurt I was. "What?" was all I afforded him.

"We can't do this because I don't trust we'd be able to stop," Will rasped, his chest heaving. "Not to mention, Nick was incredibly clear."

He was right, but I still couldn't face him. I was hurt and pissed off.

"This sucks," I blurted, throwing my hands up. "Why can't we just be a couple of normal teenagers? This is so unfair."

Will hung his head and walked into the dressing room, grabbing two towels from the warmer. He handed me one, then wrapped the other around his waist.

"This is totally unfair," Will agreed as he sat down on the beige cloth and wicker loveseat.

"I don't believe going any further can hurt us or Cristes."

"But it would go against the boundaries we set for ourselves. Plus, Nick says it amplifies our giftings, making us easier targets," Will reminded me.

"I know," I huffed. "I just...how can we become *more* amplified?"

Will chuckled and ran a hand through his wet hair. "I have no idea. I'm not sure I'll be able to stand it."

"Can we at least try, and if something crazy happens, we don't do it again?"

Will placed his hands over his face, rubbing up and down. "No," he murmured.

"You won't even try?" I pressed. "What are you so scared of?"

"Losing you!" Will shouted and then flinched, shocked at his own volume. He added, more softly, "I already lost Charlie, and not too long ago, I almost lost you." His eyes flared. "I will not risk losing you again."

My heart fluttered. "Will, you won't lose me, I—"

"Don't say you promise," he cut me off, shaking his head. "You can't promise me that. I love you and I swore to you I would do everything in my power to protect you. I couldn't handle losing you. Wouldn't you do the same for me?"

"Of course, I wouldn't want to put you in harm's way," I sighed. "But, well, this is so dang hard!"

Will's features relaxed. "Yes, but think about how sweet it will be when we no longer have to worry." I giggled, but his face sobered. "I think we should cool it on some things, scale back to lessen the temptation."

"If you insist," I responded dryly. I knew this was necessary, but it still sucked.

Will stood up and made his way to the dressing room door. "I'm going to go to my room and change. Meet me in the media room?"

I nodded. "See you there in fifteen to twenty."

"Twenty?" He arched his brow. "How long does it take you to get dressed?"

"Please. It'll probably take at least ten to walk there. Plus, I need a cold shower." I winked and closed the door on a laughing Will.

I joined him in the media room and true to his word, we didn't touch the rest of the night, even laying on opposite couches to watch *The Princess Bride.*

ϕizza

M OM AND DAD WERE AT THE KITCHEN TABLE when I came downstairs for breakfast.

"There's zucchini quiche on the stove," Mom alerted me.

"Yum!" I cut myself a large piece.

Dad, his glasses perched on the edge of his nose, looked up from behind his coffee mug. "What time are you heading to Will's tonight?"

"I think around six."

"His uncle stopped by about ten minutes ago," Dad lowered his mug, peering at me over his glasses.

My eyes widened and I dropped my chin. "Shai was here?"

"Close your mouth dear. I don't like 'see food'," Mom deadpanned.

"Ha, ha. What did he want?"

Dad leaned forward. "He wanted our permission for you to stay the night. He's hosting a Valentine's dinner and said it would run pretty late."

I swallowed hard. I had no idea why Shai wanted me to stay over and I considered this between bites of food.

Mom cleared her throat. "He assured us you'd be under constant supervision, separate rooms, and..."

"Moooom," I groaned and ticked my head at Dad.

"I know, I know. You and I have talked already... Which is why your father and I have decided to allow it." Stunned was an understatement.

"This will *not* become a habit, though," Dad cautioned. I closed my jaw with an audible snap and nodded in understanding.

Mom came and gave me a hug, and I returned it.

"I guess I better go upstairs and pack. Hey, Mom?"

"Yes, sweetie?"

"Sara no longer needs my help. Do you want to watch *Fools Rush In* with me when I'm done?"

Mom smiled, her eyes crinkling at the corners. "I'd love that."

A few hours later, I drove by myself to Will's house for the first time. Though I knew the way like the back of my hand, driving down the long gravel path to his home felt a little odd. I'm not sure if it was the trees casting shadows because of the solar lights, or the fact that Will wasn't with me.

I parked next to his Wagoneer and walked to the front door. I expected Nolan to greet me before I even reached the first step. So when I knocked on the mahogany double doors, and there was no answer, my chest and stomach tightened with dread. *What is happening?* I knocked again, harder this time, shaking my hand out from the sting in my knuckles. When *still* no one answered, I rang the doorbell. Finally, Nolan answered, his hair disheveled.

"My apologies, Madam Lydia. Please come in. May I take your coat?"

"Is everything alright?" I asked as I allowed him to help me out of my coat.

Nolan seemed preoccupied and didn't answer my question. "Lord William is in the library. Lord Abishai and Prince Nicholas will be joining you shortly."

He scurried off and I headed to the library. When I walked in, Will and Pree sat on the couch, leaning in and whispering to each other. A sudden rush of jealousy flitted through me, remembering their kiss from a few months ago, and I forcibly swallowed it down.

"Hey. I didn't expect you to be here, Pree."

"I can't say I'm mad about it." She laughed. "It's not like I had Valentine's Day plans."

Will stood and gestured to the cushion next to him. "Sorry, Princess. Nolan got here with her only about ten minutes ago. It was a surprise to me, too."

I sat down in the middle of the soft, velvety couch. "So, does anybody know what's going on?"

"Nick and Shai are in the basement," Will said.

"From the state Nolan looks to be in, one or both of them must be in a foul mood," Pree observed.

"I agree. This was the first time the front door wasn't opened before I even reached it. I had to knock twice and ring the doorbell."

"Sorry." Will gave me an apologetic smile. "By the time I

heard the doorbell, Nolan whizzed by and shooed me out of the way."

I laughed picturing the scene. Sitting next to Will, a palpable desire to lean into him, to touch him washed over me, but he maintained a safe distance. I guess keeping boundaries extended beyond last night.

I turned to face him. "Does your girlfriend get a proper hello?"

Will looked at me, confusion contorting his face.

I prompted him. "You know, a hug or maybe a kiss on the cheek?"

Will flushed. He leaned in and whispered in my ear, "I thought we decided last night to take a break from all of that?"

"Yeah, *only* last night," I whispered. "A hug won't hurt anything."

"I don't want to tempt anything." He leaned away and into the arm of the couch.

I shook my head and sighed. *Well, this is awkward.*

Pree sat slouched, with her arms folded over her chest, her left foot tapping the floor. "How long do you think Nolan's going to make us sit here?"

"Who knows, but I'm starving," I sighed, shooting a sidelong glance at Will. "I was under the impression he and I were having a *date,* and part of that included dinner."

"Hey, don't blame me." Will raised his hands. "Nolan was gone all day, and when he arrived back here, he was with Uncle Shai and Nick. They all stormed through the kitchen almost two hours ago. Then Nolan left and came back with Pree."

"And your parents were cool with that?" I turned to her.

She shrugged. "They weren't home. Apparently, Will's uncle set them up with some fancy evening away, and they were thrilled to go. They threw some money at me for takeout, and told me they'd be back tomorrow afternoon. My brother Sanj was supposed to be in charge, but we all know how *that* goes." She rolled her eyes. "He wanted the house to himself with his new girlfriend and was eager to see me leave."

A packed duffle bag sat by her feet. "So, I guess we are all spending the night. This could be fun." grinned.

Nolan appeared by the door; the tiniest hint of shadows colored his under eyes. "They will be ready for you shortly. I haven't had a moment's rest to prepare any food, unfortunately." Even his voice sounded exhausted.

Poor Nolan. "Can I help with anything?"

"Nonsense." He waved away my offer. "The pizza should be here any moment. I hope Rosati's is acceptable?"

"Perfect!" Pree and I shrieked in unison.

"I haven't had it in ages!" I exclaimed.

Will laughed. "That good, huh?"

"Better," Pree said.

Our excitement brought a smile to Nolan's face. The doorbell rang and he excused himself. I barely finished pulling my hair into a low pony when he returned carrying a couple of two-liter Pepsi bottles and a plastic bag full of paper plates and napkins. The delivery boy followed behind him hefting four extra-large pizza boxes, his face awestruck as he took in his surroundings.

"Please set them on the coffee table," Nolan instructed.

"Holy cow, Nolan. Are we feeding an army?" I asked.

He shrugged. "Did I order wrong? I have never had pizza

before." Nolan paid the delivery boy and escorted him out.

"Never had pizza?" Pree gaped at a retreating Nolan. When he came back to the library, she said, "We are definitely going to have to rectify that." She scooted herself onto one of the large floor pillows. "Nolan, sit right here. I need to bear witness to history being made."

Nolan peeked back over his shoulder and down the hall.

"Oh stop, they are big boys and can handle you not being at their beck and call for a few minutes." Pree flapped a hand.

"I am not quite as confident as you." Nolan smirked. "But I am willing to try a piece. I ordered all different toppings. Which one should I try first?"

I lifted the flap of each box and spotted the one I wanted. "Let's start you with an easy one— plain cheese."

Will handed out the paper plates and napkins and Pree poured the pop. We each held our breath as Nolan took his first bite. He sat there for a long moment, chewing in silence.

"Come on, man. Don't leave us hanging." Will leaned forward in his seat, his hands in his hair. "What's the verdict?"

Nolan paused to dab his mouth with a napkin. "It is...not unsatisfactory."

"Not unsatisfactory?" I scoffed. "Dude, this is an American staple."

"Truthfully, I would not eat it often, but I would enjoy it on occasion."

For someone who thought pizza was just 'OK,' Nolan polished off half an extra-large pizza all by himself, devouring three square slices from each of the four different pizzas.

When we were all too stuffed to eat another bite, Nolan condensed the leftovers into two boxes. "I think it is time we head downstairs."

We followed him to the kitchen, each of us carrying part of our dinner mess. Nolan placed the pizzas in the fridge, Will tossed the garbage, I placed the extra plates and napkins on the counter, and Pree put the Pepsi in the sub-zero fridge.

"Right this way, please." Nolan gestured to the door in the back of the kitchen.

We all filed out one at a time into the small hallway Nolan had led me and Will down the night he healed my foot. He laid his hand on the same rose as the last time, and the hidden door swung open. The faint voices of Nick and Shai emanated from somewhere deep in the basement. Nolan climbed down first, followed by Will, then me, and finally Pree.

"Girl, did you see that secret door open like it was straight out of *Clue*?" Pree whispered to me.

I stifled my laugh. We reached the fork in the stairwell, and the door on our right led to what I now knew was the apothecary room. But Nolan continued to the left, and as we made our descent, Shai and Nick's voices grew louder. They were definitely arguing about something.

Tension rolled off of Will in crashing waves. A few paces from the bottom of the stairs were a set of immense metal doors. Again, Nolan placed his hand on a Christmas Rose applique in the wall beside the door on the right. It unlocked with a satisfying click, and Nolan pushed it open.

Upon entering, towering ceilings at least fifteen feet tall, greeted us to what appeared to be a training room. The gray walls were constructed from slated cinder blocks. The floors seemed to extend on and on, covered in a red wrestling mat.

For the most part, the room was bare except for a small

lounge area complete with kitchenette. Nolan headed for a small terrarium filled with Christmas roses, displayed on the counter next to a mini fridge. On one of the nearby sofas, Nick and Shai sat facing one another, talking heatedly.

"Well, this is kind of a letdown." Pree elbowed me. "I mean, compared to the rest of the house."

Nick fell silent as he noticed our arrival. When Shai continued to yell, he cleared his throat and gestured to us.

I'm not sure what compelled me, but I rushed Nick and hugged him tightly. Only when he embraced me back did I relax.

I pulled away. "You look so much better. You had us worried there for a minute."

He mustered a faint smile. "Thanks to you and William. Your swift actions saved my life. I have survived another successful trip to and from the borders of Cristes."

"Traveling to Cristes is what almost killed you?" Pree gasped.

"Yes," answered Nick. "Things haven't been quite as hostile in the past, though." A deep crease formed between his brows. "I'm afraid the situation is becoming more dire."

"Quit scaring the youngsters," Shai complained.

"We agreed we would speak the truth," Nick stated, slowly enunciating each word. When Shai protested, Nick hit the heel of his hand on his forehead, then ran his hand down his face. "Shai, we have tried it your way. Let us start anew."

Shai huffed and stood. "Fine... William, Lydia, friend of William and Lydia, welcome to my home. This is the training room." He spread his arms and walked around in a circle. "I had the room specially designed and reinforced with gifting so our people could train without fear of being seen, heard, or inflicting permanent damage."

"You can do all that in here? Where is the equipment and the weapons?" Pree asked bluntly.

Shai smirked at her. "Right here." He jabbed a thumb at his own chest.

She frowned up at him. "I see nothing. Are they hidden?"

"My dear, *we* are the weapons," Shai stated patiently.

Pree gulped and took a step back from him.

Nick laughed heartily. "No need to fear us, Pree. Watchers do not harm humans... Well, most Watchers don't." He winked at her.

"William, Lydia, your training begins with Nick and I tomorrow morning. Pree, is it? Your training begins with

Nolan tomorrow as well."

Pree blinked. "Um, what training?"

Will glared at his uncle. "Excuse me, I don't mean to interrupt, but you were insistent we all meet tonight. Can I ask what this is all about?"

Shai's nose twitched. "Apparently the old man couldn't wait," he gritted out, his eyes igniting as they bore into Nick.

"Correct, I could not," Nick countered. "I almost died and realized I would have failed them and our home, Cristes." He turned to look at me and Will. "I've apologized before for my vagueness, but again, I was forbidden to speak more freely." Nick flicked his gaze to Shai briefly before continuing. "This lack of communication has been hard for the both of you. I knew it would be, but what we did not anticipate was Mara's strength and the pace at which she is moving." His eyes narrowed. "I will not stand to put you in further danger any longer."

Shai scoffed. "She's not moving *that* quickly. We need to

be careful how we are stressing this to the children."

"May I remind you that constantly underestimating her is how we got here in the first place?" Now Nick's eyes sparked at Shai.

"We are not children," Will postured through gritted teeth.

Shai rounded on him. "What was that, nephew?"

"I said, *Uncle*, we – are – not – children." A subtle ripple of tension crossed Will's jaw.

Nick flashed Will a grin, then tipped his head expectantly at Shai, waiting for his rebuttal.

"I beg to differ, young man. You are only seventeen, and there is an entire world out there you have yet to experience. It can be a harsh place, and you have been shielded from much of it."

"Yeah, thanks to you!" Will seethed.

"You are welcome," Shai retorted with a smug expression.

"You have kept me sheltered thinking you are protecting me, but in reality, you're leaving me vulnerable, without any ability to protect myself, or Liddy for that matter!"

Shai's expression turned to stone, every angle in his face accentuated as a shadow cast over it. "Everything I've done, I have done for my family. I've always done what is necessary. Do not think for one second it came without sacrifice."

Nolan, who had remained quiet off to the side, stepped forward and placed his hand on Shai's shoulder. Shai shrugged it off. Nolan tried again, and this time Shai allowed his hand to stay there, immediately calming.

Nick spoke softly. "This has been difficult for everyone and we all acted based on what we felt best. Now that we are all here, let's determine if we can work together. Everyone is striving for the same goals, after all."

I felt the need to say something. "Mr. Jamison?"

"Please—" He held up his hand. "Call me Shai."

"OK, *Shai*. Will and I can't pretend to know much about what has gone on over these past years, and obviously, there is a lot we need to learn. I know seventeen may seem very young to you, but I promise that nearly dying a few months ago at the hands of a friend possessed by Mara, seeing what she's capable of, well..." I drew in a deep breath. "I'm going to be honest; I'm scared. Please...*please* help us to learn about who we are and what we're capable of." I lowered my gaze to the red padded floor. "I... I don't want to be afraid anymore."

I looked up, and Nick and Shai were exchanging glances. Shai looked thoughtful while Nick wore a mask of sadness.

"Shai, it is time," Nick said solemnly.

Shai loosed a breath and sat down on the couch. "Nolan, would you mind bringing down the extra pizza and drinks?"

Nolan gave a curt nod, then turned on his heel and exited the room. Shai leaned forward with his elbows on his knees, steepling his fingers.

"Brace yourself, kids," he warned, locking gazes with each of us in turn. "It is going to be a long night."

History Lesson

WE ALL TOOK A SEAT on the worn leather couches facing each other.

"Where shall we begin?" Shai asked.

"At the beginning." Nick answered

"The First Fall?" Shai cocked an eyebrow. Nick nodded his approval.

"What the heck is that?" asked Pree.

Nick chuckled.

Shai looked at her quizzically. "I will tell you everything you need to know, if you don't mind."

"Oops, sorry." Pree blushed. "I tend to speak as I think sometimes."

"No matter. A thousand years ago, Cristes looked much different than it did...when I was last there anyway. Every

Watcher is born with a unique gifting that falls into specific categories, easily discernable by the color of the infant's eyes.

"Green indicates strength, resolute power, and soldiers," Shai continued. "They typically hold strong political positions and are lords over regions. Pink represents the healers and pacifists; they love to serve and help others." Shai's green eyes found Nolan and returned to the three of us.

"Brown giftings are responsible for maintaining our environment, such as keeping our atmosphere at the right temperature and preserving and cultivating the land for farming and gardening. Gold designates our record timekeepers—" Shai gestured to Nick— "Nothing escapes their memory; they can recall any images they have seen or words they have read. They follow traditional roles of scholars, educators, and scientists."

Shai's gaze landed on me. "Violet, a rare gifting, presents in only a small percentage of Watchers. They obtain coveted roles as entertainers, wielders of musical talent, and have the ability to always choose love. Blue is even less common," he added. "This is the most elite and powerful of all the colors. Blues are bestowed titles of royalty because their giftings fall into more than one category. Take Nick, for example."

Nick bobbed his head. "I am the son of King William Gabriel Klaus, and Queen Nicole Noel Klaus. They became king and queen soon after the First Fall, when Cristes needed a special union to unite the kingdom."

"Eh, more on that later," Shai interrupted.

"Of course, I digress," Nick bowed his head. "As a Blue, I express giftings of the Green, Pink, Gold, and Brown classifications."

"So, that is why you are able to grow Christmas roses by the entrance to your home," Pree concluded. Nick's eyes twinkled. "Precisely."

Shai clasped his hands and rested his chin on them. "As I was saying, Watchers are born with an innate gifting. However, we are capable of learning skills from other color factions, but are limited in those abilities. There are a few of us, apart from Blues, that can naturally exhibit one other color faction to full potency."

"Like how you're a Green and a Pink," I said.

Shai nodded. "Correct."

"What exactly is a Watcher?" Pree asked.

"We are a race, like any other really, inhabiting the realm of Cristes. A passionate people full of love, we cherish hope and light." Nolan answered surprising me as he strode out of the shadowed corner. He placed the pizzas on the table along with the drinks and sat next to Nick.

"Yes, what Nolan said," Nick chimed in. "After the First Fall, we also would add guardians of Mortalia to our obligations."

Shai ran his hand through his hair, reminding me of Will. "Pardon me, but I thought I was tasked with sharing our history?"

Nolan averted his gaze.

"After you, friend." Nick dipped his head and swept out his arm.

"Thank you," Shai retorted. "About a thousand years ago, the land of Cristes divided its people based upon their color classification. Each sector was assigned a lord who reported to the king on a monthly basis. His noble family secured protection from a private army composed of highly trained Greens. They also had their own throng of Golds, Pinks, Browns, and one Violet. Gifting talents vary in ability and, therefore, decide one's entire future. School was only for the wealthy. Thus, one could not improve their station in life; if you were poor, you would remain poor. If you were wealthy, you would remain wealthy."

Pree dropped her chin then snapped it shut. "Like a caste system?"

"Yes," Shai answered. "Instead of remaining downtrodden, though, some from lower stations chose to risk their lives via expeditions, employed by their noble family as paid mercenaries and explorers, for these nobles looked to expand their territories, influence, and power. Others explored of their own accord, seeking avenues leading to a better life. All this exploration introduced the people of Cristes to Mortalia; a land, we discovered, completely surrounding Cristes, and full of treasures beyond measure.

"It was on one of these journeys the human race was discovered. Humans were viewed as fragile, but beautiful, creatures. So naive they were, Watchers found them utterly loveable. They had no knowledge of the power they possessed right at their fingertips— Hellebore Niger. The Christmas rose was rare in Cristes and highly coveted. Cristes' tropical climate in most locations is not a suitable habitat for their growth. Since humans had no use for them, Watchers thought it their right to take these flowers and, in return, leave gifts of wealth and protection.

"Many more well-to-do Watchers began traveling to see and dote upon humans— especially children— for entertainment," Shai continued. "They deduced December as the ideal time to visit since that is when the roses bloom in abundance. However, as Watchers devoted extensive time and resources to Mortalia, the lower classes of Cristes were neglected. Tensions festered like an open sore and escalated as the years passed.

"The desire to possess power from the Christmas rose and infatuations with humans distracted many nobles from their duties to their own people. Consequently, many Watchers grew resentful of humans, meeting in secret and soon, whispers of rebellion floated amongst the winds of the outer sectors. Some of the oppressed desired to dismantle the tiered class system. But others..." Shai's expression darkened. "Others wanted more than just their basic needs met; they coveted supreme power over Cristes. These extremists formed the Black Roses, a rebel group who sought to overthrow the government of Cristes and establish themselves as the leaders of the new realm order."

Shai lowered his voice. "They aimed to make all nobles suffer as they, and generations of their families, had. The Black Roses believed the best way to incite insurrection was through secret missions to Mortalia to study the land and its people. Rebels intended to eradicate all Hellebore roses and 'human pets'; their words, not mine." Shai paused as his gaze swept over me and Pree. "I apologize if this makes any of you uncomfortable," Shai added, shifting in his seat. "It was a dark time in our history, and it is difficult to share."

"I find it all fascinating," Pree marveled, leaning forward in her seat. "It's not like our world hasn't had rough times. Heck, we literally have a time period labeled the *Dark Ages*."

Shai turned to Nick, a dimple peeking through his barely there grin. "You are right. I do believe I like this girl."

Pree smiled and straightened in her seat.

"As I was saying," Shai continued, "the Black Roses visited Mortalia often, befriending the very people they wished to destroy; something about keeping your friends close, but your enemies closer. At first, they had no intention of outright killing humans. No, they wanted their lords and ladies to witness their beloved creatures' suffering.

"Now, I should mention that the tradition of visiting Mortalia every December became a celebration in both Mortalia and Cristes. The humans didn't know who we were. Watchers are more beautiful, physically superior, taller, and stronger than most humans. We also possess light magic, although the human eye can detect only a faint glow around us when we allow them to see it. Initially, we had no reason to hide our powers from humans, but soon it became necessary as their lust and infatuation with us became dangerous.

"Some Watchers couldn't do their jobs of harvesting the Christmas roses because the residents of Mortalia would want to host them all night. Some desired us to stay forever and tried to hold us captive, or attempted seduction to bond us forever through mating.

"Scant few humans feared us, however, and even attacked some Watchers. Afterward, we realized the importance of guarding our giftings. So, we made ourselves virtually invisible to them. We only traveled at night, careful to remain in the shadows when harvesting the Hellebore rose. We left bountiful gifts, and humans began to anxiously await our visits each year. Stories circulated that Watchers would only visit the homes of well-behaved children. Little did they know we only visited houses with roses. Soon those stories morphed into fairy tales about elves that would come only while people slept; this part, minus the elves, was true of course, for reasons I stated before. Eventually, our celebration of the Christmas Rose became what the three of you know as Christmas—how Santa, a magical elf, could fly around the world stopping at every home and leaving gifts for all the good girls and boys."

My jaw dropped, and I saw the same expression on my friends' faces. I grew up believing in Santa and the magic of Christmas. I couldn't believe what I was hearing— that my childhood fantasy was surprisingly grounded in reality, yet was even more magical than I could have ever imagined.

"What does all that have to do with the Fall?" Will cut in.

"I'm getting there," Shai murmured. "As I said, the Black Roses wanted to hurt both humans and Watchers alike. One Christmas, they had plans to poison both humans and their Christmas roses."

Pree gasped. "What happened?"

"Nothing," Shai said nonchalantly.

"Nothing? I'm confused." Pree frowned at him.

"Well, the Fall did happen, but nothing harmed Mortalia," Shai explained. "The king's spies received an anonymous tip about the cult's plans. On Christmas Eve, King Alaric sent out a myriad of guards to protect all possible routes to and from Mortalia. Seeing their plans had been thwarted, the Black Roses remained hidden, biding their time to plan another attack.

"Years passed, and the anti-human sentiment grew larger and stronger. The Black Roses worked tirelessly to raise money, often going without, bribing the upper echelons to bankroll the cause. As a result, lower-class Watchers that did not sympathize with the Black Roses soon found themselves beaten and thrown out into the wilderness."

"How horrible!" I cried. Will squeezed my hand.

Shai nodded and continued, his voice softening. "Their following grew so large, they posed a true threat to the crown. For five years, their message of hate and bitterness contaminated every corner of Cristes. In that time, they were able to gather the funds necessary to amass their own soldiery of Green lighters, appealing to their senses of entitlement.

"On Christmas Eve in the fifth year, when most of Cristes focused on the Christmas celebration, the Black Roses marched on King Alaric's castle. Many of the royal family lost their lives that day, including that of the king and all heirs to the throne.

"The weeks after their death were complete chaos. With so many in the royal lineage taken out at once, there was no one left to replace the king. More fighting and loss of life continued as noble lords and their loyalists battled each other for the crown.

"In the end, the Pinks and Golds appealed to both sides, forming a sort of oversight committee. Much like you all do here in Mortalia, we hosted our first and only election. All families, no matter their gifting, would have the chance to put their bid in to be considered for the position of King of Cristes.

"From that point on, the elected king's lineage would rule over Cristes with some additional changes. Now, it would be up to the ruling king and his advisors to decide whom he would marry, rather than being obligated to marry another

Blue." Shai's brow furrowed. "I should note, Watchers live much longer than humans, by at least four hundred years. Some have lived upwards of six hundred."

My jaw dropped and my eyes flicked to Will; he looked as shocked as I felt.

"In any case, far too many citizens put their hat in the ring for that election. The committee decided that whoever would rule Cristes should be able to read and write and would require at least two hundred signatures as a show of support. Although some complained about this turn of events, many were pacified because they still had a voice in choosing their leader. Through this new set of qualifications, roughly seven potential leaders emerged.

"Over the course of a week, the candidates took their time campaigning in each province, discussing how they would implement changes and rebuild Cristes to be stronger than ever. Ultimately, they elected Nicholas's grandfather as king, and my family lineage became lords over the northeast sector of Cristes.

"The remaining candidates received provinces to govern. However, their new roles included serving as representatives to the Watchers residing in their respective sectors. Representatives had a duty to the people, not the other way around. In other words, individuals could communicate directly with their lord, who would then raise citizens' concerns to the king. During King Gabriel's rule, Cristes enjoyed peace for another two hundred and fifty years. He was a great and fair ruler," Shai added.

"This has all been an in-depth and very detailed history lesson," Pree said. "But how will this help us defeat Mara?"

Nick cocked an eyebrow at Pree and answered for Shai.

"Patience, my dear. Shai is getting there."

I yawned and leaned further back into the couch, my body inching toward Will. His energy, his gifting humming just beneath his skin, called to me. He feigned a cough and inched away from me. Shai's gaze caught the movement, but he didn't say anything.

Nolan cleared his throat. "I think it may be time for a snack and bathroom break."

"Yes, I guess it's about time," Nick agreed. "Nolan, do you have those cookies I like?"

Nolan smiled and gestured to the kitchenette. "Of course, Your Highness. They are on the counter."

Shai stood. "I shall return in a few moments." He strode out of the training room, closing the door behind him with an audible click.

"Where is the restroom?" Pree asked.

"In the far-left corner," Nolan responded pointing from the kitchen.

Pree winked at me and padded across the long mat, disappearing behind the weightlifting equipment.

Will had barely spoken to me, let alone looked at me the whole night. I nudged his knee with my own.

"Hey, stranger. Sorry, our Valentine plans were ruined, but it is pretty cool hearing more about our history, isn't it?"

"I guess." Will shrugged. "Kind of sucks they had a civil war and revolutionary war all in one, don't you think?"

"Yeah, but it made them better, right?"

"True."

I leaned against him and whispered. "So, I can't even snuggle you?"

Will stiffened. "I don't think that's a good idea."

"I think you're overreacting. We're not alone, and that's enough of a reason to be able to handle ourselves," I said pointedly.

Will heaved a deep sigh. "I guess you are right. I think I just freaked out over how fast things can progress between us, and I want to—"

"I know, protect me," I finished for him. "But you don't want me to be in pain, do you?"

"Of course not!" he gaped.

"Well, you know how it feels when we are close and can't touch each other."

Will nodded, clearly not catching what I was throwing.

I pouted. "It's driving me nuts! Seriously, it's almost painful."

Understanding dawned on his face as he laced our fingers together. Pree waltzed out of the bathroom, and I stood, plucking my hand back.

"Hey, I thought you said you wanted this," Will stated, wiggling his fingers at me.

"I do, but nature calls."

Let Me Show You

I EXITED THE BATHROOM and found Nick leaning up against the weightlifting equipment.

"Lydia, may I speak with you for a moment?"

"Of course." I nibbled the inside of my cheek.

He walked to the corner hidden by large, rolled-up mats. "Do you still have my white journal?"

Initially, I'd carried the journal around with me the first few weeks we checked on his place after Christmas Eve. When I wasn't sure he'd return, I hid it in a boot tucked in the back of my closet. But I'd made sure to pack it tonight.

"I do. It's in my bag upstairs."

"Could you please bring it to me? I am ready to share the contents with you all."

"Sure. But I'm not sure how Nolan opens the big door to

get back in here."

"All you have to do is place your hand over the third Christmas rose and then use your gifting to impart your power into its internal mechanism. Once it recognizes you, the door will open."

I strolled past Will and Pree and out the door. Before I reached the stairs, Will caught me around my waist.

"And where might you be off to, Princess?"

I peered at Nick and he nodded his permission. I leaned in closely and whispered, "Nick asked me to go grab the journal I found in the back of that book he gave you when you first moved back here. Remember it?"

Will responded, "His and Mara's journal, right?"

"Yeah, want to come with me? I left it in the library."

"After you." Will gestured up the stairs.

We reached the library, only to find my bag missing, along with Pree's.

"It's not here." I huffed, placing my hands on my hips.

"Maybe Nolan moved it to your room?"

"Do you happen to know where that is?"

"I do, actually." He tucked me under his arm and led me up the grand staircase. I'd never been up there before. I peeked over the wrought-iron railing and a bird's-eye view of the atrium greeted me. The plush carpet squished and sank under my socks as Will ushered me to the entrance of a room a few doors down.

"How come we've never been up here?" I asked him.

He shrugged. "We've never had a need. Not to mention, you've never asked."

"What are all these rooms?"

His face contorted in thought as he ran a hand through his hair. "Some of them appear to be guest bedrooms. I say 'appear' because with all the secrets this place holds, who knows what really is and isn't based on looks alone?"

I smiled back at him. "True. So, is this my room?" I pointed at the door behind him.

"I think so. I've never been in the doors on the opposite side, but this one is Nolan's," Will said, gesturing to a walnut door at the far end of the hallway.

I opened the door to a luxurious guest bedroom. "It looks like Pree and I will be sharing a room tonight." There were two queen beds and our bags were sitting on them. My duffle was on the bed closest to the bay window.

"Here it is," I called happily to Will holding the journal.

He stood frozen in the door jamb. I searched his face, waiting for that warm, familiar feeling I had come to know as his presence. All I felt from him, however, were nerves.

I walked toward him but stopped about a foot away. "Why are you nervous?"

"I'm not nervous. I just..." Will dropped his gaze. "Can we go back downstairs?"

"No. You've been distant since, well...since the other night in the pool. You explained why we should take it slow and I respect that. But honestly, I didn't expect you to be *this* distant." I closed the gap between us and placed my hand on his arm, giving him a little squeeze. "Can we really not let it go back to how it was?"

"I'm sorry, Liddy. This is so dang hard." He connected his forehead with mine and closed his eyes. "I find it hard to stop once we begin, and I feel like...like I can never have enough of you."

"But we do have self-control. It doesn't have to be all or nothing."

"I'm glad one of us has self-control." Will sighed and pulled away.

"I think doing this is going to make it harder in the long run." Will looked incredulous, baiting me to explain myself. "Hear me out. The more we deny this Watcher attraction, the stronger and louder it grows, for me anyway. I say if we don't feed the beast at least a morsel, then when it gets ravenously hungry, it will demand a feast."

Will smirked at me. "A feast, huh? Well, when you put it that way, I say 'snack time'." His eyes shimmered to life, and a blaze of heat rippled through me.

"Only a snack," I teased.

Will's eyes followed the path to my mouth, and his tongue peeked out over his lips in response. I rose onto my tiptoes and pressed my lips to his, every nerve ending kindling, anticipating a spark that would set us on fire. A few minutes later, we pulled apart.

"Oh, no!" I breathed.

"What?" Will asked, searching my face.

"We're glowing! Nick wanted me to be quick about it, and now we have to wait up here until this goes away," I moaned, plopping on the edge of Pree's bed.

Will grabbed my hands and helped me to stand. "We are in a Watcher's home now. We don't have to hide."

"But, they will know we were doing...something."

"What, kissing? Who cares? Kissing is nothing to be ashamed of, but let's really give them something to wonder about." And then he kissed me, hard and deep, for a brief moment more before pulling away. He grinned wickedly. "Come on, Princess. Everyone's waiting for us downstairs."

I opened the door as Nick had instructed. Carrying the journal in my left hand, I held Will's hand in my right as he guided us down the stairs.

Nick shook his head, a smirk playing on his lips. "Well, no need to guess what you two were doing."

Nolan smiled at us from the kitchenette as he poured Pree a glass of water.

"*Humph.* Teenagers," Shai grumbled.

"Don't be such a zib," Nick razzed. "Do you need reminding of what you were like, Mr. Gal-sneaker, going after all the jammiest bits of jam?"

Shai shook his head and smiled as Nick nudged him. "Fine. I just don't know how I feel about it in my own house."

"We didn't do anything to disrespect your house," Will argued.

"It's not so much what you did as much as the fact that you are literally wearing your actions," Shai scolded. "The problem is that you do not possess the erudition to conceal it from others."

"Yeah, thanks for that, by the way," Will said sarcastically. "School has been a real treat because of it, especially dance class."

"My apologies," Shai gibed. "I shall teach you after our history lesson is complete."

"If both of you are finished, I would like to pick up where we left off. Our little history lesson is important, as it sheds light on how the Second Fall happened," Nick said. "Pree,

William, Lydia, to the couch please," he instructed.

"So, is Shai not going to finish the lesson?" Pree whined.

"Of course I am." Shai smiled at her. "Where did I leave off?"

Pree chimed in, "Cristes basically encountered both a civil and a revolutionary war at the same time." She flicked her hair over her shoulder. "This led to the downfall of the caste system and a more democratic approach to government. Oh, and we learned that humans are special to Watchers because they unknowingly provide some sort of magic fuel for Cristes through their ecosystem, and thus Christmas was born. Is that about right?" She cocked her head at Shai.

Nick relaxed against the sofa, stretching his arms out across the backrest. Shai stared wide-eyed at Pree briefly and then continued, "Albeit in human terms and references, you are, indeed, correct."

Pree held her hand up and we all turned to face her. "I do have one question, though. What happened to the radical cult members? Crazy like that doesn't just, like, disappear."

Nick slapped his hand over his knee, whooping, "Did I not tell you this one is afternoonified?"

"Yes— Y-Yes you did." Shai wheezed, nearly choking on his water.

Pree leaned back into the corner of the couch, crossed her arms, and propped her feet on the table. "This is gonna be good." She smirked.

Nick let out a belly laugh, and everyone couldn't help but join along. When the laughter finally died down, he said cryptically, "The story of the Second Fall is much darker, my dear."

I looked over to Nolan, who now sat on Shai's right side, somberly studying his own hands. A muscle in Shai's jaw twitched. Pree brought her knees into her chest at the sudden coldness that swept through the room. I snuggled into Will's side as he wrapped his arm around me.

"You are correct, Pree. Some could not accept the new ways of Cristes, especially the continued traditions involving Mortalia."

"I thought it was limited to Christmas Eve?" I blurted.

"Yes, that was when Watchers dispatched by their lords came to Mortalia. However, over the years of peace after the First Fall, the interactions with human adults in Mortalia became more normalized. Human and Watcher friendships were made, and after a time, King Gabriel would allow some Watchers to visit their human friends in Mortalia or bring them to Cristes to visit for a day or two at a time."

"As you can imagine, the idea of humans in Cristes posed some problems as well," Nick interjected.

"So, Watchers were really upset that humans were still well-liked? I mean, didn't their quality of life improve significantly after the fall?" I asked.

"It is not so much that they were liked, but rather, they were treated as equals. There were those in the Black Roses who saw humans as an inferior species. Humans, after all, contain no magic. A new storm was brewing within the radical group. They hoped to take over Mortalia and make the humans their slaves."

"So how does Mara fit into all of this?" Will asked.

"Mara is the daughter of Bronwyn, her Brown-gifted Watcher mother, and Hul, her human father," Nick answered.

Pree and I both gasped, and Will hugged me tighter.

Nick ran a hand across the back of his neck. "Bronwyn's father died in the First Fall when she was only a child. Her mother became mixed up with one of the radical sympathizers who brainwashed her." He stroked his beard once, then cupped his chin. "Bronwyn grew up believing humans were evil and inferior, a species to be dominated if not exterminated. However, Bronwyn fell in love unexpectedly with a human man named Hul on one of his visits to Cristes. You see, she was out on her first assignment, and he was her target. She was meant to befriend him and report back any of his weaknesses. Life has a funny way sometimes. She fell in love rather hard and fast, soon learning humans were not all what she had been led to believe.

"Bronwyn and Hul had quick, intense meetings. She convinced her family and the other cult members she was making great progress with her assignment. They gave her permission to visit Mortalia, and while there, their romance blossomed. Bronwyn soon learned she was with child."

Pree moved as if she were about to speak, but I grabbed her wrist and shook my head.

Nick continued. "After she told Hul, the couple seemed genuinely happy, but then he disappeared, and she never saw him again. When she could no longer hide her growing belly, she was forced to confide in her mother. Unfortunately, her stepfather overheard her confession and threw her out of their home."

I couldn't help the gasp that escaped from me. "I'm so sorry. Please, continue."

Nick gave me a sad smile and nodded. "Her fellow Black

Roses shunned her for what they believed was the ultimate defilement of the purity of Watchers, mating with a human. Bronwyn was also turned away from the lord of her province—not just because she was a known supporter of the aggressions toward humans, but because no one knew what to expect of the child she bore. A Watcher-human child had never been seen before.

"Mere days from birth, Bronwyn found herself in King Gabriel's city, Bradwit Waterford. She disguised herself well enough, although this would prove unnecessary, for most people who lived in Bradwit Waterford were not familiar with the inhabitants of the other provinces." Nick inhaled deeply and huffed through his nose, steepling his fingers. "She secured herself some shelter amongst some outcasts in a district named Abaddon. It housed those who dabbled in black magic, those considered mentally unstable, and those with less desirable reputations such as thieves, whores... you get the idea.

"It was in this squalor that Bronwyn gave birth to Mara, and she remained in that small community of misfits. Bronwyn's mother died without ever seeing her grandchild. Her stepfather made it a point to find her and accuse Bronwyn of being responsible for her mother's death. He heartlessly claimed that her mother died of disappointment and even went as far as spitting on the baby, Mara." Nick's gaze moved from us to some faraway place, his eyes unblinking. "Bronwyn was never quite the same after that. It was as if she'd cracked, and the last bit of hope she had, evaporated."

"That's so sad," Pree said, wiping a tear from her cheek.

"So you see," Shai said, "Mara was born into a home

with a mother whose heart was too broken to properly care for her. Her only family despised her for what she was, while the community her mother placed her in was full of less-than ideal role models."

"I could see why Mara had a hard time," I said softly.

"*Humph.*" Nick blinked and his attention joined us once again. "That is not even the worst of it."

Shai's eyes flickered to life like a small flame as he faced Nick. "We agreed to only tell them the basics."

"This next part counts, does it not Cousin? No one but you believes you are to blame. You must let it go. I promise none of them," Nick said, gesturing to us on the couch, "will think you are to blame either."

Shai reached his hands up to massage his temples. "If you must. I do not wish to hear it all again, though."

"Nolan, would you please help Shai upstairs?" Nolan did not hesitate to come to the aid of his lordship.

Shai turned his attention to me and Will. "I guess I will be seeing you both for training first thing in the morning."

"Good night, Uncle," Will said as he stood, strolled over to him, and gave him a hug. At first, Shai stood still, his eyes wide; but then relief washed over his face and nearly broke my heart as he warmly returned Will's hug, blinking away wetness from his eyes.

Shai cleared his throat and pulled away. "Whatever Nick shares with you, please know that I love you, your parents, and your brother very much. I would do anything for any one of you," he added with conviction. Then he left the training room with Nolan at his heels.

Pree sighed and sank her chin into her palm. "This is like

one giant telenovela."

"Can I have my journal, please?" Nick asked, holding his hand out to me. For a moment, I'd forgotten that I had it and I wordlessly handed it over to him.

"As I mentioned earlier, I can present as a Gold. This journal details my friendships when I was a young lad through the Second Fall," he shared while flipping through it.

"But the pages are blank," Pree said flatly.

"Not quite." Nick smiled. "No human can read this. No ordinary Watcher can read it, either. I enchanted it to allow Lydia and William the ability to read it if something ever happened to me. But now, I will be able to *show* you my history instead."

"Come again?" Will asked, his brows pinched in confusion. "Are Watchers able to time travel or something?"

"Something like that." Nick smirked. "Thanks to my Gold giftings, I can recall any memory in vivid detail. I can also show you my memories."

"So, like a movie," Pree said.

"Exactly. A movie within your mind," Nick said.

Nolan returned with a few vials of chartreuse-colored liquid and passed one to Nick, placing the others on the end table. Nick thanked him, and Nolan bowed the same way Nick did before he left on Christmas Eve; with his left arm at his heart, his right arm crossing over.

"Care to join us?" Nick asked him.

Nolan shook his head. "I need to stay with Abishai. Ring if you need me."

As Nolan left, Nick returned his attention to the three of us. "We will all need to hold hands and form a chain so my power can flow through each of you. Lydia, I was able to make a clear connection with you the other day when you found me; I will place you between William and Pree to help strengthen the images."

The three of us did as instructed, then watched Nick expectantly.

"I will not be able to talk to any of you during the process," he continued, "and will need one of my hands to flip the journal pages so as to not stop the story."

"This is so cool," Pree squealed. "It's just like *Back to the Future*, you guys."

I laughed nervously while Nick arched a brow. "I warn you, some parts are difficult to bear witness to, and you will not be able to look away."

"Then I'm glad I have you both to hold onto," I said to Pree and Will. They responded by each squeezing one of my hands.

"Same." Pree smiled at me.

"Same," Will said as he kissed the inside of my wrist.

Nick offered his hand to me, and I took hold. His strong hands were soft except for the few calluses that lined the top of his inner palms.

Nick flipped the pages of his journal. "We will start from when I first met Mara. When I was honing my skills, she allowed me to record some of her memories in this journal, so you will see those parts as if she is telling the story."

My heartbeat quickened, and my pulse raced in prestissimo tempo with Will's.

"Do not be alarmed," Nick said, as if he could hear my thumping heart. "She will not know we are viewing this."

I released a breath to calm the adrenaline rushing through my veins.

"If you have no further questions, I am ready to introduce you to Cristes as I experienced it, along with my once-angelic friend, Mara." Nick's smile faltered. "Close your eyes."

And then I was spinning and flipping so violently, I thought I'd be sick. The moment passed, and my feet were planted on the earthen ground. I looked around, marveling at how I was no longer in Shai's basement, but in a tropical paradise.

Part II

CRISTES

Nicholas: The Day I Met Her

I STEPPED OUT OF MY PARENT'S SUMMER ESTATE. School ended last week, and I could not wait to spend the holiday with the guys, hanging out at the beaches and exploring the caves by the water's edge. I'd been in Sint Natal for a few dreary days, but the last of the tropical storm had finally cleared. I woke early, took my breakfast in the kitchen and left for the beach. I kicked my leather sandals off. Rolling my linen pants up to my shin, I buried and wiggled my toes in the sand. I sat watching the water for a while, then walked along the shoreline. My friends Shai and Gavin would be here tomorrow, so today I would enjoy the quiet.

The salty air kissed my face with each breeze. I trekked north, and gradually the dunes on my left rose to large hills, then climbed to cliffs full of cavernous spaces. As I approached the second cave, my favorite one, it emptied its belly from the tide. This cave always held sublime treasures. One summer, I found a plethora of green and blue sea glass and filled a jar with it to present to Mother. It still sat on a table near her beloved chair on the wraparound porch. I was curious to see what trinkets awaited discovery this time. When I neared the cave's mouth, the most beautiful singing greeted me.

"Hello?" My voice echoed, and I secretly hoped I'd find a mythical mermaid. The singing immediately ceased. "Hello," I called again. I closed my eyes and stretched out my right hand, imagining my hand were a flashlight. When I opened my eyes, a light blue glow ignited my palm and illuminated the space. I had learned this, how to control which segment of my body my gifting emanated from, in school this past year. Now that I was eighteen, I would attend university in the fall. There, over a two-year span, Gavin, Shai, and I would all finish our intense abilities training.

"Please, do not be afraid." I tried to reassure the angelic voice once more.

She did not respond and I stilled, trying to determine the direction from which it had come. And then it was there; the low, pulsating, tangible energy of a creature. I had heard rumors but had not yet experienced this phenomenon as a Watcher. The older a Watcher becomes, the more adept they are at feeling energies, especially from those in which a primal bond is present. I slowly backed out of the cave and hid behind a large rock on the side of the entrance. I waited, and waited, and waited. Finally, I heard a faint splash— something moving through the water, creating small ripples. I grew eager with anticipation. As the tide crept in, the creature carefully exited the cave.

A beauty as I'd never before seen stole my very thoughts, along with the air I breathed, upon seeing her golden blonde hair glimmering in the sun. She did not see me, but I definitely noticed her as she carried the full apron portion of her tattered, damp dress. The young woman had danced along the sandy shore at least a few yards away from me, before I finally regained my senses.

"Excuse me!" I hailed the beautiful maiden. She slowed and stiffened, her back to me, but continued walking. I chased after her, too enthralled by her presence to think clearly about how she might perceive a strange man running at her. "Madam, please wait!" She picked up her pace. I ran full speed ahead and only stopped when I had gained some ground on her. I abruptly turned around forcing her to a dead stop roughly two feet from me.

I was again taken by her beauty. So much innocence and light painted her round face and lavish cheekbones. Her pouty, salmon pink lips only added to her purity. But it was her eyes, the depths of which informed me that she was a wonder to be treasured. Her energy vibrated through me; she was scared.

I held my hands up in front of me. "I did not intend to frighten you. I mean you no harm." Her eyes, a medley of pastel colors, bore into mine from behind her thick lashes. She remained frozen like a statue, and so I bent my left arm and crossed my right over it, a bow of respect and honor.

"My name is Nicholas, but my friends call me Nick." I flashed her my most sincere smile. Though I had not yet been taught this, I attempted to control my energy and send her little surges of reassuring calm.

She seemed to ease up, though just a hair, and returned my greeting with a small smile. Still, she spoke no words.

"What do you have in your apron?"

She answered, her voice quiet and melodic, "I didn't steal these. What the water offers, I do not have to pay for."

I splayed my hands. "I do not mean to offend or imply that you stole whatever it is. I am merely just curious. I, too, like to seek out treasures from the caves." My admission piqued her interest, so I proceeded. "Last year, I unearthed some beautiful sea glass and gave it to my mother as a gift." Her face softened. Her eyes changed from their kaleidoscope of pinks, purples, greens, and blues to the exact shade of glass I had gifted my mother, returning just as quickly to their rainbow.

Her knuckles clenched tightly onto her wet, sandy apron. She opened the cloth, inviting me to have a look; I took a step closer to her, careful to keep my hands in my pockets, and peered in. Roughly two handfuls worth of fully formed seashells of all shapes and sizes were nestled together. Their iridescent and pearlized coloring were mesmerizing. I looked up, and my eyes were immediately captivated by the girl's beautiful smile, her pink cheeks full and reaching up to meet her sparkling eyes.

"What did you say your name was again?" I pursued it once more.

"I didn't," she said quietly, biting her lip. It was easy to read her; she was contemplating whether or not to trust me. I stayed patient and didn't push, but again tried to send her reassurances through the bond between us. The wind started to pick up. She grappled up her smock in one hand and used the other to swipe and hold her hair by the nape of her neck.

Looking up at me through her lashes, she replied, "Mara. My name is Mara."

I knew at that precise moment this woman was someone I needed in my life forever and ever.

She allowed me to accompany her back to the village square. I of course offered to see her fully home, but for the split second when her eyes flitted to orange and fear seized my gut tight, I knew not to force the issue.

"Nicholas!" A familiar voice beckoned from a local shoppe. I waved Mother over, but when I turned back around, Mara was gone. I only hoped that she would grace me with her presence again.

Mara: The Dark Mood

"MAMA," I SANG when I skirted around the tilted door to our cottage. She wasn't inside, and I worried. I had been gone longer than usual due to meeting that persistent boy, Nicholas. I paused to untie my apron and lay today's treasure on the uneven table. Because of him, I had to take extra precautions— through back alleys and brush and bramble— to make sure I hadn't been followed. Mama would have been furious. I was to talk with no one, especially strange boys. I quickly shook my head as her words came to mind. *We cannot depend on anyone but ourselves.* But then, his face, with those piercing blue eyes like a cloudless sky, distracted me, and I couldn't help but smile. Nicholas was harmless. I skipped out the back looking for Mama.

She still sat in that same old rocker I helped her into this morning, staring unblinkingly into the open field before her. I often wondered if she was waiting for someone. But every few months, when she got into her *dark mood*, she refused to speak or eat. I came up beside the peeling, white-painted chair and placed my hand on her forearm.

"Mama, I found a lot of shells today. I plan on using them to create beautiful necklaces and selling them at the market now that I'm old enough to have my own booth."

Mama's sad brown eyes turned to me, but they did not *see* me. Then she returned her gaze to the field of wildflowers. I sighed. "It's OK, Mama. I'll take care of you. Let me help you inside and make us some supper."

After completing my chores, I brushed and braided Mama's hair before helping her into bed. Tomorrow, I would search for more of those beautiful seashells, and seagrass to braid into chains.

Nicholas: Above Water

MY EYES SNAPPED OPEN and I nearly fell out of bed as I rushed to get up. I wanted to hit the beach as soon as possible. There was no telling if or when Mara might be there, and I did not want to waste one minute without her. I had the kitchen staff pack me a picnic basket and scurried straight out of the house, and down the long, pebbled trail that led to the village. I jogged through the square, waving and nodding at all my favorite vendors.

"Nick!" My name chorused from behind me, just as I exited the beaten path to the shore. I skidded to a halt and spotted Shai and Gavin rushing toward me. A large smile spread across my face, and I dropped the basket to embrace them both.

"You gents finally made it!" I cried, clapping Shai on his

shoulder.

"Did we miss anything?" Gavin asked.

"Not at all." I waved off his concern.

"Two weeks nearly felt like an eternity," Shai groaned. "I thought my father would never finish training his new regiment at Ardenthan Academy."

Shai's father, my uncle Ethan, was head warrior of Cristes. He trained all the soldiers at the castle and only came to stay here in Sint Natal for a few days each week during summer.

"Same here," Gavin said. "My mother had to finish her volunteer work readying donations for this year's Christmas excursions, while my father had meetings to attend." Gavin's father was a financial advisor to the king, my father. He also governed Mount Saffron, a neighboring city to the capital.

"Yesterday was the first sunny day since I have been here. Nothing has happened worth noting, though something tells me that will no longer be the case now that the both of you are here," I razzed them.

"You, my cousin, are one hundred percent correct." Shai grinned as he ruffled my hair. "I am ready to blow off some steam from school and have some fun."

"Me, too," Gavin said. "Hey, what's with the basket?"

Heat rushed to my cheeks and I hoped they weren't red. I couldn't lie to my best friends, and yet I wasn't sure if Mara would want to meet them. Maybe I didn't want them to meet her. "I was bored and thought I'd have lunch at the beach, but now that you two are here, that sounds...unappealing. Why don't we go to Silver Snow's and grab some food there?"

Gavin cocked a brow at me. "A picnic for yourself?" He pursed his lips. "Shai, I suggest we pay a visit to the beach. What say you?"

A smirk lifted the side of Shai's mouth. "I say, off we go!" He snatched the basket and darted off.

I chased them down. Just before I caught Shai, he handed off the basket to Gavin.

"Gavin, stop!" I yelled when we reached the sand.

To my surprise, he actually did, and I had to dive out of the way to avoid tackling him.

"Dude, what are you staring at?" Shai asked Gavin as I stood and shook sand from my hair and clothes.

"Gavin?" I asked, my brows pinching together when he did not respond.

"Who is that angel?" he whispered, seemingly entranced.

Whether it was sports, academics, or girls, Gavin always seemed to come out ahead and I never once felt jealous or begrudged him for it. However, as I witnessed the way he looked at Mara just now, my heart sank and I didn't care for it one bit.

"Let's just go back to my house," I suggested. "My mother would love to see you both."

Shai finally caught sight of Mara. "Uh oh, Gavin has his eye on another girl." He sighed heavily, shaking his head. "Gavin, control yourself. I thought we agreed this summer was to be solely us chaps— no dames regardless of how beautiful."

"Shhhhh." Gavin planted his index finger over Shai's mouth, still not taking his eyes off Mara. "I'm going to go talk to that gorgeous maiden." He removed his shoes and threw them over his shoulder. With a boatload of confidence and his aquamarine eyes glinting, he strode over to her. She was too busy combing the sand for more ocean treasures to notice him at first.

I stayed frozen in place, unable to peel my eyes away

from the inevitable train wreck before me. Minutes passed, although they felt like hours. Gavin worked hard to capture her attention. I watched as his mouth moved, and boy, did it...a lot. But Mara didn't utter a single word in return; she just stared at him.

This had to be a first, because Gavin could charm anyone. He leaned down to whisper in her ear, and she jumped back, throwing sand and shells at him. I laughed as she ran for the caves while he just stood there, disbelief etched on his face. Shai joined me in laughing. As he walked toward Gavin with the picnic basket, I flung my shoes off and quickly followed.

"Wow, I think you've lost your touch," Shai teased, clapping Gavin on the back.

Relief washed over me, but then Gavin shot me a look.

"What are you so relieved about?" He grumbled.

Sometimes I greatly detested how easy it had become for my friends and I to read each other. I would need to work on shielding my emotions. "Nothing," I lied. "We should really head to Silver Snows or my house."

"I'm not leaving the beach. She will have to walk past us sooner or later." Gavin sat down and opened the flap of the picnic basket. I reached in and pulled the green and white checkered blanket off the top and laid it out for us. We took turns reaching in and setting all the food out.

"There's not much in here," Gavin mused.

"I told you I was just going to have lunch by myself."

"Looks more like lunch *for two*." Shai wiggled his eyebrows.

"Yeah, it does. How about you lads go to Silver Snows and I'll wait here for the angel." Gavin shifted his body, leaning on his elbow as he gazed in the direction of the caves.

Shai stopped short. "Whoa, don't you think you are getting a little too hung up?"

"Never. I know what I want." Gavin sucked in his bottom lip, catching it with his teeth.

I quickly changed the conversation to other topics, like what we could expect at university next year, what sort of adventures we may have at the lagoon and Carnival this summer, and whose manor we would sleep at for our first night here. Every now and then, I stole some glances in the direction of the caves.

The sun sat low in the sky, burning red and orange. The ocean waves inched closer and closer with the tide taking the beach with it; before long, it would fill the belly of the cave we had seen Mara enter. My throat immediately dried. I couldn't sense her at this distance, and that worried me. If that cave filled with water, not even an exceptionally seasoned swimmer would likely make it out alive. I wanted to get us all out of here so she could escape.

"Hey, are you still hungry," I asked Shai.

"Starving," he replied. "Can we please go grab some food?"

Gavin pinched his bottom lip, his eyes squinched in thought. "Maybe the princess is a little more sly than we thought. Those caves are almost filled with water and she has yet to come out, which leads me to believe that she somehow got past us." He smirked. "I can dig *playing hard to get*."

"Give it up, friend." Shai rolled his eyes so hard, I was sure he could see behind him. "I do not think whipping sand at you and running away means what you think it means."

My gifting suddenly screamed at me down my bond with her; Mara would be in trouble in only a few moments. *I need to think of a diversion.* "Last one back to the square is a wilted Christmas rose!" I yelled and jumped up.

Gavin and Shai never ignored a challenge. They both sprang up and bolted, sand launching behind them. I kicked it into high gear and reached the wooden planks of the boardwalk just ahead of Shai and Gavin. I slowed my pace and they breezed past me, flinging sand onto my shirt.

When they were yards away, I hollered to my friends, "I'll be right there! I forgot the basket!"

"Guess we know who's going to lose," Shai whooped over his shoulder.

"Let me know who wins!" I yelled back.

I tore off my shirt and ran like the wind to the second cave. I entered its mouth, carefully grasping the jagged wall with my fingertips. "Thundernation!" I gasped as I plunged into the cold water that barreled against my chest.

"Mara! Mara, are you in here? It's me, Nicholas!"

"Yes," a weak and terrified voice responded.

"Are you alright?" I called out, using the wall as leverage against the crashing waves.

"I— I can't swim and I cut my hand badly on a rock."

I waded deeper into the cave until I spotted her. A dull orange glow surrounded her frail figure as she huddled atop a large smooth boulder, cradling her right hand in her left. The water engulfed her feet and continued to rise rapidly.

"I'm going to get you out of here, do not worry." I tapped into my gifting, letting myself burn brightly enough to illuminate the cave. With better visibility, I could assess the situation and determine the best way to get us both out. My scan of the cave told me I would need to act fast. I reached for Mara and urged, "Take my hand."

She shook her head and hugged herself even tighter. The water now sloshed about her knees.

"Mara, look at me. I will get you out of here, but you have to trust me."

She cocked her head to the side, her large, beautiful eyes examining me for a long moment, like a hunted animal unsure of whether or not to trust the potential danger in front of her.

"I'll make this easy for you," I asserted sternly, our time running out. "You can either do nothing and drown, or you can risk taking my hand. What's it going to be?"

My approach seemed to free her from the fear that held her captive. With her good hand, she reached for me shakily.

"Quickly, Mara; you're going to have to do better than that. I can't come to you or I'll lose my grip on this wall, and I need it to push off of if I'm going to get us both out of here."

She unfurled herself and lunged for me, but slipped on the rock and fell, disappearing beneath the rising tide.

"Consarn it!" I cried. I took a breath and submerged my head underwater, keeping my eyes open, grimacing against the sting, and hoping the light from my gifting would allow me to see. Mara was there, fighting against the pull of the crashing waves, still holding out her hand. I grabbed it and pulled hard. She came up and gasped for air and I wrapped my arm around her waist, securing it like a vice. She shook violently as the frigid water lapped at our necks. Her eyes were wide with fright, her lips stained blue, and she trembled so hard, I thought her bones might break.

If she's too cold, she won't be able to move to help me save her. I instructed my body to warm up, sending the impulses through her body as well. Her violent shaking simmered to a shiver. The water teased our chins, eager to claim our mouths. Time was up.

Looking her straight in the eye, I said, "*You* are going to help me get you out of here, understand?"

Mara nodded.

"Alright, ready? On the count of three, tilt your head back, take a deep breath, and hold it. Kick your legs hard and fast. Do not stop, and I promise I will never let you go. One... two...three..."

We ducked under the water together, and I pushed off the cave wall with all my might, using the momentum and strength of my legs and free arm to swim against the current. But the waves were powerful and I was not gaining ground fast enough.

Being a seasoned swimmer, I focused on remaining calm. I knew firsthand that panicking only leads trouble quickly. But as Mara's kick started to falter, so did my resolve. I squeezed her into my side more tightly. I would not let her die. Channeling my gifting into my strength and speed, I sent a blast of light through the waves, more than enough to help me gain the momentum my body demanded. My lungs burned, and Mara went limp in my grip. In a few heartbeats, we were out of the cave, our heads above water. After a few more yards, we were back on the beach.

I laid Mara on the sand, sweeping her hair out of her face. I placed my ear to her mouth; she was not breathing. I folded one hand over the other, positioned it between her breasts, and began pumping. *One, two, three, four, five.* I covered my lips with hers and blew life and healing into her body. *One, two, three, four, five.* My mouth found hers again, and I held nothing back as I breathed healing into her.

On my knees, I prepped to pump Mara's chest once more, but her eyes fluttered open as violent coughs seized her. I placed her on her side to make sure the water and vomit were properly expelled. Only when I was certain she would be all right, I collapsed back onto my heels, my arms numb, and just stared at her. After a while, when her body finally relaxed, she sat up and met my stare.

"You, you kept your promise," she rasped, her eyes blinking rapidly.

"I am a man of my word," I responded.

Her face hardened. "I owe you."

I shook my head. "You don't owe me anything."

Mara tilted her head, scrunched her eyes, and pursed her lips. "But you risked your life to save mine. I'm indebted to you. That's how it works where I live."

"Well, that's not how it works with me. Friends are never indebted to each other, especially when it comes to saving the life of someone you care about."

"Thank you," she whispered, her eyes glossing over one more with tears; those doe-eyes that sparkled in the setting sun, flicked to the horizon and back to me. "I—I really do need to be going home now."

"It would be my pleasure to accompany you home."

Mara wrangled her hands together with such force, her knuckles went white. "Not today."

"You just nearly drowned. Surely you may need—"

"Not today, but maybe another time," she hastened to add as she stood and wobbled.

I sprang to my feet and caught her elbow, righting her.

She smiled up at me. "Will I be seeing you tomorrow at the market, Nicholas?"

I looked at her for a long moment, torn between chivalry and being overbearing.

Finally, I grinned at her and acquiesced. "You can count on it."

Mara: Into the Woods

H E SAVED ME. *He kept his promise.* I couldn't help but think about Nicholas on my way home from my near death experience. Most Watchers, as far as I knew, would have chosen to save themselves, rather than risk their life for...someone like me.

I approached the worn grass that trailed to my front door, dread pooling in my aching stomach as I clasped the cold handle. Would Mama know what happened? I'd been taught not to talk to strangers outside of the customers at the week's end market. My fear of Gavin— charming, wickedly handsome Gavin— had sent me running into that cave. As a result, I had been unable to go on a treasure hunt to find more shells and turn them into beautiful pieces of jewelry. My negligence would cause Mama and me to starve.

Mama still sat on the worn wicker chair in the garden where I'd placed her this morning. She gazed out across the fields that stretched as far as the eye could see. Her shawl, which I pieced together from scraps of material I'd fished from the trash in the town square after the market closed last fall, was wrapped loosely around her thin shoulders. A single strand of her ash-colored hair floated up and down, tickling her cheek with the warm breeze, but her eyes remained unblinking.

I helped Mama into the house and sat her in the faded pink wingback chair by the hearth. I opened the ice chest and pulled out the heavy cast iron containing the remaining few inches of watered-down soup. Grabbing the large wooden bowl off the cracked stone counter, I went to the rusted spigot at the back of the garden to collect fresh water.

The field lay empty of anything edible, as I'd been foraging there since our food stores ran out months ago. Thank Eira it was now summer, promising abundant growth. And even if nature didn't cooperate, the warm season lured more city folk to vacation here, offering me more sales opportunities at the market.

Shadows covered most the cottage, the sun having nearly gone to sleep for the night. I only had a few more minutes of sunlight left to try and find something to add to the soup. I raced across the garden to the small forested area on the side of the house. I hated going in there, especially in the dark.

Before I stepped through the thick brush, I spotted a single tan mushroom sprouting in the grass. *Thanks be to Eira!* To think I'd almost crushed it! Using a twig, I severed its head from the base of its stem and placed it in the partially torn pocket of my apron. I trudged forward. Twigs snapped under my feet, and squirrels and other woodland creatures rustled amongst the bramble and trees, making me jump.

Something hard pressed into the arch of my foot through the sole of my worn slipper. I stepped back and looked down, breathing a sigh of relief at the sight of a few scattered acorns. I gathered a handful and slipped them into my pocket. A patch of small bushes on my right still held a few berries that the critters had not yet gotten to; those, along with a few bright pink and blue flowers, completed the ingredients for my foraged soup.

The wind blew and with it, the moon rose high above, a nightlight guiding my path back to the garden. Prickles emerged on my skin as the temperature dropped. I picked up the bowl of water that rested on the wicker chair and returned to the single-room cottage. I pushed hard against the door with my hip and it scraped along the stone floor, following the groove of the semi-circle worn into the plank flooring. On the table I'd salvaged at the end of last summer from Florist Merryweather, I set the bowl down and emptied the contents of my apron pocket into it, thankful for the meager rations that would fill my belly tonight.

In the hearth's grate, only two logs remained. I sighed at the obvious reminder that we were at the end of our provisions. *I must do well at market tomorrow.*

I lit a fire in the hearth and hung the cast iron pot over the blaze, then transferred the contents of the bowl into it. I watched as the orange, yellow, and blue flames took turns licking the pot's base. My stomach growled, pulling me from the trance of the fire's dance. I glanced at Mama, who hadn't seemed to notice me or the fire. She sat still as a statue, hugging herself.

It was not long before the soup was hot. I dipped the ladle in twice for Mama and managed to fill it one and a half times for my own bowl. Sitting on the floor at her feet, I chatted with her about my day, careful not to mention the cave incident, while I spoon-fed her. I could have sworn her eyes flickered at the mention of Gavin, but it could have been the sparks from the fire. I finished my chores and helped Mama to her bed. When she was nestled in, I unwrapped the satchel that held the seashells I'd collected yesterday. I lit our final candlestick and set to work.

Dawn came, the sunlight peeking through our torn curtain, warming my face. My head lay heavy on my arm which still rested on the table. My eyes refused to open on their own, so I sat up and massaged them. My stomach was tight with hunger, but there would be no food unless I could sell the three necklaces, two bracelets, and single wind chime I'd crafted at the market today.

Nicholas: Our Cave

I OWE YOU. Mara's words echoed in my mind until sleep claimed me. Her words were laced with scorn, their self-deprecating meaning heavier than the humid air. This morning I came to the distinct conclusion that Mara did not view herself in the same light in which I saw her. What must she have experienced in her short lifetime that would make her believe she was not worthy of saving without a price? I shook my head and raced down the back staircase that led me into the kitchen.

"Prince Nicholas! What can I get yah this fine morn'?" Chef Berrouet asked, smiling. When father was away, mother did not mind me having breakfast in the kitchen from time to time.

"Actually Chef, can you please prepare me a basket with

lunch for two?"

Chef's brow rose high on his forehead. "Again for two? Who is joinin' yah, young man?"

"A...new friend."

"Sure, man. A 'friend'. With cheeks as red as yours, one would think it's a sweetheart." He winked.

I worried my bottom lip. "Just a friend," I reiterated. *For now.*

Chef laughed deep and loud, and I couldn't help but join in.

"OK, man. Leave it 'tah me."

Chef placed two basted eggs, toast, and a handful of sun kissed orange slices in front of me on a platter. I ate as he and Clara, his sous chef, prepared the picnic basket.

"Here yah go, my man," Chef said, smiling as he handed me the basket. A blue and white checkered cloth peeked out from its clasped top.

I grinned widely. "Thank you."

"Go 'ave fun, Nicholas." Clara smiled warmly.

I grabbed the basket and bolted out the back door, down the pebbled path, and through the picket fence.

Halfway to the market, I slowed my pace. Although it was still morning, the air was already wet and clingy, and I didn't want to show up a sweaty mess.

The market was very crowded today, which was not unexpected as many families' summer holidays began this week. I worried I wouldn't be able to find Mara as I'd never seen her at the market before. I perused all the shops around the perimeter, unable to locate her. At the center of the square stood a towering fountain carved from white glittering stone depicting a massive bouquet of Christmas roses. Water from one of the mountain's springs jetted, bubbled, and cascaded from the sculpted fountain. Numerous patrons sat at its base enjoying a rest in the shade it provided as well as the cool water that misted from it, offering them relief from the day's heat.

I looked for a clear spot and found one on the fountain's ledge. The sun beat down on me as I stepped up on to it, shielding my eyes with my hand as I scanned the crowded market for Mara. Something glinted in the sun and, like a bear to a honeycomb, I was drawn to the source. There, sitting on the ground between two grand tents, was Mara. I grinned and hopped down from my perch.

The crowd parted for me as I made my way over to her. Unlike the other vendors who had colorful tents to catch customer's attention and chairs to sit on, Mara had nothing. She sat on the cobblestone ground. Laid carefully before her were a few beautiful pieces I assumed she'd created. I was pretty sure my mother's ladies would love the handcrafted jewelry, but the sea glass wind chime was something I was confident my mother would adore. Its opalescent pearls shimmered while shades of turquoise and sapphire did not just shine, they sparkled.

Mara examined me as I studied her creations. "How much for the wind chime?" I asked, finally letting my eyes meet hers.

"Three silvers," she said softly.

"I'm sorry?" I asked, not because I could not hear her the first time, but because I could not believe how little she charged for something so beautiful, so original.

Mara worried her bottom lip. "Would you accept two silvers?

"No, Mara..."

Tears welled in her eyes, but she blinked them back.

"Here..." She held the fragile piece out to me. "...A thank you for saving my life." I placed the picnic basket down and enclosed her hand with mine.

"Mara, I told you that you do not need to thank me for that. And, it was not that three silvers was too much, it was that it was too little a price for something this exquisite."

Mara's cheeks turned a rosy pink, and my heart fluttered in response. She'd unknowingly inspired a new lifelong goal within me; to create opportunities to make *that* happen more often.

"It's not worth much." She shrugged. "I make these with what I find at the beach."

"Are not most of the vendors here selling things they have made? What difference is it if they are made with their hands or machines or giftings?"

"Stop." Mara shook her head in disbelief. "You don't have to lie to me for my sake."

"I'm not. I honestly would like to purchase this for my mother. But do not insult me by trying to give me a friend's discount. I will pay you nothing less than five milled notes."

Mara dropped her gaze. "Why are you doing this?"

"Doing what?"

"I don't need your pity. Please, just go." She wrapped her slender arms around herself. "People are staring and I don't want to make a scene."

I peered over my right shoulder, then my left. It was true,

the market patrons and vendors alike were staring, but not for the reasons Mara might have thought. I frowned. For the first time in a long while, I was annoyed with my position as Prince of Cristes.

"Fine, don't sell it to me...yet. Can we make a deal?"

"Maybe. It depends what it is," Mara replied, skepticism evident in her narrowed eyes and pursed lips.

"I will make myself scarce. You will not see me again until one o'clock. That is four hours from now. At that time, I get to buy whatever you have left at the price I feel is competitive market value, and you will close up shop and spend the rest of the day with me, starting with lunch."

Her brow arched. "And if I sell everything beforehand?"

"Then I will suffer a great loss having missed the chance to bring joy to my mother every morning in her study as she reads by the open window, the sea breeze ushering in the peaceful music of a Mara original wind chime."

Mara scrutinized me and I zeroed in on her energy. It was obvious by the faint vibration— its rhythm fast, then slow, then fast again— that she did not know whether or I was being serious. I was, even though my tactics were a tad dramatic, and I smiled sincerely.

"Fine, Nicholas." She sighed heavily, letting me know she had given in. "You have a deal."

I bowed and backed up a few paces, disappearing into the crowd. I was good at hiding, very good, as I'd had plenty of practice evading the public eye. As I scoped out a spot to relax in, I spied the handful of guards that always trailed me, a security detail my parents insisted I have at all times. They may have been inconspicuous to everyone else, but I always knew where they were.

I made a point to walk past each of them, nod, and quickly give orders to keep patrons away from Mara's 'store.' Once I'd approached all five guards, I sat on the terrace of Carol Belle's Comforts and sipped peach-flavored iced tea. Nestled into the hillside, the cafe provided the perfect vantage point to peer down at the square. Although Mara could not see me, I was in a position where I could easily observe her, and waited patiently for the time when I could free her from her cobblestone prison.

Three and a half hours, and many cups of iced tea and bathroom trips later, I slowly made my way back to Mara. She had only managed to sell one necklace.

"A deal is a deal." I smirked.

"I guess so." Mara frowned.

"Oh, do not be so forlorn. This is a win-win for the both of us. I get the pleasure of your company and beautiful items to gift my mother and her ladies. And you will have sold out!"

Mara wrung her hands, her face screwed up in apprehension.

I tugged on one of the chains from my vest and my royal blue leather satchel popped out from the pocket of my trousers.

"Let's see, two necklaces and two bracelets... I am going to haggle you for a good price since I want the whole lot. Is four milled notes fair?"

Mara's chin dropped and without a thought, I lifted and closed it with the underside of my index finger.

"Please do not leave me in suspense." The corners of my mouth twisted.

Mara nodded her head vigorously, her eyes wide as if in shock. I wanted to laugh but feared she would automatically assume I was laughing at her for the wrong reasons. Instead, I crossed my arms and glared at her.

"Mara, that is not how market negotiations work. You are supposed to come back at me with another price, a higher price."

"A higher price than four milled notes?" she gasped, disbelief still etched in her perfect face.

"Yes. Go on, try it."

Mara twisted her tattered apron, clearly uncomfortable. "Umm, four milled notes and two bronzees?"

"Wrong," I stated matter-of-factly. I had studied Father on numerous occasions as he dealt with the kingdom's finances. I had also been shopping plenty of times with Mother and Chef Berrouet. Although money had never interested me, I did have a knack for economics and finances.

"Wrong?" Mara's face paled, and I feared she would pass out.

I relaxed my stance. "You should say three silvers or more."

"That's...that is way too much. They are not worth that," Mara exclaimed.

"You do not get to decide what art is worth to someone else. Let the buyer tell you what they are willing to spend." I crossed my arms once more. "Go on. Try it."

"Five silvers, sir," Mara said, her perfectly straight teeth smiling back at me.

"Four and a half," I responded swiftly.

"Six and a half," Mara shouted and we both doubled over

laughing. "Kidding! Four and a half is more than fair."

"Next up, how about ten milled notes for the wind chime?"

"Nicholas! That is—"

"Ah, ah, ah, what did we just go over?" A smirk tugged at the corner of my lips as I wagged my finger at her. Mara let out a deep sigh. "Twelve?"

"Eleven," I blurted, keeping my voice playful.

"Sold!" Mara beamed.

"Pleasure doing business with you," I said, placing the monies in her hand. I looked over my right shoulder and found Elden, the most tolerable guardsman, and waved him over.

"Yes, Your Highness?" he asked, his brow popped in confusion at having been called out from his disguised role of commoner.

"Can you please take these articles back to the manor for me and place them in my room? They are a gift for my mother."

"Of course, sir. I will see to it immediately."

"Thank you, Elden. I will be taking Mara to lunch at the beach now."

A gentle tug on my shirt sleeve garnered my attention.

"I can't go to the beach yet," Mara whispered.

"Why not? That was part of the deal. Besides, you must be starving."

"I am hungry and I'll go eat with you, but first, I need to go shopping for groceries and supplies."

I wondered where Mara's parents were. She always seemed to be alone, and she had an awful lot of responsibility for a young woman.

"How about we eat together, right over there?" I pointed to a shaded picnic area under a sweeping oak tree. "Then we can return, complete your shopping, and head to the beach."

"That sounds alright."

I offered my arm to Mara. She lifted her hand, hesitated, then dropped it. She glanced around nervously before finally deciding to place her hand in the crook of my arm. I led her toward the grassy area, but after only a few steps, she released her hold. Inspecting my surroundings, I was convinced that the growing stares and whispers bothered her. Time had taught me to pay them no attention, but this was all new to her. I scowled briefly and righted my face before she could get the wrong impression.

I placed the basket on the grass and unfastened the gold clasp. The two flaps readily sprang open, the contents of the basket full and pressing against them. I pulled out the blue and white checkered blanket and laid it out for us before taking a seat. Mara followed my lead.

When I finished emptying the contents, we had a nice spread, complete with pewter salt and pepper shakers and a succulent dessert.

"Wow! I don't think I've ever seen so much food all at once in my entire life!" Her eyes were liquid pools absorbing the sight. "There is at least a week's worth of food here! There is no possible way we can finish this all."

My heart sank. Mara was thin, but looking at her again, I realized her flowy smock must hide just how malnourished she truly was.

"I didn't mean to offend," Mara said, averting her gaze.

"You could never. You would tell me, though, if you were

ever hungry or needed something, right? Cristes has programs that my mother started. You don't have to go hungry, ever."

"I can take care of myself, thank you."

"Of course. Eat your fill and whatever is left over, you can take home."

Mara brightened at this, and we both dug in.

Thought I was starving, I was careful to eat only a small portion; I wanted her to take this food home. Once we finished, I collected the leftovers.

"Mara, my kitchen staff was going to toss this blanket away after today. Apparently, they got a new linens and no longer need this one. Would you like it?"

A broad smile lit up her face. "Like it? I would love it! Thank you."

"My pleasure." I wrapped the leftovers in the checkered cloth, tied it shut, and made a large loop with the ends. I stood and slung the package over my shoulder.

"Ready to go shopping?" I asked her.

"Yes, thank you."

Mara made quick work of checking off her grocery list. Candles and produce were her main purchases, along with flour, salt, and yeast. Lastly, she added matchsticks and a twelve-ounce piece of venison.

"I'm done." She smiled at me.

She had plenty of money left over from today's sale of her items. I wanted to encourage her to purchase a new dress and shoes, but I was not sure how to broach the subject without coming off as rude.

"Would you like me to help bring these to your house before we head to the beach?"

"No," Mara said hastily.

"But, do you not need to get your meat into the ice chest?" She bit her lips and fidgeted with the hem of her apron.

"What if one of my guar— I mean, friends, brought these to your house for us?"

"No, I want to bring this all back myself and then join you near our cave at the beach."

It was clear Mara did not want me to escort her home, but the words *our cave* had me beaming.

"Do you promise to meet me?"

"Of course. How does thirty minutes sound?"

"Perfect. See you there."

Nicholas: Mine

AS MY SHOULDERS ROLLED BACK, my vest slipped down my arms. I kicked off my loafers and after peeling my shirt off, I untied the string of my linen trousers, letting them drop to the sand. I stepped out of the pool of fabric, adjusted my swim trunks, and ran into the ocean. The clear teal waters promised relief from the muggy air. I dove through the belly of a wave and swam out past the crest. The water here was calm; the cool ripples lapped my muscles, which were sore from the workouts I had been doing with Admiral Colton and Father.

I stood on a sandbar, my back to the shore, fixated on the horizon.

"Mara," I breathed, her presence called to me and I turned.

I knew she was special the moment I first saw her, and spending time with her allowed me to better recognize her tangible gifting. The unique hum that strummed my veins like an acoustic guitar grew, albeit infinitesimally, with each encounter. At seventeen, my body underwent vast changes, typical for a Watcher. In their adult form, Watcher's gain full access to their giftings. However, the onslaught of sensations and sensory overload usually dialed down and became a natural part of all interactions. This was not the case for me and Mother and Father were proud.

Mara must not have noticed me, but she could never have gone unnoticed. Her golden hair lifted in the wind, curling at the ends as it caressed her face, neck, arms, and back. Her white, ruddied smock of a dress billowed in the breeze, and she carefully held her worn shoes as she made her way to the cave.

I freestyled parallel to her and when I was perpendicular to the cave, bodysurfed a wave onto the shore. I did not shy away as Mara's eyes traced my chiseled body one section at a time.

Keeping my eyes focused on her, I approached slowly. I had never before experienced such a hunger to kiss a girl before, but the connection between us told me she was my match. Just as I was within a foot of her, a breeze carried my name.

"Hey, Nick! Nick!"

I turned and Gavin and Shai bolted toward me, sand flying high behind them.

I raised my hand to wave at them, glad they could not see the grimace I wore. True, this may have been our last summer to all hang out, and yet I wanted to spend my time, all my time, with Mara.

I turned quickly to face her. "I can get them to leave if you want."

She worried her lip and peeked over my shoulder, her eyes fixed on Gavin. "It's fine. I trust you. If they are your friends, then they must be good."

I ran my hands through my hair, frustrated at the interruption. Did I misread her appreciating my body earlier? Because the look she gave Gavin now also showed interest. *Just like every other girl.* Still, I would rather have her as a friend than not have her in my life at all. And, when Gavin broke her heart, I would be here to help pick up the pieces.

"Nick, you wouldn't dare ditch us for a *girl*," Gavin said jokingly. "Granted, she is the fairest maiden I have ever seen in all the realms." He laid his best smolder on her and she blushed, that pinky rose color that was quickly becoming one of my favorite things about her.

Shai rolled his eyes and shook with laughter. Gavin elbowed him hard in the gut and he fell to the sand, clutching his stomach, still laughing.

"I did not ditch you. I was not aware we had any plans today," I explained.

"Since when do we make plans while summering? It is standard operating procedure that we convene every day."

"Sorry, Gavin. I was trying to be a welcoming host to Mara."

"No need to keep her all to yourself." Gavin draped his arm over my shoulder. "Mara, would you like to fraternize with us? We meet at the beach just about every day unless it rains, then we rendezvous at my place or Nick's manor."

"The manor?" Mara's eyes jerked to me.

"Oh shoot, you didn't tell her," Shai said as he stood.

"Tell her what?" I asked, genuinely confused.

"You are Prince Klaus?" Mara asked, her voice barely above a whisper.

I gave her a slight bow. "I am. I thought you knew when my guard referred to me as 'prince' at the market."

Mara shook her head. "I must have missed that."

"It does not change anything. I am still me."

"Nick's right. He is a great guy and surprisingly humble," Gavin said.

"Unlike some of us," Shai teased, tilting his head in a not-so-subtle move toward Gavin, who responded by placing him in a headlock and giving him a noogie.

We all laughed, but I knew Mara now perceived me differently. Though my connection to her remained strong, her link to me, the once steady hum, now barely vibrated. It was as if she'd muted her guitar strings.

Gavin joined Mara in wandering up and down the beach as she gathered more treasure for her creations. Shai came and sat next to me. "Sorry, Nick."

"Whatever are you sorry for?"

"I know you like her and Gavin swooped in. Biggest fopdoodle ever."

"Well, you know him. Always going after what he wants without any consideration of others." I smashed my lips together and pressed my fist against them.

"Maybe it is better this way. You know you will have a set list of women you are allowed to marry. You and I both know that, as lovely as Mara appears, she would not be on that list. Probably better that nothing starts between you both in the first place."

"Sure, Shai. I guess." Little did he know, my parents would not hold me to a list.

"Nick! Look what Gavin helped me find!" Mara ran toward me. Her face glowed with hard work and excitement. I stood, smiling at her. She lowered her smock and within it were pieces of neon coral, pearls of different sizes and colors, and a piece of gold.

"Seems like you found an ancient coin," I said, amazed. "You can probably trade that for a lot of money."

"She sure can!" Gavin exclaimed, cradling Mara's shoulders with one arm and giving her a quick hug. "My dad would know just how valuable it is." He turned to her to explain. "He is the crown's financial advisor and manages the Cristes World Bank. For fun, he likes to find and collect rare coins."

"Do you think your dad could get her a fair price?" I asked.

"Of course. I will make sure of it. Under one condition, Mara."

She pulled in her bottom lip and bit it and a growl rose in my throat, but I swallowed it back down. How dare he put her on the spot like this! She barely knows him!

"What's that?" She straightened her back, fists clenched at her sides, and gave him a stiff glare, just as she did with me when she assumed she would owe me for saving her life.

"That you spoil the heck out of yourself with half of the value received." A sly grin grew on his face.

Mara laughed, quiet at first, then her sweet chuckle

morphed into a real belly laugh. We all couldn't help but join in.

"I think I can do that," she finally replied, wiping a tear of joy from her eye.

"Good. I will request that you get yourself a swimsuit, shoes, a day dress and an outfit for midsummer night's Carnival." Gavin's eyes glinted in anticipation.

Shai and I exchanged looks of surprise. Gavin never made plans with girls more than a week in advance. He claimed that life could not be planned, that anything could happen, and he did not want to be tied down. Carnival was several weeks away.

"What is Carnival?" Mara asked.

"Oh, boy! You will love it!" Gavin scooped her up and spun her a few times before setting her down again.

I shook my head at him, but couldn't help a smile. "Calm down, Gavin. Carnival is a huge festival. Everyone generally starts celebrating after lunch. The scheduled events start in the evening and they can sometimes last into the early morning hours. This is the first year that Shai, Gavin, and I will be able to stay out past ten."

"The parade is the best," Gavin added.

"Do not forget the food," Shai said, licking his lips.

I smiled at her. "I am particularly fond of the dancing."

"I—I don't dance," Mara said, casting her gaze to the ground, wiggling her toes in the sand.

Gavin wrapped his arm around her and lifted her chin so that she peered directly at him. "I will teach you."

She crossed her arms over her chest, rounding her shoulders. Gavin slowly dropped his arms.

Mara moved away from him. "I never go out past sunset."

Shai stepped up this time, recognizing the tangible wave of uncertainty mixed with fear that radiated from her. "We will not force you to go, but if you decide you want to, we will all make sure you are safe. Plus, my sister will be coming down in a few weeks to stay for the rest of the summer. You will like her."

"That sounds nice." Mara smiled at Shai, though it did not reach her eyes.

"The sun is starting to set. Can I accompany you home?" Gavin offered, inching closer to Mara.

"No, no thank you." She stepped away from him. "I can get home myself. It's not dark yet."

"I insist. A lady should never walk alone whether day or night, especially a lady as refined as you," Gavin pressed.

"Gavin is right," Shai lamented. "The city is full up with everyone summering, and you never know what vagabonds might arrive each year. They tend to follow the money."

She stiffened. My friends were right, but I knew if I pushed her, I could possibly ruin all of the trust I had built with her at this point. I locked my gaze with hers and willed our connection to send her a message I had no idea she'd receive. *Allow me.*

Mara cocked her head slightly at me as if she were studying me. "Nicholas has offered many times these past few days. I think if anyone walks me home, it should be him."

I knew she could not really hear the words I sent her, but I was glad she seemed to be able to feel their intentions. "I would be honored."

Gavin wrenched me by the elbow.

"Mara, go ahead and gather your treasures. I will meet you at the top of the stairs. I just need a word with Gavin."

"Come on Mara. I'll help you collect your things," Shai offered.

As soon as Mara and Shai were out of sight, Gavin released me.

"What the heck, Gavin?" I asked, shaking my arm out, blood rushing back into my fingertips.

"She's mine," he said flatly.

"If you are referring to Mara, she is not a material item to be owned."

"*Ha, ha* very funny. I know that. It's just... I have never felt like this for a girl before."

I rolled my eyes. "If I had a steelee for every time I heard that..."

"This isn't a joke. I... I really feel like I could marry her." My chin dropped. "Close your mouth, Nick."

"You caught me by surprise, that is all. I never thought I would see the day when one of my boys would settle down."

Gavin smirked. "I know, right? I am shocked, myself. She needs a little work to fit in with our parents' social circles, but I know my mom would love her. I can teach her procedures and protocols over the summer."

"She is not a puppy that needs training, Gavin." My words sounded harsher than I intended.

Gavin sighed. "Nick, I know you like her. But we both know what obligations you have as prince." He gave me a few pats on the shoulder. "The people would never accept her as their future queen. I can give her a good life. Please, let me have her."

"It is her decision—"

"Please, Nick," Gavin pleaded.

"I will not stand in your way or hers. And I *will* remain her good friend and you will *not* say anything about that. Are we clear?" I allowed my gifting to flash, asserting the seriousness of my words.

"Crystal." Gavin slapped me on the back and ran off.

I took one last look at the sun setting on the horizon, sighed, and followed him to catch up with Mara.

Gavin gave Mara's hand a lingering kiss after which he and Shai left.

She gave me a self-deprecating smile. "You don't have to walk me home, Nick."

"Please, I like it when you call me Nicholas."

"Don't all your friends call you Nick?"

"The ones closest to my heart don't." I smiled back at her. "And I'm walking you home. It will be dark by the time you make it back." Mara wrung her hands.

"If you keep that up, you will tear a finger off." I laid a hand atop hers. "What has you so distraught?"

Mara ambled in the opposite direction of the bustling town center. *She must reside near the farms.*

"I have never shown anyone where I lived. Mama and I moved here a few months ago, so the place still needs a lot of work."

"Are you worried I will not be your friend anymore once I see where you live? Because that would never happen."

"Never is a long time."

I shook my head. "Do you feel I am the type of man who would judge you?"

"No. I suppose not. Just, you can't come in, alright?" She stared intently at me, almost desperate. "Mama, well...she's sick. She would be embarrassed if anyone saw her in this state."

I kept her talking as we walked further and further, the sandy ground gradually changing to scattered patches of grass. Eventually, the patches filled and the grasses grew taller.

"I understand. I would never invite myself into your home. I just want to see you to your door safely. You have friends now— friends who care about your well-being."

"Thank you. I—I've never had friends before."

"I find that very hard to believe," I said, but I knew she wasn't lying.

"We move around a lot... This way." Mara made a sharp left down a small path through a dense brush.

I came out on the other side, my arms and shoulders scratched, while Mara emerged unscathed. Off in the distance stood a small shackle of a house, silhouetted against the setting sun. White paint peeled from every shingle, and the roof had been poorly patched. No glass filled the panels of the windows. I worked hard to hide my shock — both in my face or through our connection — at the squalor she called home.

"Is that your house?" I pointed.

"Yes. It has the most wonderful garden in the back and the views of the plains are beautiful." Her eyes gleamed in appreciation.

"I bet. It is very quaint. Perfect for you and your mom."

"Like I said, there is much work to be done before it feels like home, but it has been good to us."

"If you ever need to borrow any tools or scrap material, I would be happy to provide them."

"Nicholas, I said..."

I held my hands up in surrender. "I know, I know. You can take care of yourself. Listen, I am not trying to fix anything for you, just offering you a hand if you ever want it."

"Thank you." She smiled at me. "I've got it from here."

She stopped before what once was a cobblestone pathway leading to the front door of her dilapidated cottage. The path was now crooked, stones completely cracked or hidden under layers of soil and dense grass. Weeds grew between the cracks all along the walkway. Inside the cottage, a faint orange glow emanated from every nook and cranny.

"What's glowing in there? It resembles fire, and yet does not have quite the same color or flicker."

Mara turned to peer at her house. "Oh, that?" She faced me and flicked her wrist as if it were no big deal. "It's how I keep my food fresh."

I lifted my brow. "Oh, so you can use your gifting for food preservation?

"My what?" She scrunched her nose.

"Your...gifting."

"I was told I don't have one, but I was able to use some herbs from the garden to cast a desirable over the meat from the market today, so it won't spoil."

"A desirable?" I tilted my head at her, not understanding what she meant. I knew Watchers were able to access their natural giftings, sometimes coupled with elemental magic, to produce enchantments, but I'd never heard of this.

"A spell." She smiled. "Don't worry. I'm not very good and

have very limited abilities. Her smile morphed into a frown. "What's wrong?"

I realized my eyebrows had been pinched together, my lips tight. *No gifting?* But her power stirred, wanting to get out. Whoever told her she didn't have one was seriously underestimating her.

I shook my head. "Nothing. Will I see you tomorrow, at the market?"

"Yes, after twelve." I wanted to argue but she held her hand up to stop me. "I don't want my customers to avoid my booth because the Prince of Cristes is there. Oh, and Nicholas?"

"Yes?"

"Thank you for walking me home. Please bring Shai and Gavin with you tomorrow."

She had caught me off guard. I hadn't expected her to accept my friends so easily. Though I was thankful she did, I frowned because she had welcomed Gavin so readily. I realized when she hugged herself with one arm and chewed on the inside of her lip that my reaction to her last comment was out of place.

Forcing a smile, I said, "Of course. Goodnight, Mara."

I waited at the end of the long narrow path until she was inside. I made it a few yards before three of my guards emerged from the brush. Each sat astride their horse, leading a white one for me.

We rode in silence to the manor. Music greeted me when I walked through my front door. It grew louder as I strode across the open corridor, past the kitchen, and into the parlor where I knew Mother would be hosting her friends. I approached the entryway to the room and paused. The night breeze lifted the organza curtains and danced about freely like ghosts. Nolan was at the piano while Mother and her ladies chatted on the settees.

"Hello, dear." Mother stood to greet me, but I made no move past the entrance.

As soon as her gifting brushed against my face, I knew she'd be able to discern something was wrong. I turned, slipping into the library across the hall. Mother was at my heels, closing the doors behind us.

"What is it, love?" Mother palmed my cheek.

"I need your help, with a friend." I needed to be careful of the words I used, knowing Mara would never accept my mother's generosity if she felt as though she were a charity case. "I have met an exceptional young woman. She is amazingly gifted. I sensed the power within her immediately." I laid my hand over Mother's that still cradled my cheek and stared fixedly in her eyes. "I could...*feel* her abilities."

Mother's grin was warm and bright and she dropped her hand. "Oh dear, that is fantastic. Maybe you will be able to choose your wife after all." She took my hand and led me to the tufted couch.

We sat and I shook my head. "Let's not get ahead of ourselves. I came to you with this because this young woman is poor and living in awful conditions."

Mother crossed her legs and steepled her fingers. She fixed her gaze on me, listening intently.

"The problem is, she has never had anyone to take care of her; at least, I think that is the situation." I sat back and draped my arms over the couch. "She is proud and lacks trust. It took substantial effort on my part to build her confidence in me enough to see her home safely tonight."

Mother gave me a knowing smile. "You are one of the kindest souls I have ever known, Nicholas. Of course, it would only be a matter of time for her to trust you." Mother leaned in and patted my knee. "How can I help?"

"I know you care a great deal for our community in the capitol. What do you think about an outreach here in Sint Natal as well?"

Her brow arched and the corner of her mouth lifted giving her a conspiratorial look. "What do you have in mind?"

"Well, Mara— that is her name, by the way— is a fantastic artist. She sells her work at the market on weekends. I was thinking she could take tutoring lessons here at the manor, and we could provide her with a studio where she can safely create. If she shows promise, maybe she can attend university in the fall on a full scholarship, room and board included."

Mother surveyed me and I could feel her abilities flit through me, albeit not intrusively. Nevertheless, she would be able to ascertain how determined I was, and perhaps even glimpse Mara in my memories.

She smiled, stood up, and came to grasp my hands. "I think that is a wonderful idea. And do not worry; I will make sure her creations are sold out each day at the market so that she can come here for lunch and lessons. She will never go hungry, and her mother will be well taken care of with the leftovers I will provide— no, insist— that Mara take home with her."

I pulled Mother into a big bear hug, lifting her off of her feet.

"I have gifts for you and your ladies."

"Oh, Nicholas!" She giggled. "Put me down, you silly, sweet boy. Now, go grab our presents and join us in the parlor. Leave the details to me."

I kissed her cheek and ran to my room.

Nicholas: The Apprentice

A S I MADE MY WAY TO THE KITCHEN, the sound of tinkling glass stopped me short. Mara's creation already hung in the window of Mother's lounge, its shimmer as beautiful to look at as the melody it played with every breeze. I smiled. Mother genuinely fell in love with my gift, just as I knew she would. Deciding I would have breakfast in the dining room today, I changed my path and was glad to see her there.

"Hello, Mother." I kissed her cheek before sitting down on the tufted, cream-colored parson chair.

"To what do I owe the honor of your company this morning?" She smiled at me, delighted I had joined her. She wore her blonde hair extra soft today, swept behind one ear and pinned with a pearl-studded barrette.

"*Ha, ha*; very funny. Can a son not join his mother just because he wants to?"

"Of course. I am sure it has nothing to do with Mara." Mother gave me a knowing smirk before taking a bite of poached egg.

"Honestly, I am very grateful for you and Father and all that you do for me. You deserve more than I have shown." A servant marched in with breakfast for me and set it upon the teakwood table.

"Nonsense, Nicholas. No need to make a poor, old woman cry."

"You are neither poor, nor old," I reminded her, laughing. "However, now that you mention her name, are we initiating the plans for Mara today?"

"Yes. No time to waste, especially if such precious gifting is at stake."

"What do you need me to do?"

"My son, you need to act as if you had no part in this. By not sharing my exact plot, your reactions will be much more natural. It's probably best if you go about your day as normal and head to the market when you informed Mara you would."

"Thanks." I wolfed down the rest of my plate, gave her a kiss on her soft, warm cheek, and headed to the stables. Shai would no doubt already be at Gavin's, and I wanted to clue them both in on what my intentions were.

The sunshine and wonderful breeze further heightened my good mood as I strolled to the barn.

Nolan greeted me just outside the stables. "Should I ready a horse for you, Prince Nicholas?"

"No thank you. I changed my mind... I will walk today."

As I strolled to my friend's house, I thought about what a

change Nolan had undergone over the past year. He was a few years older than I, but we practically grew up together. His parents worked for mine and Nolan had recently started as my personal butler, taking his position very seriously.

I arrived at Gavin's and ambled down the paved walkway aligned with colorful shrubs. My hand reached for the brushed nickel door knocker and rapped it three times.

"Good morning, Prince Nicholas," the butler, dressed in a freshly-pressed linen suit, greeted.

"Good morning. Is Gavin home?"

"Lord Gavin and Lord Abishai are out back at the court. Please, do come in." The butler stepped aside to let me enter the home. I headed through the back double doors at the opposite end, past the pool, and down the hill to the tennis court, where Gavin and Shai were involved in an intense game.

"Nick! The Admiral let you off early today?" Shai yelled, narrowly missing a ball to the face. He simultaneously contorted his body and swung, launching the ball back toward Gavin.

I cupped my hand over my mouth and hollered, "Nice move!"

Gavin plucked the approaching ball straight out of the air with his bare hand.

"Want to join in, mate?" Gavin turned to look at me, his usually light brown hair now dark and matted with sweat.

"Actually, I wanted to invite you guys over for lunch. Then I figured we would rendezvous with Mara. I promised we would meet her at the market just after twelve."

"I am definitely in," Gavin responded without a moment's hesitation.

Shai rolled his eyes. "I guess. So, is this girl going to be with us *all* summer?"

"Yes," Gavin and I said in unison, and we both laughed.

"Mara is awesome. Give her a chance. You will get to like her," I urged.

"I am sure she is," Shai muttered. "That's what I'm worried about."

Gavin draped an arm over his shoulder. "Relax, man. When you get bitten, you will understand."

"Um... When I what?" Shai's brows pinched together.

Gavin and I chuckled.

"Well, then I shall leave you both to it. See you at my place soon." I didn't bother to head back through Gavin's house. Instead, I traipsed through the pristine grasses to the white fence's gate. I unhooked the rod iron latch and swung it open, careful to ensure it closed behind me.

I had been home for thirty minutes when Nolan brought Gavin and Shai to join me in the dining room for lunch. We chatted about the upcoming Carnival and what costumes we might don this year.

"I don't care what you blokes decide to wear, but I will plan mine to coincide with Mara's," Gavin announced.

"Oh, get a grip, man! You have known her for all of, what, ten minutes, and you are so quick to drop your friends? It is tradition that we all dress in the same theme," Shai nearly growled.

"Easy, killer."

"No, Gavin. What is up with you?" Shai shot back. Gavin averted his gaze and bit his bottom lip.

"Shoot, it must be significant if you are at a loss for words," Shai said quietly.

"It is. I... I cannot explain it. I think she is *the one*. No, I am *certain* she is the one," Gavin sighed.

I rolled my eyes and forged ahead in the conversation before Shai's head could explode. "Actually, I thought we could surprise Mara. What if we choose a theme where all three of us are dressed the same, and Mara could complement or complete the costumes? She has moved around a lot and has never been to our festival before. I think we should save the surprise until the day we reveal her costume to her." I did not want to share Mara's financial situation with them. It was her story to tell if she wanted.

"Excellent idea," Gavin said, slapping me on the shoulder.

"Fine. Might as well include Lana as well."

"Don't sound so excited to have your sister join us," I razzed Shai.

"Prince Nicholas, it is time for you to head to the market to pick up Miss Mara."

"Thank you for the reminder, Nolan."

Our chairs slid easily out from us with nary a sound, and the three of us walked to the market, tossing out ideas on what our theme could be.

"So, where do you have plans to meet her?" Gavin stood on the balls of his feet, attempting to see over the crowd.

"At her sales spot."

"Her spot? Like her booth? She...she works here?" Shai's mouth fell open.

"She sells her art. You know those treasures she is always looking for on the beach? She transforms them into amazing pieces." I pointed to the far end of the square. "She's usually tucked into that corner, between those two tents."

Gavin took off before I'd even finished my sentence. By the time Shai and I caught up to him, he stood before some of my mother's guards, arms crossed as if posturing for a fight.

"What is the meaning of this?" I asked Lance, the head guard.

Lance placed his left arm over his heart and crossed it with his right, hands balled into fists, and bowed before answering. "Prince Nicholas. We are merely following the Queen's orders."

"Which are?" I asked, adding a layer of annoyance to my tone, feigning ignorance.

"She was so impressed with the gift you gave her last night," Lance said, looking impassive, "that she ordered us to find who made it and bring the person back to her straight away."

Gavin's grin could have lit up the entire square. "Indeed, you were not embellishing her talents."

"I have no reason to," I said defensively, unsure why my friend would not have believed me. I looked back at Lance. "What are you doing with Mara's items?"

"The Queen has purchased all of Miss Mara's inventory for today and asked us to ensure they get to the manor safely.

She also instructed that the madame's booth be properly stowed."

Her booth? Mara merely sat on the ground while selling her wares. But then I saw pieces of blue and white checkered cloth; Mara had used our picnic blanket to fashion a small tent.

"Clever girl," I mumbled.

"You say something, Nick?" Shai asked.

"Nothing." I shook my head smiling. "Let's get back to the manor and rescue Mara from the clutches of my mother's ladies."

We ran the few miles back to my family's estate.

"Mother?" I called out, my chest heaving and slick with sweat.

"In here, darling," she sang from her lounge. The boys followed me through the expansive hall, which boasted incredible ceiling heights.

We all stopped short in the salon's entryway. Mara stood on a pedestal with a wide grin on her face as she admired her reflection in the mirror. She was wearing a beautiful sea-green dress that perfectly matched the wind chime she had created which now hung in the window. My mother's maidens were holding a rosy pink frock up in front of her, nearly the exact shade her cheeks turned when flushed.

"Mara, are you alright?" I asked, not sure what she thought of all this attention.

Mother waved me off. "Of course. She is fine, Nicholas. This extraordinary young woman has agreed to be my apprentice. In exchange for creating out of my house every day, I get first pick of her art before I allow my ladies to shop, but I cannot imagine I will leave them anything to purchase." Mother's bell-like laugh was music to my ears, and I smiled. "Mara understands that as her benefactor, I wish her to study here and she is expected to dress for company at all times."

One of the maidens carried the pink gown away while another helped Mara down from the pedestal. When she turned around to face the three of us, each of our jaws dropped.

"You look beautiful," Gavin said, striding up to her. He

took her hand in his and pressed a lingering kiss to her palm. Mara's cheeks practically glowed.

"She always does," I murmured. Mother's eyes snapped to mine. It was a calculated look, as if she were working out a mystery.

"Boys, I will expect you to help Mara with her studies each day. She is well-traveled, but has not had a traditional education in any sense of the word." Mother frowned.

"Yes, Your Majesty," Shai and Gavin chimed as they crossed their arms over their hearts and bowed.

"Oh, stop, you two." She playfully swatted the air near them. "You are practically sons to me. Bowing is entirely unnecessary in my home." Both Gavin and Shai straightened. "Now, you gentlemen go wait in the guest quarters. Miss Mara and I will finish up here, and she will be with you presently."

"Of course, Mother." I kissed each of her cheeks and exited the salon, Gavin and Shai on my heels.

I turned the gold knob on the glass-paned door to the guest quarters just beyond the inground pool. The room had been rearranged to suit any need Mara may have. The space was compact, but airy and full of natural light, with a nook just large enough to fit a small bed. A pale wooden table with four chairs stood directly across from the entrance, an L-shaped white bookcase behind it. To the right was a larger workspace consisting of a few tables and some tools I was unfamiliar strewn on top. How Mother had readied this room so quickly was beyond me. She was a woman with a big heart and many talents fueled by her determination.

I claimed one of the four chairs covered in pale green fabric and took a seat at the round table, Gavin and Shai flanking me on either side.

I crossed my arms and leaned on the table, peering at my friends. "So, how are we going to do this?"

"Do what?" Gavin asked.

Shai scoffed. "Did you not hear your Queen? Has Mara made you deaf, too? Teach her, that's what."

"I have lots of things to teach her," Gavin said, a wicked smile pulling up the corners of his lips as he waggled his brows.

I snarled at him.

"I was kidding, Nick. Sheesh." Gavin held his hands up in mock surrender.

"You'd better be." I let my gifting ignite my eyes. "My mother is obviously impressed with Mara. Do not mess this up."

"Woah, Nick. Relax." Shai gripped my shoulder, but I kept my eyes alight.

Gavin rubbed the back of his neck. "I have no intention of tainting her innocence."

"Good. You can court her elsewhere. We are here to help her," I stated matter-of-factly.

"I am good with Cristes' history," Shai cut in garnering my attention. "I can assist her with that, along with writing."

I relaxed. "Thank you. I will instruct Mara in giftings and Cristes customs."

"And I can tutor her through math and economics," Gavin offered.

"That should cover it all," I said, glad to have finished divvying up all the traditional subjects.

Gavin regarded me intently for a long moment.

"What?" I pressed.

"When you teach Mara our customs, skip the dancing."

I frowned. "But she needs to know how to dance."

"True, but I don't want you getting too close to my girl."

I rolled my eyes. "And I suppose you'll teach her?"

"Yes. I want to be the one to teach her the customary dances as well as the popular ones she is expected to know at soirees."

Unexpected anger surged within me. "You know, you're acting like a real—"

A knock at the door interrupted me and seized our attention. Framed by the glass door stood Mother and Mara. We all shot up from our seats at once, and I hastened to the door. A waft of humid air clung to my body when I opened it.

Mother stepped inside, her hands clasped together at her chest. She turned and beckoned Mara to follow her in. I closed the door behind them and was thankful for the cool breeze that brushed my skin once again.

"Gentleman, please have a seat. Mara, you too, dear." Once we were all seated at the round table Mother continued. "This young woman shows great potential in being able to study at university, as she is already a fine artist. The problem lies in that she has no official transcripts to speak of since her family has moved around so much. We need to make sure she can pass all entrance exams by summer's end." Mother stared pointedly at each of us. "Can I count on all of you?"

We nodded our assurance.

"Wonderful. Every morning at ten, one of you will meet Mara here for lessons. All of the curriculum and materials you should require are on the bookshelves." She gestured to the shelves behind us. "You will break for lunch at twelve and resume studies from one to three. After that, she will need to head to the beach to collect her bounty so she can create." Mother came to stand behind me and placed her hands on my shoulders. "She should not have to lug her treasures home with her every night. So, Gavin and Shai can deliver her findings here at the guest quarters, which now Mara's art studio. Any questions?"

"I can escort her home, Your Majesty," Gavin said shyly, rather uncharacteristic for someone as confident as him.

"Thank you for your kind offer, but I have already set my mind. My Nicholas will see her home on the nights she does not wish to stay here." She smiled at him, then moved around to stand next to the wall. "Now, you need not all be present each day. The poor girl would not be able to concentrate with all your shenanigans. Thus, I have devised a schedule. Cynthia, if you please."

My mother's maiden seemed to appear out of nowhere and pressed a small button. The wall flipped to reveal a sleek whiteboard bearing my mother's handwriting.

"Memorize this schedule. Mondays, Wednesdays, and Fridays before lunch will be history and writing. Tuesday and Thursday mornings will cover math and economics. All afternoons will be reserved for giftings and customs."

"Mother, what about time for Mara to work on her art?"

"Great question. Mara knows she is welcome to stay the night here. She is also welcome to come before lessons start, and on the weekends."

"And what about fun?" Gavin asked.

Mother smiled at him. "I am sure you all can help her

with that in your spare time."

For the first time today, I allowed myself to stretch out my giftings to Mara. I no longer felt fear from her. Tiny puffs brushed all over my skin, like a flower popping open from its bud. *Is that hope I feel?* She smiled at me, noticing my stare and I smiled back.

Mara turned her head away from me. "Um, thank you," she whispered, barely audible.

Mother, who had been looking at me, shook her head and blinked. "I am sorry, dear. What did you say?"

Mara glanced at me, as if to confirm she had not said something wrong. I encouraged her to try again. "Thank you. For...*seeing* me."

Mother pressed her hands over her heart. "The pleasure is all mine." She glowed with happiness, her eyes igniting. Mara startled at the sight of her. Mother reigned in her joy and studied Mara. "My dear, have you never seen Watcher giftings before?"

"I have, but yours are much brighter."

"Of course, she is the queen," Shai stated, as if Mara's observation were ludicrous.

I gave his foot a swift kick.

"Ow! What was that for?" Shai stared daggers at me.

"True, my mother is exceptionally gifted, but you made her very happy, that is all," I explained to Mara.

Mother sighed. "Well, Mara, I think you have had enough excitement for one day. Would you like Cynthia to put your new wardrobe in the chest, or will you be taking it all home?"

Mara scrutinized her outfit and then considered the chest at the back of the room. "I will take what I'm wearing home and keep the rest here, if you don't mind."

"Of course. I am off to start preparations for Bradwit Waterford University's annual fundraiser. You all go have some fun." Mother strode to the door. "You boys are welcome to use the pool or go to the beach, or whatever else you wish to introduce Mara to." She stopped short just shy of the door and turned to us. "Lessons begin Monday. That is only four days hence."

"Yes, Your Majesty," Shai and Gavin responded, giving her the authentic Watcher bow, right arm crossed over the left at the heart. I made my way toward her.

"How many times do I need to remind you, boys? You do not need to greet me so formally in my own home." But Mother's cheeks grew rosy as she beamed.

I leaned in close to her ear. "Thank you, for everything, Mother." Then I swept her into a big hug.

"Anything for you, Nicholas; you know that."

I released her. She left the room, and her entourage of guards and maidens reappeared out of the woodwork from their statue-like positions, following after her.

Shai wasted no time in making plans. "I say we hit the beach."

"Mara will be going to the beach regularly for her art projects," Gavin responded.

"How about Azure Summit?" I suggested.

Mara's eyes widened, and excitement surged through me. I beamed at her and Gavin nearly growled at me.

"I have never been, though I've heard my customers mention it," she said.

"Then it's decided," Gavin said, taking her hand. "Nick,

can we take your carriage?" he asked without looking at me, his eyes trained on Mara's face.

"Of course," I said and realized I'd been clenching my jaw when a sharp pain stung me. "I will ring Nolan to get the carriage ready."

"Ummm, is anyone else hungry?" Shai asked, pressing a hand to his stomach.

I laughed. "I'll have him talk to Chef as well."

Half an hour later, the aqua and gold carriage led by white horses wearing large, salmon-pink feathered headdresses strolled to a stop in front of the gatehouse. I was the last to enter the carriage, plopping down on the cream and gold tufted fabric.

I reached into the top right corner and pressed the marble button. A low hum filled the interior, and specs of white began to fill the space. Quiet, soft, and slow, the snowflakes drifted onto our skin, and cool relief melted away the oppressive heat.

Mara's eyes glowed ever so slightly. She closed them, tilted her head back, and stuck out her tongue, something I used to do as a child. It was fun to watch her experience something new, and I realized very quickly that I was not the only one. Gavin sat mesmerized, not taking his eyes off of her for a second, as if she were life itself.

Nicholas: Azure Summit

THE CARRIAGE OSCILLATED IN A STEADY RHYTHM the entire way. I couldn't help but glance at Mara often, smiling at her exuberant expression. *I love that I get to witness her first time in a carriage.* The lush landscape that covered the mountain came into view. Soon, the vibrant greens of the plant life appeared close enough to touch, and the carriage rolled to a soft stop. Although I'd seen it at least a hundred times before, the blue that surrounded the mountain and glowed under the sun's rays still mesmerized me. My parents and I always spent one day together here over the summer holiday. My favorite part was cave-diving in the lagoon.

"Thanks, Evan," I said to the footman who had unfastened our cooler.

"Of course, Your Highness." He bowed. "We will be at the ready whenever you wish to return."

My cheeks heated. I hated when my parents' staff doted on me in front of my friends. Usually, the guys did not care. They spent a few years razzing me about it, but they had become so accustomed to it, they paid it no mind. However, I knew this was new to Mara, and I did not want her to feel uncomfortable, especially around me.

As if reading my mind, Gavin reached for Mara's hand, and she accepted it willingly.

A little possessive, are we? I wanted to separate them, even if only for a moment. "Care to help with the cooler?" I shouted.

Gavin ignored my outburst, but Shai turned and acknowledged me, jogging over and gripping the roped handle.

"Which way?" he asked.

"Shall we head to the lagoon?" I gestured my head to the right. "It has shade and a shallow pool area."

"It's like you read my mind," Gavin responded, but his eyes remained on Mara as he led her through the amethyst canopied entrance.

This is going to get annoying. I shook my head. Gavin really was head-over-heels gobsmacked over Mara. I just hoped he would not break her heart. Eira knows he never dated the same girl for more than two weeks.

Shai and I followed, wobbling as we trudged through the soft soil, the heavy cooler throwing off our balance. With sweat-soaked shirts, Shai and I dropped the cooler onto the sandy earth next to the blue pool deep inside the mountain.

Gavin was already shirtless, showing off as he splashed around in the lagoon. Mara sat at the edge of the pool, letting the water caress her shins. Shai and I peeled off our shirts and flung them onto the rugged boulders jutting from the mountainside. Exchanging a knowing smile, we ran and cannonballed into the water.

Waves crashed up Mara's thighs and onto her abdomen and she squealed in delight.

"You should take that cover-up off and come in. The water's perfect, like you," Gavin said, eyeing her from naval to chest from under his lashes.

Mara bit her lip. "I'm fine here."

"You are fine—" He licked his bottom lip. "But I would really love it if you joined me *in* here."

Mara's eyes sought mine, pleading.

I sent her a little pulse of reassurance down our bond. "Hey, guys, want to dive down to the cave? See if we can find something for Mara to use for her creations?"

"Sounds fun," Shai said.

Gavin squinted his eyes and pursed his lips. After a few long moments of silence, he responded, "For Mara, anything even though cave-diving is a dangerous activity, and I may not live to see tomorrow."

"Oh, please!" Shai feigned gagging and Gavin stared daggers at him, but his face softened when he gazed back at Mara.

"I would have one regret." Gavin frowned.

Mara appeared stricken, her eyes darting between me and Gavin. I know I said I wouldn't get in his way, but I could feel her fear. She had no idea he was joking.

"Mara, we'll be traveling through a long tunnel to the

underground cave. We'll be under for a little while, but there are some air pockets along the way. We're trained divers and we've done this a hundred times before."

"See, super dangerous," Gavin said again, mischief glinting in his eyes.

Mara smiled and shook her head. "And what would your one regret be?"

"That I would not have gotten a kiss from the most beautiful girl I've ever had the pleasure of laying eyes on."

Mara's cheeks bypassed my favorite rosy pink and flushed red as the corners of her mouth lifted into a bright smile. "I think I could allow that."

The chins on all three of us guys dropped. No one, not even Gavin, expected Mara to say yes, and I felt his uneasiness, a feeling I was unaccustomed to experiencing from him, as he swam closer to her.

She sat there, leaning back on her hands, her feet making lazy circles in the water. Gavin popped up between her legs, his full weight on his arms, his triceps bulging. He leaned in for a kiss, and just before his lips met hers, she turned her face and the kiss landed on her cheek.

"You got your kiss." Mara smirked, then lifted her foot and gently pushed him back into the water.

Shai and I died of laughter. This was a side of Mara I hadn't seen before— a playfulness mixed with a savvy approach to handling Gavin. For a brief moment, I was no longer worried about him breaking her heart.

"I promise to bring you back some meritorious pieces for your art," Gavin vowed, squeezing her foot before taking a deep breath and pencil diving into the lagoon. Shai followed suit.

"Help yourself to the cooler if you get hungry," I said. Then, I waved to her and dove after my friends.

As we descended, the water grew colder and darker, and the tunnel to the cave became increasingly narrow. The conditions made it nearly impossible to swim and hold our breath, especially during the last stretch when there were no more air pockets. Just as the fire started to burn in our lungs, we finally reached the end of the tunnel. Climbing out of the water, we lay on our backs, chests heaving as we caught our breaths.

Gavin, in a rush to get back to Mara, did not bother waiting until he'd fully recovered before starting his search for treasures. I turned my head and was surprised when I spotted exactly what *I* would present to her— a teal and plum conch shell with a pearlized sheen.

"Do you think she'd want these?" Shai asked, holding out his hands.

"What are strawberries doing down here?" Gavin asked.

Shai laughed. "They aren't strawberries; they are strawberry-topped seashells." We peered at his palms. The small spiral shells really did resemble the fruit, their red coats dotted with tiny specks of black.

"She will love them," I assured Shai.

"Great...you both already found gifts for Mara, but as her boyfriend, I need to top them. Help me look," Gavin pleaded, running his hand through his hair.

Within the textured wall, a slight discoloration snagged my attention. I walked over to inspect it and smiled. "Over here, Gavin."

He bounded over in two long strides and threw his arm over my shoulder to take a look. His grin widened, and his eyes lit up the wall. The heart-shaped cockle shells in muted shades of pink, purple, orange, and blue appeared to charge under Gavin's light. He shut down his ability, and the shells' hues bloomed to vibrant colors that sparkled. Using common shells we found on the sandy floor, we carefully carved out a few of the hearts.

"Perfect," he breathed. "Let's go, boys."

We made our way back through the tunnel, the water warming the closer we got to the lagoon's pool, and broke through the surface.

Fear constricted me as soon as I took my first breath. It took me a moment to realize it was not my own that I felt.

"Oy! Leave her alone!" Gavin shouted. He made a mad dash to the edge, his eyes intense and biceps bulging as he launched himself out of the water.

Mara was backed up against the vines lining the rough inner wall of the summit's base. A cluster of guys and girls— schoolmates of ours— had formed a semi-circle, boxing her in.

"You know her, Gavin?" Rudy, the tallest of the group, asked over his shoulder.

Gavin muscled his way through the intimidation ring and stood directly in front of Mara, shielding her from their view.

"Excuse me," I bellowed, and the two other guys and three girls parted immediately. "What is going on here?"

"We saw *her* going through your stuff," Charity piped up. "And?" I retorted.

"Well, we thought she was stealing. Clearly, she is not one of us. We've seen her at the market," Charity whispered the last part to me, as if that meant something.

"Oh, boy," Shai sighed, rubbing the back of his head.

"She's with us," Gavin gritted out through a clenched jaw, reaching behind him to clutch Mara's waist, his eyes glowing a fierce green.

"Easy, man." Rudy stepped back and raised his hands in surrender. "We've never seen her in these parts before. We recognized the royal seal on the cooler and saw her going through it. Honest mistake."

Gavin relaxed a bit and dropped his arm, turning around to face Mara.

"Are you alright?" he asked, cupping her jaw as he rubbed her cheek with his thumb. She nodded.

"We did not mean to frighten you," Rudy said, cocking his head to the side to peek around Gavin.

"Definitely. It was an honest mistake," Charity parroted, reaching for Rudy's hand.

I gestured toward Gavin. "I would like to introduce you all to Mara. Mara, these are classmates of ours— Rudy, Charity, Shep, Northelyn, and Christian." They all gave an uneasy wave.

Mara stepped out from behind Gavin and laced her fingers in his. The others exchanged glances, their eyes widening in silent communication.

What they had not said aloud was not lost on me. My parents were the rulers of Cristes, and parts of their unique giftings had passed on to me; thus, I could feel and understand more than most Watchers. And I knew, despite my classmates' niceties, that they did not accept Mara, nor would they ever.

"I think we were about to head home," Shai said, throwing his thumb over his shoulder. "The lagoon is all yours."

Nicholas: They Found Us

MARA HAD BOLDLY SHOWN HER COUPLING with Gavin by taking his hand, but she still did not let him take her home that night. Then again, I doubted she knew what our customs were, and what lacing fingers together in front of others meant. Gavin, as elated as he was with her public display, did not fault her for walking home with me. He, too, knew Mara did not understand the significance of her actions— that she had publicly declared them an official couple. He trusted me to see her home, confident that I would not break my word.

"Today was lovely," Mara said, her cheeks sun kissed from her time in the lagoon at Azure Summit.

"Most of it, anyway," I grumbled and shoved my hands in my pockets.

"They were trying to protect their friends." She placed her hand on my forearm and gave it a reassuring squeeze.

"I suppose though you are hardly a threat. They needn't have responded as such."

"I'm fine." She dropped her hand and smiled. "They only questioned me. Besides, if they are your friends, they must be good people."

Mara had much to learn yet, but now was not the time. The carriage began jostling and hopping, the unkempt roads indicating we were close to her cottage. She peeked her head out and stilled.

"STOP!" She yelled at the driver through the peephole.

"Whoa!" he ordered, pulling on the reins. The horses protested, but we came to an abrupt stop behind the brush still a good thirty yards from Mara's place.

I grabbed her arm. "What is it?" Her heart thudded so loudly, the sound amplified by our touch, I could barely hear her next words.

"They found us."

My brows pinched together in concern. "Who, who has found you?"

"Never mind, Nicholas. Please, do not follow me." A loud crash sounded from the house, and she swiveled her head to look back at the cottage. "Mother!" She flung open the door.

"Mara, wait!" I cried after her. But she did not stop, not even as she stumbled out of the carriage, gashing open her knee in the process; she quickly collected herself, then sprinted down the overgrown path.

"Should we proceed home, Your Highness?" the driver asked, his eyes flicking uneasily between me and the fleeing Mara.

"No, stand by," I instructed. I waited until she had barreled through her front door before I bolted from the carriage and snuck around to the back of the cottage, crouching beneath a broken window.

"Finally, your bastard daughter graces us with her presence," a gruff voice said, sarcasm dripping from his tone.

"Don-d-don't call me that," Mara stammered.

"He'll call you whatever he wishes, you little witch," a nasal, high-pitched voice sneered.

"Did you think you could really disappear and that we'd never find you?" the gruff voice asked.

I rolled onto my toes and craned my neck to peer inside the window, hoping to Eira I wouldn't be spotted.

A lady with fire-red hair clutched another, pale woman's hair in her grip forcing the woman to her knees. A tear trickled down the accosted woman's cheek.

"Leave my mother alone!" Mara shrieked. "We've done nothing to you!" She ran toward her mother but froze when the redhead yanked her mother's hair, causing the blonde woman to yelp in pain.

A sinister laugh boomed from the shadowed corner, and out walked a man with hair whiter than snow, his eyes so dark, his irises were almost indistinguishable from his pupils.

Fear. I could feel it gripping me, one cell at a time, as it raced across my chest, coiling and constricting. But it was not mine; Mara's body was screaming at me.

"We will leave you alone when you tell us where the black rose is."

"Melchior, please," Mara's mother whimpered, pleading with the platinum haired man.

Mara's round eyes flickered to her mother's face, then

swung back to Melchior.

"What is that, Bronwyn?" The male standing next to the redheaded woman sneered at Mara's mother. "Speak up, I couldn't hear you." Without warning, he slapped Mara's mother across the face, and her head snapped to the side. "Speak to me without permission again and next time, it'll be my fist."

The two lackeys laughed. Melchior held up a hand to silence them. "Mara, I know you have the black rose—"

"I don't!"

"Do not interrupt me!" Mara flinched as he ran up to her and seized her by the arms, shaking her. He stopped abruptly, rolling his neck as he took a sharp inhale through his nose. The he spoke slowly, as if his next words cost his great effort. "Roisin said she saw you."

"Correct, chief. I did see her." The redhead shot Mara a killer glare, her eyes dimly glowing red.

"Liar," Mara whispered. Melchior raised his hand as if he'd assault her, and my power pulsated in response, ready to strike. He suddenly stopped himself, clenching his fist. His gaze turned amorous and instead, he stroked her cheek with the back of his hand.

His cruel hand on her perfect face made me want to vomit.

Melchior leaned close to Mara's neck and inhaled deeply. He straightened, a smile tugging at the corners of his thin lips, his eyes glazed as if intoxicated.

"My offer still stands. All would be forgiven. No one would dare question my bride's loyalty. I and only I, could protect you from the mob." He stroked her cheek and slid a finger down her neck, caressing her collarbone with the pad of his index finger.

I shuddered with repulsion, desperate to catapult myself through the window and break the guy's neck.

A cool, heavy force crackled across my chest, shoulders, arms, and abdomen. Like a suit of armor, each piece snapped into place over my body, offering protection and strength. I'd never felt anything like this before, and had to look down at my torso to make sure I was not glowing, that I had not conjured a gifting I did not know I possessed. And then I realized— it was Mara.

"I will never marry you," she seethed, staring Melchior dead in the eyes before spitting on him. I could swear I saw the tiniest spark of orange ignite in her beautiful, innocent eyes.

He collected the spit from his angled cheek with a swipe of his hand. His eyelids grew heavy before licking his fingers, savoring each taste, his eyes rolling in ecstasy. "Roisin, Yule, help Mara understand what is at stake."

The lackeys began trashing what little there was to destroy in the cottage. The brute, Yule, hoisted Bronwyn by her hair and wrenched her arms back. Roisin stepped up and her thick red lips morphed into a sickening smile before she reared her hand back and punched Bronwyn in the stomach.

"That is for your defiant daughter. And this," Roisin punched her again in the side, Bronwyn collapsing as she gasped, her eyes rolling in pain, "is for defiling your body with a human."

"That will be enough," Melchior ordered calmly. He looked menacingly at Mara. "I do hope you'll reconsider my offer. Something tells me you will be begging me to marry you before the month's end. No one else would dare wed a disgrace like you— a pathetic, powerless, half-human Watcher," he sneered. "Face it. You *need* me and unlike anyone else in all of Cristes, I am confident that you cannot taint my power. You will serve my needs well and give me offspring that will manifest my pure bloodline. Your human traits, as weak as they are, don't stand a chance of coming through."

"Yeah, even your filthy human father wanted nothing to do with you," Yule snickered.

Mara clasped a hand over her mouth, suppressing a scream that threatened to erupt at any moment.

My guards had been creeping up toward the cottage and I shooed them away, pleading silently with them to stay out of sight. They had no idea who was inside, and our interference could bring about war.

Melchior's voice claimed my attention. "I am feeling generous. You have until the summer's end to either return the black rose or accept my proposal. You know how to reach me."

Melchior flicked his platinum hair out of his eyes and pressed a metal piece inside his black leather cuff. Black, inky clouds billowed from it, cascading to the floor with the force of a waterfall. Yule and Roisin disappeared into the ether. He held Mara's gaze for a moment, licked his top lip, smirked, and vanished.

Finally, they were gone, and it was as if the world began breathing again. Wildlife around me buzzed with life, and Mara gasped as she fell to the floor. She crawled to her mother who was huddled over her knees, rocking back and forth and sobbing.

I wondered how Mara would react to knowing I had overheard everything after she told me to leave. Much of what I'd overheard was personal; she was only half-Watcher, something I'd never known possible. Her father had abandoned her and her mother. Melchior was wrong though about her being powerless. I slipped back around to her front door and waited a few minutes.

I knocked three times, but no one answered. I wanted to pound on the door, but forced considerable restraint. It already looked fragile enough, barely clinging to its hinges. I knocked again.

"Mara? It's me, Nicholas."

She cracked the door open an inch.

"Is everything alright? I know you said to leave, and I got about halfway home before I realized I forgot to give you this week's stipend from my mother."

She eyed me suspiciously. "Queen Nicole already arranged for that."

"OK, you got me." I kneaded the tension from the back of my neck. "I couldn't stop worrying. You looked so frightened, and you banged your knee pretty badly... I just had to turn back around and make sure."

Mara smiled at me and opened the door another inch. "I'm fine. Thank you for checking on me. I—I will see you tomorrow."

"OK, just remember, you can tell me anything, alright?" When she nodded, I reluctantly turned and headed back to the carriage. The entire way home, all I could do was ruminate on ways to save Mara from the clutches of that beast's claws.

Nicholas: Six Weeks Later

MARA NEVER BROUGHT UP what occurred the night Melchior threatened her and her mother. It was as if that frightening encounter never even happened; in fact, she was thriving. As the weeks passed, she managed to gain some weight, having access to food at every meal for a change. She was happy, or at least she appeared to be. On the inside, however, she'd built up a wall that hid many of her emotions from me. *Is she even aware she's doing that?*

Her relationship with Gavin had not progressed beyond that kiss on the cheek at the lagoon and holding hands. He remained enthralled, and never once complained. In the meantime, Mara was making strides in her studies, but not in her giftings. Since she was past the age of seventeen and had yet to fully manifest her abilities, I had to assume being half-human impeded her development. My instincts, however, whispered that she was far more powerful than even a seasoned Watcher. I could *feel* her strength, and I would never forget the orange spark I'd seen in her eyes, a color never recorded before in Watcher history. Whenever she'd get frustrated or defeated, I'd take her to the pool and teach her how to swim.

Gavin stopped by during one of our many afternoon swim lessons. "Hands off my lady!" he teased. Mara's toes were curled over the smooth rock ledge of the pool, her arms outstretched and crossed above her head as she bent over, poised to dive. I stood at her side holding each of her arms tight by her ears.

Mara tilted her head. "Hey, Gavin! Look what Nicholas taught me today!" She returned her focus to the water.

"Cannot wait to see, my love," he called back to her, eagerly unbuttoning his shirt.

"Alright, you've got this. Tilt forward, fingertips first, and everything else follows." I peeked over at Gavin, who had flung his trousers with a flick of his foot and slipped into the water with barely a ripple.

"I'm ready," she said, and I could feel her determination as it entered my bloodstream and sharpened my mind.

"I am letting go this time," I warned, "but I'll count you off. One...two...three!"

Mara dove in a perfect arc, smooth as silk, disappearing beneath the water's surface without a splash. Her head popped up directly in front of Gavin, his arms outstretched, ready to embrace her.

"You did it!" He cheered, so elated that his eyes glowed

green. She grabbed the back of his head and pulled him in for a kiss.

For a brief moment, Gavin froze, his eyes bugging. Then he composed himself, wrapped his arms around her, and deepened the kiss.

I rubbed at the ache in my chest. I knew this was inevitable, given how their relationship was progressing. I'd had to shield my emotions one night last week, when Mara had let Gavin take her most of the way home— something only I previously had the privilege of doing with her. I squeezed my eyes shut and clenched my fists against the hurt. The sight of him with her taunted me, reminding me I could do nothing about my feelings for her.

They continued kissing, and I could no longer stomach it. "*Ahem*," I coughed into my hand. They paused, their foreheads pressed together, chests rising and falling.

"Cannonball!" I yelled, taking a running leap, my rear end hitting the water a mere foot from the couple.

"Nicholas!" Mara giggled. She splashed me when I came up for air, then quickly dove underwater.

She broke the surface again behind Gavin, using his body as a shield. The game rapidly became two against one as Gavin joined forces with her. I conceded, throwing my hands up in a gesture of good faith. Mara climbed on Gavin's back like a koala, and he hugged her behind her knees, keeping her in place.

"Hey!" Shai called as he walked out onto the lanai. "I forgot to tell you guys— Lana will be here tomorrow. She's staying an entire week for Carnival."

Mara's grasp around Gavin's neck loosened, and she slid

off his back.

"Do not worry, my love. Lana will adore you." So it seemed Gavin was be in tune with Mara's emotions after all; I wondered if their recent kiss had anything to do with increasing his gifting in that regard.

Her face was scrunched with uncertainty, and I stifled a laugh at how adorable she looked. "Are you sure?" Mara asked. "I mean, I haven't been able to really access my giftings yet. What if...what if she finds me unworthy?"

A muscle ticked in Gavin's jaw, and he looked at Shai for assistance.

Shai's eyes widened in surprise. "That would never happen. My sister is the most easygoing person you will ever meet. Don't fret. I think you'll be great friends." He gave her a genuinely warm smile and started to put his hand out to her, to touch her shoulder.

But Gavin quickly pulled Mara in for a hug, leaving Shai standing there all awkward with his hand out; he quickly ran it through his hair to try and save face. I pressed my lips together, turning my head to stifle a laugh.

Mara's sleek, golden hair was soaked and hung low, fanning around her shoulders in the water. Gavin played with it, letting it run over his palms and through his fingers and she relaxed in his touch.

"Lana is very easy to get along with, isn't she, Nick?" Gavin parroted as he continued stroking her hair.

"Yes, she is very nice. You will be safe with her. I promise."

Mara turned her gaze to me and nodded, a gesture of gratitude and affirmation that my words had eased her worries she really had nothing to fear.

"She is bringing a *'friend'*, Shai said, forming quotation marks with his fingers on the word "friend."

Lana was undeniably beautiful; I could not think of any man who did not desire her, with the exception of two: me, being her cousin, and her brother, of course. Lana was also unusual compared to most girls her age. She never made time for dating, always prioritizing her studies. Her goal was to become a master fighter, and it was a gifting she possessed in spades. She was deeply passionate about the history of Cristes' giftings and rare magic.

"No way," Gavin chimed in, whipping his head around to face Shai, who had slipped into the hot spring tub conjoined to the pool.

"Right? I could hardly believe it myself, but my parents seemed very pleased and relieved that she seemed to finally be dating."

I knew Shai was glad his sister had not cared to date anyone, especially Gavin. Did Gavin try, though? Oh boy, did he ever. Although, he finally gave up after a year.

"What's he like?" Gavin asked. I tasted a hint of his jealousy on my tongue. Its bitterness zinged the inside of my cheek and back of my throat, but not enough to concern me that he still wanted Lana. What man wouldn't be a little miffed at such a diss? He had made a large spectacle of himself for her acquiescence, only to be denied.

"I don't know...probably a nerd. Apparently, she met him at the academia camp she attended this summer." Shai shrugged, and I could tell that he was nonplussed, assuming this would not last. Or, at the very least, that his parents had misinterpreted things and the guy she was bringing home was, indeed, just a friend.

"Guess what Shai?" Gavin asked, his eyebrow raised, a cocky grin on his face.

"Do I want to know?" Shai responded, his face contorted in a grimace.

"Mara learned to dive today!"

Her cheeks flushed a deep pink. Shai had finally warmed up to her, and his grimace morphed into a smile that spread slowly across his face, revealing his perfectly white, straight teeth. He was proud of her.

"That's excellent, Mara. Hopefully, you'll be able to see the underground cave with us at Azure Summit before summer's end."

Mara's gaze flickered away from us, her expression souring, and Gavin gave her a tight squeeze. I knew she assumed she would be left behind when we all returned to Noorjove, the capital of Cristes for university in the fall. What she and the others did not know was that she would be joining us.

Mother had plans to grant Mara a scholarship, the first that the University of Bradwit Waterford —UBW — had ever issued. Mother worked tirelessly on good Samaritan projects in various communities around the kingdom. This scholarship, she reasoned, would not only help someone in need, but would be a great benefit to Cristes— finding hidden talent all over the realm would expand Cristes' power and greatness. Without such opportunities, those with prodigious talents would remain unknown and unutilized, a travesty to the future of Cristes. Mother planned to reveal this good news at Carnival as she spearheaded the opening ceremonies, an honorable tradition.

Mara's souring mood started to infiltrate mine and I quickly defused the situation, hoping to distract her. "Hey, there is still plenty of summer left. Not to mention, Carnival is only a few days away."

Gavin led Mara over to the hot spring tub where Shai was already soaking, his back pressed against the smooth, black stone wall. Lush orange and pink flowers framed Mara's hair as she rested her head on the pool's edge. I joined them, scooting between Shai and Mara.

"I remember you guys telling me something about needing a costume for Carnival. What should I start working on? I will need to know as there are only a few days left."

"Do not fash, my love," Gavin said, nuzzling her neck with his nose.

"How can I not? I don't want to stick out like I do not belong."

"Oh, you will stick out, but you definitely belong." The corners of Gavin's lip quirked.

"What does that mean?" Mara clutched her chest.

"It means our costumes are themed, and Gavin likes to win the costume pageant each year," I explained, hoping to calm any apprehension she had.

"My sister will assist with your costume. Oh, and I almost forgot..." He casually pointed to Mara. "She would like to spend the day before Carnival with you. The *full* day." He dropped his hand. "She wants to help you prepare. Apparently, she doesn't trust us." He scoffed so hard, his lips actually raspberried. "Something about how it's different for women, *blah blah blah*."

"Really?" Mara's eyes sparkled. "That is very nice of her."

"As I said, my sister is the best. Please don't ever tell her I said that."

"Excuse me, Prince Nicholas." Shai jumped at Nolan's sudden appearance and giggled at himself.

I sighed. "Nolan, you do not need to call me Prince Nicholas."

"Seriously, you grew up with us," Gavin said, closing his eyes as he relaxed in the water.

"Not to mention our friend," Shai added.

"Of course." Nolan gave me a quick nod. "Prince Nick, your mother would like to see both you and Madame Mara in her lounge. She expects you in fifteen minutes. Gentlemen, you are welcome to use the hot spring tub and pool at your leisure, but you are to not disturb Her Majesty's lesson."

With a click of his heels, Nolan strode through the back of the mansion, soundlessly opening and closing the sliding glass door.

Shai peeked one eye open to look at me. "Man, Nolan just appears out of nowhere. He can be so very, very sneaky." I gave Shai a conspiratorial smile. *He had no idea.*

"I wonder what your mom wants?" Gavin asked, and sensations of little needles pricked my skin.

The more I came into my giftings, the more I felt others' emotions. The one coming from Gavin was quite unpleasant, and I immediately understood why as he looked longingly at Mara. It was like the more he saw her, the less he could stand to be away from her.

"I have no idea. Don't worry. You can have her back as soon as she's done. I am sure whatever my mother wants will not take long." I hopped out of the spring and grabbed two towels from the bar, warmed from sitting out in the sun all morning and afternoon. I held one out to Mara.

"Thank you, Nicholas."

Gavin was right behind her, and snatched the towel from me before she could take it. He turned her so that her back faced him. He wrapped her hair, ringing the water out, then proceeded to pat her dry along her shoulders, down her arms, and finally her spine. He stepped closer to her, kissed her neck, and then slid down to his knees as he began to towel dry her legs.

I quickly turned away from the intimate scene, bid Shai farewell, and made a beeline for the house.

Mara: Not "No"

"**G**AVIN," I WHISPERED, whirling around to face him.

He wrapped the towel around my hips, stood, and walked backward, pulling me into the guesthouse. He didn't stop once we were inside; he marched us straight to my bed, where he collapsed onto his back, tugging me down so I laid on top of him. His eyes ignited a beautiful sea-green, and my breath caught. I loved when they did that. I loved not having to guess how much he cared for me.

Balancing on my elbows, I stared down at him, amazed that a boy such as him could love someone like me. His eyes glazed over, his body sinking into the bed as he craned his neck to reach my lips. His hands cupped my face before sliding down my back, unlatching my bathing suit clasp.

Instinctively, my arm shot across my chest to hold my top in place.

"I love you, Mara. I want to show you how much I do. I want to become one with you."

Did he mean marriage? I smiled at the thought, and kissed him again briefly before pulling away and sitting up. I grabbed a throw blanket and covered myself.

His eyes drank me in and grew even brighter. He reached for me again, but I stilled him with a hand on his chest.

"I'm going to be late, and I don't want to anger the queen."

"She'll understand." His pleading tone made my knees buckle, threatening to topple me onto the bed.

I sighed. "Go swim with Shai. When we take the next step, I want to have all the time in the world. I'm just not ready yet."

He got to his knees, cupped my cheeks with both hands, and searched my eyes. "So, this is not 'no'; it's just 'not now'."

"Exactly." I smiled. *Didn't he know how I felt?*

I waited, eager to get dressed and make my way over to the queen's salon, but he sat there staring at me, a smile plastered on his perfect face.

"Uh, Gavin? I need my privacy, please."

"Of course." He kissed my forehead and released my face. After one last look, he hustled off the bed and out the door.

I changed into a white linen dress, yanked my wet hair into a top knot, and plopped down to my hands and knees in search of my nude sandals. I found them under the bed, slipped them on, and ran past the pool and into the mansion.

Nicholas: Argentang Your Way to My Heart

"AHH, THERE YOU ARE, DARLING. Right on time as usual. Come, come. Have a seat." Mother gestured to the champagne-colored settee, and Mara obediently sat.

I was already seated on the other end. Mara smiled at me, but I could only muster a half-smile in return, unable to erase the image of Gavin's hands and lips all over her from my mind. I wondered if she realized how unsettled I was.

The salon looked different. All the furniture had been moved out, save for the settee. The expansive, cream area rug was rolled up at the far end of the room, revealing shiny bamboo flooring. Mother walked over to the golden melohymn beside the fireplace. Its wooden base, the size of a small crate, sat upon a stone pillar. The gold music box was shaped like a closed Christmas rose. It could be turned on using the brass buttons or by Watcher gifting. Mother's eyes flashed and its petals opened revealing its center that pointed skyward. She turned back to face us.

"As you know, Carnival is in a few days. Nicholas knows that his father and I usually perform the first two dances at the opening ceremonies in honor of our deity, Eira, and our home, Cristes. While King William and I will continue the tradition of dancing the Foxrumb, You, Nicholas, have come of age, and it is time for you to dance the Argentang."

I nearly spat out the crystal water I had just sipped.

"Oh, do not be so surprised." Mother waved her hand. "I was younger than you when I first performed this tribute to our people."

"Excuse me," Mara peeped as she raised her hand.

"Yes, dear?" Mother answered, smiling at her.

"What is the Argen...what will Nicholas be performing?" Mara wrung her hands together.

"The Argentang is a traditional pas de deux, a duet of passion and power joined with restraint and love— all the strengths that make the Watcher race so beautiful. Of course, Nicholas will need a partner...*you*."

"Me?" Mara clutched her chest and fell back against the couch. "But I can't dance!"

"Hush, now. I have never met someone so committed, resourceful, and artistic as you. True, normally royals with the Violet gifting would be chosen to perform this ritual. We don't technically know your gifting yet, but even if you are not a Violet, the time is ripe to *shake things up* a bit." Mother shimmied her shoulders, grinning at us. "I understand how nerve-racking this can be for a first timer, so I wanted my

Nicholas to be with someone he knows and trusts."

"What if...what if I let you all down?" Tears threatened to spill from Mara's pastel eyes.

Mother swept over to her side, wrapping her arm around Mara's shoulder, and hugged her tight.

"I promise that will never happen. I have the best choreographers in the entire realm, and their job is to make you look good, no matter your ability. Believe me, if they can make my William look good dancing, anything is possible."

Mother laughed, more heartily than I'd heard from her in a while, and we could not help but join in.

"You two will need to spend the next few days in full rehearsal, but first, I need to get you into costuming."

Thundernation. Gavin is not going to like Mara being away from him for so long.

"Cynthia and Tevo will need all the time they can gather to finish them on time," Mother said. "Mara, please meet Cynthia in the study. Son, Tevo will be here any minute." Mara rose and made her way to the door.

"Come back as soon as Cynthia is done with you," Mother called to her while fixing her hair in the mirror. "Gene will be here presently to set the choreography."

"Of course, Your Majesty." Mara curtsied. She turned toward the hall once more. Tevo nearly knocked her down as he strutted in like a peacock, yards of brightly colored fabrics billowing behind him. A small team of tailors came scurrying after him, hefting baskets that spilled over with supplies.

I stood on a pedestal in a three-way mirror, my arms and legs spread out and frozen as many hands made quick work of placing and pinning fabric on me. My shoulders were beginning to fatigue when the door swung open.

"My turn." A masculine, brawny man entered the salon as Tevo assisted me out of my pinned costume.

"I jush need 'one 'inute 'ore, 'ease," Tevo eked out, his lips holding at least a dozen pins.

"I can give you one minute, and nothing more." The man flicked his hand high about his head and smiled at Mother. "Your Majesty," he said, giving her the Cristes bow.

"Gene," she lifted herself to her full height and returned his formal gesture with a curtsy. When she raised her head, her lips were rolled into a straight line, her neck muscles strained. She and Gene let out barking laughs at the same time, ran to each other, and embraced.

"Where is this gorgeous girl you have been telling me about?" He asked after pulling himself away from Mother. Still holding her hands, he rose onto his tiptoes, searching the room behind her.

"She is in the lounge with Cynthia." Mother gestured over her shoulder. "Shall I send for her?"

He nodded. "Please do, My Queen."

Without a word, Nolan, who had been standing still as a statue in the corner, clicked his heels and was off.

The tailors had extricated the black costume with its crystal details from my body. I now stood on the pedestal in nothing but my boxer briefs, Tevo's assistant holding out my white t-shirt. I leaned down to grab it, and my attention was diverted as Mara was ushered into the room, Cynthia helping to zip the back of her dress.

Her eyes briefly locked on mine and I froze. They trailed down my face, to my torso, and back to my eyes.

I felt a hint of desire tingle across my skin, and it surprised me. But just as quickly as it came, it disappeared. I hopped off the pedestal and yanked on my shirt, pulled on my tan trousers, and tied them at my waist.

Gene took out a small, flat disc from his bag, walked over to the melohymn, and inserted it in the back. Music filled the space, and he clapped out a syncopated rhythm.

"Alright; both of you here, on your mark."

I peered down at his feet and noticed two white taped lines on the ground. Mara and I hustled over to them.

"No shoes today. No one needs to lose any toes," Gene said.

Mara's eyes widened and I laughed. Gene's head snapped to me. "You think I am kidding?"

Mara quickly slipped her feet out of her sandals. I dropped down before she had the chance, scooped them up, and placed them near the sofa next to mine.

"Now, we start with the basic hold. Prince Nicholas—"

"Nick, please," I corrected Gene.

He cocked his brow at me and crossed his arms over his chest. "Fine. *Nick*, your right hand at her waist...good. You know how to lead. Now, Mara, your left hand, just below his shoulder."

She cautiously obeyed.

"No, no, no," Gene *tsked*. Mara started to bring her arm down, but he caught her wrist.

"Like so." He placed her hand back near my shoulder. He then moved behind her, rolling her shoulders back so she stood straight and tall, tapping her elbow with the back of his hand to keep it up. "Now, your free hands will meet."

I had seen variations of this dance many times before.

I knew the hold. My arm lifted, outstretched and ready for Mara, who readily took my hand. Gene circled us, scrutinizing our shape. Without a word, he came in from the side and placed one hand on the small of Mara's back, the other on her lower belly, helping her spine into a neutral arch.

"Strong...derriere under...yes, like that." He patted her abdomen. "Strong, the entire time."

"Now, we move together. Quick, quick, slow...quick, quick, slow. The choreography will play on these movements; sometimes all slow, sometimes all quick, and any combination in between. Andrea, music please!"

The salon came alive as beats strummed through our bodies, encouraging us to move.

Gene stayed behind Mara, guiding her posture as I led her around the floor— *quick, quick, slow*— in time with the beat.

After a few measures, Mara stopped looking down at her feet, and I smiled at her. She loosed a long breath.

"You're doing great," I leaned in and whispered.

She bit her lip, clearly not convinced.

"Now, on your own." Gene let go of Mara, snapped his fingers, and walked over to the music player. We continued to travel around the bamboo flooring.

"You are doing marvelous, simply marvelous." My mother had her hands clasped under her chin, eyes shining at us.

Gene stood next to Mother, crossed his arms, and drifted toward her. "Yes, there is much work to do, but they both move well. I think I can use my plan 'C' choreo."

"Plan 'C'?" I heard my mother ask.

"Yes; I created six variations of the same routine, depending on skill level. These two," he gestured at us, "fall right in the middle. Definite potential, natural chemistry, but no Queen Nicole." He winked at her.

Mother blushed. "Well, I have many things to see to for Carnival, so I will leave you to work your magic." She swept out of the room, her cream sundress and gauzy scarf floating behind her.

Gene stopped the music. "Now that you have the hold down and the basic steps, we start with the choreography."

An hour into our lesson, my back muscles pinched between my shoulder blades, my chest soaked with sweat. Mara did not complain. I imagined she was fatigued, although she merely glistened. The sun began to set and, thankfully, without its rays blasting through the windows, the room cooled.

"Ten-minute break," Gene sang out suddenly, splaying his hands over his head. "You have the first ten measures done. Only about a hundred more to go."

I sank down on the couch next to Mara. Nolan brought me a towel to wipe the sweat from my brow, then handed both of us a glass of ice water.

She gulped hers down as did I. "Thank you, Nolan," she said breathlessly.

"My pleasure." He nodded, refilling her glass. "I shall be back in another hour with some food."

"Great, because I am starving," I announced. I turned to face Mara. She looked lost in thought as she stared blankly ahead. I realized, at that moment, that no one had asked her if she wanted to do this. My brow creased. "Mara?"

She blinked out of her daze and looked up at me. "Now that we actually have a minute to talk, do you assent to doing this?" I gestured vaguely at the room.

"What do you mean?" Her face crinkled as she looked all around us.

"I mean, no one asked you if you *wanted* to perform the Argentang at Carnival. Before any more of your time is wasted, do you wish to dance with me?"

She bit her lower lip as she studied me, a flicker of opposing emotions passing between us.

I rested my hand on her knee. "You have a choice in this."

"Do *you* have a choice?"

"I do not think I do, no." I laughed.

"Well, I would never leave a friend behind. I'm honored to be partnered with you...especially since you never told me about this secret talent of sweeping ladies off their feet."

I gave her knee a little squeeze. "Thank you. If anything becomes too much for you, do not hesitate for even a second to let me know. I will make sure this is as painless as possible, for the both of us."

"Nonsense. This is fun!" Mara's face shone with pure happiness. "When else would I ever get to learn how to dance, Let alone from the best choreographer in the realm?"

Gene, who'd just returned from break, did an about-face and beamed at her. "Well, aren't you the biggest sweetheart? But flattery will not shorten rehearsal. Now, chip-chop!" He clapped his hands twice. "Let's run it from the top!"

I stood and helped Mara up. We took our mark, and the music started once more.

"Bravo!" Gene applauded us when we finished. "A few

more days, and it will be perfect. Now, let's get to the fun parts of this dance." He waggled his eyebrows at me, and I could not help but laugh. "Stella!" he called over his shoulder, and one of his assistants pranced over. "Help me show them this middle section."

Mara and I backed up to the edge of the room to give them space. Gene looked at the melohymn, his eyes flashing purple for a brief instant, and the music started playing of its own accord. He and Stella began to dance together, and my jaw went slack watching the professional pair. By the time they finished, locked in each other's arms, lips inches apart, I did not know if I should clap, blush, or both, so I simply stood there.

At length, they broke apart.

"Did you feel the passion?" Gene tipped his chin up and puffed out his chest as he strode forward. "We need that to come alive in this dance!" He clenched his hands into fists at his sides and thrusted them out and back in. "Our people are passionate; strong, equal partners, and we *love* to love."

"But we are novice dancers," Mara squeaked.

"And these are steps that you can handle," he replied, waving off her concern.

"I'm not sure what my mother shared with you, but *we—*" *I* jabbed my index finger at my chest, then at Mara, then back at myself— "are *just* friends."

"Of course, you are." Gene winked and clicked his tongue. "Dancing is about feeling the music, not each other. It requires acting. Now, get over here. Time is ticking."

Little did he know, but I was not *just* feeling the music, nor only acting. My hands would be required to touch more of Mara than I'd ever dared before leaving me conflicted, especially now that she was dating my friend.

"Mara, now twist, twist, flick...superb." Gene stroked his chin as he scrutinized us. "Never take your eyes off your partner. On the next twist, twist, flick, Nick you will grip Mara by her waist."

I lightly placed my hands on her delicate curves.

Gene shook his head and I flinched dropping my hands.

"No! Do it again. With intent!"

Mara smiled at me, letting me know I had her consent.

I loosed a breath through pursed lips and went for it. My hands, confident and firm, gripped her hips and slid up to her waist.

"Yes, Nick! Now, lunge back. Mara, you lean forward into him...further, *further*. Beautiful! Look at that perfect silhouette." Gene clasped a hand to his chest. "Now, as you step out of the lunge, prepare for the lift and leg extension.

You remember how to get into it?"

We both nodded.

Gene snapped his fingers. "Alright, step out of the lunge... there you go. Use your leg, Nick; hands on her hips. Now hoist her into the air."

Mara floated high above me, her neck and back arching as her leg extended fully. I brought her down as she dropped into a deep lunge, grasping my leg. Everyone in the room began clapping, but one applause lingered, slow and loud, while the rest died out.

I looked over to see a weary Shai and a stormy Gavin in the doorway.

"We need to take five," I said urgently as I helped Mara

to stand.

"We just had a break," Gene growled.

"I know, I'm so sorry." I leaned in and whispered, "That's Mara's boyfriend, and he just saw my hands all over his girl."

An understanding passed in his eyes. He pursed his lips. "Make it quick."

I ran after Mara and Gavin who had already disappeared out of the room.

Shai caught me by the arm. "You could have at least warned him."

"You think I knew anything about this before I was summoned earlier?"

"Probably not, now that I can see your eyes."

"Where did they go?" I asked.

Shai pointed down the hall, toward the back gardens. I sighed and sprinted the rest of the way. When I reached the back deck, Mara stood illuminated under a porch light, clutching her arms with her head down. Gavin faced away from her.

I approached my friend. "Gavin, I am so sorry. Everything happened so—"

"Shut it, Nick."

I bristled. "No, I will not shut it. Mara and I were hoodwinked. We absolutely had no idea we would be performing the Argentang at Carnival."

"I believe she had no idea, but do you seriously expect me to believe that you did not? That you did not handpick her so you could feel her up and down at your leisure?" He wrenched his hands through his hair. "Don't be such a knave! We all know you care for her."

I snapped, my face contorting in rage. A loud roar burst from my chest as I charged him. Gavin must have sensed the threat because he whirled around and braced himself a split second before I sacked him.

We flew hard and fast into the pool, the impact sending water splashing in all directions. Gavin pushed me off him and I willingly let him go. Our soaked clothes clung to us, steam billowing from our heated skin.

"Tallywags!" Shai yelled as he rushed onto the scene. "You idiots! Nick, whatever Gavin said, he did not mean it. You know that he is out of his mind right now."

"Oh, I meant it. You gave me your word, Nick. I hope you enjoyed copping a feel because that's all you get. She's mine!"

I loathed how Gavin talked as if Mara were merely an object that could be possessed. Before I realized it, I'd ripped him off the pool ladder and punched him in the face.

"Stop!" Mara screeched.

Gavin fell back, water sloshing out of the pool and onto the deck. He palpated his jaw and then, his eyes flashed.

My head slammed back. I wiped the blood that trickled down my now swollen lip. "You coward," I spat at him. "What's the matter? Can't fight me without using your gifting?"

"Stop it, please!" Mara screamed again.

Another flash of vivid green rocked my vision and I was suddenly underwater, invisible hands holding me down. The seconds ticked by hauntingly slow. My chest burned, my lungs begging for air. Blurred faces with muffled voices rippled above me. Inky spots seeped into my vision, and my body relaxed.

Pink flames filled the top of the pool, and strong hands

pulled me from the water and laid me on my side. I heaved up pool water and finally I could draw in oxygen. Nolan stood above me, soaked from his elbows down. He handed me a towel.

Gavin, still in the water, looked at his hands in disbelief.

"Nick, I'm sorry... I am so, so sorry! I... I don't know what came over me."

I pressed the towel to my lip to wipe the vomit and staunch the blood.

"Let me, Your Highness." Nolan removed the towel and held two fingers above my mouth. He blinked twice. Within seconds, a soft pink spotlight touched my lips, and a gentle tugging sensation brushed back and forth as the skin knit together. Nolan handed another towel to me.

Gavin hoisted himself out of the pool and started in my direction.

Shai placed a hand on his chest. "Not now, mate."

"I did not mean to do that; you have to believe me," Gavin pleaded, trying to break free of Shai.

"Sure, like you believed me?" I growled.

Soft sobs finally registered in my ears. As soon as I saw her, nothing else mattered, and all my anger evaporated.

I sighed. "Gavin, I forgive you. Please believe me when I say that Mara and I are simply dancing the traditional Argentang and what you saw is acting. We are doing so at my Mother's request. I have no intention of taking your girlfriend. Mara has made her choice."

"Thank you. I do not deserve your grace." Gavin bowed.

"Don't do that. It's weird when you do." I averted my gaze, and proceeded to dry my hair. When I continued to feel

Gavin's presence, I rubbed the back of my neck and turned to face him.

He had remained bent over and I knew he was showing me respect by waiting until I dismissed him. "You may rise, Gavin." He swiftly stood and went to Mara, but she backed away, shaking her head. She was scared of *him*.

"Mara, please. I made a mistake. When I saw his hands on you, I...lost it."

She hugged herself tighter; clearly, that was not a good enough reason for her.

Gavin took another step toward her, and she could back up no further else she'd end up in the bushes. He got down on his knees and beseeched her. "Please. I made a huge mistake and I overreacted because, well... I... I love you."

A hush fell over us. Nolan cleared his throat.

"Prince Nicholas, Your Highness, I think it is time we get back to the salon. Mr. Gene is probably frantic."

Mara raised a hand to conceal her open mouth as she gasped, tears welling in her eyes. Her posture relaxed as she extended her free hand to cup Gavin's cheek. Flames swelled in my chest as Mara's emotions echoed within me, but they were quickly squelched by my own sorrow.

I could not move. My heart felt as if it had shattered into millions of pieces that now lay scattered along the beach, blending in amongst the grains of sand.

Nicholas: Final Rehearsal

THE NEXT FEW DAYS WERE A BLUR. Between non-stop rehearsals and costume fittings, every waking moment Mara and I had was spent together. Funnily enough, we barely had time to even speak. Our chemistry — or rather lack thereof — pained Gene, which he reminded us of at least once every hour.

Mara was perfect, of course, but I could not seem to shake my fight with Gavin.

"I am just exhausted. Don't worry, Gene. I'm saving my energy for the performance. I will bring the passion," I constantly reassured him.

"I know you will, because I have seen it. But I wish you would rehearse it!" He threw his hands up in frustration.

A knock on the doorframe interrupted us.

"Lana!" I cried, rushing over to her. Scooping her up in a big bear hug, I spun around with joy.

She giggled. "Put me down, cousin. I am here to meet your dance partner."

I set her down, grabbed her hand, and brought her over to Mara, who suddenly looked shy.

"Lana, this is Mara; Mara, this is my cousin, Shai's sister, Lana"

Mara's face brightened. Lana stuck her hand out in greeting and Mara shook it.

"I get these two for fifteen more minutes. Then you all can do what you want," Gene snapped.

"Yes, sir!" Lana perched on the settee, crossing her long legs in front of her. "I'm just happy I get to see the dance before Carnival!" She gave us a wink.

Cynthia and Tevo rushed in. "They are finished!" they declared in unison. Two assistants trailed after them carrying our completed costumes.

"Thank Eira!" Gene clapped. "You two," he pointed at Mara and me, "go and get changed. We need to make sure everything works perfectly. Then I get fifteen minutes of dancing."

Just then, a tall lad with blond hair wandered into the room. He anxiously whipped his head to and fro before spotting Lana. She waved him over.

Gene snapped his fingers. "And who might you be?"

The young man with blue eyes came to a complete standstill and rubbed the back of his neck. My stomach twisted as I felt his uneasiness.

"I am Brantley." When his name did not register with

Gene, he gestured toward Lana and clarified, "I'm with her."

I turned to Lana and cocked my brow. She shimmered a pale green and grinned the biggest smile I'd ever seen her wear.

Gene rolled his eyes. "Great, then if you do not mind, please take a seat. Some of us are trying to get rehearsal finished for the big event tomorrow."

Brantley said nothing and scampered over to the couch, sitting next to Lana, close enough so their legs just touched. My jaw twitched from the effort of controlling my giftings to block out the bond they shared.

"Your Highness, this way," Tevo beckoned, leading me out of the salon as Cynthia whisked Mara away.

It took two tailors all of three minutes to dress me in my all-black, supple tuxedo.

"Move your arms and do whatever big moves you have to do with your legs," Tevo instructed from a few feet away.

I rolled out my shoulders, did some arm circles, and a few lunges. The material stretched and maintained its shape, hugging every curve of my well-formed muscles. *Why do they not make all suits like this?*

"Perfect." Tevo undid the top two buttons on the black dress shirt and picked away a few specks of loose thread on the lapels. "Final touch." He draped an icy-blue ascot, the color of my eyes, over my neck and snapped it on so that it remained undone, but would not fall off.

They rushed me back into the salon and dropped me at my mark while they huddled in the corner. Apparently, Mara and I would have an audience for our final rehearsal.

I felt her enter before I saw her, but when I actually laid

eyes on her, my heart thudded and I swore under my breath. Her golden hair was pinned up with a white Christmas rose, her lips strawberry-red and glossy.

The hard notch in my throat moved with a concerted, deep swallow. Time slowed as I took her all in from the tips of her toes to the crown of her head. She glowed brighter than even my father and mother, and that was saying something. The black lace sleeves of her dress along with the hem of her asymmetrical skirt, sparkled with her every step.

She met me at her mark. "Do I look alright?" she whispered. "Everyone is staring at me."

Cotton. My mouth felt like it was full of cotton, forcing me to clear my throat three times before managing to speak. Even then my voice emerged in a low, gravelly tone, far from its usual tenor. "You look absolutely stunning."

Mara gave me the cheesiest grin and I melted. *Gavin, you lucky bastard.*

"What?" she asked, looking up at me through her now thicker, longer lashes.

"Nothing. Let's get this over with."

"If you're nervous, that is going to make me even more nervous!" she squeaked.

"No, I'm fine," I reassured her with a gentle caress of her cheek, then quickly dropped my hand as if it'd been burned when I realized what I was doing. "I just want to be done for the day so you can go have fun with Lana."

We assumed our opening positions. I reached around her and realized I touched nothing but bare skin. I bit my lip, briefly gandered at the ceiling, and tried to breathe.

Christmas roses outlined the edges of her naked back.

Goshamighty. If the costume shifted an inch, I would be able to see lines and shapes of hers I had only ever dreamed of.

Eira, may I make it through this!

Two measures. I lasted two whole measures.

"Stop! Start again!" Gene shouted.

Breathe. Just breathe. You can do this. Gavin was going to have a conniption fit, and who could blame him? Every male's attention here in the city of Sint Natal would be on his girl. Heck, even I couldn't focus and I see her all day, every day.

"You just did it perfectly at least ten times today. Do not let the costumes distract you," Gene scolded, his lips puckered as he stared at me like he knew exactly what my problem was.

Mara cocked a brow and sucked in her cheeks, unsure of what Gene implied. So, I made a funny face at her and she giggled. I breathed again, centering myself.

Gene counted us off for the last time. "And five, six, seven, eight."

When we struck our final pose, the room erupted in applause. Although I could not see her face, the pride Mara felt at this moment nearly made my knees buckle.

"Bravo! Well, done!" Lana bounded over, her dark hair swaying with each step, Brantley right beside her. "Shai told me you both learned this in only a few days, that you never danced before. It is just not possible."

"I would have to agree," Brantley said.

Gene snapped his fingers in praise. "You are dismissed. I shall see you tomorrow in costume at your curtain call for run-throughs on the stage. You will make your parents very proud." His eyes gleamed with tears that never fell.

"Will your parents be joining the festivities?" Lana asked Mara.

A dark cloud passed over my vision, and then it evaporated. I squeezed Mara's hand, and a calm settled over her as she shook her head.

"That's too bad. Are you ready for some fun? I figured you've had lots of time with the boys, but girl time is far superior." Lana winked and Mara laughed.

"It does sound nice. Let me just change and I'll meet you..." Her voice trailed off.

"How about in the guest cottage?" Lana suggested.

"Perfect." Mara waved and sashayed out of the room, followed by Cynthia and her team.

"So, what do you boys have planned for the day?" Lana turned to me.

"Actually, I honestly don't know. Gavin and Shai have made all the arrangements because every spare minute I've had has been spent in this room rehearsing."

Brantley's lips quirked. "Then it sounds like you really need to blow off some steam."

"You have *no* idea." I laughed.

"Make good choices," Lana called over her shoulder, skipping out of the room.

Mara: Carnival

S UNLIGHT STREAMED through the plantation shutters, caressing and warming my cheek. I rolled onto my back and opened my eyes. My cheeks lifted as I recalled the events of yesterday.

Nicholas and I outdid ourselves in rehearsal. And my costume... I'd never worn anything so...what was that word again? *Divine*. Giddiness welled in my chest as I recalled Nicholas's face when I entered the salon wearing it. He looked smashing in a black suit that hugged every inch of him. But such thoughts of his soft blonde hair and piercing blue eyes, his chiseled body with strong angles, were pointless. My smile faltered. I knew from the minute I'd met Nicholas that he was special. As soon as I'd learned he was heir to the throne, my belief that he was too extraordinary for me was solidified.

Queen Nicole may have been working to offer help to people like me, but that did not mean I would ever be seen as worthy of a royal if I had acted on my feelings for Nicholas. I was glad I'd followed my instincts and chosen Gavin. He was safe. Nicholas would have broken my heart regardless of his good nature and intentions. I was grateful to have him as my friend, though.

My smile returned as I thought of my handsome Gavin and how I had grown to love him; truly, madly, deeply love him. It scared me to admit that. I saw how vulnerable that could make someone; my mother was its victim, but I would not be like her. I'd chosen a wonderful man, and I knew Gavin and I would have a great life together.

I plucked myself out of bed and went to the bathroom. Lana would be here at noon so we could get ready for Carnival. I could scarcely believe she and Shai were cut from the same cloth. While it took Shai nearly all summer to warm up to me, Lana and I were instant friends. No one had taken the time to inform me that Nicholas and Shai were actually cousins on their fathers' side. When Lana showed me pictures, I saw the strong resemblance of Shai to King William; Nicholas mirrored his mother, Queen Nicole.

As I lathered the coconut and citrus shampoo, I thought about the change to the costumes Lana wanted to make for Carnival— Nicholas, Gavin, and Shai were having us dress as Primordial Angels, females of the first tribes of Watchers in Cristes. Lana was not thrilled with the color choice we were given— pink.

"What is wrong with pink?" I'd asked.

"Nothing is wrong with pink. But green is even better."

She winked and her eyes glinted a bright green glow and then it was gone. "Listen, it is fine if you want to keep pink. I only care that the color is your choice."

I thought about it for a moment. There was always a color that I was attracted to.

"I think I want blood-orange."

Lana quirked her brow. "Interesting. That gifting, according to our ancient texts, has only been seen once before."

"I didn't realize it was a gifting." I dropped my chin. "I have not come into any just yet, though Queen Nicole thinks I will be violet."

Lana smiled. "Well, then, let's get this costume dyed so it will be ready for tomorrow."

A knock at my door snapped me back to the present. Lana waved at me excitedly through the windows and I waved her in. She waltzed right into the bathroom, her light gray silk robe floating about her knees. Nicholas stood in the doorway, rigid as a statue.

"Is everything alright?" I asked him.

His hands were behind his back and he worked his bottom lip with his teeth. "Yes, everything is fine. I just wanted to thank you again, for everything this week. You are a great friend."

"It was my pleasure, and the least I could do." I gestured all around me, an effort to remind him of everything he and his family had already done for me.

From behind his back, Nicholas revealed a beautiful bouquet of orange hibiscus mixed with glowing-white Christmas roses, perfectly arranged in a crystal-clear vase.

"They're stunning," I whispered. No one had ever given me flowers before, especially ones containing giftings. Nicholas had taught me about the First Fall, and I knew how precious these roses were.

Lana sashayed over, her costume on, but only partially zipped in the back. The definition in her arms and legs, her strong core, and chiseled back commanded my attention. Her usual schoolgirl attire, concealed a hidden warrior.

"Cousin, these are lovely. I will make sure they get sunlight. Now, you need to go get ready and quit taking up my prep time with Mara." She took the vase in one hand and gently pushed on Nicholas's chest with the other.

He nodded and headed back toward the main house without complaint.

"Is there something between you two that you want to tell me about?" Lana asked, her voice light as she placed the flowers on the windowsill.

I turned from her and called over my shoulder. "What do you mean?"

"I mean, there *is* something there. I can feel it." She said, leaning against the wall and crossing her arms.

"We're best friends. I count my blessings every day that he saved me."

"Saved you? From what?" she asked.

Busying myself in the bathroom mirror, I answered, "Never mind. It's a long story for another day. Let's get ready."

I was in costume, pacing behind the stage. My nerves began to bubble and continued to build as the noise of the crowd grew louder. Nicholas appeared beside me and grabbed my hand. My stress dissipated as a cooling sensation washed over me, followed by a rush of warmth that blanketed me in comfort.

I sighed. "How do you do that?"

Nicholas shrugged. "Just one of my giftings. Besides, you were so jumpy, I could barely think straight. Mixed with my nerves, If I didn't do something to help, I thought I might hurl over the side here."

"Sorry." I cringed at my own weakness.

"No need to apologize. This is new for me, too. Just remember, Gene is the best and he taught us well. Also, we worked our butts off. We've got this."

Queen Nicole glided over to us, her arm in King William's. "There's the handsome couple. Gene tells me you both are amazing. I cannot wait to see the final piece."

Nicholas dropped my hand and enveloped each of his parents in a big bear hug. They returned the embrace, and King William's eyes met mine before releasing his son.

"And who is this, Nicholas?" The king's warm smile defrosted my shocked demeanor, and I finally remembered to curtsy.

"Dad, this is my friend, Mara."

"You may rise. It is a pleasure to finally meet you. I have loved your artwork all around my home. Well done." He extended his hand to me. Although my hand shook, I took his and was immediately set at ease. *Like father, like son.*

His piercing gray eyes — the same as his wife's — were kind, but there was no mistaking the sheer power radiating in them. A silver laurel crown sewn into his thick hair was striking against his dark locks. Teal and violet jewels, tones that matched their costumes, sparkled from it.

I smiled up at him. "The pleasure is all mine. I am beyond thankful to Queen Nicole, and, well, your entire family, really."

The queen wrapped me in an embrace and whispered, "Thank you," in my ear.

"Darling, it is time for us to start the festivities. Are you ready?" The king held his hand out to his wife.

"Yes, dear." She turned to face us. "Be prepared to come on stage as soon as we finish. Wish us luck!" She waved as the king led her to their mark behind the thick silver curtains.

Nicholas took my hand and walked with me to the side wing, where we kept ourselves hidden behind a lighting boom. The curtains sprung open. A spotlight landed on King William first, and the crowd erupted as he danced a short solo. When the spotlight for Queen Nicole appeared, the people went berserk. The sheer vibration of their cheers reverberated in my chest, and I swelled with pride that she would choose me for such an occasion, that she would find me worthy.

She was the best dancer I had ever seen. Her movements, strong and graceful, made me want to hug someone, cheer, and cry simultaneously. Every time the light hit the crown sewn into her hair, it cast sparkles all over the stage.

The royal couple moved together as one, their movements as fluid as if they were gliding on ice. I marveled at how they lit up, first violet and teal, then igniting into a rainbow of colors before bursting into a brilliant white.

Nicholas wiped a tear from my eye with the soft pad of this thumb. "They are something, aren't they?" He beamed with pride and love, and I hoped I'd have that someday with Gavin.

The music ended and the Queen and King took their bows. The crowd began chanting, "Argentang, Argentang, Argentang!" In a matter of seconds, a crew hand brought a mic out to Queen Nicole.

"Your King and I have a little surprise for you all! As you know, our son, Prince Nicholas, came of age at the end of last summer—"

High-pitched screams interrupted her announcement and she laughed. "Ladies, calm down, please. Well, he will be performing the Argentang with a lovely artist from this village." She handed the mic to her husband.

"Settle down, settle down." The king said, waving his arms. The crowd quieted to his command.

"We are so proud of our son and we know you will all feel the same about your prince. Let us not waste one more minute of this evening's celebrations with talk. Tonight, we dance!" King William roared, and the crowd joined him.

Nicholas and I walked onto the stage as their majesties waltzed off. We set up for our mark, but before I laid eyes on the back of Nicholas's head, I scanned the audience. I didn't have to search long before I spotted my friends. Gavin, Shai, Lana, and Brantley stood fifth row, center, and they waved excitedly. Gavin beamed at me, and I thought I might lose my breath staring at his beautiful face. Gene and his team were front and center and gave me the traditional Cristes salute. I took my mark with renewed confidence. I would dance my heart out and make my new family proud.

Nicholas: Roaring Like a Lion

EVERY MOVE, EVERY STEP in the choreography was performed to the utmost of our ability. Mara's passion and precision spurred the best out of me. I forgot about the crowd and that this was my coming-of-age introduction to the Kingdom. My sole focus was Mara, and I let my walls down. For these few moments, I would not have to act out my feelings.

We struck our final pose and all I could hear was my own breath, heaving in my chest, my eyes bright on Mara's perfect face.

"We did it!" she whispered.

As if my brain was finally catching up to the present, the roar of the crowd faded in from non-existent to deafening. I twirled Mara out of my grasp so we could take our bows.

Lana, Shai, and Brantley jumped for joy, whooping and hollering. Gene was...crying; he was actually crying. My eyes caught Gavin's. He stared at Mara with an adoration I had only seen on my parent's faces. But next to him was his mom and dad. I saw Mr. Frosters as his eyes flicked back and forth from his son to Mara. His brows dipped as did the corners of his mouth.

Mara and I took another bow and exited. But before we reached the stage wings, Mom entered in a new costume, pure white and shimmering.

"Did I not promise you a spectacular surprise? Let us hear it again for your Prince and his partner, Mara for honoring the Argentang and the people it stands for!"

The crowd exploded and the warm night air had a comforting breeze, tempering the heat of my body.

When the audience quieted, Mother continued. "Mara's talents were discovered at the beginning of the summer by your gifted prince. As many of you know, I have worked tirelessly the past few years in humanitarian efforts amongst the poorest and most unfortunate citizens of Cristes. Since The First Fall..." She paused, and a deafening silence fell over the crowd. "We have learned the hard way what it means to alienate people for circumstances beyond their control. For years, Cristes lost out on unimaginable giftings. For instance, Mara." She gestured toward me. "Had my son not discovered her, I would be bereft of the enjoyment her beautiful art brings to my home, nor would you all have the pleasure of watching her dance tonight."

A male's voice hooted his appreciation and the rest of the crowd, including my mother, laughed at the gentleman's enthusiasm.

"That is why I wanted to take this moment to share about a special scholarship program I have been working on that many of you, my friends, have so generously helped to fund. Although there will only be one recipient this year, I am excited for future years in which many more scholarships will be offered. Mara, will you please step forward?"

Mara watched me with wild-eyes, a torrent of uncertainty and self-doubt rained down on me. I shivered and grabbed her hand, walking with her to my mother's side. Each step of the way, I did my best to send vibes of strength, encouragement, and pride to her through our bond.

"Mara, you are a talented young lady who will do great things. Please accept this all-inclusive scholarship to Bradwit Waterford University to further your giftings under the tutelage of their two-year program." Mother held out a certificate to her. The parchment was neatly rolled up and tied with a silver ribbon.

Mara froze, her stomach plummeting, and I thought we might both hurl. I took a sharp inhale through my nose and grabbed her by the shoulders. "You deserve this." My eyes bore into hers. "No one is more deserving than you."

Her chin wobbled and she partly laughed and cried at the same time. Forgetting protocol for a second, she reached up on her tippy-toes and flung her arms around my mother, the words "thank you" trailing on repeat.

Mother startled, but then she too cried as she embraced Mara. "You are welcome."

I studied the crowd. Many wept tears of joy while others beamed brightly. Everyone except for two— Gavin's parents.

Father joined us on stage and cleared his throat. "May I have my wife back, please? We need her to get the rest of the festivities started," he said good-naturedly, and the crowd laughed.

Mara and I exited and we walked back to the performer cabins where we could change into our Carnival costumes.

I was out first and was there when my friends all arrived.

"Is Mara still changing?" Lana asked, pointing to the cream-colored cabin. I nodded. She hugged Brantley, then ran up the three steps and let herself inside.

"I had no idea you could dance, cousin," Shai said, greeting me with a congratulatory pat on the shoulder.

"Who was even looking at him? Did you see my Mara?" Gavin swooned.

Shai mock punched Gavin in the stomach. "Get a grip, man. We know you are in love. No need to make us sick over it."

"Whatever, that was the first time I got to see my girl in nearly a week, and I barely recognized her."

"I wish my sister would hurry things along. Half the parade will be gone before we get to the VIP box."

As if they had heard Shai's whining, Lana and Mara came outside. The guys and I stood with our mouths open as we took in their costumes. Shai seemed to be the only one cool enough to function under their spell. He approached the porch and assisted first Lana and then Mara down the steps.

Mara walked up to Gavin. "Do you like it?" she asked, running her hands through the large, feathered headdress.

The bright red-orange fabric commanded attention. I could feel that he liked it, and in more than one way.

"Like it? I love it!" He scooped her up around her exposed midriff, her feet a few inches off the ground, and he spun, sending her cape flying.

Mara giggled. "You can thank Lana for my costume changes."

Gavin ran up to Lana and twirled her around too, bellowing "thank-yous."

"Good grief, Lana. I know you are nearly twenty now, but come on. You could cover up a little more," Shai complained.

"What? I have more of myself covered than many of the traditional costumes we see at Carnival year after year."

Lana was right. Though the girls' midriffs and most of their thighs were exposed, there was still plenty left to the imagination.

"I, for one, think you look beautiful," Brantley kissed her cheek, "and powerful." She blushed and entwined her fingers in his.

"Whatever, can we just go to the box now? I don't want to miss the parade."

Lana rolled her eyes at her brother. "Well then quit talking and start walking."

We took the shortcut through the royal entrance; my clearance as Prince allowed for it, and it only took us a few minutes to make it into the VIP box. This would be our first year at Carnival as men, the first time we'd be given permission to enjoy the post-parade adult festivities.

"Where's Gavin and Mara?" I asked once I took my seat.

"Oh, Gavin said they would be right back. He is going to introduce her to his parents," Shai said.

The parade had been moving for over ten minutes when

I spotted Gavin across the way weaving into his parent's box, his face too-pale and stoic. *Where was Mara?*

Something was not right. "Shai, are you sure Gavin had plans to introduce Mara to his parents?"

"Yeah, why?"

"Because his parents have been in their seats since the beginning of the parade and Gavin just joined them."

"So, maybe they are all watching it together," Shai said, not taking his eyes off of the float with dancers in royal blue who shimmied their hips and flung candy and flowers at the crowd.

"Maybe, but one problem... Mara isn't with them."

Shai peeled his eyes away from the beautiful women. "You don't think..."

"With that bastard, anything is possible. I have to go find her." I stood and began working my way through the row, trying to squeeze past all the legs and feet.

"Goshamighty! The one year we actually get to join the party." Shai slammed his hands onto his knees and poised to stand.

"I'll come with you."

"No, stay here with your sister and Brantley. I am sure it's nothing."

Shai attempted to move toward me again, but I asserted my authority by giving him a quick blast of my gifting.

Shai frowned at me. "Whatever, Your Highness."

He was clearly pissed, but time was of the essence and I dashed down the stairs.

I searched everywhere, particularly places she would know from our earlier curtain call. She was neither in the cabin nor behind the stage. I took a carriage, with my guards following but keeping their distance, back to the mansion. I raced through the manor to the guest cottage. Not one light was on. I opened the door anyway.

"Mara? Are you here?"

No response. I tried again. "Mara? It's me, Nicholas. I'm worried about you." Again, no response. I closed the door and slid down it, raking my hands through my hair.

Where are you? A thought hit me. If something had happened to me, I would want to be with my family, my parents.

I shot out from the side of the house like a bolt of lightning, skidding to a stop on the rock drive, a cloud of dust engulfing my guards and stablemen.

"Take me to Mara's, now!" I ran up to Coalcott, my black stallion, grabbed hold of his reins, jammed my right foot into the stirrup and flung my left leg over the horse's back. "Yah!" I kicked his sides and he took off.

By then the night sky was pitch black and I took a deep breath, allowing my body to light the way. The other guards did the same, casting an eerie green glow all around me, encircling my blue light.

I pulled up directly to the worn walkway leading to Mara's door and dismounted my horse. I held my hands up, halting my guard.

A loud shriek pierced my ears, followed swiftly by a deafening crack. I paused for a moment, long enough to recover and get a read on Mara. Her grief overwhelmed me. My heart, heavy as a platinum rock, sank in my chest and I gasped for breath, wrestling my gifting that reached for her, back to me.

"Stay here!" I yelled over my shoulder and ran to the front door. *Bang, bang, bang!* My fist collided with old wood and left an imprint. "Mara! I'm here for you. Please open the door." A chilling silence greeted me. I pounded again, the wood of the door crackling and popping.

Without warning, it swung open, and I nearly fell in. Mara's mother, Bronwyn, confronted me with her glare as Mara sat cowered in the corner. Her eyes were dark and orange tears dripped down her cheeks.

"Mara," I breathed. But Bronwyn's hand stopped me, surprisingly strong for such a frail woman who was three sheets to the wind.

"She doesn't need ya. She's already spoken for," the woman spat, her breath reeking of spirits.

I jerked my head away at the offense. My eyes blazed, and Bronwyn stepped back as I entered.

"Mara, is everything alright?" My light illuminated her face, and my stomach knotted at the sight of her. I gritted my teeth once I spotted the red handprint seared onto her cheek and the drop of blood that drizzled down from the corner of her mouth.

"She'll be fine. He'll take care of her and provide everything we could ever need. After all, she is the reason for my pain, all of it. I used to live in luxury, but she—" Bronwyn hissed as she pointed to Mara— "stole everything from me. He has offered more than this burden deserves."

My fists clenched, my nails drawing blood from my palms. I never thought myself capable of hitting a woman, but I was dangerously close.

"How could Mara ever be a burden? She is pure light—good, kind, and extremely gifted."

Bronwyn cackled and nearly fell over, seating herself in a torn wingback chair. "So, she has you fooled, has she? Her own father left me because he wanted nothing to do with her and I was shunned by our own kind, my family even, because of her human blood."

"Mother is right. I do not deserve anything good." Mara picked at her nails, her face obscured by a curtain of hair. "Leave, Nicholas," she said flatly.

I walked right up to her and lifted her chin. I tried not to flinch at the sight of her once pastel watercolor eyes, now a clouded orange.

"Do not lie to me. I can feel you, practically reach your soul, and I know that you are good and worthy. Come with me."

"I... I can't," she sobbed, and I thought I would drown along with her.

I wrapped my arms around her and gave her a firm hug. "I cannot...no. I *will not* leave you here."

"'Bye, princey poo. You heard her, she doesn't want ya." Bronwyn took another swig of her thick, creamy spirits and wiped her mouth with the back of her hand.

Mara spoke into my chest. "I have an obligation to my mother. I have to take care of her. She's just drunk. She will sleep this off and be a different person tomorrow."

"I already called Melchior. He should be here soon."

Mara's eyes flashed, and I fell back on my heels as she stood.

"Nicholas, you must leave now. You cannot be here. He

will kill you." Her eyes jerked around and she shook with fear.

"I am not that easy to kill." The corners of my mouth lifted as I rose to my feet to join her.

"This is no time for arrogance," Mara pleaded, grasping my hands tightly as her eyes returned to their natural colors.

"I'm not being arrogant. Right outside your door is my elite retinue of ten highly skilled men and women. Additionally, as the Prince of Cristes, I am a well-trained warrior with many developed giftings."

Mara worried her lip. "Please leave...for me. I don't want to make him mad when he gets here."

I couldn't help the next words that escape from my lips. "Choose me."

She blinked at me. "What?"

"*Choose me.*"

"What does that even mean?"

"It means that my family has already given you ample opportunity to decide what you want to do with your life. You only have to decide which path you will take. I am offering you freedom. Melchior offers you a life of enslavement, and you would be nothing more than an object he owns."

"All you royals lie, you power-hungry, deceiving, manipulative bastards," Bronwyn sneered.

I spared her no attention. She was a mere nuisance, a pebble in my shoe, and I kept my focus on Mara. "Have I not been your friend? Can you not trust me?"

Mara's eyes flicked to her mother and I guided her gaze back to me.

"She can be taken care of if you'd like. But we need to leave now. I do not want to start a war." I had done my research into

Melchior and he was a decorated leader of the Black Roses, a militant group in the uprising that initiated the First Fall. The atrocities he committed were pure evil.

Mara's chin wobbled. "He will hurt her if he comes and I'm not here."

"Cobani, Ohanna, come now!" I yelled through the threshold. The pounding of boots reverberated in the tiny cottage, growing louder until they entered, their skin glowing brightly. They were on high alert and ready for my command.

I gestured to Mara's mother. "Please take Bronwyn to the horses. An adversary will arrive any minute and we do not want to be here when he does." My guards nodded and barked, "Yes, Your Highness!"

Bronwyn put up a fight, but Cobani flung her over his shoulder and ran.

"Mara, we must to leave now." My instincts told me we had seconds left before trouble arrived.

"I need to grab something first." Mara raced out the back door and I followed her to a dilapidated wicker chair that sat facing the hills of green pasture. She dug her fingertips into the top of the seat, and I winced as shards of reed and bamboo pierced her fingertips and her nails cracked. She continued as if she hadn't noticed.

The lid flung open, and she grabbed a black Hellebore rose. "Let's go."

We raced through the cottage and I helped her onto my horse before mounting behind her.

"One more thing," Mara said.

The hairs on my arms began to stand, my skin tingling with awareness.

"Your Highness," Ohanna warned.

"Whatever you are going to do Mara, do it now."

She closed her eyes and held her hands above her head, one on each end of the rose. Blood-orange gifting erupted from her, obliterating the cottage, engulfing it in plumes of fire and smoke. Then Mara went limp in my arms and I clutched her to me, ensuring she wouldn't fall off of the horse.

My company of guards rode like the wind and broke through the thick forest just before a roar, more thunderous than any lion, impaled the landscape. The air stilled and the ground shook, spooking the horses. They rose on their hind legs, whinnying together in one chorus. My thighs burned, and the reigns stung my hands as I fought to maintain control of Coalcott, all while ensuring Mara stayed securely mounted.

A soldier fell, and a noxious snap cracked through the air. He cried out, but Ohanna was off her horse in a flash, her dark braids flinging about her face. She hoisted the injured guard up and placed the reins in his good hand. "Stay strong, man. We are only fifteen minutes out. We will get you to a healer right away. Go!"

The ground shook with a rumbling that drew closer. Melchior was closing in.

"Your Highness, get to safety, now," Cobani warned.

I knew what they wanted me to do. I had a charm in my leather cuff that would allow me to teleport home. But I would not leave my guard.

I had another idea. "Hold tight, friends."

"What are you..." Cobani started, his voice trailing off as I used my gifting to enchant every horse in one swift blue lightning strike.

We took off at light speed and were at the stables in less than three minutes.

Nicholas: Aftermath

MY PARENTS WERE WAITING AT THE STABLES, still in costume, with their full guard at the ready. Father helped Mara down and passed her into my open arms as soon as I jumped down.

"What happened, son?" Father asked. "Elden notified us that we needed to meet you here post haste."

"Melchior tried to take Mara." My heart nearly beat out of its cage.

Mother gasped and flung her hand over her chest as she took in the sight of Mara. Then her eyes narrowed when they found Bronwyn. She scrutinized the frail, middle-aged woman, and then her eyes widened, quickly returning to normal.

"Nicholas, you can take Mara to her quarters. I will have

Nolan meet you after he handles this man's arm," Dad said, gesturing to the guard who'd fallen on our race home.

"What about her?" I tipped my chin at Bronwyn.

"Your Mother and I will see to it that she is taken care of." I could immediately identify the numerous truths to that statement. "We will be by in a little while to meet with you to discuss what happened."

Mother kissed me on the cheek. "The wards are up around the city as well as the extra defenses around our home. No intruders crossed through the borders. Do we need to cancel the rest of Carnival?"

"No. As far as I'm aware, only Mara's life is in jeopardy." My jaw twitched.

"Take her now. Help her get comfortable." Mother looked to Father and they nodded once at each other, concern etched in their faces.

I took the circular stone pathway at the side of the house. A guard opened the tall white gate and closed it behind me. Mara's breaths were warm and even against my chest; she was at peace, for the moment. Another guard was waiting at the guest cottage door. She unlocked it and I walked through.

The guard nearly stepped on my heel, and I stopped.

"I am so sorry, Your Highness."

"Please do not fash. No harm done. Can you turn on the lamp and then wait outside?"

"Of course, Your Highness." The guard did an about-face, switched on the dim amber light, and quietly closed the door behind her.

I carried Mara to her bed and gingerly laid her down. Mara reached for me, her hands trailing up and around my neck.

"Mara?" I whispered. She did not respond, her breathing still calm and even.

I shifted my body to the edge of the bed. Without breaking her hold, I lay down, our faces scant inches apart. At the same time, I slid my arm out from under her and repositioned it to embrace her.

I did not know how long we had been lying there when Nolan walked in.

"Pardon me, Prince Nicholas. I had no intentions of intruding. I will return if you so desire."

I turned my chin, my nose no longer catching the coconut pineapple scent of Mara's hair.

"No, please come in. She has not woken yet, but she has clung to me nonetheless."

Nolan brought glittering Christmas roses and a light green elixir. He picked up a throw pillow and placed it on the floor before lowering down onto one knee in front of Mara's beautiful face.

"Would you like to do the first part, Your Highness?"

I ran my hand down my face. "Just Nick, please. What would I need to do?"

"Place the elixir on the parts of her that I instruct."

"I can do that." I attempted to uncoil myself from Mara, but she clutched me tighter.

"On second thought, I will do it." Nolan made quick work of it. With a swift flick and swish, Nolan's finger covered the small pear-shaped bottle's opening, and he gingerly dabbed Mara's temples, eyelids, upper lip, and each side of her neck.

Mara stirred and released her grip on me. I slid her arms

down and sat up, grasping her hand in both of mine. Nolan worked diligently around me— *flick, swish, flick, swish*— until he had swiped every major energy point on her body.

Mara's eyes flickered open when Nolan held a Christmas rose under her nose. Like a Watcher, she instinctively inhaled its magical properties.

"I shall leave you two alone now," Nolan bowed. "I will return in a little while with nourishment."

"Thank you," I responded. Nolan nodded and headed out.

"How did I get here?" Mara asked as fluffed the pillows behind her, helping her to sit up. "The last thing I remember is heading to the horses."

"Well, I will get to that. Why don't we start with why you disappeared from Carnival?"

Her eyes filled with tears again. I immediately embraced her and upon contact, my heart ached as if it were dried out, tiny pieces flaking off one at a time. I shuddered.

"Please don't cry. I'm here to listen, to help if you want; but as your friend, I really need to understand what happened."

"Can...can I show you?" she asked.

Mara knew my gifting of the mind was one of my strengths. I never forgot anything, no matter how minute a detail. Although my ability was not yet second-nature, I could see into the minds of others with their permission.

"Are you sure?"

"Positive. I do not think I would make it through telling you." Mara sniffed and I handed her my handkerchief.

I climbed fully back onto the bed and folded my legs so I was situated directly across from her. Grabbing her hands, I placed my forehead to hers, instructed her to close her eyes, and poured my light into her. It traveled slowly, searching each fold and pathway of her brain until it found the pictures it needed.

"Father! Father!" Gavin called over the crowd, clutching my hand, waving at his dad with the other. "I want you to meet my girlfriend, Mara." Gavin's face lit up, and his smile actually beamed.

I offered my hand in greeting, but Mr. Frosters looked at me, then my hand, and back at his son. Gavin looked at me, a blip of confusion on his face as he noted the slight.

"Was she not spectacular in the Argentang? Our Queen thinks very highly of her to bestow such an honor."

Mr. Frosters said nothing. He snatched Gavin's shoulder and pulled him a few steps away.

Gavin's dad leaned down to his son's ear, and I watched as Gavin's face paled, the light draining from him until it flickered and died. Gavin attempted to speak, but his dad's eyes pulsed bright blue, and Gavin immediately stilled. Mr. Frosters let go of his son's costume and unwrinkled it from where he'd clutched it in his white-knuckled grip, then he stalked away.

I worried my lip, watching Gavin stand there, frozen like an ice sculpture. I approached him cautiously.

"Gavin, are you alright?" I asked, placing my hand over his heart. He seemed to come out of his stupor. His hand found mine and he rushed me toward the deserted cast cabins.

"Slow down! What happened?" I tried to catch my breath. It was not until we reached the cabin I had been assigned to earlier in the afternoon that he pressed me up against its wall and kissed me.

At first, his kiss was desperate, hard, and fast. His hands trailed every inch of me from my hips to my jaw. But then it slowed. His hand cupped my face as if he was savoring every moment. His tongue parted my lips, moving in sync with mine. He paused to suck my lower lip and then captured my mouth again when I gasped. His hands slipped to the back of my neck, his fingers trailing up and down, leaving tingles everywhere he touched.

His kiss moved to my jaw, my shoulder, my collarbone. I moaned and he ignited. I placed a hand on his hard chest to still him, to marvel at his beauty. All different shades of blue and green traveled from his heart through his hands and feet, and he found my mouth again with urgency. I kissed him back, but my gut told me something wasn't right.

Gavin finally broke our kiss and took two steps back from me. His eyes glittered as tears filled them.

"Mara, I..." He choked down a sob. "I'm not permitted to see you anymore."

"What! What does that even mean?" I rolled my lips, pressing them hard against each other to stop their quavering.

"It means you are no longer mine. I cannot be near you and my lips will never taste yours again. My hands will never touch you again." Gavin grabbed at his shirt, clutching his chest.

My chest heaved out of my control as I pressed myself against the whitewashed wood of the cabin. "I don't... I don't understand. You said-you-you-said..."

Gavin's light faded and his face turned to stone. "I know

what I said, but things have changed."

"How could you kiss me like that, like you can't get enough, and then break my heart?"

"I don't have a choice," Gavin said, his voice and gaze dropping.

I stepped up to him and ran my fingers through his hair and behind his ear. He shivered but took another step back.

"That is not fair. Please don't make this harder for me than it already is."

"Help me understand."

"There is nothing left to say, Mara. I've made up my mind."

"Coward! Say it! Tell me why the love of my life is breaking my heart when he promised me forever?"

"You can't possibly— "

"You don't get to tell me what I can or cannot ask."

"Please. Do not make me say it." Gavin pleaded, his eyes still avoiding mine.

"I need to know. I must know!"

There was a deeply pregnant pause. Then he stared at me, resolute.

"My father, he believes you are not...suitable for me, not the right match our family requires. If I do not end things now, he will make things a lot worse. For the both of us."

"Not suitable? Not the right match? He doesn't even know me!"

"You're right. He doesn't. But my mother saw you at the market before Queen Nicole took you in."

"The queen sees something in me. I can prove to your parents I'm good enough—"

"No, Mara." he shook his head.

"So, what? I will face them, for you. I won't give up on us that easily. I will fight for you, for us."

"You do not even have the height or other features he wants me to have in a wife."

"That is not a big deal. I can wear higher-heeled shoes. I can dye my hair. I can—"

"Damfino, Mara! You will never be good enough for him. Do you hear me? Nothing about you is good enough!"

I couldn't breathe. My stomach wretched as my heart cleaved in two, and I collapsed to my knees.

Gavin knelt in front of me, his eyes pleading. "Mara, it's not me, it's my dad. I'm so—"

"Go away," I choked on the tears that threatened to drown me.

His hand rested on my shoulder, but his touch burned.

"I said, go away!"

His rapid footsteps grew faint as I kneeled on the worn grass, desperately trying to catch my breath. My chest heaved and tiny sparks danced in my vision. I tore my headdress off, taking small chunks of hair with it, and ripped off the constricting tie of my cape. Nothing helped.

"Ma'am, are you alright? Do you need a healer?"

But I did not answer them as I dashed into the woods and headed home.

I sat back, removing my forehead from hers.

"Mara, I'm so sorry." I knew when Gavin first set eyes on her that he would break her heart, but I never imagined it would be like this.

Her eyes remained closed and tears rolled silently down her cheeks. I rolled her so she faced the wall and laid on my side next to her, holding her tight.

"You know none of it is true, right?" I whispered into her ear. She needed to believe she was valuable. She needed to recognize how loved she was.

"But it is. My dad, my mom, now Gavin and his parents. No one wants me. I really am not good enough."

"Are you calling the Queen of Cristes a liar?"

Mara stiffened. "I would never!" She attempted to sit up, but I held her in place.

"Well, she thought you were — no, *are* — gifted. That you are worth investing in. You have brought much joy to me and my house."

"Why can't Mr. Frosters see it, then?" she dared to ask, her heart pounding in her chest.

"Because he is too old school."

"What does that mean?" she rolled over to face me and snuggled into my chest.

"It means that he is way too concerned with title and position, something that Cristes has worked very hard to overcome. The caste system was the cause of the First Fall, after all. He has not let go of his stubborn ideals."

"If his way of thinking is *old school* as you say, why does Gavin listen to him?"

I stroked her golden tresses. "Well, Mr. Frosters is a difficult man. I'm sure he threatened Gavin with something or made him an offer he couldn't refuse."

Mara was silent for a long moment. She began to play with the button of my shirt. "Would you have made Gavin's choice if you were in his shoes?"

"Gavin is my friend and I love him. I cannot pretend to comprehend all the conditions that led to his decision.

However..." I paused.

"However...?"

"I would have chosen love a thousand times over."

Mara sighed and took a deep, shuddering breath. "Thank you." Then, she snuggled against me once more and grew still.

When she was fast asleep, I slid out from under her and walked straight to Father's office, where I knew my parents were waiting.

Nicholas: I'm Sorry

THREE WEEKS PASSED and Gavin never visited my home anymore. Lana and Brantley had tried to come and say goodbye, but Mara would not leave the guest quarters. Bronwyn was sent to live in a woman's home in a sub-city of Cristes. Mother assured Mara that she would be well taken care of and receive the medical treatment she required. Shai came to visit a few times, but our conversations were stilted. But he did tell me Gavin was suffering and encouraged me to go see him.

Finally, a week before we were to go to BWU, Mara spoke her first words since the night of the breakup.

"What is university like?" she asked me as she started work on her final piece of art, a set of earrings for my mother.

"The town is awesome. I think you will really like it. I plan on taking you a few days early so that I can give you a tour and we can set up your apartment."

"A whole apartment?" she asked in wonder.

"Yes, but do not get too excited. They are small, with just the basic necessities. But at least you do not have to have a roommate and you get your own bathroom. Your scholarship provides you with a monthly living allowance. We can go shopping for anything you need at the campus stores."

"Will you live far?" she bit her lip with worry.

I gently plucked her lip from her teeth. "No, actually I will be right across the hall from you."

She smiled and her shoulders relaxed. "You are going to do amazing, Mara. You earned your place at university with everyone else.

"Thank you, Nicholas, for everything."

"You're welcome."

Between packing for myself, helping Mara, and spending time with my parents, the night before we were due to travel to school came upon us quickly.

Mara and I were enjoying a movie in the cinema of the manor when a knock sounded on the door, followed by Nolan swiftly entering. He approached me and leaned in close to my ear.

"Sir, you have a guest waiting for you in the reception room."

"Send them in, please."

Nolan cleared his throat. "I think you will want to meet this person privately." He straightened and placed his hands behind his back.

I cocked my brow at him, intrigued. "I will be right back,"

I said to Mara.

"I can press pause if you'd like."

"No," I shook my head, "you go ahead. I have seen this a hundred times."

Nolan closed the door behind me and hurried ahead, guiding me to the small alcove in the front entryway that served as a guest reception area.

I stumbled to a halt. "What the heck are you doing here?" I growled, my anger already boiling to the surface.

"Now, Nick. Please, he has been your friend since you were both in diapers. Hear him out," Shai pleaded with me.

I nodded at Shai who backed into a corner, then addressed Gavin. "Fine. You have sixty seconds."

Gavin looked worse for wear, down in weight about a stone, with purple circles under his bloodshot eyes. *I wouldn't sleep well if I were him, either.* Reluctantly, I sensed how broken he was. A dull glow coursed my veins as I shielded myself so that I did not have to experience his pain. I needed a clear head in order to talk to him.

"Nick, when I broke up with Mara, why did that end our friendship?"

My jaw ticked as I clenched it tight, my silence fueling the growing tension.

"You have to believe me. I did not want this to happen. If I had a choice, I would—"

"Oh, you had a choice, and you chose wrong."

"And what would you know of it?" Gavin's lashed out defensively.

I crossed my arms over my chest and bit the inside of my cheek. "I saw enough."

"She— she let you *see*?"

"Yes and I realize your dad is...tough." I relaxed my arms.

He scoffed. "Yeah, that is putting it mildly."

"Regardless, I would have chosen Mara over and over again, no matter the consequences."

Gavin paced as he threaded his hands through his hair. "You say that, but when you are threatened that you will be disowned and thrown on the street, that is a different story."

I recrossed my arms over my chest. "Mara was worse off when I found her. Look where hard work and ingenuity can get you."

Gavin stopped pacing and dropped his hands. "Maybe, but it is clear as day that she will never be totally accepted in the elite circles."

"Who cares? Why does that matter to you so much?"

Gavin turned away from me. "You will never understand. Your parents would never make you choose. They would support you in anything you do."

"That is because they raised me to be a man," I said coolly.

"Say that again, you varlet!" Gavin spat, lunging for me.

I ignited like the powerful prince that I am, bright like the beacon of a lighthouse.

"Whoa!" Shai shouted, placing himself between us. "You guys are practically brothers. You both have to figure this out."

I pinched the bridge of my nose. "You took the easy road, Gavin. You always have." I leveled him with my gaze. "Shai is right; you are not like a brother to me. You *are* a brother to me. Do you believe for one second I would ever have let you go broke and homeless?"

A muscle in Gavin's jaw twitched. "I do not need your

charity or your pity."

"Love does not equate to either of those things. That is what makes it love." I stepped toward him, arms open.

Gavin tore his eyes from mine and wiped them with the back of his hand. "I messed up brother, big time."

"What's going on?" Mara asked as she came to the entryway. I immediately extinguished my gifting, transferring Gavin to Shai's arms.

I intercepted her a few feet outside of the alcove before she could see Gavin. "Nothing. Let's go back and finish our movie."

"Who were you arguing with?" she asked as I placed my arm around her shoulders and tried to guide her back toward the cinema.

"An old friend."

Her body stiffened.

Thundernation.

She turned around and met Gavin's eyes.

"Mara." His voice broke on her name. "Mara," he said more clearly and stepped toward her.

She backed up and put her hand out to stop him. "Don't. Don't come any closer, or I'll... I'll scream."

He froze. "I won't. I will stand right here." His shoulders slumped. "I just wanted to say, I made a *huge* mistake. I am so sorry I hurt you." He attempted to look at her, but the moment his eyes found hers, he dropped his gaze. "I realize I've probably lost you for good, but I hope you can forgive me one day."

Mara turned and walked back to the media room with her head down, hugging herself.

"Gavin, we'll talk at school, alright?" I said, patting him on the shoulder.

He seemed to perk up a little at that. "I am heading there tomorrow with Shai so I can help you move in later this week if you'd like."

"Actually, Mara and I are moving in tomorrow as well."

A sudden jolt of jealousy hit me as if Gavin had punched me directly in the gut, and I crumpled over.

"Not moving in together, you idiot," I gasped.

Shai had his hand over me and in a second, the pain subsided and I stood tall.

"She will be living in our building, across the hall from me. You will be a few floors above her, across from Shai." I explained.

"I'm sorry." Gavin dropped his head in his hands. "I'm a mess. I can't seem to function."

I held my hand up, silencing him. "Go home and get cleaned up. Get some sleep. I'll see you tomorrow."

Mara: Promise Ring

NICHOLAS HAD BEEN A DREAM. He never left my side as I mourned Gavin. I feared that when we got to university, he would become too busy with responsibilities, obligations, and friends, but I was stupid to think so little of him.

Together, we explored the beautiful campus. Though we were both first-year students, Nicholas had visited many times before with his parents. He took me to the admissions office and, due to his title, we were given our schedules early. We had no classes in common, but I tried not to fret about it.

He helped me shop for my apartment, and within two days it transformed into my home away from home. On Friday night, Nicholas and I hung out, as usual, eating a takeaway dinner from Mistletides. Exhaustion clung to me, as it became harder and harder to avoid Gavin.

When I lay alone at night in my room, sleep never came as I fought against the pull of his body calling for mine a few floors above me. It was nearly impossible to ignore the tingle of my lips as I remembered our last kiss.

"Mara? Hello... Did you hear anything I said?" Nicholas asked.

"What? Sorry. I'm just so tired. It's been a very exciting week."

He smiled at me and laid his hand over mine. "I think we should call it a night."

"But it's only eight-thirty? That is so early!"

"Yes, but if you get to sleep tonight, we can go do something really fun tomorrow night."

"Really! Like what?" I asked eagerly.

"It's a surprise," Nicholas smiled coyly.

I rolled my eyes, hating surprises, and he knew it, but I also knew it was no use trying to pry it out of him. He embodied unwavering patience, resolute in pursuing his goals.

I kissed him on the cheek. "Will I see you tomorrow in the cafe for breakfast?"

"You can count on it." He smiled and it crinkled his eyes.

He watched me from his doorway as I walked a little way down the hall. I waved before entering my room and closed the door behind me.

I stepped into the aqua-tiled bathroom and pulled back the white shower curtain. While the water warmed, I brushed my teeth and twisted up my hair. When the silver-framed mirror started to fog, I undressed and slipped under the hot water.

I stayed under the steady stream until my muscles relaxed. Thick clouds of steam saturated the bathroom, and I could barely see my towel to grab it once I turned off the water. I dried off and put on my fuzzy peach robe. It may have been seventy-eight degrees tonight, but I still wore it nearly every time I was in my apartment. Nicholas purchased it for me, and I wondered how I ever managed to live without being wrapped up in a constant, warm hug.

A gentle knock sounded on my door. Thinking it was Nicholas, I flung it open. A clean-shaven and well-dressed Gavin stood before me, a glowing Christmas rose in his lapel. The door swung, although I did not recall pushing it. Just before the mechanism clicked, Gavin jutted his foot out. Before I had time to protest, Gavin let himself in my room and shut the door behind him.

"Please, hear me out," he begged.

I opened my mouth numerous times to speak, to yell at him, to tell him to get out, but no sound came. I huffed and crossed my arms.

Gavin dropped to his knees and waddled a few paces over to me. His gorgeous green eyes looked up at me through his thick lashes, and I almost caved right then and there.

"Mara, please forgive me. I cannot stay away. I cannot live without you. You are my sunlight, my joy, my better half. I— I love you."

I broke eye contact and sucked in my bottom lip. How I'd craved to hear those words from his lips. How desperately I wished he'd chosen me that night at Carnival. I turned my gaze back to him, his face pale, his breathing frantic, and his eyes filled with wild intensity.

"I'm not sure I can," I whispered.

Gavin flung his arms around my waist and started to cry.

Instinctively, I wrapped my arms around his neck and bent my head to kiss the top of his. Gavin's body went rigid like I'd shocked him.

"I promise, I will never hurt you again. I am my own man and my father cannot bully me anymore." His muffled voice sent shivers into my abdomen.

"How can I ever trust you?"

He grabbed my wrists and looked up at me with eyes that still shed tears. "I will do the work to earn it back. And, I have a plan. We do not have to tell my parents we are together. Once I graduate and my future is secured soon after, we can be free to marry."

I couldn't help but wipe away his tears with the cuff of my robe. "I don't believe in secrets. The truth always comes out."

"I have no right to even ask this of you, for your grace. But my feelings for you have never changed. I fully believe you see that; there is no doubt in my mind that you experience our bodies' pull. Watchers can't hide their mutual attraction, especially when they are as connected as we are." He nuzzled into my wrist.

My cheeks heated. That was something none of the boys had taught me in my lessons over the summer.

Gavin reached into his pocket and procured a single, white-gold band, twisted into an infinity knot design. He held it out to me.

"This is a promise ring; a promise that we will get married after graduation. When we leave here, I will propose to you properly, and with a stone larger than you've ever seen."

My hands covered my heart. "You... you're asking me to marry you?"

Gavin stood and as he towered over me, his eyes sparkled as they darkened.

"This is my promise that I will ask you to marry me properly when my father can't punish me anymore."

I flung my arms around his neck and kissed him. It took no time for Gavin to respond and his lips swelled under mine.

For about a year and a half we were blissfully happy. Of course, Nicholas and Shai were immediately told of our mended relationship and our future marriage. But Gavin and I guarded our secret from anyone else. The anticipation of sharing with all of Cristes that Gavin was mine consumed me! I eagerly awaited the day when our union would be celebrated.

Gavin and I spent every waking minute with each other until one day, he started to withdraw from me. I tried to excuse it away but after a week, worry became an unwelcome guest in my thoughts.

It was when we were in his apartment and he had ignored me yet again by engrossing himself in a book, that I mustered the courage to approach him. "I know you. I've learned to sense and trust my giftings and I can feel that you are keeping something from me."

He looked at me and quickly put his head back in his book. "It's nothing. I'm dealing with it."

I grabbed his arm, and pleaded, "Don't do that. Do not shut me out again."

He put the book down and sighed. "Fine, I did not want to upset you." Gavin walked across the small room to his dresser. After he opened the top drawer, he reached his arm in and prodded around. In his hand was a small green envelope with a large "F" in the wax seal, his family crest. He took out the parchment from it and handed it to me.

Son, graduation is only four months away. Soon you will be a respectable man at the Realm Bank. That is right, Gavin! I have procured you a mid-level role at my branch! No child of mine will have to start at the bottom of the barrel. There is one catch, which I trust will not be of issue. In order to procure such an established position for someone as young as yourself, the VP and I thought it in your best interests if we were to arrange a marriage between you and his daughter, Ellasyn. Your mother and I took the liberty of meeting her over dinner and she is perfect, absolutely your match in every way. I cannot wait for you to meet her when you come home this week. To make myself crystal clear, you will come home for spring break, and you will wine and dine Madame Ellasyn. She needs to agree to this in order to ensure your future success at the bank.

See you soon, Stephen

I shot to standing as my heart sank and I crumbled the parchment in my hand.

"Mara, you, you are glowing!" Gavin said excitedly. "I have never seen this color before. It is gorgeous! What does it mean?"

I grew a little self-conscious. I'd only been able to do this one other time with Professor Avent.

"We think it means that I can access all the giftings, but they are weak on their own. I need a physical connection to magical items in their most natural form to strengthen them."

"That is wonderful! Is this why you have been in the lab so much?"

"Yes, but quit changing the subject. What are you going to do?" I asked, pacing in front of the bed.

"Do not fash, my love. I obviously have to go home for the two weeks. We cannot afford to raise my father's suspicions. I will meet this girl. Then, I will make it so that she and I do not establish a Watcher pairing connection, but that she will still hold me in high regard, enough to still sway her father into giving me the position."

"What if...what if she *is* your perfect match?"

Gavin grabbed my hand and tucked a piece of hair behind my ear. "You see, this is why I did not want to tell you and why I was trying to play it cool this week. She is not an option. You saw what happened to me last time we were apart. I simply cannot live without you." He smiled and kissed my forehead.

"When do you leave?

"Tomorrow, late morning. I'm going to miss you so much."

I pushed him onto his light-gray comforter. Taking a few steps back, I slid the bolt of the door into place. Gavin sat at the edge of the bed, following my every move.

My hips swayed a little more than usual as I came to stand before him. His breath hitched as he watched me guide one strap of my sundress down my shoulder.

"Mara," he choked out, "What are you doing?" But it was as if he couldn't help himself. Without blinking, without taking his eyes off of me, he reached up for the light on his nightstand and turned it out. His glow lasted all night.

Mara: Broken Promises Make for Broken Magic

THE TWO-WEEK BREAK passed at a snail's pace and I had not heard from Gavin, though I knew I wouldn't. Still, I missed him terribly. He was supposed to be back last night. We had plans to hang out before classes resumed.

On the following Sunday afternoon, I approached Gavin's and knocked on the door, but no one answered. Feeling deflated, I headed downstairs. And as I reached the landing, a wave of uneasiness crept over me. Something was very wrong. I spun back on my heel and climbed the stairs once more.

"Mara, this is a nice surprise." Shai greeted me.

"Hi. Sorry to bother you. Do you happen to know where Gavin is? I was really looking forward to seeing him last night for the first time since break, but he never showed up. I'm starting to get worried."

Shai's face scrunched in confusion. "He's been back since Friday. I just left his place less than ten minutes ago."

Two days. Gavin had been back for two days and yet he'd been avoiding me. Like a punch to the gut, bile shot up through my esophagus, but I quickly covered my mouth with my hand, forcing it back down as I retreated into the hall.

Shai followed me out of his apartment, concern etched on his face as he placed a hand on my shoulder and bent down so his eyes were level with mine.

"Mara, is everything alright? You look like you're about to be sick. Come in and have a seat. I'll get you some water."

I stepped back, deliberately moving out from under his touch. "I'm fine," I forced a smile, "I really must be going."

Shai scrutinized me for a long moment. "Maybe you should check in with Nick."

"Yeah, maybe. Thanks, Shai. See you around."

I took the back staircase two at a time. The stairwell light was burned out and I could barely see. Goosebumps tickled my flesh as I felt the energy of another person with me. My body said to run, so I did...right into something hard.

"Ooof!" A deep voice I'd recognize anywhere huffed out.

The room filled with a dim sage glow and Gavin's face stared back at me before he dropped his gaze.

I bolted past him to my room and slid the bolt on the door with a satisfying click before I flung myself face-first onto the bed. I couldn't remember how long I lay there when a soft knock at my door dragged me from my state of nothingness.

I opened the door a crack, and there Gavin stood.

"May I come in, please," he asked, barely looking at me.

I said nothing and held the door open wide enough for

him to enter, then slammed it shut.

His eyes flicked to the bed, undoubtably remembering our last night together before he left me to go home, the night we had become one. Something registered over his face. Regret? Longing? I couldn't be sure.

He swiped his face from forehead to chin in slow motion.

"Gavin, what is it?" I asked, bringing him to sit on the loveseat.

"My dad suspects."

"What do you—"

"My dad suspects that we have been together."

"So, let him suspect. He can't be certain."

"That is not entirely true. He knows I have given myself to someone because he can see it."

I searched frantically over my shoulders, expecting to find someone watching us, some hint of magic that could share our secrets outside of these walls.

"Look at me, Mara." I did as he asked, and after a moment, I relaxed. Gavin's eyes always drew me in, but they were even brighter today. I placed the palm of my hand on the side of his face and stroked his cheek with my thumb.

"My eyes have changed. It is not permanent and has already mostly calmed down. But, when you and I...gave ourselves to each other... the power of our love unlocked my giftings to their fullest potential. My dad recognized it immediately, knowing I'd been with someone I loved deeply."

"But still, he just assumes."

Gavin sighed. "You're right. But—"

"Is this why you have been avoiding me?" A muscle in his jaw ticked and he promptly looked down at the ground. "I need your honesty, Gavin."

"Yes, because I think we need to keep our distance from each other...at least for now. I do not want to risk anything happening to our plan. We are so close."

"Couldn't you have told me all of this? My gosh. When I found out that you'd been back since Friday, my mind drew some dark conclusions."

His gaze snapped to mine. "I'm sorry. How do you tell someone you love that you have to stay away? This is tortuous."

I stroked his forearm absently, up and down, with the tips of my nails and he shivered. "Well, this sucks, but no matter the difficulties, we are in this together."

He stiffened. "There is one more thing I have to tell you." I braced myself and held my breath. "My father requires that I come home every weekend now to properly court Ellasyn."

I bolted upright. "I thought that you were going to persuade her to give you her blessing, but not your hand in marriage?"

"I tried, believe me, I tried." He sighed deep and long. "My father was not convinced that I was trying hard enough. He thought that more time would help me along in my efforts." He frowned at me.

I cupped his face. "But you are mine and I am yours. She doesn't get to have you." I kissed his forehead.

Gavin stood and wrapped his arms around me. "I love that little orange spark you get in your eyes when you are passionate. And, of course, I am only yours."

"Good, because I have been dying to show you how badly I've missed you." A smile tugged at the corner of my mouth.

"Oh, really?" He smirked, pulling me onto the bed.

When I woke the next morning, I felt the absence of Gavin. Mondays were his early lab days. I had until ten before I needed to meet with Professor Avent to continue testing more parts of my gifting and determine which elements it best responded to.

I rolled over and plucked a pristine white envelope from Gavin's pillow. I broke the wax seal and read:

My dearest love,

Since we cannot be together as much as we would like, I figured we could start writing to each other every day. I left you stationary supplies and wax stamp on your desk. The seal's sea shell design will be our identifier, keeping our names secret, just in case. As you can see there are two colored wax sticks. White is for everyday use. For times that we cannot go another minute without seeing the other, or we shall perish, apply the red wax to mark it urgent. However, we need to keep emergencies to no more than once a week to diminish the chance of discovery. Eager to hear from you,

~Yours forever,

G.

I crushed the envelope to my chest as I squealed and kicked my legs. Though I wasn't going to be able to see him much, I loved his ingenuity in keeping us connected. I promptly sat at my desk and opened the carton of bright white stationery. Dipping my quill in the pot of ink, I scrawled away a note to Gavin. It occurred to me that slipping a note under his door would be too risky. Instead, I decided to take a detour to the mailroom and placed the envelope in his mailbox on my way to the lab.

Over the course of four weeks, I wrote Gavin at least a dozen times, while his correspondence had been few and far between. I knew it was simply that he was doing his best to stay on top of his studies with graduation so close. I also sympathized that seeing his dad taxed him, and the three-hour travel to and from home every weekend didn't help his already busy schedule. But still, I missed him.

I nibbled at my toast, not feeling very hungry, when Nicholas joined me at my table in the cafe.

"Hey. I know you said everything is fine, but it's got to be hard to be away from..." He leaned in and whispered, "... Gavin, but school is almost over. You should be out living, having fun, and enjoying your last days at university. How about we go dancing tonight? For old times' sake?" He nudged me with his shoulder, his eyes glinting.

I couldn't help but smile when Nicholas looked at me with those clear blue eyes that sparkled with joy.

I groaned. "I'm tired. It's been such a long week."

"So, sleep in tomorrow. You have no classes in the morning. Please join me. It will be fun and will keep your mind off him."

Nicholas did have a point— a very good point. "Fine."

He fist-pumped the air. "Pick you up at seven?"

"Perfect."

At exactly seven, I opened the door on a stunned Nicholas, his hand frozen mid-knock.

"You're getting good at that." He smiled.

"Maybe, or maybe it is because your gifting is so dang

powerful, it's hard not to know when you're close."

He chuckled, which morphed into a deep belly laugh, a laugh I loved and one that I could not resist joining. He wiped the tears from his eyes with the heels of his hands.

"This is for you." he pulled a Christmas rose from his lapel and handed it to me. As soon as my hands touched it, the flower glowed and I placed it in my hair.

Nicholas stood there, his mouth hanging open in shock. "Where did you learn to do that?" he breathed.

"Here at school, silly." The black fringe of my skirt tickled my thighs as I walked to grab my purse. Nicholas held out his arm and I took it.

Every inch of the dance floor was full of bodies. It appeared we weren't the only ones seeking relief from final exams through unabashed dancing. The air in the club thickened as perspiration mingled with body heat. I was sweaty and having the time of my life when Shai surprised me. He strode into the club with Lana and Brantley in tow. I squealed in delight and ran up to them, grabbing Lana's hands and pulling her to the center of the dance floor.

"Do you remember any of the moves I taught you that day before Carnival?" Lana leaned in and yelled over the music.

"The ones that women traditionally only do for other women in celebration?" I asked.

"Yes!" Lana's eyes ignited. "I'll be right back." She weaved in and out of bodies with such precision, it was as if she had no bones in her body. She reached the music master and talked animatedly with him. Within a few minutes, she was back at my side.

We all continued to dance. Well, all of us except Shai, who

leaned against a pillar on the sidelines, a drink in his hand as he watched. A gorgeous, voluptuous redheaded woman with aqua-colored eyes tapped him on the shoulder, then pointed to the dance floor.

I giggled as Shai's face looked horrified. He hated dancing, or so he said. Nicholas informed me it was because Gavin used to make fun of him for it. Shai believed he was a terrible dancer when in reality, he was amazing and Gavin was just jealous.

I felt bold tonight. Maybe it was the sweet drink I'd had or maybe it was all the dancing. Regardless, Shai needed to let go a little. I walked over to them.

"Hi, I'm Mara." I held out my hand to the mystery woman.

"Noeleen," she responded, her ruby red lips spreading into a smile.

"What a pretty name. Shai, don't be rude. Bring her over."

"Mara," he said, his eyes wide and pleading.

"Sorry, Noeleen. Shai is, well, shy. He needs some guidance with dancing."

"I am a patient woman." The corners of her lips quirked.

Shai scowled at me, but I could sense that he fancied this woman. He allowed her to pull him to the center of the checkered floor. They danced well together and I smiled so hard, my cheeks lifted, obstructing my sight. After watching for a few minutes, we all joined them. We carried on this way until the music master made an announcement.

"Men, form a circle around the room. All ladies to the center of the dance floor, please." Everyone looked at one another, confusion settling over our brows, but we moved as directed.

Doom, da, doom, doom. The bass rattled, reverberating in my chest. Doom, da, doom doom, ting! Doom. Da, doom, doom, ting ting, badda doom. Without hesitation, Lana and I fell into step, our hips lifting and dropping to each bass note, our heads sliding side to side on the high brass notes. More and more women joined as the men whooped and hollered in approval, encouraging us.

The music continued to add to the beat, increasing in tempo. Our bodies undulated, stomped, shimmied, slid, lifted, and dropped.

When we finished, the crowd of men erupted and all the ladies bowed. A sudden pull in my belly, a longing ache, flustered me. I searched over my shoulder and found Gavin standing in one of the booths that overlooked the dance floor from above, penetrating me with his gaze.

He said nothing but held up an envelope with a red wax seal on it, then vanished.

"I have to go, guys," I yelled over the raucous crowd.

"Right now?" Lana asked.

"Yes, I'm sorry." I worried my bottom lip and turned to Nicholas. "Thank you for a great night. I'll see you all tomorrow."

I sprinted in the direction I last saw Gavin. Following his trail, and relying on the connection between us to guide me. It led me outside of the club, where I expected to find him, but he was nowhere to be seen. I raced back to the apartments and reached the elevators and as I pressed the call button, time seemed to stand still. I abandoned the elevator and forcefully swing open the doors to the rear stairwell propelling myself up the six flights of stairs to Gavin's floor. I peeked out into the hallway, making sure the coast was clear.

I raised the back of my hand to rap on the door, but it swung open and I was pulled forcefully inside. The lights were off, but I was not scared. I could recognize Gavin's gifting anywhere and under any conditions.

Gavin stood behind me, his chest so close to my back, the heat of him warmed me and his breath tickled my ear as he whispered, "I thought I might burst if I went another second without you in my arms."

Calmly, I took a step forward. Keeping my back to him, I reached behind me and slowly slid the zipper of my dress down.

"Light for me, my love," I said over my shoulder.

And he did.

Gavin played with my hair. "I wish you could stay the night, but my dad is coming tomorrow instead of me going home. He will be here early."

My stomach sank a little knowing I would have to soon leave the cocoon of his warmth.

"Five more minutes?" I asked.

He snuggled in closer and gave me a lingering kiss on my neck. "I will never get used to how you always smell like fresh oranges and ocean breezes."

Mara: Full of Surprises

I SAT BRIGHT-EYED AND SMILING at the cafe with Nicholas, Shai, Lana, and Brantley. They recapped the latter parts of the night I'd missed.

"Shai, how did things end with you and Noeleen?" I asked.

Shai's cheeks turned bright red.

"She gave him her number," Lana answered. Then, she reached over the table and tore yanked down the collar of his shirt. A number scrawled in black ink covered his chest.

Lana giggled.

"That well!" I laughed, and the table joined in.

Nicholas's body stiffened next to me, although he schooled his face. "Go for a walk with me?" he asked.

I scrunched up my face and dipped my brows. I didn't know what his problem was but my body knew Gavin was here.

My belly started doing this fun little flip recently when he was nearby. I smiled as I searched for him over my shoulder and then froze. Like winter's first frost, a thin sheath of ice formed around my lungs, and I instantly found it hard to breathe.

Gavin stood across the small cafe, laughing with his father and holding a woman's hand, his fingers entwined with hers. She had dark hair, curves for days, and brilliant violet eyes. She looked at Gavin through her long lashes, as if he was her whole universe, and he bent down to place a brief kiss on her hand.

When his lips touched her skin, the frost reached out from my lungs and encased my heart. I clutched my chest and Gavin froze.

"What is it, Gavin?" the young woman who was practically my exact opposite in every way asked. His eyes found mine, and he simply looked right through me. I could not register an ounce of recognition on his face.

"Nothing important," he said as he looked away. "Let me show you around campus."

As Gavin walked away, every bit of joy and love I had for him clouded over. I could see it happening, but couldn't access the emotions to feel anything. Nicholas gripped my arm, but he sounded too far away. Voices grew louder, but it was all just noise as I stared at the place Gavin had just vacated with *her*.

My view of the café flipped and rushed past me. In an instant I found myself outside. Nicholas set me down on a bench and crouched down, his eyes meeting mine directly. They glowed pink as he placed one hand on my heart and the other on my forehead. Then, everything went black.

My eyes fluttered open. *It was all a dream.* I smiled and stretched, turning onto my side. However, my smile slipped into a frown as four worried faces watched my every move.

I shifted to a seated position. "Why is everyone staring at me?"

"You don't remember?" Brantley asked, his brow furrowed beneath his thick-framed glasses.

"Remember what?"

"The part where you unleashed black smog and nearly snuffed out all the light in the cafe," Shai responded.

Lana punched her brother's arm and came to sit beside me. "Mara, you saw something at breakfast— something that seemed to really upset you. And then, well, we're not exactly sure what happened."

I bit my lower lip. "So, it wasn't a dream," I whispered. "Gavin really was with Ellasyn."

"That bastard," Nicholas growled.

"I think I just overreacted. I mean, he is just pretending. We have plans to get married just after graduation, once he secures a job at the World Bank."

Shai looked to his sister and she shook her head, her eyes wide. "She deserves to know," he said to Lana before addressing the room. "It was announced to the elite families today, that Gavin is betrothed to Ellasyn Cherith of Winchercheste Faction."

"You're lying." I dipped my hand under the collar of my shirt and held up the ring I wore around my neck. "He promised me we would be together. We..." My cheeks grew warm and I averted my eyes, suddenly feeling ashamed of what Gavin and I had shared.

"Go ahead, Mara. You guys, what..." Lana encouraged me.

I lifted my eyes to meet hers. "We became one," I confessed, instinctively placing my hands over my abdomen and chest, as if I could still feel his body pressing against mine, his warmth like the sun in my belly.

Lana's hand lifted to her mouth.

"I'll kill him," Nicholas spat through clenched teeth as he stormed out of the room.

"Go after him before he causes an even bigger mess," Lana fretted, addressing Shai and Brantley.

The boys hurried after Nicholas and Lana took my hand in hers. "I'm here for you. Whatever you need."

"I need to hear from Gavin, from his mouth, what is going on."

"Consider it done." Lana closed her eyes, and vibrant green lines emanated from them, tracing every vein in her body until she was consumed with light. I closed my eyes shielding myself against the intensity. When I reopened them, I saw two Lanas. One still sat on my bed with her eyes closed; the other stood, a warrior clad in a forest green cloak, typical attire of Cristes soldiers. The soldier nodded to the seated Lana, then raised the hood of the cloak and vanished through the apartment wall.

Beads of sweat formed on Lana's forehead and her chest rose and fell in a controlled rhythmic pattern. I sat there, awestruck, unsure of what was unfolding before me. I knew Lana was gifted, but I had never seen or heard of anything like this before.

My hand moved involuntarily to touch Lana's arm, but at the last minute, I snatched it back. I didn't know what would happen if I disrupted her. A scuffle resounded in the hall, and Lana's soldier-self materialized through the wall like a ghost before merging back into Lana's body. Lana stretched her neck, smiled, and opened her eyes.

"I was going to bring Gavin in here, but—"

Nicholas burst through the door, gripping Gavin by the scruff of his neck, and cutting Lana off.

"Everyone out!" he ordered. I knew Nicholas was a royal, and more powerful than any of us, but I had never seen him use his giftings to command a room before.

Lana rose swiftly and left, Brantley following. Shai took a step closer to Nicholas like he wanted to say something, but Lana's arm reached into the room and plucked her brother out, slamming the door shut behind her.

"What the heck, Nick? You cannot just barge into my room and take me against my will."

Nicholas growled at Gavin. "You owe her an explanation."

Gavin briefly glanced in my direction, but he didn't make eye contact before turning back to Nicholas. "Can you give us a few minutes alone, please?"

"No."

"It's OK, Nicholas." I interjected. "It will be fine. You don't live far if I need you." I nodded in assurance and tried to give him a sincere smile.

"No. I will go nowhere." To prove his point, he defiantly sat on the loveseat and crossed his arms. "I want to hear the tinsel and berry excuses you give her. She makes excuses for your fopdoodle too much as it is."

Gavin's eyes ignited, but Nicholas flicked his hand and they immediately returned to normal. Gavin flinched and it was the first time I saw a flicker of fear in him.

"Tell him, Gavin," I pleaded. "This has all just been a misunderstanding. I told our friends that you have just been pretending and I showed them the ring."

I stood and took a step toward him, my belly again pulled for him, like an invisible string yearning to tether to him. But Gavin refused to meet my gaze, and my anger splintered, causing tiny cracks within my wounded heart.

I dug my heels into the ground. "Tell-them-you-were-pretending. I am the one you are marrying."

Gavin looked at me then, his eyes glassy as tears filled them. "I was... at first," he whispered.

"And what *doessss* that mean." I hissed and I barely recognized my voice as my own.

"You know I didn't have a choice. My father is a stubborn man, but he really does love me and wants only the best for me."

I sank to my knees. "I don't understand." The frost enveloped me once again, swift and numbing. This time, I welcomed its chilling embrace.

"I still love you, Mara. But I would be lying if I didn't tell you that I have started to develop feelings for Ellasyn," Gavin confessed.

"Choose me," I nearly begged.

Nicholas sat bolt upright as if something I said shocked him. "Mara, why do you keep cradling your abdomen. Do you need me to bring you a bucket?"

"No. It's just my gifting getting stronger. Or perhaps I'm learning it better. I am more attuned to Gavin," I tried to explain.

"What do you mean, more attuned?" Nicholas's expression turned serious, leaning forward, his hands pressing into his thigh as if my answer would make or break him.

"Like a magnet... I feel a constant pull toward him, like I need to be near him at all times."

"And does that feeling disappear when you are right next to him?" Nicholas inquired.

"Yes." Relief washed over Nicholas and Gavin. "But only after my stomach does a little happy flip, with like little bubbles, and then it settles."

Nicholas swiftly moved to me and placed a hand on my abdomen. After a moment of concentration, he stood and deftly punched Gavin square on the jaw.

"Nicholas!" I screamed.

Gavin fell to the floor and spit blood. Our friends, who'd been waiting in the hall, burst into the room.

"What in thundernation, Nick?" Shai exclaimed, running to Gavin's side as he knelt on all fours.

Lana rushed over to me and helped me back to the bed.

"She's with child!" Nicholas bellowed.

"That's not funny," Shai said.

"Does it look like he's joking?" Lana shot back, shaking her head in disbelief at the naivety of her brother.

"Dang it, Gavin, you jobbernowl!" Shai muttered, helping him to stand.

Gavin used the sleeve of his shirt to wipe the blood from his lip. He walked over to me, an odd expression on his face. Then he sank to his knees before me and pressed his ear to my abdomen, his arms encircling me. Slowly the frost melted from my lungs, but it continued to encapsulate my heart, remaining cautious.

"We're going to have a baby," he breathed, his face brimming with joy.

"I don't know what you're so happy about, you jerk." Lana scooted away from him.

"Don't you guys see? This solves everything. I don't have to marry Ellasyn. Once my parents learn about the baby, they will have to give me their blessing."

"No," I said.

"What do you mean, no?" Gavin's brow furrowed, his chin jutting out in confusion.

"I don't want to be your second choice. I don't want the baby to be the reason you choose me. Choose me because you want to be with me more than *her*. Choose me because we are your family—" I gestured to our friends in the room— "And because you trust that we will love and support you, despite your father's threats and persuasions."

Gavin's gaze softened. "You are only my second choice because this baby is my first choice. I won't do to you what your father did to your mother."

Just like that, he had me wrapped around his finger again. I flung my arms around his neck and squeezed him tight.

"Nicholas, will you please heal his jaw?" I asked, but when I looked up, all I saw was Nicholas's retreating back as he stormed out of the room. Reluctantly, I stepped away from Gavin.

"It's fine. I deserved it." Gavin rubbed at the red splotch on his jaw that was quickly turning deep blue. "I've been a jerk. I won't see Ellasyn again. I'll figure everything out during my last few trips home." He pulled me back in for a hug. "Our original plan still stands. We just have to be patient a little longer, and then we can get married and do this right." I smashed my lips to his.

"Ow." he winced, his smile peeking through his pain.

I pulled back. "Oops. Sorry."

"Is it just me or is anyone else feeling a little whiplash?"

"Mind your business, Shai." Lana punched him in the shoulder. "Let's check on Nick and give these two some alone time."

As the door closed behind them, I turned to Gavin and asked, "Where is your dad staying?"

"He left for home about an hour ago. Ellasyn went with him."

My instincts prodded me to ask why he hadn't come to me as soon as they left, but I kept my mouth shut and pushed the thought away.

The next week, he came with me to see the university's maternity healers who confirmed the pregnancy. Thankful for doctor-patient confidentiality, we did not have to worry about our news reaching Mr. Frosters before we were ready to share it. According to the healer, I was only about eight weeks pregnant, and he reassured us it would be a while before I would start to show.

We were overjoyed to hear the strong heartbeat. The healer's assistant gave me the recording of it, and I couldn't wait to play it over and over again. This child was already cherished. It would have a mother *and* a father who both loved it and did not see it as a burden.

The next month flew by. We still had to keep our distance, but Gavin had been very attentive, writing me at least two letters a day. We were only a day away from graduation, but I found myself even more depressed because Gavin and I would be separated for most of the summer. He'd be back home and I would stay on campus in my apartment. At least I had full access to the labs under the permission of Professor Avent. Gavin would have offered to stay if he hadn't felt so strongly about securing that position at the bank. It was important to him that he provide the very best for me and our baby.

Shai kept his distance. Tensions were high between Nicholas and Gavin, and Shai likely didn't want to be put in the middle of them. At least I still had Lana. She called regularly to check in and see how I was doing. It was nice to share with her how I really felt about being pregnant. Because once the shock wore off, I got a little scared. Talking with Lana helped me through that.

Now, I was overjoyed about my upcoming wedding and becoming a mother. But these weeks had been hard on me and a piece of my heart felt as though it were missing. Nicholas had not spoken to me since he discovered my pregnancy and I knew he was deliberately avoiding me. Because his giftings were so attuned to me, they allowed him to sense my presence from a great distance. This gave him the advantage of being able to ensure we never had to cross paths.

On graduation day, a day that was supposed to be full of joy and celebration, I found myself utterly alone. Gavin's family was in attendance, so instead of sharing in each other's joy, we had to pretend like we didn't even know each other. I had to watch him march across the stage, collect his accolades, and worry that I'd let my eyes linger on him for a little too long. The only thing keeping me going was hope. Soon, our plan would come to fruition, and we could openly be together.

Graduation was also the first time I'd laid eyes on Nicholas since he ran out of my room. He looked a little leaner, the air around him palpable with authority. I walked up to him after the ceremony, but one of his guards halted me.

"Nicholas, please. Can we talk?"

He looked at me and dropped his head before turning his back to me.

Queen Nicole gave me a sad smile. She looked over her shoulder and when Nicholas was distracted by the king, she glided over to me.

"He just needs a little time, dear. You mean a lot to him. Your shoes have really never been easy to wear, have they?"

I shook my head, averting my gaze to try to blink the tears from my eyes before they could spill down my cheeks.

"Come now, no crying. I am so very proud of you." The queen hugged me. "For you and the baby." She smiled as she released me and handed me a note and a key with a ribbon on it. Then she patted my belly and walked away.

I spent the rest of the day and evening alone in my apartment.

Mara: Fall of Mara

THE SUMMER HAD BEEN ANNOYINGLY HUMID, and I suspected my newfound intolerance to heat was due to my changing hormones. Something else that annoyed me? Nicholas still would not speak to me, even though he, too, remained in his apartment right down the hall from me all summer. He was angry with me for so easily accepting Gavin back into my life, but deep down I knew he still cared and wanted to keep an eye on me. Why else would he choose to stay here over the summer while everyone else had left?

I was lonely. The last time I had seen Gavin was when he visited me in the wee hours of the morning the day after graduation to say goodbye for the summer. Now, six weeks later, my abdomen was starting to protrude, but only enough for me to notice. I only had to hang on for just one more month. Then Gavin and I would be reunited.

Why do these last weeks feel like an eternity?

I made my usual stop at the student mailboxes, just as I did every day after lab. Today, though, I was in a particularly good mood because I had been making great progress with my giftings. I was on the precipice of figuring out how to amplify my powers to an extent greater than had ever been seen before. My confidence soared. I inserted my small gold key into the lock and turned it, then reached inside and pulled out a pristine white envelope. A red wax seal donned the back. Giddy excitement rushed over me, and I hurried to my apartment to open it.

Mara:

I cannot in good conscience continue this charade. I tried, I really did, to choose you, for the sake of the baby, but Ellasyn has won my heart. I cannot pretend to be yours any longer. I fought it with everything I had, but my father was right. Though we had an undeniable match, Ellasyn is my true mate, a bond that trumps even the best of matches. I now realize that we would have never worked. We would only be settling instead of achieving greatness for ourselves.

Ellasyn and I will be united in a public ceremony in just a few short months this November. My parents know about the baby. For your cooperation, we will always make sure the child is well taken care of. It will want for nothing. I can only hope that you find love like I have one day. A true mated pairing is a special gift, and I could not live with myself if I got in the way of your happiness. We can discuss how we will share time with the baby once I return from my honeymoon.

With love,

Gavin

I didn't remember going to Nicholas's. In fact, there was a whole week of time that just vanished. I finally understood my mother's pain. How she could just sit and stare all day at nothing and when she'd come to, she'd have no recollection of the day or time.

"Nicholas?" I whispered. My throat burned with the effort of his name.

He stirred awake from the chair he'd been sleeping in next to my bed.

"Mara? Thank Eira you're back. I thought I'd lost you," he breathed, his eyes red and voice rough.

"I want to shower."

He ran to the bathroom and started the water. He came back for me, lifting me from the bed and then carried me. His hand slipped into the water and when he seemed satisfied with the temperature, he sat me on the vanity. "I'll be right outside if you need anything."

I only had enough energy to nod. He walked out and I slowly turned to face myself. A stranger with bright orange irises stared back at me. I placed my hand on my cheek, my nails much too long. And my hair... No longer was it golden like sunshine. Instead, it was devoid of color, white like snow. I screamed.

Nicholas burst through the door. "What is it? Are you alright?"

"No, I'm not. What— what happened to me?" I asked, staring at my face in disbelief as tears streamed down my cheeks.

As if it pained him to say, he answered, "We are not exactly sure."

"Who is 'we'?" I choked out.

"I got in touch with my parents and they immediately sent Nolan. Shai, Lana, and Brantley have come too. We are all here for you."

"He, he left me. He...left me." My voice, a mere whisper, bore the crushing weight of my shattered heart.

Nicholas took small, slow steps toward me. He looked exhausted. Worse, I could feel his fear bubbling to the surface of his skin like I'd scream again or run away if he moved too quickly.

"I know. Let's get you showered, alright?"

"Can you help me?" Normally, I'd have been embarrassed at the idea of a man, let alone my best friend, seeing me naked. But I felt nothing, the numbness a welcome reprieve from anguish.

Nicholas looked uncomfortable, but then he stood straighter and schooled his face.

"I can get Lana in here."

"No. It has to be you. I only trust you."

Slowly he peeled away hair that had crusted onto my skin from dried tears.

Next, he stood behind me and bent to grab the hem of the shirt I had worn the day I got the letter. As if changing a baby, he moved swiftly and with care. It was over my head in a brief moment and I inhaled deeply, feeling as if a weight had been lifted. His fingers deftly pulled my skirt down and he paused. He reached around me and placed his strong hand over my swollen abdomen.

"We will get through this, together. Your baby needs you. I will be here, always. You are not alone and you *both* will be loved. You are family." As if the baby liked what he had to say, it gave his hand a little nudge.

Nicholas let out a small chuckle. I guess I laughed a little on the inside. But I was just cold. Too cold. I began to shiver. He quickly finished undressing me and led me into the shower. He stepped in fully clothed in his joggers and t-shirt and proceeded to wash my body and hair for me.

I closed my eyes and when I awoke again, it was night and my abdomen was a little bigger. I spotted Nicholas, who was fast asleep.

"I should have chosen you."

Nicholas stirred in his chair. "Hmmm?" he mumbled, clearly exhausted.

"I should have let myself choose you. When I first met you, there was no question you were good. I also knew that you liked me and it scared me. I liked you, too. A lot. But you were special. That was obvious. Someone as special as you deserves the best. You were and always have been too good for me."

Nicholas shifted uneasily. "That's not—"

"Please, let me say this. You need to hear it." He pressed his lips into a hard line and I continued. "I wasn't sure what to make of Gavin at first. Sure, he was attractive and persistent and charming..." I choked on the last words. Nicholas handed me a cup of water without saying a word and I greedily took a sip. "And he was your friend. By default, I felt I could trust him. I was not fully into the relationship with him until I found out you were heir to the throne, the Prince of Cristes. At that moment, it was clear that you were made for greatness, so I made the decision to go all-in with Gavin."

Nicholas looked as if I had struck him, and tears fell down

my cheeks. Black stains hit the comforter like ink drops on the pages of a diary.

"I fell hard, really hard for him."

"Time. You just need time. I'm still here." Nicholas reached for my hand and held it firmly. "I've never stopped caring for you, Mara. I... I love you. Please, let me in. You are my everything, and my parents have already accepted you as their daughter."

"I wish I could turn back time," a sob burst forth from me, "but it's too late."

Nicholas squeezed my hand. "It's never too late."

"It is for me!" I screamed and he flinched away, clapping his hands over his ears. A crack formed down the mirror in the bathroom. "Gavin broke me. I gave him my whole heart and now, I'm...empty."

Fear radiated off of Nicholas like the stench of stale garbage clinging to the can long after it had been taken out.

"You don't have to love me," Nicholas whispered. "It will be enough if you just let me love you."

I pretended I didn't hear him, and so I continued. "I want to leave here. I *need* to leave here. Everywhere I look, I see, smell, and taste *him*." I finally let my eyes fall to Nicholas.

"We will do whatever you want, but one last thing—" He wrapped his arms around me— "On my honor, I will make sure he will never be able to hurt you again. I will give my life before I let you hurt because of him."

I nodded. Little did he know, but Gavin would be the one to hurt next time. I would make sure of it.

Nicholas: Something Dark

MARA HELD A SPECIAL PLACE in Mother's heart. The key she gifted Mara on graduation was to one of our apartments in Noorjove with a breathtaking view of Berfin Park, our capital's largest and most enchanting park.

Mara was right. Moving back to Cristes, away from anything reminding her of Gavin, seemed to help her. She appeared to snap back to her old self, though her physical changes — the orange eyes and platinum hair — remained. I worried for her daily. By all appearances, she acted normal, laughed, and looked like she slept well, but I felt in my gut a darkness lingering, a wisp teasing me of her brokenness.

Mara would disappear for long periods of time and claim she was out getting exercise in order to maintain her fitness during pregnancy. But she never smelled quite right when she returned. Instead of smelling like the outdoors and her signature scent of fresh oranges, a charred aroma clung to her. Her bright orange eyes began to dim, and with irises so dark they were nearly indistinguishable from her pupils. I needed to find out what sort of trouble she was getting herself into.

"Can I join you on your walk today?" I asked, hoping she would accept my company.

"I prefer to walk alone. It allows me to clear my head and go at the speed that I want." Mara responded quickly as if she'd rehearsed this answer.

"Are you sure? I would follow your lead."

Her eyes sparked like she was momentarily frustrated by me, but calmed immediately. "I appreciate the offer, I really do. But no, thank you."

"Alright then. See you Friday for game night?"

"Of course! I wouldn't miss it." She smiled at me and stood, one hand on her lower back.

She was definitely showing now. "May I?" I extended my hand toward her belly.

"You know you are welcome to greet this baby anytime you want. It already loves you."

I kneeled and held each side of her protruding stomach in my hands and spoke directly to the baby. "Hi, little one. It's me, your Uncle Nick. Be good for your mama. I will be back tomorrow." The baby kicked and punched where my hands laid and I chuckled.

"This baby already has you wrapped around its finger." Mara laughed.

"I wouldn't want it any other way. Oh, and Nolan will be by early on Friday for your six-month check-up."

I left the apartment but did not go home. I met up with Shai around the corner.

"Are you ready?" I asked him.

"Yes. Are you sure this is a good idea? She won't like it if she finds out what we are doing."

"Then don't get caught," I remarked.

"*Ha, ha,* very funny."

"Alright, you know what to do."

"Yes, we've been over this a hundred times. I follow her to find out where she goes every day. If anything suspicious happens, I am to contact you immediately," Shai rattled off.

"Exactly. And, there she is. Go! Talk to you later."

The rest of the week dragged. I spent my days in the castle shadowing Father and Mother, learning what it took to be a ruler. Friday came at last, and I took the carriage over to Mara's with Nolan.

"Nolan, Nicholas! Come in." Mara wore a navy-blue sundress, its empire waist accentuating her belly and its neckline emphasizing her much fuller breasts.

"Would you like to know the sex?"

"You can tell that?" I asked, surprised.

"Not always, but this little one is quite loud." The corners of Nolan's mouth rose and his eyes crinkled.

"Yes!" Mara clapped her hands.

"You are...having..."

"Oh, come on man! The suspense is killing me," I said impatiently, my hands gripping the hair on the sides of my head.

Nolan and Mara laughed, and I hit my forehead with the heel of my hand.

"... a girl!" Nolan exclaimed, removing his hands from her

belly. "And she is very happy and healthy. She also loves you, Nicholas."

I could not contain my grin and nearly crumpled into a sobbing mess. Nolan continued his exam of Mara, checking her heart, her feet, and measuring her belly.

"Well, I am finished. I shall return in a month's time for our next checkup and to discuss your birthing plans."

"My what?" Mara asked.

"Do not stress. I will go over all of your options, and Nicholas will be here to help you decide," Nolan assured her.

"Thank you both for coming." Mara yawned and stretched. "I think I'm just going to nestle up here on the couch and take a nap. Are you alright to let yourselves out?"

"Of course, Madame Mara." I eyed her suspiciously.

"What is it, Nicholas?" she asked.

"Should I stay for game night?"

"Oh, for Eira's sake. I completely forgot!" she tried to sit up on the couch. A knock on the door diverted my attention, but Nolan was already on his way to answer it. I turned back to her.

"No, you seem exhausted. I will just tell Shai—"

"Tell me what?" he came bounding in, holding a small stack of games and case of fizzy sodas in his hands.

"Mara needs some rest. How about you and I go visit the pub, just us guys tonight?"

The old Shai would have complained about having made a trip all the way to the center of town. Instead, he stepped around me to get a clearer view of Mara, worry etched in his furrowed brows. "Are you feeling alright?"

"Oh, I'm fine. Just tired from growing this little princess.

Want to say hi to her before you leave?"

"Your intuition says it's a girl?" Shai asked, sitting on the edge of the couch next to Mara.

"No, Nolan told me just before you got here."

Shai beamed and placed his face near Mara's belly. "Hello, sweet girl. I cannot wait to meet you." He pressed a hand to her belly and lit up softly when the baby nudged him.

Nolan took the carriage home, as he was unable to join us at the pub, so Shai and I walked to Tasi's to grab a cup of cheer and dinner.

As the hostess led us to a table in the front, Shai stilled, wringing his hands.

"Would it be too much trouble for that private booth in the back?"

"Of course, Lord Abishai. Anything for you and the crown prince."

We sat and Shai swiftly caught the elbow of the young lady. "We are not to be disturbed for at least ten minutes. When we close our menus, that will be your cue that we are ready to order."

The dark-haired girl bit her lip, curtsied, and rushed off.

"Well, great. Now you scared off the staff."

Shai leaned in, his eyes dark and focused. I bent toward him.

"I have found where Mara goes every day. Nick, you are not going to like this."

My brows shot up. "What is it, cousin?"

"She is visiting the same building day after day...in the Abaddon District."

My heart sank. The Abaddon district was mostly

unoccupied. Many of the buildings became uninhabitable after The First Fall when my grandfather and his armies dismantled the uprising. The only reason it still stood was to act as a visual reminder of what rebellion against Cristes looked like.

The gifted service guardians were called there every now and again to respond to various incidents that all had one thing in common: suspicious or dangerous activity.

As if he knew what I was about to do, Shai grabbed my forearm and sent a jolt of warning into me, effectively stopping me from jumping out of my seat and running to Mara.

"Do not make a scene," he warned under his breath. "We have to be careful about this. I was not able to see anything concrete...yet. We need to get inside and figure out what we are dealing with here. If she suspects us, we may never know."

I ran my hand through my hair. "Critosi," I muttered.

"Easy there. You never curse."

I crossed my arms over my chest and quirked an eyebrow. *Seriously? You are going to comment on that of all things right now?*

Shai shook his head and smirked. "Listen, the sun is almost set. Let us eat and have a drink. We can use the time to plan, maybe scope it out tonight, and go in another time."

"No way. We go in tonight."

"Nick, we are not prepared."

"So be it. Every moment Mara continues with whatever it is she is doing is one moment too many. We both saw what happened that day in the cafe when Gavin walked in with Ellasyn. Then he broke her heart again with that letter, and..." I trailed off and gulped.

Shai shuddered. "Fine. We go in tonight."

On our way to Abaddon, we stopped in Rein's Pro Shop. With ten minutes to closing, Shai and I decided to split up. I grabbed dark clothing and sacks while Shai gathered tools.

"How do you want to play this?" Shai asked. "If anyone sees us, it could be very bad for—"

"Yeah, yeah. I know. We wouldn't want anyone to think you and I were up to something."

"Well, yes. But also, it could cause a headache for your parents. I may be a royal too, but *you* are the crowned prince and an only child and if anything were to happen to you..." he sighed heavily. "Are you sure you want to risk all that for her?"

I sucked in my cheeks to stop my jaw from twitching. He was right. If we got caught, the consequences would be far reaching. Technically, I had been the model citizen and leader in training since birth. One infraction on my record would not mean my imminent downfall, but it would be a serious offense nonetheless. And if I were caught sneaking around an area where rebellion against the crown occurred, it would cause much gossip and doubt as to where my loyalties lay.

"If you think any harder, you are going to have a permanent crease between your brows," Shai joked, trying to lighten the mood.

I shifted my attention back to Shai. "You don't have to do this, but I do. If it was you in Mara's situation, I would not hesitate."

"I figured you would say that. I am definitely coming with you. And it just so happens that I have a plan."

Shai ran up to a street vendor on the outskirts of the town center and procured two more large drinks of cheer.

"Follow me."

I did as he commanded and trailed him down a narrow alley void of any artificial light and Watchers.

"We should change into our gear here," Shai said. "The less recognizable we are as we walk to Abaddon, the better."

"You do realize that I have a small guard on me at all times, right?"

Shai rolled his eyes. "I know. That is why I chose this alley. The black pants, shirts, and hooded cloaks will camouflage us. Not to mention, it's in stark contrast to what we are wearing now." He gestured to our light-colored khakis and sweaters.

"Now what?" I asked after changing and shoving my clothes into the velvet bag. Shai responded by handing me a heavy sack and clip. I copied him and fastened it securely around my waist.

"Follow me."

"Are you going to actually tell me what we are doing instead of ordering me around?" I asked, a hint of irritation lacing my words.

"The less noise we make the better," he whispered, then grabbed my arm and we slowly disappeared into the shadows in the back of the alley.

He looked once more over his shoulder and then ducked behind a large pile of crates.

"Help me lift this."

I squatted and saw a large metal grate. My muscles tensed and bulged as we pulled together. With a creak and moan, the grate lifted, and Shai slithered in. I joined right after and together we pulled the metal lid back down.

Shai's eyes ignited, providing light. I followed his lead

and my eyes created a soft glow to match his.

"Where the heck are we?" I asked, somewhat amazed by the sight before me.

"This tunnel was dug by the Black Rose rebels. It leads straight to the district." Shai answered as he trudged ahead.

"How do you know that?"

"I like architecture. Plus, my grandad spoke about them. I taught myself all about these tunnels a few years ago."

I smirked at him. "So, all those times I wanted you to work out with me early in the morning, you actually *were* studying."

"I wouldn't say *every* time." We both chuckled.

We continued through the tunnel, careful not to run our hands along the rough surface. I'd already cut part of my hand on a stone that jutted out. Shai was able to heal it for me, but we did not want any more incidents slowing us down.

Time passed with no way to determine how long it had actually been, but it seemed to take forever as my back ached from having to hunch down. Finally, a cool breeze brushed our faces.

"We must be getting close," I observed.

"Yes. I think it should be just around that small bend up ahead."

We reached the end and I was finally able to fully stand. I stretched as I eyed a metal door that stood askew from having broken off one of its hinges.

Shai tried to open it, but it would not budge. I offered my assistance, but still the door did not move. Upon further inspection, I discovered it wedged between the rock ceiling and floor, nestled within perfect notches.

I closed my eyes and took a deep breath. The energy of the room buzzed in anticipation and I felt Shai readying his powers to match mine.

"On the count of three. One, two, three!" We opened our eyes, and a blast of blue and green light hit the door. Unknowingly, we had both focused on the same upper notch.

"Move!" I yelled at Shai and tugged his cloak with such force, we both somersaulted backward.

BOOM!

"I'm not sure if I should thank you or punch you," Shai said, rubbing his shoulder and neck.

"My vote is *thank you*, seeing as that heavy door was half a second from crushing you."

"Thank you," he mumbled.

"You are most welcome. Now, let's go uncover Mara's secrets."

We climbed over the door and entered what looked like a dilapidated basement. Cobwebs painted the rafters, their silk and the eyes of its spinners glinting in our light.

"I hate spiders," Shai grumbled.

I was already on my way up the stairs when I approached a wooden step that was completely missing.

"These are definitely not safe. We should go one at a time."

"Agreed. Lead the way, Your Highness," Shai teased.

I stepped gingerly, tapping the wood with my foot first to check for rot. I made it to the top without incident, and Shai met me a moment later.

"This appears to be the Black Rose's headquarters."

"How could you possibly know that?" Shai asked.

I pointed to a faded canvas over the broken mantle of a fireplace where a large Black Rose insignia had been painted.

"Good observation, cousin." He gave me the side eye.

Soft shuffling sounded above us, and our heads jerked up. "Animals?" I whispered.

Shai shrugged then pointed at himself, then to me, then to the upstairs. He was right; we needed to check it out to be certain.

We dimmed our eyes so that we could just see where we placed our feet. The main floor was vacant. Every window's glass was broken; shards were strewn about the floor, glittering in the moonlight.

The shuffling noise sounded again, clearer this time. I placed my finger over my mouth and pointed to the next flight of stairs. Shai gave me a curt nod.

We moved slower than a sloth chasing a snail as we climbed the stairs. We could not afford for even the slightest moan to escape the stairs we treaded.

When we reached the top, my stomach coiled tighter. A flash of platinum hair at the end of the hall flickered in my vision, and I crouched behind a large drape-covered chair, pulling Shai along with me.

I shut off my internal flashlight. On my hands and knees, I peeked around the chair's wooden feet and focused my gaze on the small opening in the door at the end of the wide hall. Sandpaper coated my tongue and throat, my nerves soaring as I waited. I prayed I was just seeing things. But then, Mara walked past the open door.

Nicholas: Secrets

THE ACHE IN MY KNEES clued me in to the fact that we must have been in our crouched positions for a long while. Odd gifting colors of red and orange, sometimes by themselves, sometimes in combination with an unfamiliar green, flickered in from the hall. The room we were hiding in was large and nearly fossilized; each piece of furniture, decor, and tapestry covered in dust and cobwebs and frozen in time.

I had not moved from my position, but Shai had shuffled behind me to the back wall, where a large chest obscured him from view. His head was tilted back, his eyes closed. As we waited, I realized my connection to Mara was completely blocked. I attempted to use my gifting to connect with her and gain a sense of what she might be doing, but each time I tried, an invisible, impenetrable wall prevented me from reaching her.

After numerous attempts, I tried to rely on my other senses instead. I could see nothing through the walls, and could only catch a brief glimpse of Mara every now and again if she passed through the small opening in the door. My eyes slammed shut in frustration. *What in Eira's realms are you doing, Mara?* My head tipped to the side as I strained to listen for clues, but the only sounds that registered were faint mumblings.

I bit down hard on my bottom lip, directing my focus to the sharp pain and metallic taste that coated my tongue; otherwise, I feared I would burst through the room and confront her right then and there.

Both my knees and my nerves were shot. Slowly, I slid over to Shai and joined him at the back wall. He remained still and silent, like a statue that had always been a permanent fixture in the room. My breathing slowed as I focused solely on counting my breaths.

When a loud creak sounded from down the hall, it took every ounce of training I ever had with my father's top spy not to react. I was surprised that Shai, too, remained motionless, wondering if he'd actually fallen asleep. Determined to keep my emotions in check, I cautiously opened my eyes and witnessed Mara nearly floating across the room to the stairs, her eyes an eerie blood-orange. She moved without sound, swift and agile, as if she'd been to and from this room a million times before, effortlessly navigating through the darkness.

My heart crashed against my ribs, and pressure throbbed in my temples.

"We can go in now," Shai whispered to me. I didn't know

how he knew it was time, but I trusted him enough to follow his lead.

I made my way over to the door, placed my hand on the rough wood, and gently pushed. A gush of air exhaled over me, as if the room were alive. A sickly-sweet scent clung to the air and I doubled over, choking down vomit. Beads of cold sweat formed on my brow and the back of my neck, nausea creeping around my skin over and over again.

Shai lifted his hands in the air, his body dimly lit, then he began to brighten.

"No!" I warned. "We don't want to draw any attention."

Shai nodded and dialed down his wattage to a muted pink. He hustled over to me and held one hand over my nose and mouth. I instantly felt better, and when he removed his hand, a thin cloud of pink remained.

"These will not last long, so we need to hurry," Shai said as he formed another cloud to shield his breathing from the scent of decaying flesh that permeated the air.

My guard was officially up, my instincts leading me where I needed to look. I took two long strides and stood in the center of the room. At first glance, everything appeared normal, but the place hummed with a strong magic. I called on my golden gifting. Without warning, my right arm shot out to my side, followed by my left. I fought to bring my hands together in front of me, my muscles straining as the lingering magic in the air resisted my gifting.

"Shai, a little help, please?" My arms vibrated with effort as I continued to force my hands toward each other.

Shai was in front of me in a flash, his hands over mine, pushing them together. A sphere of crackling, golden light sparked between my hands.

I waited, my body near collapsing, until the faintest trickle of a recent memory from the room floated by— a tiny fleck no larger than a speck of dust. I did not hesitate and threw the golden orb at it.

The orb flew true and when it made contact with the memory, it exploded. Glittering flecks settled onto every surface revealing the loose shape of a body. The shape took on more detail as it morphed into someone we recognized, and Shai and I gasped as we watched a gold-dusted Mara flit about the room.

She sat on her knees, writing fiercely in a black leather book. Just to her side laid an envelope. I crouched down to inspect it and flinched. It was Gavin's breakup letter to her.

The memory that had taken shape shimmered and changed to show Mara plucking a petal off of the flower I'd seen her take out of her cottage the night she'd burned it down. The black rose she swore to Melchior that she did not possess. She placed the petal in a bowl and used a pumice stone to grind it. She inhaled, her eyes wildly igniting a blood orange. As soon as the light extinguished itself, she fell forward onto her hands and wretched, but instead of vomiting the contents of her stomach, she expelled black tendrils of shadow.

I walked over to peer into her notebook. I reached down, my hand disrupting the memory's shape for a moment, like I'd put my hand into a sand timer, and pulled up the floorboard where she sat. I reached into the hole and removed the black book.

I'd seen enough. I stood with my hands fisted and crossed my arms in front of my face. With one quick yank, my arms flung out and down, successfully slicing through the rain of glittery sand. The room went dark, save for the muted pink glow around our faces.

My hands trembled as I walked to a podium in the corner of the room, set the notebook down, and flipped through the contents. Mara's handwriting filled every inch of space. At first, the words looked like nonsense, just random scribbles of chaos. As the pages progressed, the writing began to flow like a song, and my skin crawled at its haunting melody.

"That can't possibly be—"

"Witchcraft," I answered for Shai, who was peering over my shoulder.

"But I thought..."

"That it died with the first generation? It would appear we were wrong." I sucked my bottom lip into my mouth and bit down.

"This can't be good."

"Mara has no idea what she is getting herself into." I sighed.

"What do you think she wants with all this?"

"Power. To feel in control." I scratched my chin. " Do you remember while working closely with Professor Avent in her last year, Mara learned that she could use natural elements to strengthen her power from them?"

"Yeah, but then why all the sneaking around?"

"Because she is experimenting," I answered.

"So?"

"Isn't it obvious? She is using materials of a dark nature to access her power and—"

Shai snatched the book from me. "She does not want us to

know what she plans to do with that power." His eyes fixated on what mine could not believe they were seeing.

"I have to stop her."

Nicholas: Public Humiliation

SHAI AND I MADE IT BACK THROUGH THE TUNNEL, to the alleyway, and back into the clothes we'd been wearing previously. Shai picked up the full glass of amber spirits he'd stashed and expertly gulped half of it. He let the rest spill down his shirt and onto his shoes. I followed suit.

We stepped out of the alley and shuffled back toward the pub, our arms flung over each other's shoulders like we were holding each other up. We only made it a few steps before my guards swooped in.

"Your Highness," Cobani's rough voice growled.

"Oh hey, Cooobi. Evvvverything alriiight?" I faked a slur and goofy smile.

"We are on strict orders to bring you back home. Lord Abishai, we had better see you home as well."

Shai stood gazing at the indigo sky, his eyes hooded as if a naked woman lay in the clouds. I could not help but truly laugh at his goofy grin. My guards cocked a brow at each other, then led us to the waiting carriage. Once the wheels and hoofs of the horses clicking and clanking against the cobblestone path provided enough noise to mask my voice, I leaned over to Shai.

"We should talk to Mara tomorrow."

He pointed at me. "*You* should. As I said, I need to warn Gavin."

"Fine. It's probably better this way. She won't feel ambushed."

I arrived home, expecting my parents to be livid that I'd slipped by my guards.

"Son, in here please," Father beckoned as the guards led me down the east wing to my chambers.

I continued the drunken charade and slapped on another goofy grin while barely opening my eyes.

Father paced in front of the brick fireplace, his hands clasped behind his back. He stopped short when he took in the sight of me.

"You may leave us," he spoke to the guards once they deposited me into a chair.

The door clicked and I closed my eyes.

"Ahh, to be young again," Father sighed. "Son, you have been such a blessing to your mother and me. You work hard, you train hard, you study, you're respectful, and you love the people you will one day rule over. I understand the need to blow off some steam and I can only assume you slipped your detail because you needed a little normalcy. Am I correct?"

I tilted my head back and sighed. "Am I that obvious?" *I hate lying to him.*

"I figured." He smiled, his eyes and face lighting up. He sat across from me on the small rounded ottoman and patted my knee. "I won't tell your mother about this. Promise you will not make it a habit, alright?"

"Courrrrsse, fahjur," I slurred.

He chuckled. "Let's get you to bed, son."

He helped me into my bed and I feigned instant sleep. After he left, I rolled over and stared up at the ceiling, trying to anticipate the many ways Mara might react when I revealed I knew of her plans and tried to stop her. Both defensive and offensive plays streamed through my mind, my brain conjuring up several different scenarios. However, none of them ended the way I wanted.

The castle was silent save for the *tick-tick-tick* of my clock charm embedded in the leather cuff at my wrist. Small trickles of dread seeped over my brain as each minute passed.

My room lightened and I turned my head to the window. The sky was streaked with oranges, reds, and pinks. I could not remember the last time I had been awake for the sunrise, and allowed myself to get lost in the beauty of the vivid colors. I showered and dressed for the day, waiting impatiently for a decent hour to strike so that I could go to Mara's.

My carriage rolled to a stop just outside the entrance to her apartment building. "Do you need assistance this morning, Your Highness?" My footman broke me from my trance.

"No, sorry. Just a little tired this morning." I gave him a tight smile and entered the building. I approached her door, lifted my fist, then turned back down the hall, repeating this process at least ten times. At this rate, I would leave a matted path in the carpet from her door to the lift. I shook out my appendages and rolled my neck, mustering the courage to face this head-on.

Mara, my sweet Mara, would confide in me and turn from this dark path. She would want to be and feel light again. She would accept the love my family and I, and our friends, were waiting to offer her with open arms.

I raised my fist again, but this time, the door swung open before I could knock.

"Ahhhh!" Mara jumped back.

I startled, tripping over my feet, and fell on my bum.

"Good grief, Nicholas! You scared me half to death!"

I did not move. My heart felt like it was lodged in my throat.

Mara doubled over laughing. "You-should-see-your face!" she breathed between snorts of laughter. I immediately relaxed and joined her.

"You're here early," she said when she'd finally calmed down. I stood and brushed off my rear.

"Yeah, I figured I would check in on you and see how you were feeling, make sure you were able to rest up."

"That is very sweet of you. Yes, I feel much better now, thank you. I was going to go for a walk in the park. Care to join me?"

My stomach growled. "Actually, can I treat you to breakfast first?"

"That sounds wonderful."

We strode through the park, Mara sipping on orange juice in her to-go cup, her free arm linked through mine. It was another gorgeous day and I chastised myself for worrying myself sick all night.

The sun warmed our skin, but the air held a slight crispness that awakened my senses. Fall is when the trees really showed off. Flowers of every color, shape, and size decorated them, their alluring scents floating on the air, waiting to bless the next person who walked by.

"Mara, there is something I wanted to talk to you about."

"No, the baby cannot be named Nicholas."

I laughed. "That is not what I was going to say."

"What do you think about Nicole?"

I stopped short. "That— that's my mother's name."

"I know." Mara leveled me with her gaze. "I owe her everything."

"She would love that." This was the Mara I knew. Maybe last night, something had happened that Shai and I couldn't see. Maybe Mara had learned just how bad witchcraft could be.

"I cannot wait to tell her. When will she be back from her tour?" Mara asked.

"My father said she should be back from Sint Anahera Island at the end of next month. Father is going to visit for a week and bring her home."

"I'm sure you miss her."

"I do. A lot, actually." I wished she were here with me right now. She would know what to say and how to help.

Mara stiffened against my arm, and I immediately ceased my steps.

"What is it?" I followed her gaze. "Cristosi." About fifteen yards in front of us stood Gavin, his fiancée, and their families.

Mara attempted to walk toward Gavin, a murderous intent darkening her eyes. I planted my feet and held tight to her, pulling her to a bench on the side of the wide, tree-lined path.

"Let me go," she seethed through gritted teeth.

"No. We need to talk."

"Let me go, or else—"

"Or else what? You will use your witchcraft on me?" I snapped. I had never spoken to her like this before.

Her face fell. "How did you—"

"That does not matter. What are you doing? You cannot harm Gavin, and Ellasyn has done nothing to you. That spell that you have conjured up— it will not end well. Witchcraft was banished for a reason."

"And why can't I? He has done worse to me." Tears welled in her eyes.

I clung to her hands. "He is a coward. He is not worth tainting everything you have worked for. Everyone will know it was you. Witchcraft changes a person. There is no going back from dark magic."

"I just—" She hiccupped. "I just want him to *see* me. To *see* our daughter."

"He is a fool. He doesn't deserve you. Furthermore, your daughter, my niece, deserves better. You remember what happened to your mother when she got mixed up with the Black Roses?"

Mara flinched as if I'd slapped her. I grabbed her hands again, stroking her knuckles with my thumbs.

"Gavin is like a brother to me. I may understand the why of his choices, but that does not mean I agree with them. I chose you. Please, bring back the Mara I know and love. Let her come back. She has a bright future."

Tears slipped down Mara's cheeks and she flung her arms around me. I held her close and stroked her hair, letting her sob into my shoulder.

"I've ruined your jacket," she sniffed. Red outlined her sad, puffy eyes.

"Nonsense. They are just tears. Come, let us get you back home." We stood but when we turned, Mr. Frosters blocked our path. I stiffened and rose to my full height.

"What are you doing here?" he snarled at Mara. I pushed her behind me.

"Please watch your tone, sir," I said flatly.

His lips ticked up in a sly grin. "Of course, Your Highness. I am sorry, I was caught unawares, is all. It is not every day your son's lying temptress tries to ruin his engagement."

"First of all, *sir*, Mara is not a temptress. You owe the lady an apology. Secondly, she is not a liar."

"I will not apologize to a halfling who spews lies and possesses my son's mind. My Gavin would not have chosen so poorly had she not engineered it that way. And that baby could be anyone's. A true Watcher would keep her legs closed until marriage."

Red. I saw red. "How dare you!" I bellowed. I charged at him, reeling my arm back to punch him square in the face. A hand encased my fist holding it prisoner.

"Nick?" Gavin stood before me. "What is going on?" Ellasyn and her family rushed over.

"Ask your father," I spat between clenched teeth.

Gavin brought my fist down and turned. "Father?"

"Nothing son, let's get back to the gazebo." Mr. Fosters put his arm around Gavin's shoulders, trying to move him away from me. "We do not wish to keep the photographer waiting."

I scoffed. "He owes Mara an apology. Scratch that— many apologies."

Gavin shrugged out of his father's hold and for the first time, he noticed Mara. His widened eyes traveled down her body and lingered on her swollen abdomen. She crossed her arms over it protectively and his face fell.

"Father—" Gavin's voice pierced the air. "Why is Mara still pregnant?"

Mr. Frosters narrowed his gaze at Mara. "It's not yours, son. It's been months. She is a whore."

"You told me she lost the baby on purpose, to spite me."

Mara came to stand next to me. "I could never have done such a thing and you should have known that." She opened her coat and cradled her belly. "Your daughter is alive and growing every day."

I felt Gavin's rage come to a boil in seconds as he advanced on his father.

"How could you?" I thought he'd scream bloody murder, but his voice, low and gravelly, was far more chilling.

"Gavin?" Ellasyn took a few careful steps toward him, entwining her fingers with his.

"Nick, can you help us have a private moment, please?" he asked.

My mind was reeling. Could Gavin really not have known she was pregnant this whole time? Did he really believe she would hurt their child? I guess now was as good a time as any to get some answers. My eyes ignited as I called on my giftings and I gave anyone within fifteen feet of us a shove backward. I let Mr. Frosters stay. He still needed to apologize.

"Ellasyn, this is Mara. The woman I told you about."

I thought Ellasyn might pass out, but then she shook her head and stood tall.

"It— it is nice to meet you, Mara."

Mara just stared at her trying to keep a brave face, but I could feel the pain she was in.

"It appears my father lied to me. Mara is still pregnant with... my daughter."

Ellasyn flicked her eyes to Mr. Frosters and then back to Mara. "We are so sorry. We had no idea."

"I got a letter. Right here. It says you knew and did not want anything to do with her." Mara reached in her bag and pulled it out. She handed it to Gavin.

He took it, his face paling more and more with each moment that passed as he read it.

"I did not write this," he whispered.

Mara bit her bottom lip and snatched the letter back.

Gavin whipped around to face his dad.

Mr. Frosters held his hands up in surrender. "Son, I only did what was best. I knew you loved Ellasyn, but you are too nice for your own good." He shook his head and again, leveled a menacing glare at Mara. "You would have stayed with this *trash* out of obligation and ruined your life."

"If your dad made this all up, then that is good news. Gavin, we can be together. We can be a family." Mara's face lit up. Gavin released Ellasyn's hand and as if in a trance, he reached out toward Mara's pregnant belly.

But then he stopped himself and took a step away from her.

"No, Mara. It's too late. I— I have fallen in love with Ellasyn. My father did not lie about that. But I would still like to be in my daughter's life. Let me—" he grabbed Ellasyn's hand again, "Let *us* take care of you and her."

Mara began to vibrate. Soon, her body shook as she processed what he said.

"I know you love me." She reached for his hand and he shook it off.

"I do love you. But, not like that."

"When? When did you stop loving me in *that* way?" She hugged herself and Gavin dropped his gaze.

"Mara, please. Don't ask me that. It's not going to help anything."

"Answer me. I deserve... No, I need to know." Mara's lips quivered.

"It's not that simple." Gavin tried again.

"Answer me, consarn it!" she shrieked and Ellasyn flinched.

Gavin tucked Ellasyn behind him and he turned ashen, like he would be sick. "The first time I met Ellasyn, I knew I already loved her, too because—"

"That cannot be true! You kept coming back to me. You would not have kept coming back if you didn't love me." Mara's sorrow was now full-fledged anger as her eyes burned into Gavin.

He set his jaw but refused to look at her. "I know you weren't brought up with much Watcher history—"

"Don't patronize me."

Gavin looked back at Ellasyn and she shook her head, pleading with him to stop. Silent tears streamed down her face as she tugged at his hand, urging him to leave with her. He caressed her cheek and turned back to face Mara.

"You can't escape a fated bond. Eira knows I tried. But Ellasyn is my true match, Mara. While I still value our friendship and will forever be grateful to you for giving me a child, it is Ellasyn who will be my wife," Gavin declared.

A knife felt like it pierced my heart. Gasping in pain, I spun on my heel searching for the source.

"Mara, don't!" I warned, noticing the black rose that she now gripped in her hand. But if she heard me, she made no attempt to heed my warning.

"You cannot play with heartsssss like they are toysssss to be disposed of once you grow bored," Mara sneered.

"I did not grow bored. I did not mean for this to happen. Please, believe me!" Gavin pleaded as he tried to reach for her.

Mara snarled and he immediately dropped his hand. I peered around her, expecting to see someone else, but no. That menacing sound came from my Mara, and I shivered.

"You are a coward," she spat at him. "This is your father's fault. He needs to learn his lesson first."

She bit into the black rose, chewed a few petals, and swallowed. She turned her now blazing orange eyes on Mr. Frosters. He took a step back. Mara smiled, black ink staining her lips and teeth. She held up her index finger and with a swish, the sleeve of his crisp white shirt rolled up his arm. With another flick, he began writhing in pain.

"Stop it!" Ellasyn took a step forward. "I'm sorry this did not turn out in your favor. Gavin and I will decide what to do about his father, but—"

Mara's eye twitched and her head whipped to Ellasyn in a disjointed motion. Her eyes blazed and Ellasyn's words were silenced. Ellasyn grabbed her throat and fell to her knees, her eyes wide in horror. Gavin dropped to his knees, trying to wrench her hands off.

"Mara!" I called out to her. She studied me, a hint of recognition in her eyes, and Ellasyn heaved, taking a weak, shuddering breath. Gavin hugged her, his eyes closed tight. The shock seemed to have worn off the crowd and they rushed over, eyes flashing as they hurled giftings at us, but nothing seemed to penetrate Mara.

She leaned back and laughed, the quickly threw her hands out and bodies went flying.

"Mara! Enough! This is the rose...this is not you! Fight it!" I yelled.

She glared at me. "But it is, Nicholassss. This life here in Cristes holds nothing for me anymore. I will not let my daughter grow up feeling like she is unwanted or lessss than."

"But she won't. You have me, my family, Lana. Even Gavin said—"

Her sinister laugh cut me off. "Gavin? The little boy who can't say 'boo' to daddy? Whose love is so fickle, it can change with the wind? I cannot trust that when he has a child with his newest toy, that he will not forget about my daughter and choose to not love her. I will not be a weak, pathetic mother. I will show my daughter what strength lookssss like."

Mara bit off another large chunk of the rose, and her chest heaved. I wrapped my arms around her and tried to pry her mouth open.

"Spit it out! You are not in control. The dark magic is controlling you!" I shouted. But she broke my hold as if I was nothing but a piece of spun sugar. The air went still, but Mara's hair floated about her face, the ends turning black; it seeped into the strands as if she dipped her hair in ink, and then... the inky hair caught fire.

Gavin walked to her, his hands up in surrender. He looked around him, assessing the situation. "Mara, please. I'm sorry. You are right. I love you." He stood in front of Ellasyn, shielding her from Mara's view. "Let's go home, to your place. We can be a happy family there."

"Do you think I'm an idiot? You mistake my generoussss heart for a fool." She raised her arms behind her and as she took in a breath, she lifted a few inches off the ground.

The square had grown eerily quiet. Ellasyn and Gavin's families, as well as my guards, banged on an invisible barrier, but I could not hear the pounding nor the words their mouths were forming. Gifting attempts to break it were unsuccessful.

Gavin's father rushed toward Mara, flinging his body at her, knocking her to the ground.

"Go, son! Get out of here!" he bellowed.

Gavin helped Ellasyn up. They made it a few feet before they froze, like statues. Mara smirked with her hands held high and as if they were attached to strings, she turned the couple and walked them back over to her. Mr. Frosters lay on the ground, panting, blood seeping from a wound over his heart.

I rushed over to him, placing my hands over his chest to staunch the blood. I tried to remember everything I'd ever seen Nolan and Shai do. I closed my eyes and tapped into any healing gifting I had. The blood slowed and Mr. Frosters coughed, a wet cough that left a dribble of blood on his lip. And then, the life drained from his eyes.

I whipped around to Mara, my hands bloodied, tiny splatters of blood on my cream sweater, and stood letting the full power of my gifting come to the surface. "I love you. I love you too much to let you harm yourself, let alone anyone else."

But Mara was keeled over, holding her stomach.

"Nicholas," she whimpered, her eyes back to their bright orange. "Help me. Something, something is wrong with her."

My giftings extinguished as I dropped to my knees. I held my wrist to the sky and shot a flame of red light above, a royal distress signal.

"I'm sorry," Mara whimpered. "I'll do anything, just save my daughter, please." She winced in pain.

I placed my ear on her belly and detected a weak, slow heartbeat.

"Hang on, little darling," I whispered to the baby.

Mara began to sing as she rubbed her belly. I sat on my knees, anxiously waiting for Nolan to arrive.

But then Mara grunted in pain. "She's coming, Nicholas! It's too soon... I still have seven weeks to go!" She groaned, louder this time. "Please, help us!"

I had no time to think. With Mara's wards up, we definitely had our privacy. I lifted her skirt to her knees. Locking my eyes with hers, I spoke with an authority I faked to the best of my ability. "Baby Nicole is going to be fine. Nolan will be here any minute. You can do this, and we will rush her to the healing nursery."

Time passed in agony as minutes seemed like hours.

Mara cried out and arched her back.

"Push, Mara. We need Nicole out and away from the rose's poison." Mara bore down with vigor. "That's it. I see her head!" I smiled up at Mara. "She's got a lot of blonde hair, like you!" I tore my sweater off.

Mara pushed a few more times and passed the shoulders. The rest of the tiny miracle slid out into my hands, and I cradled her into my sweater. I handed the tiny bundle to Mara, tears streaming down my cheeks.

I patted Mara's knee after pulling her skirt back down. "Well done. She's the most beautiful thing I've ever seen."

Mara cooed, never taking her eyes off of Nicole's face. Then Mara's eyes changed *again*. To my astonishment, I shed even more tears of relief at seeing those beautiful pastels again.

"Mommy loves you, darling. I will take excellent care of you. You will never know cold. You will never know hunger. You will always know..." She trailed off, looking at me, and grabbed my hand. She returned her gaze to her baby. "You will always know unconditional love, especially from your Uncle Nicholas."

The baby let out a small coo. A deep brown marking began to spread from her chest, following the path of her veins. When it finished covering her body, she let out a gasp and stilled.

"Nicole?" Mara whispered. But the only movement the precious bundle made was when her tiny hand released its grip on her mother's finger.

"No, no, no..." Mara repeated over and over. I wrapped my arm around her and bit my fist, trying to stifle the sobs that wracked my body.

"Nicole, stay with Mommy. I'm sorry. I am so, so sorry. I won't make any more mistakes. Never again. I want to watch you grow and dance with you in the fields. I can take you exploring in the caves and Uncle Nicholas can teach you to swim."

I squeezed Mara tightly into my side and kissed the top of her head. Mara stilled and I released her. She re-swaddled Nicole in my sweater and cradled her. Her slender fingers closed Nicole's eyes. Then she traced the now charcoal veins that marked the baby's ashen skin. Her fingertips trailed over Nicole's features, as if tracing them enough times would concrete them to memory. Mara sat singing and cradling the baby.

Much of the crowd dissipated. I looked at the stricken faces of my guards who were still trapped outside of the invisible barrier set forth by Mara's dark magic. Many had grown to care for her and now they'd have to arrest her.

Gavin and Ellasyn sat huddled together, grief trying to break through the shock that seized them. Their families, too, sat at the invisible barrier, a mixture of anger and disbelief as they were unable to tear their gazes away from the death in our group.

I placed my hand on Mara's shoulder. "We should go and get you some healer attention."

Mara looked at me and screamed. The high pitch shattered the protective casing she had erected around us and the immediate surrounding area. Slowly, little tinkling sounds, like pieces of strung sea glass blowing in the wind, resonated as fragments of the once invisible dome fell.

When Mara stood, she was no longer *my* Mara. Her eyes were devoid of the once angelic soul that I loved from the moment I saw her. She laid Nicole in my arms and before I could stop her, she wolfed down what remained of the black rose.

She pushed me aside. I did not recognize this creature.

With black hair that floated like ash around her, her pale skin glowed a putrid green, and her nails resembled red knives. Her gaze flicked to a spot over my right shoulder. I turned. *Gavin.* My gifting screamed they were in danger. Ellasyn sobbed into Gavin's chest as she clung to his shirt. Mara stalked over to him and flicked a tear that strolled down his cheek, leaving an angry red gash on his face.

To Mara's right, a flicker of black diverted my attention. Without warning, that little flicker grew to a small hole and she sneered at the grieving couple. The bench nearest the hole lifted from the ground and disappeared through it. I stared in alarm at Ellasyn and Gavin as their bodies began to drift toward it. I knew what Mara's plans were. I knew what spell she would cast. I knew what I had to sacrifice to save them all.

I'd absorbed all her memories in that room last night. I was not powerful enough to stop her, not after what I had witnessed, but I could put a giant wrench in her plans. An arm flung around my chest, a hand clasped over my mouth, and someone took Nicole from my arms. Shai and Brantley positioned themselves on either side of me, and I had never felt such immense relief in my entire life.

"Do not make a sound," Lana whispered in my ear.

Mara's lips moved with speed and she again hovered over the ground. The black hole now swirled with shades of orange and red and grew larger. Mara lowered herself back to the ground and moved to stand in front of Ellasyn and chanted:

"Ellasyn, Ellasyn, it's a shame for you

But your first-born daughter Will just not do.

Upon its birth, it shall never wake

And your position as wife

Another will—"

Brantley and Shai charged Mara and tackled her to the ground. I sprang into action and released Gavin. Black lines protruded from the gash on his face. He ran over to where his father's body lay, but I caught him around the waist.

"No. You cannot take him with you. You need a healer, a strong one." I motioned to the gash on his cheek. "I do not know what toxin is traveling through your veins." Gavin placed a palm over his cheek.

"Not without her," he said, pointing to Ellasyn who was still tethered to the ground.

I ran to her, and with the same steps, I gathered what was left of my strength to release her from Mara's spell.

Ellasyn collapsed into my arms and I helped her to stand.

"Both of you, go now! Gavin, tell my parents I love them."

Gavin gave me a swift nod and started to run, Ellasyn clutched to his side. Without warning, a dark laugh rang in my ear, too close. I turned and Mara's nails sliced my face, narrowly missing my eye.

With one hand held over me, her magic forced me to the ground. With her other hand, she flung a tendril of flame at Ellasyn. Her body jolted, and Mara reeled her back in.

I wiped the blood from my face with my t-shirt. Gavin lay sprawled on the ground, his leg bent at an odd angle. Brantley was knocked unconscious, Shai as well and Lana was bent over on all fours breathing heavily.

"I wassss not finished yet!" Mara screeched.

Just before Ellasyn reached Mara's arms, I flung my body between them, grasping Ellasyn's wrist with one hand and locking elbows with Mara. I used a gifting I was told never to tap into, to briefly borrow the power of another. I drew in a deep breath, taking some of the poison that flowed through Mara's veins. It weakened the black magic's hold on her, but I knew it would not last, for darkness could not survive in my light. Gripping Mara's shoulders, I devised a prayer in hopes of undoing the beginnings of Mara's curse.

"Eira of Cristes,
Son of love
Hear my plea
To save all thereof
Ellasyn's first-born child
Shall not perish
Dormant the genes will be
Until a daughter born cherished
A pair who is worthy
And bear the unique mark
Together they will defeat
Within Cristes, the dark
I renounce my title
To rule the land
And with your decree
May this plea stand."

"No!" Mara shrieked.

I let her go and held fast to Ellasyn. My brief physical

connection with Mara allowed me to see what she planned to do with Gavin's fiancée and my stomach churned at the malice of it.

"Give her to me," Mara commanded.

"Never."

"So, you choose her, too?" Mara sneered.

"That is not what this is!" I shouted over the wind that roared like a freight train.

Mara sank her nails into my arm and I cried out.

"Fine. Then you are both coming with me!" Her preternatural strength pulled me and Ellasyn easily toward the cavernous portal.

Something flipped past me and I was startled when it landed next to me. "Lana!"

She glowed a green so bright, I could barely look at her. But then there were two Lanas, and I couldn't comprehend what I was witnessing. The cloaked Lana fought Mara face to face, keeping her distracted. The other Lana forcefully pried Mara's claws from my arm with a sickening crunch, her nails scratching through to the bone. I howled in pain but did release my grip on Ellasyn.

With a swift kick, one of the Lana's sent Mara into the portal. I stood gaping as it began to close. I didn't even quite know how I was standing, especially with a shuddering Ellasyn who could barely stand herself, clinging to me.

"Lana, a little—" But I did not get to finish that sentence. An orange flame shot out from the closing black hole, wrapped around Ellasyn and me, and catapulted us into the swirling abyss.

Part III

BACK TO THE PRESENT

Time

LIKE THE GRAVITRON AT THE ANNUAL CARNIVAL, a two-ton weight settled on my chest as the last scene disappeared and blackness swallowed me whole, pulling me down, down, down, until the sensation that I would be pulled apart stopped. But the ache in my heart persisted.

I opened my eyes and peered around. Will and Pree wore expressions on their faces that I was positive I wore, too. Mostly, I was in shock at how rapidly everything descended into chaos. I watched Nick, whose eyes were still closed, and followed a single tear as it fell down his exhausted face. The tears that I had been trying to blink away furiously streamed down my cheeks.

"If you'd let go of my hand, I'd like to wipe those tears away."

I looked down. My knuckles were white and hands numb from squeezing Will so hard. I released him and he gave me a half-smile, his own eyes watery. He took the cuff of his sleeve, wiped my tears away, then kissed each cheek.

"How long were we in your memories for?" Pree asked, her voice hoarse.

Nick opened his eyes and glanced at his wrist.

"Just shy of twenty minutes," his voice was like gravel.

"You're kidding, right?" Pree's scoffed.

Nick only stared back at her, his mouth pressed into a hard line.

"But it felt like years. How can that be?" she pressed him.

"Not even the most advanced of those with my gifting comprehend the distortion of time within memories," he responded.

Will bit his bottom lip, a rigid crease forming between his brows.

"What is it?" I whispered to him.

Will looked up at Nick. "I have some questions."

Nick chuckled, almost self-deprecating in manner. "I have no doubt that you all do."

Pree blinked as if she were still in a daze. "Oh, I definitely have questions, but I think Liddy and Will should ask first."

Nick nodded at her, then looked back over at Will. "Ask me anything."

Will's lips twisted downward. "Why did my uncle not want us to see this?"

"Ah, an interesting choice for the first question." Nick played with his beard. "Actually, this was not the part he preferred you did not see."

"There's more?" Pree choked out, clearly shocked by the prospect.

"Yes. Much more...it's true, Shai is haunted by the fact that he was not able to stop Mara that afternoon in the park. But the part that he cannot bear to see again has to do with your brother, Charlie."

I watched Will swallow, his Adam's apple dipping slowly and popping back up. "I—I think I need some water." Pree tossed him an Evian. "Thanks." Will twisted the top until he succeeded in breaking through the seal. Just as he brought the bottle to his lips, I decided to ask my question.

"What happened to the baby?" I don't know why I asked this. The scene, full of blood and pain, so vivid, I would never forget. I felt the sudden heaviness of my question and cast my eyes to the floor.

"The dark magic from the black rose..." Nick's voice cracked and he cleared his throat. "...the price of Mara's use of it was the life of her baby."

Everyone went silent, their gazes far away as if they were seeing the moment all over again. The ache in the center of my chest throbbed, and I rubbed it in circles, trying to get rid of it.

Anxiously, I continued, "So, Mara pulled you into that swirly—"

"It was a portal," Pree interrupted.

"OK, so Mara pulled you and Ellasyn into the portal," I amended. "What happened to Ellasyn after? How did you get here? And Mara, well, where is she exactly? How did she get to wherever she is now?"

Nick held up his hand, as if to say, *One question at a*

time, please. "The force of Mara's magic nearly tore my limbs from me as I fought to disentangle myself from her hold while maintaining control of Ellasyn." He shook his head, as if still bewildered by this all. "I am still not quite sure how it all happened, but somehow I was able to break from her clutches when I saw an exit—" His brow furrowed— "A glittering light that called to me, a strong pull I needed to go to, my body unrelenting in its desire. Once through, I recognized immediately that Ellasyn and I were in Mortalia..." he spread his arms. "Your world."

"And Mara?" I asked.

"She is in Beldam, and underworld of her creation."

A collective shudder rushed through the room.

"So how is Liddy connected to all of this?" Will asked, placing his hand on my knee.

Nick hoisted himself off the couch and picked up a teacup from the tray Nolan had set out. The rest of us remained silent as he prepared his cider, then joined us back on the couch.

"Ellasyn lived with me for many years at Hill House, where I currently reside. It was a common spot where Watchers stayed for their annual Christmas rose gatherings—" Nick breathed in some of the steam from his cup and took a sip of his cider— "In any case, we tried to get back to Cristes but were unsuccessful. The path I had taken a few times before on my sanctioned travels no longer worked. It was as if something broke in Cristes when Mara—"

"Lost her freaking mind?" Pree quipped.

"Pree!" I chided her, smacking her arm with the back of my hand.

"What?" Pree shrugged. "It's not like that bastard Gavin

didn't give her a reason."

Nick cocked an eyebrow at us and continued. "Ellasyn was scared at first, then angry, and then...depressed. After the third year, she gave up trying to find a way home. After the fifth, she resigned herself to the fact that Gavin was not coming for her. Finally, After the eighth year, she asked me for a favor." Nick closed his eyes and massaged his forehead.

"You can skip this part if it's too much," I whispered.

"No. You need to hear." Nick pressed his lips together, his expression resolute. "She asked me to take her memories and place a shield on her giftings. As you saw just moments ago, I had enacted a counter prayer against Mara's spell— Ellasyn's child would be the one to break Mara's curse."

"Unless Liddy is adopted, how can she be Ellasyn's child?" Pree cocked her head at him, her mouth agape, her teeth and tongue visible.

Nick scrunched his nose at Pree's *duh* face. "My dear. Child is not a literal interpretation. Lydia is her great, great *grandchild*, the first female born that carries Ellasyn's blood."

"I wish I could have met her." I lamented, hugging my stomach against the unexpected hollowness.

Nick patted my knee. "I wish I'd had the chance to know her under different circumstances. She was lovely." He slapped his thighs. "Right. Where was I? Well, Ellasyn knew that by staying with me at Hill House, she would not have children and knew that Cristes could be lost forever. I am not a chemist, but I had been collecting Christmas roses and experimenting on them to help slow down our aging. I felt they were almost ready. But Ellasyn knew I could not make any guarantees."

Nick turned his hands so his palms faced up. "Time for Watchers in Mortalia is not as kind to us as it is in Cristes for Watchers age more quickly here, on par with humans. She could easily blend in with them and did not want to risk losing her fertility window."

Nick's eyes glimmered with unshed tears. "Alas, I took Ellasyn's memories of Cristes so she would not mourn the loss of what once was. She no longer knew she was a Watcher, and I took her ability to access her powers so she'd remain hidden. I always kept tabs on her. Within a year, Ellasyn married and started a family.

"For years, I kept myself busy tending to my Christmas rose gardens and experiments. And when children started disappearing around Mortalia, I found myself drawn to their cases and began tracking them, trying to find a connection." His brow crinkled. "They were all random, or so I thought, except for the month of the year they occurred in. Then, one day," he continued, "Brantley, a newly pregnant Lana, Shai, and Nolan dropped into Arbolias. I was hopeful that travel to and from Cristes was once again possible, but their globital broke on arrival. When Lana gave birth, imagine our surprise when her son bore the markings of a whitelighter king."

His voice wavered with emotion. "And I knew, *I knew* that the baby girl I had prayed for, the one who would join with Lana's son and break Mara's curse, had finally come to snuff out the dark." Nick's eyes cut to me, a twinkle in them. "And we began our search for her immediately."

Wow, What a Coincidence

PREE INHALED, long and dramatic as if she were watching a live Telenovela.

"I understand my connection now to all of this," I gestured to the room. "Nick spelled it out for me pretty clearly...though I still have some questions."

"Hold, please," Pree stated. She moved her lips, talking to herself as she waved her finger and pointed here and there, orchestrating her thoughts. "Ah, ha!" She rounded on Nick. "So, you were the one who took Will and Liddy's memories, and their families' as well."

Will dropped his hand from my knee and shot to his feet. "What! How could you!"

Nick heaved a heavy sigh. "And now we get to the part that Shai could not stand to be here for."

I grasped Will's hand, tugging it gently, encouraging him to sit back down. But he stood strong.

"Liddy, he took us away from each other! He erased our memories!"

I stood and wrapped my arms around him. "I know. And that sucks. But he didn't permanently erase them. He temporarily hid them."

"Same difference," he grumbled.

I pulled away and sandwiched his cheeks between my palms, bringing his face level with mine.

"No, it's not. Look, none of this is easy. But let's hear Nick out. I'm sure he had good reasons." I entwined my fingers with Will's, and this time he sat with me.

Nick nodded appreciatively. "Once I had figured out that Mara was behind the disappearances, Shai, Lana, Brantley, Nolan, and I started strategizing. We believed it was only a matter of time before Mara found one of the Jamison boys... or you, Lydia."

"Please, call me Liddy."

"Of course."

I thought on Nick's words, then blurted, "But you had Will and me searching for a connection to the disappearances... why, when you already knew?"

Nick shook his head. "The disappearances have always been completely random. Without directly communicating with Mara, there is no way to determine who she takes and why. I was hoping fresh, young eyes may be able to spot something we could not see."

"But we do know that she uses the kids, thanks to Liddy's dreams, to access more power," Will said, pulling me in closer to him. "And from your memories, we know that she needs an element to harness the power of her giftings."

Nick's jaw twitched as he worked it. His eyes glazed over for a moment, but when he refocused, he looked sad. "Yes, now we know why she takes children. But my instincts tell me there is more to it than just siphoning power for herself. A plan was set in motion when she targeted William."

"I'll be right back," I whispered to Will before moving to sit beside Nick.

Sensing the burden he carried, I reached out and grasped Nick's hands.

"Nick, I trust that whatever you have to tell us, I know you did it because you felt it best. We want you to continue and we promise to not get angry."

He slid one hand from my grasp and placed it back over mine. His hands, warm and calloused, encased mine like a warm hug.

"Thank you." he breathed. "Lana and Brantley were understandably busy raising their boys. That left Nolan, Shai, and me working, trying to figure out how to find you, Liddy."

"But there are billions, literally billions, of people in our world. How the heck did you find her?" Pree wondered aloud.

"Well, we are very powerful Watchers." Nick released me and spread his hands. "With my prayer cast over Mara's spell, I had to believe that it brought me and Ellasyn where we needed to be in order for it to bear fruit. So, Nolan, Shai, and I all split up across northern Illinois, scouring every town, dwindling our supplies of Christmas roses as we used them to try and entice Watcher giftings to show themselves in any child we came in contact with at our behest."

"Wow," Pree breathed. "That is...that is dedication."

Nick shrugged a shoulder. "What alternative did we have? In any case," he continued, his eyes flicking to mine, "Shai was the one who found you. He had run out of Christmas roses and was headed back to Hill House, deciding on a whim to check a neighborhood on his way home. Turns out, he did not need the help of an enchanted rose. When he passed you riding your bike as your mother walked your brother in a stroller, he sensed a nudge from you." He waved a hand. "This can happen with powerful Watchers who share a connection somewhere—past, present, or future."

"Oh, my, gosh," Pree gasped. "Like, some people would be like *wow, what a coincidence.* But no way...fate was on your side."

The corners of Nick's mouth ticked up, and he chuckled.

"Shai hurried back to Hill House and called Nolan and me to return. He held a meeting and before the night was over, he had Lana and Brantley in agreement to move onto Liddy's street. I argued against this. Shai felt that if we could get you both together, it would speed up the process of fixing everything and, at the very least, get us all back safely to Cristes. I, on the other hand, had no real justification for not wanting to bring you both together, but rather another hunch."

"Obviously, Shai's plan did not work out," Will said quietly.

"No, it did not." Nick shook his head. "As we already know, the opposite happened; your connection to Liddy was immediate. In that, Shai was not wrong. But what he nor anyone else considered was that bringing you two together would create a bond strong enough for any Watcher to feel. We never anticipated that Mara would be able to detect it all the way from Beldam; but she did, and as a result, she purposefully sought you two out." Nick sighed and played with his beard. "Shai has never forgiven himself for Charlie's kidnapping; his idea made each of you a target."

"Poor Shai," I whispered, dipping my chin.

"Is that why we moved? Uncle Shai could not deal with his guilt?" Will asked, more curious than angry.

"No. We had to separate you from one another to mute your bond, to keep you hidden," Nick explained. "I had Nolan move your family to Florida that very night. Once I was sure you were safe, I tried to convince Shai to come with me; but he refused, stating that Lydia needed someone to watch over her."

Nick paused, his brow furrowing deeply, as he continued to stroke his beard. "When I arrived in Florida, Brantley and Lana were unwell. After a week of mourning, they begged me to lock away their memories of Charlie, of this entire calamity, until the time came to put a stop to Mara and get Charlie back. Although they kept the knowledge that they were Watchers, they decided to take on the personae of humans and raise William as such, so as not to draw attention to him."

Pree snorted, loudly.

"What?" Nick asked.

"Ummm, have you seen the boy? *William* draws attention wherever he goes."

Will's neck reddened Nick barked an unexpected laugh.

"Precisely why, after he completed 'the change' as all adolescents experience, though it is more extensive and intense for Watchers, I convinced him to come to Illinois. His parents could no longer keep him from notice, yet Nolan and Shai could with my help.

Will bowed his head. "But Shai barely spoke to me. No one, not even Nolan, attempted to help me understand what was happening to me. Not to mention..." he trailed off, his gaze arresting mine.

"Ah, regretfully, your uncle did not agree with me that it was time to bring you and Liddy back together. Fear motivated his stubbornness, and I knew he could not see clearly. He believed that in bringing you and Liddy together, we would again paint targets on your backs, one of you would be taken, and Cristes would crumble." His lip twitched. "Your uncle had no idea I had unlocked your memories and the hold on your giftings. He truly thought you just wanted to come up north," Nick added, glancing at Will. "He stayed away from you only because you are a reminder of his failure."

"But he didn't fail," I interjected. "There was no way anyone could've known Mara would take Charlie; she was after Will!" I fisted my hands. "And even that was weird because, at the time, it made more sense to assume that she would come after *me*."

Nick sighed. "His words, not mine. I agree with you, Liddy. Shai needs forgive himself."

We sat in uncomfortable silence for several minutes, processing what we'd just heard. I tried to get a feel for what Will was thinking, but as I reached out to him with my gifting, a kaleidoscope of emotions swirled through me, the temperament changing too quickly for me to make any sense of them.

Will bolted up from his seat, startling everyone. "I—I should go talk to Shai." He pivoted toward the door. As I watched his retreating back, my heart flipped.

"Want me to come?" I called after him.

Will stopped and looked over his shoulder at me. "No. This is something I'd like to do on my own."

Power Rangers Sans Costume

I T DIDN'T FEEL RIGHT talking about anything more with Nick and Pree without Will there. And yet, I still had questions, ones that were stuck in my throat like a piece of taffy I hadn't quite chewed well enough.

Pree had pulled out a notebook and appeared to be taking copious notes in between chewing on the end of her pencil. Nick just sat there, his eyes glazed over, staring into nothingness. I hated to interrupt him.

"Ni—?"

"Um, excuse me? Is no one going to mention how you all are basically like Power Rangers?" Pree blurted, interrupting me.

I sputtered a laugh and quickly slapped my hand over my mouth.

"Hmm?" Nick hummed as he blinked once, then focused on Pree.

She gave him another *duh* face. "You know, Power Rangers? A.k.a. color-coded superheroes."

Nick's brows arched high on his forehead. "Should I know of these 'rangers'?"

I sighed. "Pree, I doubt he's had much time to watch TV."

I swiped my hand across my throat. "Ixnay on the angers-ray."

"I mean it is *so* obvious, but whatever," Pree muttered, returning her focus to her notebook.

I cleared my throat and tried again. "Nick, I wanted to ask about my family."

"What about them?"

I lowered my hands to my lap, where I'd laced my fingers together. I twisted Will's promise ring around, the cool metal warming against my palm. "Are they...like me?"

Nick tilted his head, scrutinizing me, or maybe my words. "Do you mean, are they Watchers?"

"Yes." I sat up straighter. "Am I the only one in my family with these giftings? Are they able to help? Did you take their memories?"

"Whoa." Nick put his hands up, the corners of his mouth quirking. "First of all, yes, you have been the only one in three generations to express giftings. However, that does not rule out the possibility of other Watchers who merely lacked the guidance Mara had. Secondly," he ticked off on his fingers. "Your kin are human, so, unfortunately, they are not able to help. And, finally, I did not take their memories."

I sucked in my bottom lip and averted my gaze. Again, an

ache in the center of my chest pulsed, but this time I couldn't pinpoint why.

A small beep and a loud swish of the door over the mats redirected my attention. Will, Shai, and Nolan all walked in together. Will looked calm. Shai, who usually wore a smug expression that read *I'm better than everyone else and my poop smells like roses*, actually smiled. He appeared lighter than I'd ever seen him before.

"Shall we get started on the training?" Shai bellowed.

Nick flinched. "Well, look who is all excited now? But you do not need to yell."

Shai laughed, a slightly lower baritone than Will's and I joined in.

"Ladies, Nolan has some gear for you," Shai continued.

"I get to train?" Pree asked. Her body wiggled as she clasped her hands near her chest.

"You know everything now. Might as well try to teach you how you can protect yourself."

"Heck, yeah!" Pree pumped her fist and jumped over to Shai, gave him a big hug, and then stood in front of Nolan, dancing like she had to pee really bad.

I stood up from the couch and walked over to Nolan. The gear he handed me was surprisingly heavy for just a long sleeve black tee and leggings.

As if he read my mind, he leaned forward and whispered, "They are enchanted. No gifting can truly affect your body when wearing this." Then he straightened and clasped his hands behind his back.

Nick yawned. "Shai, it's late. I think we should get the kiddos to bed. Training will be better received on a good night's rest."

"Noooo," Pree whined. "Don't be a grumpy old man. Come on, we can work for at least an hour."

"Preethi, it is after one in the morning," Nick replied through his teeth, his patience worn thin.

Everyone seemed to be holding a collective breath while watching the exchange. Nick was right; I was exhausted, and everything we'd learned tonight was a lot to process. At the same time, I was eager to see what Watchers could do.

"How about showing us one move?" I offered. Shai's lips puckered as if he'd eaten a handful of *Lemonheads* and was trying not to laugh.

Nick grunted and shook his head. "Fine. Just one."

"The first thing you would normally learn is how to access your giftings. However, recent events have taken care of some of that. There is much more for you to learn, but tonight, let us look at how to block an attack." As Shai spoke, he grabbed me gently by the shoulders and led me over to Nick, who leaned against the wall. Then he returned to stand next to his nephew.

"Miss Pree, I will take you back to the apothecary." Nolan offered his hand. "It would be more prudent for you to learn the alchemy of the Christmas rose."

"Can't I just see this one thing tonight, and then we go to your indoor arboretum tomorrow, pleeease?" She batted her eyes at Nolan on the last word. He smiled and offered his elbow to her. She hooked her arm in his, her eyes narrowed in distrust. He led her toward the door a few steps, but then circled back to the kitchenette where he helped her sit on a stool.

Nick and Shai positioned themselves on opposite ends of the rectangular room. They moved a few paces toward each other but were still separated by nearly half the length of a football field.

Without any words spoken between them, they exchanged Cristes' traditional salute. The room became charged with power, my hair lifting away from my body. The air thickened around us like the cloud canopy of a tropical rainforest about to unleash a torrential downpour.

Nick threw his hands down at his sides and an audible crack filled the room like a thousand glow sticks all breaking and splintering at once. Fluorescent blue light flowed through his veins, creating a web from his eyes, down his neck, racing toward his open palms. Seconds later, his hands held a glowing orb between them.

I flicked my eyes to Shai and suddenly felt nervous for him. Nick had never looked so intimidating as he did at that moment, and Shai appeared unbothered, if not completely unprepared. I reached for Will's hand, my eyes never leaving the dueling men, but my hand found no purchase. I had forgotten that Will stood across from me and instead had to fist the bottom of my shirt against my nerves.

I obviously hadn't given Shai the benefit of the doubt. His eyes burned bright green. Heat shimmered off of him in oscillating waves, providing an invisible shield and warming my skin. Had I been standing closer, it would have been uncomfortable. He smirked and beckoned to Nick with his index finger then mouthed, *bring it on.*

Faster than Jet Li could throw a roundhouse kick to your face, Nick launched the glowing orb straight at Shai's chest.

Shai braced his feet, and with a swing of his arms, the orb hit the shimmering wall in front of him and exploded, a shower of sparks raining down, disappearing just before hitting the mats.

Pree jumped from her seat and applauded wildly. "That was so freaking cool!"

I looked at Will and a smile tugged at the corners of his mouth.

"Can you believe that you and Will are going to be able to do things like that?"

I started at the proximity of Pree's voice. "No, I can't."

Pree assessed the room and then my wide-eyed stare. "Yeah, I can totally see how this might be a little jarring."

"A little?"

Pree linked elbows with mine and brought me before Nick, Will having already walked over to his uncle. Nick wore a smile that crinkled the skin near his eyes.

My intuition nudged me. "Something tells me that was slowed way down for our benefit." My lips spoke the words before my brain decided if I should say them or not.

Nick tilted his head and cocked his silvery brow at me. "You are not completely wrong." Without taking his eyes off of me he continued, "Shai, I think it is time for these kids to get some sleep. And Nolan?"

"Yes, Your Highness?"

"Give them a nightcap, would you please?" Nick winked.

"Of course. The three of you, this way please."

Nolan led us out of the secret training room, through the long hall, and up the stairs to our rooms.

"Ladies, your room awaits. Lord William, I shall give you

a moment to say goodnight to Madam Lydia." He abruptly turned his back, light pink clouds encasing his ears.

Pree gaped, and I widened my eyes at her, gesturing my head toward the open door.

"I'm going, I'm going. I can take a hint." She grabbed her bag off the foot of the bed and disappeared into the bathroom.

"That was something, wasn't it?" I whispered up at Will.

His sea-green eyes twinkled back at me. I could feel my cheeks grow warm as he gazed at me.

"That is one way to describe it." He smiled and placed his hands on my hips, pulling me closer to him. I gasped a little at the contact, not realizing how much I needed it.

"I'll never get over the cute sounds you make, nor the blush of your cheeks." Will's finger caressed my face and he leaned in, his lips barely brushing mine when he said, "I cannot wait for the day when we say goodnight and it means goodnight...not goodbye for the night." And then, he kissed me.

Right before I completely melted in his arms, I pulled back just enough so that our foreheads touched.

"See you in the morning."

"Sweet dreams, Princess."

I rose on my tiptoes, wrapped my arms around his neck, and put my all into this next kiss. He pulled back, gasping, his body aglow, and I bit my bottom lip in satisfaction.

"As you wish, my Prince." I blew him a kiss and closed the door.

Mortal Kombat

I ANTICIPATED NOT BEING ABLE TO SLEEP regardless of how drained I was. When I'd gotten out of the shower, I discovered Nolan had visited again. A tray with tea cups and a teapot sat steaming on the desk. Pree and I sat for a few minutes, each of us cross-legged on our own beds facing each other. Barely into our tea, we were both suddenly overcome with complete exhaustion. I barely got the cup on the nightstand and myself under the covers before I zonked out.

Just before I shut my eyes, I turned my head to the left and giggled. Pree had not made it under the covers; she was sprawled out, her chin hanging open.

"Pree... Pree!" I called out when I woke the next morning, but she only responded with a snort. I flipped back the covers and stretched. I'd slept so deeply, I didn't even dream. I swung my legs over the edge of the bed and went to my duffle bag, grabbing the black gear Nolan gave me last night, then locked myself in the bathroom. I had just finished dressing when a knock sounded on the bedroom door.

I walked over and opened it a crack.

"Oh, good morning, Mr. Jameson."

He smiled wide. "You may call me Uncle or Shai, if you wish."

"Sorry." I bit my bottom lip.

"I wanted to inform you that Nolan—" A loud snore from Pree erupted, and Shai's brows shot up.

"She doesn't normally snore. I'm guessing Nolan put something in that tea?"

"I have no idea what you are implying." Shai was more playful and less business-like than ever. I could see by the way he pressed his lips together that he was suppressing a laugh.

I pursed my lips. "Sure, you don't."

"As I was saying, Nolan will have breakfast ready in the kitchen in fifteen minutes. My nephew is in the library should you wish to see him before training."

I peered over my shoulder at Pree. "I better stay and help her wake up," I said, hitching my thumb in her direction.

"Go down and meet with Will. I'll tell Pree where you are when she wakes."

A rush of flutters flitted in my stomach and Shai grinned. "Go."

I tore down the stairs anticipating an entire fifteen minutes of Will, all to myself. He sat on the couch that we'd spent so much time on this past winter, reading.

I leaned against the doorjamb, watching his beautiful face as he pinched his bottom lip. He released his lip.

"Don't just stand there like a creeper. Come say hi." He placed the book down on the coffee table and opened his arms wide. I flung myself at him and gave him a huge hug.

"Good morning." I inhaled his citrus scent. "Yum."

"Yum?"

"You always smell good."

He laughed. "Well, you always smell delicious yourself. What are we going to do with ten whole minutes to ourselves?" he asked, a hint of rebellion in his tone.

"Well, I am a little nervous about training, and then of course how we'll fit training in with our duet and showcase rehearsal, and college applications, and—"

Will cut me off when his lips connected with. His urgency ignited me, and all thoughts of my tedious to-do list disappeared.

Will pulled away and his tongue slid against his bottom lip. "Now, what was it you were fretting about?"

I balled his tight, black shirt into my fist and brought him back to me, and that is how we stayed until...

"*Ahem.*" Someone cleared their throat and we jolted apart. "Breakfast is getting cold, though that may be a good thing."

"Thanks, Nick," Will said, not taking his eyes off mine. I could feel my cheeks flush. I moved from Will and stood. He followed and we walked hand in hand to the kitchen.

"Geez, are you carb-loading us or what?" Will remarked as we took in the spread before us.

"You will need the calories after today's training, Your

Highness," Nolan answered.

My mouth watered as I spotted French toast, bagels, blueberry pancakes, warm maple syrup, eggs, hash browns, and bacon. I loaded my plate with a sampling of everything.

"Hungry?" Will asked, smiling.

I nodded and did a little happy dance with each bite. When I'd had my fill, I scraped my plate into the garbage and placed my dishes in the sink. Will shoveled the last of his food into his mouth and we walked to the entrance of the training room while holding hands.

"You nearly gave Nolan a heart attack," Will said, his words garbled around the food stuffed in his cheeks.

I laughed. "I know. I saw him get up and knew he was coming for my dishes, but I acted like I didn't see him."

Will shook with laughter as he pressed his hand on the etched Christmas rose. The door opened with a silent greeting. We traveled down the stairs until we came to the large doors.

Nick was waiting for us in the center of the training room. His gear was much like ours, only white.

"Shall we get started right away? We only have Liddy until dinner before we must return her home."

"Yes," Will and I said in unison.

Nick clapped his hands together once, a loud smack echoing throughout the bare room.

"Great, Liddy on my right, William on my left."

"Just Will, please."

"Of course," Nick nodded. "Today, we are going to focus on conjuring our giftings and using them for defensive measures. When Shai joins us, we'll work on blocking. You witnessed this last night. Though your giftings will present differently, you can achieve the same goals.

"Close your eyes and relax your arms at your sides with palms facing out. I am going to cease speaking in a minute and when I do, I want you to focus on your body. Focus on the way your blood flows through your veins, like water flowing through a babbling brook. Focus on the elements around you, the light, the sounds, or the lack there of. Can you sense the air? Its movement or temperature? water? Can you taste or smell anything? You will begin to see colors before you. Your gifting will highlight the color of elements unique to you. When an element calls to you, reach for it and connect it to your heart. Your gifting will flow from there."

I closed my eyes and did as I was told. The silence was hard to ignore, the magnetism of Will even harder to block out. *Focus, Liddy.* I rolled my neck and relaxed my jaw, then my shoulders, my arms, and finally my fingers. I inhaled and let my breath out slowly.

For several minutes, nothing seemed to happen. I had to keep talking myself out of opening my eyes or asking for more guidance. I tried to picture the currents of magic, millions of fibers flowing together, each element on its own path. As hard as I focused on trying to see colors, I could not conjure them.

When I stopped trying is when I heard them. Different melodies at first and then they were accompanied by mists of colors that surrounded me. I smiled at the symphony that played loudest for me and attempted to tune the others out. It was blush pink in color and had a soulful accompaniment, the bass drawing me in. I reached out with my mind and plucked out a pink droplet, placing it in my heart as instructed.

Suddenly, my body vibrated with each note of the bass.

The first beat was rather pleasant, but then, the tempo began to increase as well as the volume, and I couldn't wait to release it.

"Hold onto it and keep your eyes closed, Liddy," Nick's voice sounded in my mind. "Turn a little to your left. Good. When I say go, open your eyes, find the target, and release the energy you are holding. Ready... Set... Go!"

My eyes flashed open. At the far end of the mat stood a tree. I had no idea where it came from, but the huge knot in its trunk looked like a target. With a large exhale, I unleashed my power.

"Bullseye!" Nick bellowed.

I turned to him, a huge grin on my face. Then my eyes flicked to Will's and he beamed at me, literally.

"You both are quick studies," Shai said, clapping as he entered the room. "Are we ready to move on to defensive tactics yet?"

"Not quite," Nick responded. "They have only completed the task once; they need to be able to repeat their success two more times before I'll let them move on. They can practice the speed later."

Each time, we were able to conjure our gifting and hit our target. Will and I took turns so we could observe one another. When he burned with his gifting, color ignited along the path of his veins, whereas, according to Will, I became encased in a blur of light, my body appearing like a shadow within it.

"Alright Nick, we need to move on before lunch," Shai said, moving to the center of the room. Nick nodded and stepped aside. "Defense is your lifeline, but there are many layers to it. The first is actual physical, hand-to-hand combat;

this is where Greens tend to excel. Another layer involves what you saw last night, and that is blocking an attack. Third is the ability to change the power's target, otherwise known as deflection. Finally, defense can include a combination of any of the aforementioned layers."

Shai stood tall, his hair gelled perfectly. He grasped his wrist behind his back as he paced back and forth between us.

"Today, we are focusing on halting an assault. When you are in combat with innocents nearby, you do not want to merely deflect the attack, as that can result in their peril."

"That makes sense," Will chimed in.

"Good. Now, you two will start at opposite ends of the room. This shall give you time to see the threat and react."

"But how do we extinguish it?" I asked.

"Your body's natural fight or flight response. Most Watchers must train to face their attacker, when their normal reaction would be to run away. You must be able to access your gifting and shape it to your will, commanding it to invade the attack. Personally, I like explosions and fireworks." Shai smirked.

"So, I shape my gifting in a way that will respond to whatever is being sent my way?" I ventured.

"Yes." Shai continued to pace before us. "For example, say Will sends a wall of fire your way. Water might be a natural choice, but obviously a simple drop won't do."

"What about a large wave or monsoon?"

"Those could work, if you can conjure them," Shai answered Will. "Practicing helps, especially with others whose giftings differ from yours. No two Watchers are the same, but their defenses tend to have a theme based on their giftings. Your job will be to memorize those themes. Seeing as though you and Liddy have whitelighter promise, you both have access to at least two giftings. Hopefully, those giftings complement each other."

"Hopefully? What if they don't?" I hated how small my voice sounded. There was no reason for me to be afraid.

"Well, you can always practice with me, Nolan, or Nick, or the occasional rogue Watcher who comes around."

Nick spoke up. "Liddy, rest assured that we will not leave any stone unturned when it comes to training the both of you."

"Thank you." I said.

Shai steepled his fingers at his chest. "Nick is right. There is no plan B for Cristes."

I couldn't tell whose stomach dropped first, but I definitely felt Will's uneasiness through our bond.

"Now remember, the outfits you don are enchanted. Nothing will hurt you."

I could still sense Will's apprehension. I smiled at him and mouthed, *I'll be fine.* I didn't want him to go easy on me; I wasn't going to hold anything back with him. We needed this training to be authentic. Too much was riding on our shoulders.

Shai gestured to Will and me to take our marks. "Liddy you're going to attack Will first. Think of something you can create to distract and challenge him, then aim and shoot it at his torso. He will have roughly five seconds to process what you send his way before he needs to block it."

Will and I exchanged a Cristes bow and Shai began the countdown. In my mind, I shaped my gifting to resemble a football, and I concocted a cacophony of the cheesiest cheers by the most annoying voices one could expect at a game. I smirked at my cleverness and when Shai whistled, I let go.

Will laughed when he realized what I'd done. However, the football grew ten sizes as it spiraled through the air, hurtling toward him, and the voices nearly ruptured our eardrums. We all slapped our hands over our ears, except for Will, who quickly flung out his hands. With no time to spare, the glowing football hit a net he conjured and went silent. As the ball rolled down, it deflated slowly into nothingness.

"Well done! Well done! That was excellent work, both of you!" Shai cheered.

My cheeks hurt from grinning so much. The exhilaration of it all made me feel powerful, and more like myself than I ever had.

The apples of Nick's cheeks nearly touched his eyes.

"Will, your turn to attack."

From where I stood, I could see Will had paled some.

"It won't help to go easy on me," I shouted across the way.

Will ran a hand through his hair. With no idea what to expect, I tried to clear my mind as Shai began the countdown.

Moments later orange eyes and black crystal lips on a blood-orange envelope called my name as they hurled toward me, growing louder and more sinister. I froze.

The jolt knocked me flat on my back and I momentarily lost the ability to breathe. I couldn't hear from the ringing in my ears, but soon Will's worried face was in front of mine.

"She'll be fine. Just give her a minute," Shai's muffled voice registered.

Will had his hands on my chest, my ribs, my abdomen, carefully assessing for injury. I took a breath and sat up.

"You scared the heck out of me." Will sprang forward and wrapped me in a tight embrace before he rocked back on his heels. "Are you OK? What happened?"

"She froze," Nick answered for me.

I dropped my head in shame. Will's finger crooked under my chin and brought my face up so he could look directly into my eyes. "Don't do that. I'm the one who took it too far, especially for the first go. You sent me a rowdy football game and I literally sent you your nightmare. I'm such an idiot."

"No. You did as I asked. She is who I will face, after all. And I'm fine. I promise."

Will turned his frustration on his uncle as he helped me to stand. "I thought you said we couldn't get hurt?"

"She is not hurt," Shai retorted, calmly.

"Yes, she is."

"She just got the wind knocked from her. There will be no lasting injuries, and she cannot die."

Will's neck turned red and I could see his jaw working.

"I'm done for the day." He grabbed my hand and began leading me to the doors. Shai and Nick just stood like two mirroring statues, their legs spread apart, arms crossed over their chests, lips pressed into a hard line.

I yanked my hand from his. He reached for it again, but I dodged him.

"Will, stop! Please hear me. I am fine. I need practice.

Would you rather the next time I be alone with Mara?" That halted him in his tracks.

"Fine. We can continue." Will crossed his arms over his chest. "But first, I need to mentally recover. I'm going to lunch." He turned and strode through the door.

"That sounds like a great idea. We shall reconvene in an hour."

I looked at Nick and mouthed *thank you* before I raced to catch up with Will.

Blindsided

MY ALARM WOKE ME EARLY ON MONDAY and I groaned, bracing myself for a jam-packed week. Will and I would be rehearsing our duet during class, staying after school for dress rehearsals ahead of this weekend's show, all the while carving out time to practice our newfound Watcher abilities.

"Orchesis, this is it! This week will be grueling, but your creativity and the hard work you put into making your dance creations come alive will be celebrated this weekend!"

We all cheered at Coach R.'s words, excited for the show to finally be here.

"Now is not the time to sit back and relax. Now is the time to push yourself, to dance harder than ever, and take care of your bodies with good food and lots of rest. Class time this week is reserved for lighting and setting pieces in the theater. I have put the schedule on the whiteboard. If you are not on stage, you are quiet in the wings helping with lighting or here in the studio rehearsing or finishing costumes and stage props. Understood?"

"Yes, Coach R.," we all replied in unison.

"Good. Liddy and Will, you can still rehearse in the rec room. But first, Will, I need you in the theater so I can set the hip-hop piece you're in. I'll get it done first so you can meet Liddy straight away."

Will nodded. "Sounds good."

"I'll grab the boombox and try to figure out that ending." I smiled at him.

Coach R. clapped her hands twice as she said, "Chip-chop! *Ghetto Superstar* dancers, you are up first! I expect you on stage in you're starting positions in five minutes!"

The rec room blinds were still closed from the last time Will and I rehearsed in here. I pressed play on the boombox and turned the volume all the way up, drowning out the noises from the gym classes swimming below. Then, I tied on the blindfold we would use in our routine.

My body moved with the music as I marked each step of our choreography. On the third listen through, inspiration finally blossomed, and I had part of the ending set. I held down the rewind button to practice the new steps a few times, committing them to muscle memory.

I began the dance from the beginning. Shortly after starting, a pair of warm hands slid down my waist, gently squeezing my hip bones. I smiled. "Hey, babe. Done already?"

Will didn't say anything. Instead, his hands slid across

my stomach, engulfing me in a hug. The corners of my mouth ticked up and I let my head fall back on his chest. We stood, cradled in each other's arms, swaying to the music.

"What the heck?" A male's voice, Will's voice, rang out from somewhere in the room. I flinched, majorly disorientated.

Suddenly, those warm, strong arms were gone, replaced by a torrent of rage and jealousy. I whipped off the blindfold. Standing before me was Will, his eyes sparking, the veins in his hands bulging.

Slowly, I turned my head and saw Alex, his lips pinched between his fingers as he tried to hold in his laugh.

"You jerk!" I whirled and swatted him hard on the arm.

"Keep your hands off her," Will said through clenched teeth.

"She seemed to really enjoy it."

I rolled my eyes. "You wish. It's obvious I thought you were Will. Don't you have somewhere to be?"

"Awww, you guys know I was just messin' around.

Everyone knows you are practically married."

My cheeks flamed with heat and I looked to Will. Although he'd unclenched his hands, his eyes still crackled with anger.

"Anyway, I'm free this period and thought we could all hang out. Maybe, I could see this dance you've been—"

"No." Will stated this as its own complete sentence, offering no further explanation to Alex.

I owed my life to him and it bothered me that he and Will weren't getting along.

"Sorry, Alex, but Coach R. would have our heads if she found you in here. You're still planning to come to the showcase this weekend, though, right?" I smiled, hoping to soften the tension.

Alex bit his lip and rubbed the closely buzzed hair at the back of his head.

"Everything OK?" I asked, my intuition piquing.

"Yeah, I'm totally cool." His feeble smile lasted all of two seconds. "Guess I'll catch it this weekend then. See ya around, Liddy."

When the door to the pool closed behind him, I spun around to face Will.

"I know you don't like him, but did you have to be so rude?"

"Let me get this straight. I come in and he has his hands all over you and I'm the one who is rude?"

I sighed. "You know, Alex. He would never take it far. He basically does it to push our buttons."

"Why are you justifying his bad actions?"

Will just didn't understand. I shook my head and took a deep breath.

"Let's just forget about it. On a brighter note, I finished choreographing the ending and I think you'll like it."

The next few days whirred past. I think Nolan must have put something in the delicious shakes he had Will deliver to me each morning. Any normal teen would have already crashed from exhaustion between school, dance rehearsal, and combat training.

Alex hung around me more than usual during the day, though he was unusually quiet. By Thursday, I could no longer ignore him. The dark circles under his eyes only intensified his solemness.

Orchesis dance ensemble was hanging out in the commons area after changing into costume, waiting on Coach R. to let us into the theater for the final stage and lighting tweaks. I saw Alex pass by on the far end of the hall, walking toward the athletic corridor.

I shot up from the carpeted bench seat and ran after him.

"Alex, wait up!" I yelled just as he disappeared around the corner. I barreled around the corner and nearly slammed into him, my sneakers squeaking loudly in protest at the sudden stop.

"Liddy, what's wrong?"

"Nothing with me. What is wrong with you?" Alex cocked his brow and pursed his lips.

"Sorry, that came out wrong. I just get this feeling that you are not OK. Do you want to talk about it?"

Alex's eyes widened and then he threw his arms around me.

"What is it? You can tell me," I said into his shoulder.

"I can't, not here," he whispered.

Fear enveloped me. "You're freaking me out."

He squeezed me tighter. "I'm not gonna lie. It's not good."

"What can I do?" I made to release him, but he only held me tighter.

"Meet me after your show on Saturday, at the park?"

"Husky Park?"

"No, Carousel Park. It's near my house." He let me go, and his eyes resembled fish bowls brimming with water, his tears on the edge of spilling.

"Are you sure you don't want to meet tonight? It seems important."

"It is, but it can wait until after your show." He smiled weakly at me.

"OK. I should be able to meet you around nine."

"Thanks. See you then." He leaned in, gave me a lingering kiss on my cheek, then walked away.

My gut was screaming at me. Something was very, *very* wrong. I turned to head back to the theater and my heart dropped to my stomach. Will stood at the end of the hall, his arms crossed over his chest. For a second, with his eyes blazing and ripples of adrenaline pumping out of him and into me, he appeared like a menacing soldier, not the loving Will I knew, and it frightened me.

I boldly strode past him as if he hadn't been standing there like a jealous boyfriend.

But Will grabbed my elbow and spun me to face him.

"Why do I feel like I'm in trouble when I haven't done anything wrong?" I spat. My patience was stretched too thin this week.

"Why *do you* feel like you are in trouble? I didn't even say anything."

"You didn't have to!" I threw my hands up in frustration. "I can feel everything, remember?"

"Can you? Because you sure as heck couldn't *feel* it wasn't me in dance class when Alex had his hands all over you."

He was right. *Why didn't I feel that it was Alex and not him?* "I'm sorry for raising my voice and getting defensive. I have no idea why that happened. Maybe I was too distracted? There is quite a bit going on. Or maybe I'm just so used to you that I didn't check for our connection."

Will's face was hard as stone. "How would you feel if you stepped in on Jackie doing that with me?" he countered.

A hot surge of jealousy threatened to turn me green, but I blew out a long breath to cool down. Will smirked.

I lifted my chin. "I would hate it. But... I trust you."

"I of course trust *you*, but this is not about that."

"Then what is it about?" I huffed, my frustration returning.

"I don't trust *him*."

"Yeah, and why is that?" I shoved my hands on my hips. "I mean, if it wasn't for him, I would not be standing here today."

Will squeezed the bridge of his nose. "How long are you going to let him guilt you by playing that card?"

"I'm not letting him play, Will."

"How long am I supposed to stand here and watch Alex disrespect me over and over again?"

"He may be arrogant, but he means well."

Will snorted and rolled his eyes. "Stop making excuses for him."

"Stop trying to tell me what to do!"

He placed his hands on my shoulders and brought his eyes level with mine. "You are my everything. I wish you would respect me, no, *yourself* enough to know when someone needs to be put in their place. He knows you and I are together, Liddy, and I want to rip his arms off every time he dares to touch you."

"So the real issue is jealousy."

Will raked his hands through his hair in a rough, swift motion.

"NO!" He finally raised his voice. "That upsets me, of course. Didn't we just go over that with the Jackie example?"

"You know, come to think of it, I have felt this before, only you were actually kissing a girl...not just any girl, but my best friend." It was a low blow, but something had come over me and all I could feel was a pettiness mixed with anger.

Will's mouth dropped open. After a moment, he snapped it shut. "You know what happened, Liddy."

"I do. And I forgave you, but it still sucked. Alex and I never have even come close to that. We are just friends and right now, something is going on with him and he needs me."

"And I am telling you that my gifting is warning me, sirens blaring, that something is wrong and he is a danger to you. Why do you find it so hard to trust me on this?"

"He saved—"

"Again with that card! You do not owe him because he happened to be in the right place at the right time."

"Is everything alright?" Pree asked, looking between the two of us. I startled at her sudden proximity, not knowing when she'd arrived nor how much she'd heard.

"We're fine," Will and I said in unison.

"Riiiiight. And bears don't poop in the woods." Pree dropped her voice to a whisper. "Listen, luckily everyone else is in the theater, but you guys are getting loud. And if that wasn't concerning enough, may I remind you..." Pree trailed off and pointed with two fingers at her eyes and then at ours. "You don't want to let people in on your little secret."

I closed my eyes and took in a few deep breaths, calming myself. When I opened them again, I knew my eyes were back to normal, but I still was angry.

"Now, will someone please tell me what the heck is going on?" Pree asked, her hands on her hips.

"I'm done explaining myself. Will can fill you in. I'm going to the theater. Do me a favor. Don't follow me." I stormed off. As soon as rehearsal ended, I grabbed my bag and rushed out to the parking lot.

Spring Showcase

WILL DIDN'T CALL ME THAT NIGHT and I was glad. Well, my brain was glad, but my heart was sad.

So when he stood at my locker the following morning, waiting for me, a rush of relief swept over me at the sight of him. I wrapped my arms around his waist and gave him a big squeeze. "I'm so sorry. I don't know what's come over me."

"Same. I don't know why it escalated so quickly. If you need to be there for a friend, I won't stand in your way."

"Thank you," I said and brushed a soft kiss to his lips.

He smiled and then handed me the shake from Nolan. "Are you ready for tomorrow tonight? You don't seem nervous."

"I know, right? This time, all I can think about is how I

cannot wait to dance with you and knock everyone's socks off."

Will smiled and took my hand as we strolled to Sara's locker. "Uncle Shai is giving us the weekend off from training."

"Thank goodness! I have tons of homework to catch up on."

"Me, too. Also, I stupidly forgot about a big physics project due Monday. I am going to have to work double time to get it in on time. Nolan promised to help me tonight."

I deflated a little knowing I wouldn't see him, but then the corner of my mouth lifted.

"What's the little grin for?" he asked as he gently pinched my cheek.

"Since the winter formal, there hasn't been a single day that's gone by without us seeing each other, and I can't help but think how much more authentic it will feel for us when we dance the duet."

"You're right. Definitely something to look forward to."

I soaked up as much time with Will as I could during the classes we shared. At the end of the day, we waited for the parking lot to clear out so we could give each other a proper *see you later* kiss.

The evening's homework flew by thanks to the mixed CD Sara had burned for me. I had just crawled into bed when my phone rang.

"Hello?"

Only silence answered back.

"Hello?" I tried again, louder this time.

Unsteady breaths greeted me and then the line disconnected. My skin prickled and I set the phone on its base. I jumped when it immediately rang again.

"Who is this!" I said, clutching my chest.

"Liddy, what's wrong?"

I let out an immense sigh of relief upon hearing Will's voice. "Did you just try to call?

"No."

"Someone called, but they wouldn't say anything and then they just hung up."

"It was probably just a wrong number," he reassured me.

"You're probably right," I agreed, though my skin still crawled.

"Well, it's late. I was just heading to bed when our bond alerted me that you were scared. Now that I know you're alright, I just want to say sweet dreams and I love you."

I smiled. "I love you, too. See you at curtain call tomorrow."

The next day, Pree, Sara, Dani and I chatted excitedly as we headed to the dance room to grab our costumes. Then, we proceeded down to the black box, the room behind the stage, where female performers prepped. The few guys on the team would be next door, readying in the music room.

Dani had just finished applying my false lashes when a stagehand called out to me through a crack in the door.

"Liddy, someone is here to see you."

"Thanks, Megan. I'll be right there." I slipped through the door and was met with a surprise. Will stood with his hands behind his back.

"Hi, beautiful." I could feel the heat rising up my neck.

His compliments would never get old.

"Hi handsome," I replied coyly.

"Who, me? This bronzer and cheek stain doing it for ya?"

he teased, turning his head and puffing out his chest.

I burst out laughing. "If spider leg lashes and fifteen layers of makeup do it for you."

"Still beautiful," he said and when he leaned down, his lips tickled my ear. "But your naked face is my favorite."

I clenched my hands, my nails biting into my palms to distract myself from jumping on him.

"These are for you." Will presented me a beautiful bouquet of blush pink peonies with a few Christmas roses sprinkled in.

"They're gorgeous and they smell heavenly!"

"Break a leg. See you at curtain call." He wrapped his chiseled arms slowly around my waist and leaned down so his lips were mere millimeters from mine. "If you weren't wearing lipstick, I would kiss you until you glowed brighter than a thousand spotlights."

Curse this red lipstick! My bottom lip jutted out.

"I promise that when the cast party is over, I'll kiss you until you ask me to stop." When he pulled away, I nearly toppled from weak knees.

He smirked and walked to his dressing room. I took a steadying breath and headed back to my friends.

"Holy crap, Liddy. Did Will just propose to you?" Pree laughed.

"Something like that," I teased.

"Fine, fine. Sit your butt back down. I need to add the winged eyeliner," Dani ordered me.

"Yes, ma'am."

Twenty minutes later, the entire ensemble was spread out on the dimly lit stage. All the girls wore lilac or mint dresses, and the boys khaki pants with white button downs, for the opening cast number. Coach R. led us in warmups as we stretched on the black marley flooring that had been laid down and swept clean. Before I knew it, we were all ushered into the wings, next to the boom lighting, waiting for the heavy blue curtains to open.

"Welcome, ladies and gents, to the thirteenth annual Orchesis Spring Showcase!" Coach R. announced over the speakers. The entire audience erupted in cheers and my heart hammered in my chest, the anticipation driving it to near bursting.

As Coach continued with announcements, I felt Will's eyes on me from across the stage. When I looked up, I found his gaze. A gentle pressure wrapped around me and then released. My eyes widened at the surprise hug and he smirked. I mouthed *I love you* and blew him a kiss. The next time I'd see him would be onstage for our duet to close out Act One.

My skin was hot and sticky as I flew past the boom lighting to the quick-change area, where Sara was waiting to help me into my duet costume. In less than sixty seconds, I needed to be back on stage.

"I'll be rooting for you in the wings!" Sara whispered to me as she checked that my two clasps were securely fastened. Once released, they would turn my dress from white to black to purple as planned. She placed my blindfold into my hand and I rushed onto the stage.

Will stood waiting for me on our mark. He helped tie my blindfold around my neck, ready for the part in the choreography where we would be blind and separated, relying completely on muscle memory. His fingers brushed my neck and arms, trailing down to my hands. He brought one to his mouth and kissed it. The auditorium was silent except for my heavy breaths. For a moment, just before we were announced, it was just me and Will, swallowed by the darkness. Our bond hummed between us and I relished the secure, weighted comfort it brought me.

With the staccato strum of a guitar, the stage lit up. Bright lights streamed across our bodies, snow falling on the back canvas thanks to lighting effects. And thus, through movement, we told our story.

In the final four eight counts, we turned and our chests slammed into each other, our arms extended out. Slowly, we relaxed them, swaying and sinking to the floor as we held onto each other. Then he stood as I sat on the ground and turned to him. With both my hands in his, I exploded from the floor into a split jump. Will caught me as I wrapped my legs and arms around him and he spun. I released my arms from his neck, the momentum carrying me as I dove back and around in a wild dip, still secured in Will's strong arms.

Finally, Will kneeled after one pirouette and postured toward me as I rose onto my toes. With my chest and arms lifted to the ceiling, I free-fell into his waiting arms. His hands at my waist quickly turned me and he held me as he dipped me over his knee. My arms came around to brush the sides of his cheek. The final strum of the guitar blasted through the speakers, and as the vibration faded, we were only supposed to cling to each other, but one look at that spark in his eyes and I could not help but kiss the young man who was my world.

The stage lights cut out, and the audience erupted into a standing ovation. But Will and I continued our kiss until the curtains closed. We broke apart as the ensemble swarmed the stage to congratulate us. Amid the celebratory wishes and pats, I could hardly hear or feel anything as Will helped me to stand, my gaze locked in his.

A good yank on my arm broke my stare.

"Ow!" I complained.

"Someone had to snap you out of it," Pree chirped.

Will laughed and placed his hand on my shoulder. His hand warmed and a tingling sensation flitted over my skin, then sank deep into the muscle. He was nothing if not thorough when healing me.

As I listened to Sara, Dani, and Pree highlight their favorite parts of the duet, I felt eyes against my back. I looked over my shoulder.

Alex stood in the wing furthest upstage near the exit doors clutching a bouquet of purple roses. He gave me a small wave and beckoned me over to him.

"I'll meet you all backstage in a minute," I said to my friends. Then I jogged over to Alex. "Everything OK," I asked him.

"I just had to let you know, you are seriously the most beautiful dancer I've ever seen."

"Oh, please. You just haven't seen many dancers."

"No, I mean it. You pulled up feelings I didn't even know I had to the surface. Shoot, I almost cried."

Heat crept into my cheeks. "Thank you."

He stared at me for a long moment and shook his head. "Here, these are for you. Unfortunately, I have to leave." He handed me the flowers.

"Thank you, they are beautiful!" My body alerted me to the distinct vibrations of Will before he appeared at my side.

Alex stiffened, not taking his eyes off of me. "Are we still on for tonight?"

"Of course. Carousel Park, right?"

"Yeah. See ya then." Alex gave me a hug before exiting.

"I know I said I wouldn't interfere, but—"

"Yes, you did say that."

Will's hands rested on my shoulders, his gaze intense, as if pleading with me to better understand him. "I'm not trying to be a jerk, but I don't want you meeting him tonight."

I shrugged out of his hold. "Well, too bad. Alex is counting on me, and I can't let him down. Besides, I don't know about you, but when my friends need me, I'm there."

A surge of Will's anger coursed through me, expanding my veins, the blood pulsating with vigor on its journey to and from my heart. I ignored him for the rest of Act Two.

The Coward

"**L**IDDY, STOP. THINK ABOUT THIS. I know you're angry with Will, but running off to be with Alex?" Pree waved her hands wildly. "Red flags *all over* the field."

Of course I was angry with Will. He managed to turn one of the best nights of my life into a downer. After the show, as I was gathering my things, he approached me yet again to question my seeing Alex.

"Darn straight, I'm mad." I wadded up my discarded costume and shoved it into my duffle bag. I spotted the flowers Will gave me and my eyes stung. "He basically told me I was an idiot."

"He *so* did not." Pree clucked her tongue. "He said his magical Watcher powers—" she wiggled her fingers at me— "were giving him serious danger vibes."

"Whatever." I adjusted the waist of my black track pants and zipped up my team jacket. I tried to leave it at that, but Pree would not let the subject drop. She prattled on and on, from the changing area, out of the auditorium, all the way to the near-empty parking lot.

"I'm just sayin'," she said as we approached my car, "my Spidey sense is tingling, alright?"

I released an exasperated sigh. "Alex simply needs a friend right now, alright? It's the least I can do for him after everything, you know?" I ducked into the driver's seat of my car before she could respond.

Pree flung open the passenger door and dropped into the seat as I turned the key. "What's so important that you have to ditch the cast party for?"

"I don't know. And I'm not ditching the cast party. I'll be...fashionably late."

"Then you won't mind me joining you."

"Of course not," I replied, backing out of my parking spot.

"Just wait in the car. It seemed like it was personal."

"He's probably going to profess his love for you," Pree mumbled.

I rolled my eyes. We'd been over this, more than once.

"Don't roll your eyes. I'm serious," Pree scolded.

"Don't tell me what to do," I snapped back. "I do not like Alex. I—"

"I know!" Pree cut in.

"Don't interrupt me! As I was saying, for the hundredth time, Alex is a friend. I owe him my life."

"You owe him nothing. You said 'thank you.' That should be enough."

"Ugh, now you sound like Will."

"Good." She pursed her lips and cocked her head. "That means I have my head on straight!"

I snarled, my eyes burning with the temptation to destroy something. I took my frustration out on the steering wheel, nearly crushing it with my grip, and refused to look at Pree. We were silent the rest of the drive. I pulled into the closest parking spot and turned off the car.

Pree turned to me. "Liddy, I'm sorry for yelling. Please, just be careful."

My lips twisted. "You all act like I'm incapable of making good decisions."

"You are capable, but there is something up with Alex. At the very least he likes you, but he's also using you...or something."

"He's not using me." I closed my eyes, not wanting to lash out at her again.

"Fine, manipulating, playing you like a fiddle. However you want to put it. Ever since he *saved* you, you bend over backwards for him. *All-the-freaking-time*." She slapped her thigh in sync with each word.

I looked askance at her while white-knuckling the steering wheel. "Alex wouldn't do that."

"Are we talking about the same Alex?" Pree smacked her forehead. "Because the Alex I know *definitely* would. If it were between you and him, he would choose himself every time."

"Are you done?" I glowered, keeping my gaze trained straight ahead.

"Almost." Pree bounced slightly in her seat. "Didn't you learn anything the night Nick shared his memories with us? It was like when he saved Mara from the cave. She felt she didn't deserve to be saved. Do you feel the same way about yourself? Is that why you are trying so hard, in your own way, to make it up to Alex?"

I just stared at her. "I don't know," I whispered.

Pree pried my hand from the wheel and squeezed it. "I'll wait here. Just be careful, please."

I tried my best to muster a smile, but the corners of my lips barely quirked. I got out, slammed the door, and walked through the mulch.

Alex stepped out from behind a slide and I gasped.

He gingerly touched a spot near his eye. "It looks worse than it is," he said, averting his gaze.

I walked up to him and cupped his chin, gently turning it. "Who did that to your face?"

He stepped back. "No one. I have a big mouth. Don't worry about it." Though he smiled at me, I could only detect sadness and pain behind it.

"So, that's not the emergency?" I furrowed my brow confused.

"No, it's not." He shook his head. "Walk with me?"

"Sure, but I can't go far. Pree is with me," I said, turning to my car and then back again to face Alex.

More uneasiness rippled off of him, and my gifting began thrumming deep inside, alerting me to its potential necessity. Something told me the grimace he wore had nothing to do with his black eye and cut cheek.

"That's fine, we'll just go around the field," he said as he checked his watch.

"OK."

We walked for a few minutes. Alex stopped in the middle of the field a few yards behind the park equipment.

"Liddy, I need to sh—" his voice cracked and he bit his lip. "I need to share something with you."

"What is it? You're making me nervous."

"You know I...care for you, right?"

"Alex, you've been a good friend to me."

His usually bright eyes went dark. "No, I mean, I really care for you, more than just about anyone I've ever met. You're special. The way you treat everyone with such kindness. That's why what I have to do pains me so much." He looked at his watch again and darted his eyes toward the playground.

"What do you mean? What do you have to do?"

"Let's go take a seat."

We walked in silence, Alex worrying his lip the entire way. He climbed a few steps to the landing in front of the slide and sat down. I hesitated for a moment before sitting directly across from him. Darkness rapidly descended upon us. The park lights were not on yet, and the shadows lingering around him troubled me more than the darkness creeping in from the elements.

Alex's knee bounced faster than a basketball in a Globe Trotter's hands. I touched his knee to still it, and his eyes met mine.

His lips moved, but no sound came out.

"I'm sorry?" I prodded him.

"It was me," he whispered.

"What was you?"

He cleared his throat, his hands now clenched so tightly in his lap that his knuckles turned white. "The winter dance.

It was me."

"I know. I'll never forget how you saved me."

Hurt registered on his face. "Liddy, you don't understand. If it wasn't for me, you'd never have been in that predicament in the first place."

I stared at him, blinking, trying to understand the words that came out of his mouth. "Alex, it's not your fault that I chose to go with Justin."

Alex's hands flung to the sides of his head and he nearly ripped his hair out. A groan of frustration escaped his throat. I scooted back a few inches.

"Why do you have to do that? Why do you have to be so dang nice?"

"Alex, you're freaking me out." And for the first time, I realized we were hidden from Pree's sight.

"You should be scared of me. You should hate me, but I've been too much of a coward to carry out my orders, and now my time has run out."

My gifting was suddenly on high alert. I could feel the energy around me begin to change to something familiar and dark. I started to get up.

"I'm so sorry, Liddy, but you're not leaving."

"Very funny, but you don't get to order me around. I *am* leaving...now."

He grabbed my wrist. "I said, you cannot leave." A familiar color flashed in his eyes. He shook his head, blinked, and it was gone. "Not yet," he said, talking to someone over his shoulder.

I froze. My stomach sank and my heart raced.

"Alex, is that you, or was I speaking with someone else

just now?"

"Yes, it's me. She would never possess me like she did Justin and Pree."

She. Every hair on my body stood up as wave after wave of panic washed over me. I closed my eyes and reached out to Will. I didn't know how far he was from me at this point, but I had faith that he'd be able to find me.

"When you say *she*, you mean Mara?"

"Yes," he responded flatly, "though I have to call her *my queen.* You see, I'm the one who poisoned Justin."

I made a go at trying to escape off the metal platform, but Alex's stealthy reflexes snatched me before I moved even an inch, like he knew I was going to move before I did.

He had me pinned beneath him with his hand over my mouth. "Please don't make this harder for me. We don't have much time, and I need to explain."

I tried to bite back the tears of betrayal, but couldn't. Alex sighed, and rested his forehead on mine.

"I'm sorry, Liddy." The pad of his thumb brushed away my tears as they fell.

"Mmmm suuuueurrrr," I struggled to speak, but my voice was muffled by Alex's hand. He removed it and I repeated myself. "I'm sure you are."

Hot tears, Alex's tears, fell on my cheek, and I wanted more than anything to get them off my skin.

"When? Why?" I asked, nearly choking on the sobs that escaped my throat.

"She's the reason my family moved to Wheeling. Every summer I go 'away' to sports camp, but really, I have to live in that hell hole. She threatened me that I'd have to stay in her cave permanently after I was unsuccessful in getting you to go to the dance with me. That's when I came up with the brilliant plan to drug Justin instead and let him be the bad guy. I could still fulfill her demands without having to hurt you myself. But I couldn't go through with it."

Sharp pains bit into my back as the honeycombed metal of the platform pressed into my skin under Alex's weight. "Is that when you hit Justin?"

"Yes. I thought Mara wouldn't know. I made sure to approach Justin from the back so she wouldn't see me, but she was still angry nonetheless. I had failed in killing you."

"So, you're going to kill me?"

"No..."

"Thank God. I knew you were a good—"

He placed his hand over my mouth, cutting off my words as tears continued to stream down his face.

"*I'm* not going to kill you. *She* is."

A Good Drama

"LIDDY? ALEX?" Pree's voice called. She was close. "I know I was supposed to wait in the car, but it's been like thirty minutes and we have to get to the cast party. Plus, look who I found going for a run in the neighborhood. I totally forgot he lived here."

Alex stilled and placed his finger to his lips, a warning. "Hey, Pree. Can you give us a few more minutes? We are...in the middle of something important."

I closed my eyes and tapped into my power for strength. The heat was immediate, but something hard hit my cheek, cutting off the surge. Before I could cry out in pain, Alex's hand stifled my sobs.

"Oh, no you don't. You're not going to use any Watcher magic on me, or I'll have to hurt Pree." Alex's breath was hot against my ear and I recoiled.

"What was that?" Pree asked. Silence greeted her.

"Liddy?" A male voice, one I hadn't heard in far too long, was like music to my ears. *Justin.*

"Why can't people mind their dang business?" Alex hissed. "Go away, we are indisposed."

"Oh hellz no! Liddy, have you lost your freakin'— What the heck!" Pree screeched, Justin right at her side.

"Get off her, now," Justin growled, his eyes moving as he took in Alex sprawled over top me, holding me down and covering my mouth.

"Liddy, what are you doing? Use, you know..." Pree ticked her chin and stomped her foot. "Use your *gift.*"

My eyes were wide with terror and Alex released his hand.

"Tell her why you won't be using your Watcher gifts on me," Alex said coyly. The emotional boy from just a few moments ago was now a lion ready to enter the ring. He quickly checked his watch and smiled.

Pree's face scrunched. "Wait, he knows about—"

"Obviously. Gosh, you really are *such* an airhead," Alex mocked, getting to his knees, one pressed into my chest holding me down.

"Pree," I mustered through the sobs that choked my throat. "He says if I do, he'll hurt you."

"Not if you pulverize him first!" she smacked her fist into her palm.

Alex's head whipped to the side. "Justin, take one more step and you'll regret it."

"What the heck is wrong with your eyes, Alex?" Pree gasped. "Liddy, call Will."

"He won't make it on time," Alex said, the fight leaving his voice as he gazed at me. He finally lifted himself off of me and clutched my elbow. "Stand up, Liddy. I need to get you in the right spot." When I didn't, he wrenched my arm and forced me to stand.

"Alex, you don't have to do this. We can help you. We know people who can help you," I pleaded.

He sighed. "You won't beat her."

"You don't know that," Pree countered. "There is no way you can know the future."

"She's too powerful. She always gets what she wants. Always." Alex used the back of his fingers to caress my cheek. I whipped my head away. "See, I told you you'd hate me."

I forced myself to look at him. "I don't hate you. Just disappointed in your lack of courage, and your lack of fight." I braced myself, expecting another blow.

"I tried! I really did!" Alex bellowed. "Nothing worked. She was always ten steps ahead of me. If you only knew what I've been through, what I've witnessed." He still had a tight grip on my elbow. "I told you I care for you, I really do. But if I don't do this, I will turn into *one of them*." I could see the absolute horror in his eyes, and I knew he was referring to the shadows in my dreams. "I'd be better off dead."

Without further preamble, Alex produced a crisp white envelope from his jacket pocket and tore it open with his teeth before tossing it onto the ground in front of us. At first, nothing happened. I began to back away, but Alex came behind me and wrapped his arms around my torso, an impenetrable vise. He was shaking.

I couldn't think straight. His betrayal was too much. He

had been working for Mara all along. All this time he had planned to deliver me to her, essentially sealing my fate. I *trusted* him. I guess I really couldn't be counted on to make good decisions.

I looked at my friends who stood there, not sure what to do. Justin had no idea what was even going on, and yet he didn't back down or run away. Even after all he'd been through, he still chose to stay and try to help me.

"Pree, go with Justin. Tell Will what happened and that I'm sorry."

"No, Liddy! You can't! Use your gifting, now!" Pree begged.

Tears streamed down my face. "I will not risk something happening to you, to either of you."

"I don't know what you guys are talking about, but Alex... just let her go man," Justin chimed in.

The envelope began vibrating so quickly, I almost missed when it began to float above the ground. A dull glow started within the seal and leaked out around the envelope's seams before exploding into brilliant orange. When my vision adjusted, a large portal stood before me, blocking my view of Pree and Justin. I would know those cave walls anywhere.

My body hummed as each fiber and nerve ending screamed at me to run away when a dark shadow walked toward us from deep within the portal.

"Please forgive me, Liddy. You'll be alright. Just do what she says and it'll be over quickly." Alex tucked a loose strand of my hair behind my ear. "She promised you won't feel a thing."

"Do you honestly believe that?" I grimaced.

"It's the only thing keeping me together," he said somberly.

Pree and Justin emerged on opposite sides of the portal so that once again they were in view.

"I'd stand back if I were you," Alex warned. "She'll take anything she can grab."

Justin stood with his jaw clenched, his eyes calculating the situation before him, but he didn't say a word. He kept his gaze locked on mine in silent communication, and it brought me some comfort.

Finally, the shadow drew close to the portal's entrance. Momentary relief flooded me when I saw it wasn't Mara, after all. I cocked my head and my heart flipped in recognition. It was the boy from my nightmares. But then my heart sank. This was the same boy who came to my house and tried to deliver one of Mara's envelopes to me after she possessed Justin and forced him to attack me.

Alex's eyes narrowed as he pushed me a little closer to the portal. "Jamie? Where is Mara?"

"She has other matters to attend to at the moment, so she sent me," Jamie answered impassively, his gaze fixed on me. I could swear I almost saw him frown.

Alex started shoving me toward Jamie. I dug my heels in.

He grunted. "Liddy, please. You are making this so much worse...for both of us." His voice was full of regret.

But I didn't care. How dare he? If our roles were reversed, I would never intentionally hand my friend over to their death. Rage surged through me, and I stomped on Alex's right foot with my combat boot.

"Damn it, Liddy!" While he was still stunned and hopping on one foot, I elbowed him in the gut. Alex wheezed and crumpled forward.

Jamie just stood there and watched, like a gargoyle sentry.

"Jamie, dear, what's taking so long?" A singsong voice echoed from down the cave. Shivers ran along the length of my spine, and everyone froze. I turned to face Justin. His furrowed brow told me he was working out how he knew that voice.

But then Alex recovered and snatched my arm, dragging me forward.

"My queen, we are in need of your assistance," Jamie said, looking bored.

I was only a few feet away now, my palms sweaty, as the shadowy form of Mara emerged in the depths of the portal's window. She must have saw me because the shadow gained unnatural speed. I was out of time.

I screamed, kicked, anything I could do to slow down Alex, to break his hold on me. I saw Pree, crying, trying to inch toward me.

"Interfere, and she'll come for you too," Alex sneered.

"Go, Pree!" When she didn't budge, I planted my feet and stiffened my legs, focusing my gaze on Justin. "Justin, please! Take her back to my car. Get out of here, now! She will know where to take you." Justin came up behind Pree who sank into his arms and cried even harder.

A loud cackling assaulted me. She was here. My body vibrated with pure natural instinct, wanting to explode, but I quickly squelched it. I would not risk my friends.

"My, my, my. Don't we all jusssst love a good drama." Mara brought her fists up to her chest and shimmied in a little dance. "Jamie, dear, help Alex. As per her usual, Lydia is playing hard to get. But we've waited long enough." Her smile resembled an asp's. "Seize her!"

Jamie took a single step out of the portal, careful to keep one foot in the other world. Alex shoved me with all his strength toward Jamie. Everything that happened next seemed to unfold before me in slow motion.

"Trust me, Liddy!" Pree screamed.

I darted my head in her direction as I fell toward Jaime's outstretched arms. Without warning, Justin's body slammed into me, the force sending me skidding across the ground and away from the portal.

"Noooo!" Mara screeched.

I scrambled onto my hands and knees just in time to see Alex roar, his eyes flashing, as he charged at Justin and forcefully shoved him.

In Mara's eagerness, she accidentally bumped Jamie, who stumbled out of the portal. Her gaze focused on Justin who was about to land in her arms. Mara slowly licked her champagne lips, the flesh turning to marcasite everywhere her tongue touched. Pree, who'd only been a few seconds behind Justin, skidded to a halt. She looked at Justin, then at Alex, then her eyes swung over me, holding my gaze. Her lips moved, but I couldn't make out what she said. She reached out and grabbed Justin's arm, never taking her eyes off of me. I stared back until bright green flashed in my vision. When I finally wrenched my eyes open, the portal was gone.

So were Pree and Justin.

I Can't Leave

S OMEONE WAS SCREAMING. Loud, incessant, gut-wrenching sobs for what seemed like eternity. They wouldn't shut up and I couldn't tune them out.

Alex's face came into focus. He was saying something, but I couldn't comprehend his words. His face contorted and then he began shaking me.

Everything came back to reality and I realized I was the one wailing.

"Liddy, what did you do? What did you do?" Alex yelled over and over again, shaking me, my body like a limp noodle.

In the parking lot, tires screeched and car doors slammed.

Will was finally here. "Get your hands off of her!" he bellowed.

Alex let me go, and I slumped to the ground, curling in on

myself. The ground vibrated with thudding footsteps as dirt was kicked up at my legs.

"I've got her!" Will yelled. "Someone get him!" Will knelt at my side. "Liddy," he said with all the protectiveness of a guardian angel watching over their charge. "Liddy, I'm here. Are you hurt?"

But I couldn't answer him through the dark fog of shame that clung to me. How could I explain that not only did Mara nearly capture me because I was too stubborn to listen to anyone, especially Will, but now Pree and Justin were at the witch's treacherous disposal because I failed in my duties as a Watcher to protect them!

He stroked my hair, then ran his hands over every inch of my body, making sure I was unharmed.

"Is she injured?" Nick asked, his voice deep and gruff.

"A few scrapes," Will responded.

"You should get her to the car."

Will reached under me to lift me up, but I flailed. "It's OK, Princess... It's just me. I'm going to get you out of here."

I continued to thrash unable to voice the words racing through my mind. *I can't leave. Not without them.*

Will let go. "OK, I'm not taking you anywhere." He helped me to sit and straddled himself behind me, drawing me close. I turned and clung to his chest.

Shai dragged Alex by his coat collar. "Does someone want to tell me who this boy is and why he ran from us?"

"What did you do, Alex?" Will asked, his words cold. I shivered and he hugged me tighter.

"It was so crazy. I— I asked Liddy to meet me here because I got into a fight—" He gestured to his eye— "and I needed someone to talk to."

"You lying jerk!" I screamed and lunged at him. Rage consumed me and, like a rabid dog, I tried to bite his leg.

"Well, obviously he's lying," Nick said flatly.

"Easy, Liddy." Will coaxed me back into him. My body shook as I tried to reign in my gifting's desire to unleash itself on Alex. As much as I wanted to right now, I knew I'd never forgive myself if I killed him.

"Looks like you're coming with us, kid." Shai smiled with a wicked turn of his lip.

"That's kidnapping!" Alex bellowed. "Help! Help!"

Shai's leather gloved hand successfully silenced him. "Nolan, if you could."

Nolan shoved a twinkling purple vial under Alex's nose. Within seconds, his head slumped forward. Shai took Alex's arm and brought it over his shoulder, then bent and lifted him in a fireman's carry.

Shai turned to speak to us before trekking to the car. "We need to be going. Although it's dark, we can't risk being seen."

"Come on, Princess," Will coaxed. "Let's get you back to my place, warm you up, and grab a bite to eat. Maybe you'll feel like sharing what happened then."

"I... I can't leave." My cheeks were tight from salted tears that had dried in the frigid air.

"Sure you can. I'll carry you."

"No!" I whimpered, sobbing all over again.

"I don't know what to do," Will said, and I could feel the utter confusion and nervousness as it coursed through his system.

"Liddy, why do you not you want to leave?" Nick pressed.

In all of the chaos, no one noticed Jamie walk up to us until he spoke. "I believe I know."

Nick turned to face Jamie. He cocked his head, assessing him, then his eyebrows shot high on his forehead and he fell to his knees.

"Nick, what is it?" Will looked at Jaime and frowned. "And who are you?"

Jamie stepped into the glowing light Shai and Nick's powers produced. After a few minutes, Will gasped, and I felt his body go into shock, the mild numbness dousing my bloodstream like I'd received a small dose of Novocain.

"Hello, brother," Jamie said, staring directly into Will's face.

"Charlie?" I took one look at the boy's face, and I knew. *How could I not have recognized him sooner?*

"Hi, Liddy," he responded. No smile. No wave.

A thousand emotions rained down on me like a monsoon in a dessert. Guilt for not knowing who he was and for not saving him sooner. Pain at knowing only a fraction of the horrors he'd had to endure. Grief so heavy it would crush me that this sweet boy lost so much, and how we were denied time with him. Fear, anger, surprise, shame, regret...the emotions swirled and crashed.

"I-can't-breathe!" I huffed out. My chest heaved as I tried to catch my breath. My body rebelled against all attempts Will made to console me through our bond.

"A little help, Nolan?" I heard Nick say. A moment later, the purple vial was under my nose, and I quickly went to sleep.

Taken

FLASHES OF CONCERNED FACES. Fragments of hushed voices. Shivers of every emotion under the sun. My surroundings blurred in and out of my consciousness. Then, quiet.

"Madam Lydia, open your eyes."

I tried to blink, but everything felt heavy.

"That's it. Here, take a sip of this." Something cool and smooth touched my lips and I drank. Bubbles of heat slid down my throat and through my limbs. As they burst, more and more feeling and energy came back to me.

My eyes flung open and I tried to make sense of my surroundings.

"Welcome back." Nolan smiled down at me.

"Where am I?" I croaked, sitting upright.

"Easy now. Swing your legs over the edge of the bed... That's it. Sit there for just a few moments. You are in Lord Abishai's guest room, where Lord William's parents used to sleep."

I'd not been in this room before. Shades of cream and gold met my gaze as I surveyed the room. My fingertips brushed against the soft, green velvet bedding.

"Tell me I was just having another nightmare, Nolan."

His face fell. "All is not lost," he said quietly, placing his hand on my shoulder. I felt a small ripple of calm ask permission to enter my body, and I allowed it.

I took a deep breath. In...two...three..., Out...two... three... four. "Where is everyone?"

"His Highness and Lords Abishai and William are downstairs in the family room with Charlie."

"Take me there, please."

"Of course. As soon as you finish this drink I made you."

I chugged down the rest of the bubbly drink. "Done."

Nolan chuckled. "Alright, follow me."

We traveled down the main stairway and I used the elaborately carved banister for support. Not because I needed it physically, but because emotionally, I needed something to hold on to.

Nolan took slow, purposeful strides. I couldn't be sure if it was for my benefit or his. Maybe both. Regardless, I was thankful for the pace with which he led me as it allowed me a few extra moments to try and at least process the idea that Charlie was back.

Jamie is Charlie. Charlie is Jamie. That young man whose gaze bored into mine during my dreams... I'd simply forgotten him. I knew he looked familiar, but... My heart sank. Eight years he'd lived with that witch, with the shadows, cloaked in a cave of darkness. The bright-eyed, fun, and lively Charlie I knew was no longer.

Totally lost in thought, I collided into Nolan's back at the entryway to the family room. It was like hitting a rock. Nolan barely budged except to turn.

He steadied me, then leaned down and whispered, "Are you alright?"

"Yes, sorry. I guess my thoughts wandered."

He removed his hand from my elbow and took my hand in his. Looking at me straight in the eyes, he said, "I have a strong feeling everything is going to be alright."

I smiled back at him and wished I had his confidence. I stepped into the family room and immediately tuned in to Will. He looked up, gave me a half-smile, and patted the couch cushion next to him. Though he was elated to see me, he was still rather numb.

Uncomfortable silence blanketed the room. Shai couldn't take his eyes off of Charlie, who had his hands in his lap and his head down. Nick, though physically present, seemed to be lost in the recesses of his mind as he sat back against the couch, arms crossed, staring blankly at the wall.

I scurried over and leaned into Will's ear. "What did I miss?"

He draped his arm around my waist and pulled me in close. "Nothing. I guess we are all in shock."

"You could say that."

My eyes swept the room again and swiftly fixed on Charlie, as if staring at him could make me believe he was truly here and not merely the ghost of a boy who once was.

Charlie tilted his head and peered up at me through his lashes. His eyes, once so alight with life and adventure, were now empty and tarnished by dark circles underneath. All traces of his father's blue had vanished, replaced by an orange film. Shadows marred his ashen skin and his once bright blonde hair had turned the color of dirty dishwater. He literally wore his time with Mara, and my heart cracked under the weight of that revelation. The radiant light within him had been extinguished. I could only hope it wasn't permanent.

Charlie dropped his gaze and worried his lip, just as Will often did. I cleared my throat and Nick stirred from the sound.

"Liddy, I am so glad you are feeling better." He smiled at me, but it didn't crinkle his eyes like usual.

"Are you able to tell us what happened at that park?" Shai asked.

Will sensed the utter guilt that unloaded over me again as the earlier events came rushing back. He squeezed me tighter around the waist, as if by bringing me closer he could take some of the burden from me. However, I knew he had no idea yet as to why I felt this way.

"Yes," I answered Shai, taking Will's free hand in mine.

"You kept saying you couldn't leave," Will said softly. "Why?"

I took a deep, shuddering breath, readying myself to share out loud for the first time that Pree and Justin were... gone.

"Her friends were taken by the queen," Charlie mumbled, keeping his head down.

Nolan, who was pushing his silver cart full of drinks and snacks into the room, came to an abrupt halt.

"What do you mean?" Shai knitted his brows.

"Mara, she took Justin and Pree." I choked on Pree's name and Will wrapped me in his arms.

Hands grasped my shoulders and knees and I suddenly felt lighter. Not completely, but not ravaged by emotional turmoil either. I placed my hand on Will's chest and pushed myself to a sitting position. Nolan was at my shoulders, and I was surprised to see Shai at my knees.

My eyes darted to Nick. For the first time, I saw anger. His lips were pressed into a hard line as he rolled up each of his sleeves to his elbows in quick, sharp movements.

"What happened?" he growled, a tone I'd never heard from him before, the fierce warrior in him emerging.

"Do you need me to stay here?" Shai asked me, a small smile warming his eyes.

I shook my head and he returned to his seat. "I'll start at the beginning. Alex asked me...wait, what happened to Alex?" I twisted, searching the room for him.

"He's in our care at the moment," Shai quickly responded. "Please continue."

I blew a strand of hair out of my face. "To make a long story short, Alex confessed to being the one who drugged Justin at the winter formal and to doing Mara's bidding. Then he apologized for planning to hand me over to her. But, Pree spotted Justin on a run. They saved me from being shoved into Mara's hands, but were taken instead."

Just when I thought I would lose it again, another surge of energy flowed through me, calming my racing heart.

Will released me and shot to his feet, emerald eyes gleaming.

"Sit down, William," Shai cautioned, coming to stand by his nephew.

Will shrugged his uncle off. "No. I think we need to have a chat with Alex."

"Sit. Down!" Nick ordered, his voice reverberating off the walls, and I flinched.

Will stumbled back a few steps, his face contorted in anger, his head cocked with annoyance at having been scolded.

"Nick, relax." Shai held a hand up to him. "He obviously has no plans to jeopardize our operation. He's a young man who just wants to avenge his match."

Will glanced at Shai and the light in his eyes dimmed. I grasped Will's forearm and he sat back down.

Nick turned to face Shai. "Cousin, the time is ripe. We need to make plans—"

"Not yet." Shai cut him off.

"Now." Nick rose to his full height. "We are making plans to leave, *now*."

Time to Wake Up

"**U**M, EXCUSE ME."

"What?" Nick bellowed as he swiveled to face me.

I simply pointed at Charlie, who sat still as stone. Nick's scowl melted; he looked exhausted as heck.

Like talking to a wild animal that might scare, Shai gingerly approached Charlie, his arms low and hands splayed. "You probably don't remember me, but I am your uncle— Uncle Shai."

Charlie looked up then, but whether or not he remembered Shai was still a mystery as he merely stared at him.

Shai continued, "We are so glad to finally have you back with us. We have been looking for you ever since you disappeared."

"But you knew I was with the queen," Charlie said, ice lacing his words.

"Well, yes, but—"

"But you never came for me." He dropped his gaze. "Then again, no one gets in without her knowing."

"We tried. Oh, how we tried." Shai wiped at his eyes with the back of his hand. "We have no idea where exactly Mara is nor how to access her, but we never let that deter us."

Charlie lifted his head. "Speaking of, she is going to be very angry. You need to return me to that park. She'll be back to collect me."

"You will stay with us now." Shai wore a pained smile. "You never have to go back there again."

I would think Charlie would be relieved, or show some sort of emotion now that he was out of Mara's clutches and Beldam. But his next words surprised me.

"I need to go back. She trusts me. I..." He worried his lip. "I help the others."

I knew exactly who he meant, and suddenly, I was a pumpkin whose innards had been scraped too many times— the realization hollowed me out. The blinking orbs that I learned were children flickered across my mind as I recalled my dreams. I got up from the couch, knelt in front of Charlie, and gave him a big hug. Although he did not return it, I did not let go.

"Of course you would be helping those children. I knew she couldn't steal your heart. You have always been brave, a true light," I whispered. Charlie relaxed under my hold. Within minutes, stronger arms were around the both of us, the top of my head now wet with Will's tears.

"I've missed you, little bro," Will said, his voice gruff.

I began to pull away, hinting to Will that we should back off and give Charlie some space. Will wiped his tears with the inside of his wrist as we returned to the sofa.

Shai, Nick, and Nolan were crying too, their silent tears trickling down their cheeks.

Charlie looked torn, a tinge of pink coloring his wan cheeks. "As much as I'd like to stay, I do need to go back. As I said, those kids need me."

"My friends Justin and Pree are there now. They sacrificed themselves to save me. They will definitely take care of those children," I reassured him.

"Your mom and dad will be so happy to have you back safely. We must go to them immediately," Shai exclaimed.

Nick's eyes flashed subtly, but his voice remained calm. "Nolan, would you mind taking Charlie to the kitchen to get something to eat and drink?"

"Right away, Your Highness."

Shai's shoulders lifted with a huge inhale, and he released it slowly, as if he knew exactly what Nick was going to say.

Nick waited until Nolan and Charlie had been gone for a few minutes before speaking. "Shai, you know we cannot just waltz into Lana and Brantley's home. We promised them we would only do that if Charlie was *unharmed*."

"He is better than I expected after being with that witch for so long."

Nick shook his head. "We have no idea yet how he has been impacted. We do not know if his being here right now is even part of her orders."

"I was there," I said. "I saw Mara accidentally push Jamie,

I mean Charlie, out of the portal when she snatched Justin. I do not think he's here on purpose."

"Maybe, or maybe Mara wanted it to look that way," Nick countered, his brow raised.

"Wait—" Will leaned forward onto his elbows— "I didn't remember my brother until Nick gave me the Christmas rose. I still cannot remember my parents mentioning Charlie in all the time we've lived in Florida. What gives?"

Nick and Shai stared at each other. "You tell them," Shai said as he leaned back in his chair, arms crossed.

Nick crossed his ankle to his knee and his frown deepened. "The pain of losing a child is a chasm that no one should have to cross. Your parents, as strong as they are, nearly put everyone at risk with how desperate they were to get Charlie back. We all—"

Shai cleared his throat.

"Well, your parents and I thought it best if their memories of Charlie were locked up until he returned," Nick explained.

"Why would they want such a thing? That's horrible." I gasped.

"Do not judge others for how they handle their grief," Nick admonished me.

He had a serious stick up his butt tonight, and I was about over his inner werewolf.

"She's right." Will's hand moved to my knee. "I didn't get a choice to remember Charlie or not. The pain of losing him was a lot, but I would never have chosen to forget my brother."

Nick brought his foot back down with a loud thud. "They knew that they posed a risk to all of us, to saving Cristes had they not forfeited their memories. Your mother is an extremely gifted warrior, your father one of the best elementals I know. Together, they are lethal." He steepled his fingers and leaned toward Will. "They nearly went crazy with grief. If not for me, not only would they lose Charlie, but you would be with Mara."

"You don't know that," Will growled.

"You are correct, but we were not going to take that chance," Nick growled.

I knew it was selfish of me to ask, but I had to know. "Why would you take Will away from me without so much as a goodbye. I mean, I get why we had to separate, but you couldn't let me keep a little of him?"

Nick didn't even blink when he answered. "We felt it necessary."

"Who's we?" I demanded.

This time, Shai uncrossed his arms and fidgeted with the collar of his shirt.

Shai's fidgeting didn't go unnoticed by Nick. His attention flicked to Shai for a second and then back to me. "Shai and I. As we shared with you previously, Shai bringing you two together so quickly instigated things...things we were not yet prepared to handle. We could not keep you both anywhere near each other and risk your powers becoming amplified to the point where astronauts could see you from space!"

"Fine. You moved Will and his parents. You still didn't answer. Why? Why steal my memories? I was a kid. It's not like I could have gone to find Will in Florida."

"You...died," Shai responded before Nick could, his eyes vacant as if he saw something else besides the room we were presently in.

I frowned. "No, I didn't."

Shai shook his head and looked at me. "Not physically, no. When Nick went with my sister's family to Florida, I agreed to stay here to keep an eye on you. I couldn't... I couldn't let you live like that."

"Like what?"

"Like you died. You were a shell, devoid of any light." Shai's eyes glazed over as if he was reliving it all. He shook his head. "Nick came back and helped you."

"I could have gotten over it. You didn't need to do that." I crossed my arms and sank into the couch.

Shai leaned forward, but Nick caught him on the shoulder and shook his head. "Shai failed to mention that you were also a liability. You are quite strong-minded, and we could not risk you convincing your parents to come visit Will. Once a Watcher pairing has been decided and the bond linked, nothing can keep you away from each other, not even most giftings."

"Will and I are...mated?" I looked at Will and back at Nick.

"I don't know for certain, but I believe so, just not in the traditional sense."

"Great, like vampire mates?" I scoffed.

"Something like that." Shai smiled, his lips. "Only there is no blood involved."

"Some good news at least," Will chimed in. "What does it mean to be matched? How can we be *absolutely* certain we are?"

Shai went red in the cheeks and suddenly had to bend his head to rub the back of his neck.

Nick answered for him. "There are pretty clear signs when you initially meet. You can more easily feel them and your desire to be with them all the time grows stronger; like a force is physically pulling you to one another. However, to be absolutely certain...the wedding night."

"The wedding night? Ohhhh." Will's cheeks burned red and he ran his hands through his hair.

"You and Liddy should not fuss. I have shared that you both show promise of immense power, and much of what you have already experienced...sensing each other when the other is close, feeling one another's emotions, and so on, are what fully-marked matches experience. We assume that your connection happened when you both first met. However, we cannot be certain of your whitelighter pairing until you both, shall I say, become one."

Normally, Nick talking about consummating the marriage would have me flustered and embarrassed. I couldn't help but notice the way he always used phrases like *shows promise, we aren't certain, you're a good theory.* What if all of these efforts were wasted on me, and Will's true mate was still out there?

I stiffened. Will picked up on my mind shift immediately and he squeezed my knee offering reassurance.

I gave him a half-smile, but my worrying continued. What if I wasn't the one Cristes had been waiting for? What if Will and I combined did not produce the power needed to defeat Mara and save the realm?

"OK, so why are you worried about going to my parents?" Will asked Nick.

"Because we should be making plans to head to Cristes

instead. I already shared that I am not sure Charlie, or this version of him anyway, can be trusted."

"It's Charlie, for Eira's sake!" Shai spat, his fists clenched.

"I promised Brantley and Lana that I'd bring Charlie to them only if it was actually Charlie," Nick countered.

"I get to have a say this time," Will declared, his chest stretching his shirt with each breath. "I trust him. He has been to hell and back and deserves to be with me, with my parents. It is time for them to snap out of their little bubble and start helping us defeat Mara.

Shai grinned, flashing his pearly whites. "I could not have said it any better." He clapped Will on the shoulder. "With their help, we can come back here and plan our return to Cristes. Nick, we will do what we can for Charlie here. Nolan is a gifted healer; we can all help him. But we should get to Florida, stat. Will, spring break starts Friday, correct?"

"We are not ready," Nick said flatly.

"Pree and Justin are down there with Mara!" I cried. "Frankly, I don't care if you feel we are ready or not. We need all the help we can get." Hysteria began to boil within the deepest parts of me. With Nolan not here to help calm me, I clenched my fists and hoped my breathing exercises would keep me in check.

"Don't you think I know that? If we go to Florida and wake Lana and Brantley, they are going to want to march on Mara immediately!" Nick's eyes shone, and I thought he might be pleading with me.

"Going straight to Cristes would set Will and Liddy on a swift course. We have not had enough time to train them yet, and their giftings could overwhelm them," Shai argued as he fidgeted with his cuff.

"But training in Cristes would be more productive. Charlie would be able to heal faster there. Not to mention it would keep them most safe," Nick countered. "Then we come back for Lana and Brantley."

"I know better than anyone that moving these two—" Shai jabbed his thumb in my and Will's direction— "too quickly can have dire consequences. I won't let that happen, not again. Besides, how do you propose we get to Cristes without the help of my sister and brother-in-law?" Shai crossed his arms, his brow quirked in smug satisfaction.

Heavy silence permeated the room, weighing on all of us. Will squeezed my hand so tightly, I felt as if it might break.

Nick turned directly to me and Will. "How do you both feel about a trip to Florida for spring break?"

Will shot up off the couch with a loud *whoop*. "Yes! I had plans to visit my parents, anyway. I've been dying to show Liddy where I lived all this time."

"Wait, I'm coming, too?"

Will pulled me up from the couch and gave me a great big hug. He released me only enough so I could see the elation on his face. "You better believe it. I'm not leaving you here alone. Who knows who else Mara has working for her that is already in your circle? And I am not letting anything happen to my girl."

"My nephew is correct. We cannot leave you unwatched. That would be great foolery."

"Will... Shai, would you mind going to the kitchen to check on Charlie and Nolan for me, please?" Nick rolled his neck, then arched his back.

Shai's eyes flicked from me back to Nick and his brow furrowed.

"Sure thing," Will said. He planted a kiss on my forehead and walked out of the room, Shai close behind.

Nick came and sat next to me, staring at his steepled hands.

"Liddy, I want you to be prepared."

My stomach tightened. "What do you mean?"

He sighed, but still didn't look at me. "I mean there is a significant chance that we will not be returning to Illinois after we visit Florida."

I gulped. "Why wouldn't we return?"

"Because..." Nick finally faced me. "I have no doubt in my mind that Lana and Brantley will want to finish this as quickly as possible, and that means going straight to Cristes." His gaze fell again to his hands in his lap. "I just wanted you to have the chance to say your goodbyes."

Honeycomb

S AY MY GOODBYES? I knew I'd always felt called to somewhere else, that I never felt like Illinois was my true home. Heck, I even had plans to move out of state after graduation. So why did this news strike me right in my gut?

Nick patted my shoulder. "It will be alright, kiddo. It doesn't have to be forever. It just may be longer than you want, and I thought you should be prepared."

I smiled at him, but when he stood, I knew he felt my uneasiness. "Stay here a few moments. I'll return presently."

The quiet afforded me some much-needed solitude to digest the idea of not seeing my parents anymore. At least with college, I had another year and a half to prepare for the departure, and I knew that I could always visit home whenever

I wanted. I drew my legs up and hugged my knees. What would they think? And what about Mickey? It's true the little bugger knew how to press every single one of my buttons, but I still loved him. And what about Sara and Dani? How were they going to react to Will and I just, *poof...* gone?

I didn't hear Will come into the room. Though my senses already knew he was close, his warmth still surprised me when he laid his head in the crook of my neck and rubbed my arms up and down.

"What's wrong, Princess?"

"I'm worried about Pree and Justin's already been through so much because of me."

"He's a true hero," Will said. "He made a choice in the moment, and he chose to help you."

"And so did Pree. Oh, gosh, her mom is going to be devastated!" I rubbed at the tension in my temples. "How do we keep what we know to ourselves? What if we don't get them back in time before Mara does something horrible to them?"

Will jumped over the back of the sofa and easily lifted me onto his lap, cradling me. "We won't let that happen. Charlie is back. We still have Alex. They can help us find a way into Beldam and bring them back."

"And if they don't?"

"We just won't accept that possibility."

"But it *is* a possibility; a real one. And it's all my fault." Tears welled in my eyes and I buried my face in Will's chest.

He patiently stroked my hair. When I finally settled my sobs to a more manageable sniffle fest, he said, "You and I both know that is not true."

"What?" I croaked.

"Pree and Justin falling into the portal. That is *not* your fault."

"But if I'd only listened to you, to Pree, I wouldn't have agreed to meet Alex, and none of us would be in this mess."

Will drew languid circles on my back. "Alex would have just found another way to get to you, *if* Mara let him live. Listen, I know it sucks that Pree and Justin are with Mara, but their sacrifice returned Charlie to us and kept you safe. I couldn't be more thankful."

"*Ahem.*"

I peeled myself from Will's chest and turned my head. Nolan stood at attention in the door frame.

"Lord Abishai wanted me to inform you, Madam Lydia, that you are most welcome to stay here tonight."

"I don't think my parents would allow it."

Nolan's eyes twinkled, and he brought his hand to his chest. "Let me rephrase; Lord Abishai insists that you stay under our roof for maximum protection. I, of course, have already sought and received permission from your parents."

I tugged at my shirt. "But... I don't have any of my things."

Nolan smiled. "Not to worry." He clasped his hands behind his back. "I took the liberty of shopping for you once you started spending so much time here with Lord William rehearsing for the duet. Do you mind taking dinner in your room?"

"Uh, sure. That would be great."

"You will be staying in Lord William's parents' room. You seemed very comfortable there." Will cocked his head at me.

"I'll tell you later," I whispered to him.

"I shall be up within the half-hour. You are welcome to

your room now." Nolan stood with one arm behind his back as he extended his other in a graceful sweep, encouraging me to exit the family room.

I took Will's hand and led him up the main staircase. Instead of turning right, where I'd stayed last time with Pree, I turned left. This was the side of the upper atrium Will had informed me he'd never investigated. I stopped at the first door on the left and opened it.

When I first woke up earlier, I hadn't taken the time to fully appreciate the room. It was simple, yet elegant. The tufted headboard, along with the chaise lounge at the foot of the bed were covered in matching cream and gold spun fabric. And the clean, uncluttered walls opposite the bed were bedecked with shabby-chic, yet classic, board and batten. I turned to find that Will had only taken one step into the room.

"I can't believe my parents lived here," he said as he took in the room, his hands in his pockets.

The room's soft amber glow and large, luxurious bed made me crave sleep. On the seat of the bay window, I spotted toiletries, a pair of folded pajamas, and an outfit for the next day. *Dang. It's like staying at a resort.*

"Will?"

"Yes?"

"Will you stay with me tonight? You know, like you did at the hospital?"

His eyes flashed and a flutter of excitement brushed my skin, but then it flitted away. He worried his lip and ran a hand through his hair.

My shoulders drooped and I looked away. "It's OK. You don't have to."

"I just don't want to risk anything when our situation seems pretty dire right now."

"Can you at least stay with me until I fall asleep?" I asked over my shoulder.

Will clapped his forehead with the heel of his hand. "How could I be so ignorant? I will definitely stay with you...all night."

I ran over and gave him a great, big hug. "Thank you!"

He squeezed me as if he remembered that he'd almost lost me tonight.

"I'm going to take a hot shower and get into my PJs so I'm ready when Nolan comes up with dinner."

"OK. I'll go do the same and meet you back here. I should probably let Nolan know that I'll be having dinner with you."

Will closed the door behind me and I grabbed the purple pajamas from the window seat. They were a little cold from the draft, but I still snuggled the soft fabric to my chest as I entered the bathroom.

I reached into the walk-in shower and turned the water as hot as it'd go. I stepped in and as the water rained over me, I barely registered the drops hit and stream down my body. I closed my eyes, rolling my neck and encouraging my muscles to relax. But images of Justin and Pree being swallowed up by Mara's burning black hole came bursting forward. Suddenly, guilt struck me, its weight so heavy, I slumped to a crouched position and hugged my knees for support.

It's not fair that here I am, safe in a Watcher's mansion while Pree and Justin are probably being tortured.

My stomach lurched with reminders of their sacrifice, a sacrifice driven by loyalty and love I didn't deserve. I leaned over the drain, prepared to heave whatever scant contents remained in my stomach.

A knock sounded at the door. "Lid, just wanted to let you know I'm here."

"I'll be out in a few minutes," I called back to Will.

I quickly washed my hair and body. Although I wanted to stay in for much longer, I sighed and slid the nozzle to "off." I wrapped the soft, oversized towel around me, then flung my head over to wrap my hair. At the vanity, I used the hand towel to swipe the fog from the mirror. The faint scar on my chest left by Mara when I was a kid snagged my attention, and I whirled away from the mirror.

I ignored the fear that threatened to paralyze me and began to towel-dry. Another knock, further away this time, sounded, followed by muffled voices.

"Liddy!" Will called after the clanking of dishes stopped. "Food is here!"

"Thanks, I'll just be another minute!" I grabbed the satin underwear, trying not to think about Nolan having picked it out, and slipped it over my legs and hips. Then I slid the slinky, velvety pants on and tied them loosely. I went to grab the shirt, but it was nowhere. I flicked out the towels and moved the floor mats. *Crud.*

I held the cream towel over my chest. Opening the door a crack, I spotted Will sitting on the upholstered bench at the end of the bed, his head in his hands. He looked like I felt, like today was just too much and it left him drained. I peeked at the window sill and with my eyes, I traced my footsteps from there to the bathroom. About a foot away was the button-down pajama top.

I held my breath as I opened the door, hoping it wouldn't creak and draw Will's gaze to me. The last thing I needed was for him to feel as if I were trying to move things along too quickly again. Like a doe on the soft forest floor, I stepped light and swift to my goal. I swooped down to pick it up and was about to turn around when...

"What the..."

I froze standing stiff as a board. Clutching my chest, I quickly explained, "Will, it's not what you think. My shirt must have fallen, and I—"

Will was at my side in a flash, his hands tracing patterns on the skin of my back.

"What the heck happened?" he asked.

"What do you mean?" I responded, heat flushing my cheeks, chastising myself for enjoying his touches so much, especially at a time like this.

"These bruises," the pads of his fingers continued their gentle exploration," they form a weird honeycomb pattern across your back."

As much as I wanted to step back and inspect myself in the bathroom mirror, I wanted the comfort of Will's touches more.

"Why didn't you say something? You must be in a lot of pain. I'll call Nolan to—"

I whipped around and grabbed Will's wrist. "Please don't. I'm sure he is busy attending to other things. It doesn't hurt, I promise."

As if Will had just registered the fact that I was naked under the towel, he took me in from face to navel and back up and his eyes flamed brightly.

"I'm sorry, I didn't mean...uh..." I stepped back, hastily raising my shirt. "I'm just going to finish getting dressed." Avoiding eye contact, I rushed over to the bathroom and quickly closed the door. But Will managed to grab the door just before it could shut completely.

I gazed into his eyes. They were still bright, a beautiful teal that only meant one thing and my pulse quickened in anticipation. As he moved to enter the bathroom, I took a step back making room for him. He nudged the door shut with his foot, his focus remaining steadfast on me. And when he closed the distance between us, I did not back away.

Gingerly, he drew me closer against him, and I could sense the restraint he was using through our bond— a protective shield against the relentless and demanding pull of emotions threatening to overtake him. He carefully gathered my hair in one hand and slid it over my right shoulder. A sigh escaped my throat, but I refused to close my eyes, wanting to watch him. This appeared to amuse him as a little surge of light flitted within his irises. Slowly, his lips curled into a craving smile, and then they were on my neck.

I'll Kill Him

INEARLY COLLAPSED UNDER THE SENSATIONS that bubbled through me, overwhelming after the numbness I had just experienced. I flung my arms around his neck and swept my fingers into his hair. A low moan rattled in his throat and his lips met mine. Soon, the taste of him consumed me, and before I knew it, his hands were on my hips and my feet swept from the ground as he sat me on the edge of the vanity.

Suddenly, Will pulled away, but kept his forehead against mine. "One day, you will be mine...in all ways," he whispered, "and I yours. And that day cannot come soon enough."

"Before I excuse myself, can I please heal you?" he asked, his fingers again drawing on my back.

I turned my neck and looked in the mirror. "Oh," I gasped, just now realizing where they'd come from. I stiffened as I again felt the weight of Alex pressing me into the cold steel of the playground.

"What is it?" Will asked, his eyes darkening.

"The bruises. They're from earlier. At...at the playground."

"What are you not telling me?"

I knew better than to lie to him. He would know. "It happened when Alex held me down, when Pree and Justin came to find me."

"I'll kill him," Will snarled, pulling away from me and reaching for the door.

"Please don't go," I choked out. Some of the fight left Will as his shoulders relaxed.

He returned and hugged me, his fingers resuming their long caresses on my back. I quivered as tiny pulses zinged over my skin, first tightening, then loosening my muscles. Then Will's full hands were on the small of my back, inching their way up. Cold seeped into each purplish hexagonal shape. With a final stroke down my spine, I was warm again.

"There." Will smiled at me. "All better. I'll step now so you can dress. Don't take too long. Our food is getting cold."

He ducked out and I twisted my body in the mirror to see that the bruising was gone. *Wow. He's definitely getting better at this healing thing.* I whipped my shirt on and joined Will, sitting crisscross on the bed.

I'd just finished forcing down the last bite of my sandwich when a soft knock at the door caught our attention.

"Come in," Will called out.

"Sorry to be a bother. Lord Abishai and Prince Nicholas would like to see you both, in the family room."

Will and I followed Nolan to the end of the hallway, a

place I'd never ventured to before. We stood before a wall with a half-pedestal table leaning against it and three wall sconces. Nolan reached for the one on the far left and pulled it down. The once plain wall transformed into a door right before my eyes.

Nolan slid it open and ushered us inside. Once in, he pressed the star button that glowed bright white, and the floor began sinking. It took me a second to realize we were in an elevator.

The sleek steel doors slid open into a small hallway. Nolan walked out first and we followed him right into the family room, where Alex sat front and center. Will wrapped his arm around protectively my shoulder and hugged me to his side.

"Young man, you must have seen it in Beldam," Nick insisted with an impatient snort.

"Seen what?" Will interrupted.

"The missing piece to the broken globital," Nick answered without looking at him.

Alex rolled his eyes. "I've already answered you, old man. I have no idea what you're talking about."

"I think I know where it is," a quiet voice spoke from the shadowed corner. Charlie stepped out, his eyes not knowing quite who to look at. When they found mine, he dropped his gaze.

"I thought you had gone to bed for the evening."

Charlie peered at Shai. "No, Uncle. I knew I would be needed."

"Come sit by me," Shai patted the seat cushion next to him, and Charlie obliged.

"You were saying you have seen the missing globital

piece," Nick prodded.

"Yes, but only once. It was on her desk when she was writing a letter."

"And you're certain?" Shai asked.

Charlie dropped his gaze from his uncle and wrung his hands. "Well, if not a piece from a globital, then certainly something from Cristes. The thin crystal piece glinted and sparkled in the candlelight as if it had been fabricated from sunlight itself. It was impossible to overlook."

Nick and Shai exchanged glances, and I could swear they spoke to each other telepathically.

"What is a globital?" I asked.

"A globital is what Cristes explorers used to help them travel safely between realms," Nick answered. "We will need it to get back to Cristes and then, eventually, to Beldam. The one in my possession is the only one remaining in existence here in Mortalia."

Shai added, "To common folk, a globital would look just like a snow globe or an extremely large marble. For us Watchers, it represents the protective encasement of Cristes. Like a snow globe, Cristes is contained within the walls of protection as put forth by Eira, the creator. Within the walls, Cristes flourishes in a rich, tropical climate. Outside those walls, however, are conditions not suitable for habitat."

"Did the encasement crack the day you were dragged out of Cristes by Mara?" Will directed his question to Nick. "I remember from your memories there was a loud noise, and now that I think about it, the sounds remind me of ice cracking on a frozen lake. But then, a little later in the memory, it shifted to a cascade of shattered glass."

"Yes, it did," Nick answered.

Something was nagging me. "If the globital is broken, how did you get to Cristes on your last trip?"

Nick finally stopped his pacing and relaxed against a wall. "I still use it, regardless of its impending risks. You see, each trip I take places a little more pressure on its infrastructure, weakening it—" he shrugged— "I suppose on this last journey, enough of the structure gave way and left me suspended between the realms for too long. Nevertheless, given the number of people we need to travel together, it needs to be completely intact."

Shai interjected, "We have no idea what we will be returning to in Cristes. Things were already bad when I left to come here with your mother and father."

"All the more reason we fix the globital and get to Cristes as soon as possible," Nick said.

"Agreed." Shai slapped his thighs. "We need to infiltrate Beldam and find the encasement piece."

"Too risky," Nick growled.

Shai rubbed his temples. "What do you propose?"

"She figured out a way to cross the realms without one. If I can just meet with her, I am sure—"

"You have had your chance, *many* times may I add," Shai cut him off. "It is far too late for a change of heart from her. Now, Alex, I am sure you know exactly how to sneak into Beldam."

Alex's face paled. "No."

"Excuse me... *No*?" Shai blinked.

"That is what I said." He jammed his hands in his pockets. "No dang way. If she even thinks I helped you in any way, I'm done for."

"You should have thought about that before you helped her almost kill Liddy," Will snarled, his skin brightening. I placed a hand on his forearm to soothe him.

"I didn't have a choice, man! It was either work for her or—"

"Or what?" Will interrupted.

"Stop it!" Charlie's hoarse whisper was enough to silence the entire room. His vacant eyes stared into a horror none of us could see.

"We cannot use the children as bait, Lord Abishai." Nolan spoke up for the first time, placing a hand on Shai's shoulder.

"Of course not. Nor was I suggesting such a thing. I merely want to know how to gain access to Beldam so that Nick and I may repair the globital."

Nick cleared his throat. "Lana and Brantley, they were making great progress on the globital before..." Nick trailed off. "We don't need to risk going to Beldam. We will see them first. Let them hear everything and help to weigh in on our next steps. If ever a bright mind and fierce warrior were to succeed, it would be them."

"Fine." Shai mumbled something unintelligible under his breath. "We leave for Florida in the morning."

"What about waiting for spring break?" Will asked, sensing my unease.

Shai peered over his shoulder. "Nolan, please speak with Liddy and Alex's parents."

Alex's jaw dropped. "You can't just keep me here! I'm not a prisoner."

"Think of it as an extended vacation," Nick said, clapping

him on the back.

"But spring break is still a week away. I don't think my parents will go for this," I stammered.

"Just leave everything up to me, Madam." Nolan winked. "Everyone up to bed. I shall make all of the arrangements."

Alex and Charlie looked confused, but Nolan was at their side in a flash. Will kept his gaze on his brother; it was clear from the expression on his face and the emotional overload coursing through me that he wanted to hug Charlie, to muss the hair on top of his head. But he just didn't know if that was OK to do now.

I took Will's hand and led him upstairs. As he stood in the hall in front of my door, his face still showed a flurry of conflicting emotions.

I cupped his cheeks in my hands. "What's wrong?" I asked.

"I don't think it's a good idea anymore...to stay the night. You know I would in a heartbeat, but—"

"I'm not asking for more than you to just hold me, and I you. It's been a long day."

Will grasped my wrists and brought my face to his, giving me a kiss. He led me to the bed, tucked me in, and tenderly nuzzled my nose with his.

"I'll stay until you fall asleep."

Hammock Dunes

WHEN THE PRIVATE PLANE lifted off the tarmac at Palwaukee Airport, dawn had broken over the horizon. Will and I sat in lush, ivory seats near the front of the plane with a mute Charlie. Alex sat in the back, tethered to his spot via a wisp of gifting at his ankle. Shai studied paperwork while Nick dozed. Nolan roamed the galley and offered service wherever and whenever needed.

"Mr. Jamison and company, this is your captain speaking. Prepare for landing in T-minus five minutes."

A vast ocean with a beautiful coastline filled the windows as the plane tilted, readying for descent. Excitement coursed through me, but one look around the plane, at the somber faces, had me wishing we were visiting under better circumstances.

We landed at Flagler Airport, where a white limo awaited

us. We drove toward the beach and turned onto a street that led us to a large gated community called Hammock Dunes.

After checking the driver's ID, the security guard ushered us through. The limo followed the twists and turns of the streets lined with palm trees and plants with large blooms in bright shades of orange, pink, and red.

I sighed, staring out the window and squeezed Will's hand. "I don't know how you were able to leave this place. It's almost *too* beautiful."

"Key word is almost. Something more beautiful and way more important lured me away," Will murmured, and my skin heated under the spotlight of his stare.

"Gag me," Alex grumbled.

"With pleasure," Will sneered.

Shai smirked, and Nick let out a belly laugh.

The limo came to a stop in front of an impressive home on a large plot. An orange-tiled roof sat atop a pristine white stucco home adorned with arches...lots of arches. Dark wood shutters framed the windows, echoing the same wood that made up the entrance and the trio of garage doors.

The driver came around to open the door for us and Nolan looked stunned, his hand hovering over the door handle like he couldn't understand how it opened before he got to it. I pressed my lips together in an effort to stifle my laugh.

"Shai, Nick, we are so glad you are here!" Lana's voice sang out from the front porch.

Will stepped out of the limo next and held my hand as he escorted me out.

"William!" Brantley rushed down the steps. He embraced his son and pulled back. "Looks like you've grown a few more inches. And who is this?" Mr. Jamison's eyes landed on me and he extended his hand.

I dropped my arms, feeling awkward that I nearly hugged him. *That's right. He wouldn't remember me.* I gave him my hand. "Hi, I'm Liddy. It's nice to meet you." He smiled brightly at me. When Charlie exited the limo, both the Jamisons' eyes landed on him, their brows scrunched, as if trying to place him.

"Shai, you were not being facetious. You truly do have a limo full." Lana came down the steps and greeted us all. "Hello, everyone. I am Lana. Welcome to our home."

I marveled at her calm facade. Mom would have had a heart attack at the prospect of last-minute guests, let alone a stretch limo full.

"Come, come." She waved us along. "William, you can show these two gentlemen—" she gestured to Alex and Charlie— "the guest bedroom off of yours. Shai, Nick, and Nolan, please follow Brantley to the guest cottage out back. Liddy, follow me, dear."

Lana led me up the cylindrical turret to a bright and airy room. Back doors lead to a rounded balcony.

"Your home is stunning, Mrs. Jamison, and the view is breathtaking," I said, awestruck.

"Thank you. I count my blessings every day. And call me Lana, please." She sat on the edge of the bed and crossed her legs. "So, tell me, how long have you and my William been dating?"

"How did you—"

"I am his mother. I see the way he looks at you. So much love there. I am happy he was able to find another Watcher.

Who is your family descended from? How did they get here to Mortalia?"

I just stood there with my mouth hanging open.

"Oh dear, where are my manners? We have the whole week to get acquainted, do we not?" She smiled and reached for my hand, giving it a gentle squeeze.

I regained my composure. "Since just before Christmas."

"What was that?" She blinked at me.

I smiled sheepishly. "You asked how long Will and I have been dating. The answer is since Christmas."

"And what a nice Christmas present you were for each other." She sighed happily. "Well, I will leave you to it. How does ice tea on the veranda sound in about fifteen minutes?"

"Sounds lovely."

I had just finished putting away my toiletries in the ensuite bathroom when Will walked in. I rushed out to greet him.

"I *love* it here! You should have kidnapped me out of Illinois and brought me here!"

Will laughed. "Yeah, right! Because that would have gone over so well." He placed his hand on the small of my back and led me out to the balcony. He wrapped me in his arms, and nuzzled his nose in my hair.

"How's Charlie adjusting?" I asked.

"I wish I knew. He barely talks to me. Do you think the true Charlie can come back?"

"I think he is still there. He is incredibly brave, even willing to go back to Beldam for those kids still enslaved there."

Will rested his chin on my shoulder. "Maybe when he knows he is truly safe, he'll be able to tear his walls down and trust again. Come on. Let's head downstairs."

Will and I were the first to sit at the long table on the veranda, although the rest of the group was only moments behind us.

"What brings you for a visit, Shai? Nick?" Brantley asked, setting glasses down on the table while Lana shooed Nolan away.

"Is my visit unwelcome, brother?" Shai asked, a teasing tone in his voice.

"Not at all. It has just been so long since you have been able to get away. You are always so busy."

"I am glad to see you have taken the time for some rest," Lana said, filling the glasses with iced tea. "It does not hurt one bit that you have brought my son back home to me and his father. We were not expecting him until next week!" She placed her hands on Will's shoulders.

Nick cleared his throat. "We have something special planned for this evening. Nolan is going to prepare the meal for us. Is there any place where we could find some Christmas roses here?"

"Brantley and I grow them in our back shed. Can we help with anything?"

"No, no. Opening your home to us is more than gracious."

"We have no time to waste." I froze as I heard Nick's voice, but his mouth hadn't moved. His eyes bore into mine, and I tried to relax as I focused on the words he spoke. "You and Will need to help bring back his parent's memories tonight. Come to the cottage shortly before dinner for the details."

I gave a small nod and flicked my eyes to Will, who seemed to be hearing Nick as well.

"What do you all wish to do today?" Lana asked.

Without missing a beat, Will answered, "I plan on taking Liddy to the beach. I'm going to introduce her to surfing."

I choked on the tea I'd just sipped, coughing loudly. All eyes turned to me.

"Is everything alright, dear?" Lana asked.

"She's just afraid of sharks." Will laughed, patting my back.

Brantley's eyes twinkled. "Nonsense. You'll have so much fun, you won't even notice they are there." Lana swatted his arm.

"Aren't we needed here?" I tried, hoping to get out of surfing.

"I cannot think of anything, can you Shai?" Nick asked.

Shai smirked and shook his head. "Not a darn thing."

"Well, that settles it," Brantley said. "Be back with enough time to get cleaned up before dinner. The Jeep is in the garage ready to go," he added.

My arms hugged my chest the entire way. When Will parked near the pier, I unfurled myself and hopped out of the front seat before he could open the door for me. He laughed and went to the back to pull down the surfboards.

We laid out a large blanket and set down our small cooler full of bottled water and sandwiches. I appreciated that we basically had the beach to ourselves except for a few people fishing and sunbathing.

I untied the strap around my neck and slipped out of my white sundress. "Can you please help me with sunblock? I'm so pale and I don't want to burn."

Will bit his bottom lip and raked a hand through his hair.

"Sure." His voice shook slightly as he accepted the bottle from my hand. He took his time, making sure he didn't miss a spot, even applying in areas I could have done myself.

"Your turn." I smirked. Then I, too, took my time. Yes, I enjoyed the feel of his muscles under my hands, but also, the more time we spent on land, the less time we had to spend in the water.

"Alright, Princess. I think I'm good."

"Can we practice on the sand for a while?" I asked.

"But the water is so perfect."

"I know, but I don't want to be shark bait."

A muscle in Will's jaw twitched. "Do you trust me?"

"With my life."

A corner of his mouth turned up. "Let's leave the boards here and take a dip."

"I like that compromise. And guess what?"

"What?"

"Last one in is a rotten egg!" I screamed, kicking sand behind me as I raced to the shore. The cool water teased my feet when strong arms wrapped around my waist, sweeping me into a cresting wave.

I popped my head up. "Hey, that's not—" but Will's lips silenced my protest.

He pulled back only far enough so that his lips tickled mine when he said, "I have been wanting to do that since last night."

"Well, don't stop," I complained.

When we broke apart, I gasped. "Will, we are too far."

"Too far? What is too far?"

I looked all around us. We were surrounded by endless

ocean, glittering in the sun. It was equally beautiful and terrifying; a sobering reminder of just how small we really were in the grand scheme of things. *Talk about a reality check.* And then, I spotted it.

"Will!" I shrieked, clawing out of his grip.

"What, what?"

"There!" I pointed. Roughly ten feet from us, a gray fin broke the surface of the water.

"Liddy, calm down. You don't want your light to attract it. If we just stay here, chill, it will leave us alone."

But my heart shot into overdrive and the fin was getting closer. Another fin appeared and my adrenaline spiked.

"Liddy, look at me." Will cupped my chin and brought my face to his. "Take a breath for me." Tears streamed down my face. Will kissed me, soft and tender. But not even this could distract me from the imminent danger. I tried to pull away, but his hands moved up my neck and traced down my spine. His fingertips caressed the sensitive skin of my hips.

Fire consumed me. Not in the burning to death painful sense, but one full of desire and want. My hands trailed across his strong shoulders, to his chest, and then...

"Liddy!" Will breathed. "Look!"

My eyes, glazed and heavy, darted to where he pointed. A small pod of dolphins chased each other. I giggled. "They're amazing!"

"See? No sharks." Will beamed, his skin glowing aqua. I hoped any passerby would reason it away as a trick of the sun glinting against the water.

"You look amazing," I murmured.

"As do you."

We treaded water, watching the dolphins. Eventually, Will's smile faded, his face vacant. "Now that Charlie is back, I wonder if...never mind."

But I knew what he was alluding to. "Will, it's not your fault."

"It is. I was the one who brought the envelope into his room."

I hugged him, threading my hands through the back of his hair. "Mara is at fault. Not you. You were just a kid."

"But—"

"But nothing. You can't foresee the future." I kissed his shoulder. "She wouldn't have given up. Imagine if she'd found you or me instead. You should try to talk to Charlie. He may not say anything, but he will hear you." Will dropped his forehead to mine.

"Forgive yourself, Will. The sooner you do, the sooner you can be there for Charlie."

"How'd I get so lucky to have you as not only my best friend, but also my girlfriend?"

I shrugged. "We are blessed, that's for sure."

"Let's swim back. We have a surfing lesson we are late for."

After a few hours in the sun and many falls into the water, exhaustion overcame me. We packed up and Will drove us home.

When I woke, I was in bed at Will's parent's house. Will was snuggled behind me and we both still wore our swimsuits.

"Will?" I croaked.

"Hmmm?"

"How did I get here?"

"I carried you," he mumbled.

Heat rose to my cheeks. "Don't we need to meet Shai and Nick?"

"Crud. What time is it?"

I looked over to the digital clock on the far nightstand.

"It's a quarter to five."

"Oh, we don't have to meet them until six."

I sat up and stretched. "I need to shower and get ready. I want to make a good impression on your parents."

"You already know they love you. They just don't remember that they do."

"Still."

"Pleeease?" He held his arms out, opening and closing his hands, beckoning me to lay back down.

"Fine. Five more minutes, and then I'm kicking you out so I can get ready."

"Ten and I won't beg for more."

After Will left, I showered and styled my hair. With my towel wrapped around me, I opened my suitcase and grinned. Nolan packed many sundresses for me, all stunning. I chose a periwinkle spaghetti strap number that billowed around my ankles. The color popped against my sun-kissed skin and brought out my eyes. After a dab of watermelon Lip Smackers and a few coats of mascara, I made my way downstairs to meet Will in the breezeway.

The wind tousled his hair as he stood leaning against a pillar waiting for me. His tank was the exact same color as my dress. I expected the night air to be humid and uncomfortable, but it was the exact opposite.

Will's smile lit up his face when he saw me. "I guess we

are twinning tonight." We walked hand in hand to the guest cottage and knocked on the door.

Nolan answered. "Good evening. Please, come quickly. I need to get back to the kitchen."

We hurried inside and joined Nick and Shai in the family room.

"Lana and Brantley will be getting their memories back tonight. Do you remember how jarring that can be?" Nick asked us.

Nick's and Shai's somber mannerisms made me realize how self-centered I had been today. Honestly, the thought hadn't even crossed my mind, and I suddenly felt ashamed.

"Yes," Will responded, squeezing my hand.

Nick nodded. "It is a much more pleasant experience when you have others who can help you process." Will stiffened significantly. He'd had no one.

Nick's jaw ticked as he took in Will's posture. "Still, it will be quite difficult for them to have lost eight years with their son."

"Not to mention, they have little time to get acclimated," Shai added.

"OK, so what's the plan?" Will asked.

I admired how he swallowed down his anger at having to navigate his new memories on his own before moving back to Illinois.

"When Nolan serves the soup, after your parents have each taken three sips—" Shai held up three fingers— "I will need you both to get up and place one hand on each of their shoulders, and with the other you continue to hold each other's hands."

"That seems relatively easy." I shrugged.

Nick's lips quirked. "Not entirely. You will feel some of what they do. Your job is to remain a strong conductor for them so they can use you both to process the assault more easily. Your bond will help strengthen them, and since Will is their son, they will have an easier time accepting it all."

"And what will you be doing, Uncle?"

"Nick and I will shield Charlie until we feel your parents are ready to see him. We will also make sure everyone is safe, ready to step in should our giftings be needed."

Will stood. "Well, no time like the present. Let's get this over with."

We joined the dinner party on the veranda. The Rat Pack crooned from the living room stereo out to the patio.

"A toast to our hosts. Salud!" Nick cheered, his cheeks rosy, as he held up his wine glass.

Everyone held up their glasses in return.

Salad came out first, followed by the soup. I watched as Lana and Brantley ate, counting how many times the spoons hit their lips. When I counted three, I stood up, along with Will.

"What is it, sweetheart?" Lana asked, her eyes landing on her son's face.

Will smiled at her. "Nothing, Mom. Just wanted to share something with you and Dad." Will placed his arm around my waist and led me over to them.

Lana took Brantley's hand. "This is it," she spoke only loud enough for Will and I to hear.

"What do you mean, Mom?" Will's brow crinkled and he cocked his head.

"Oh, stop with the pretenses. Please tell me you are getting married and that I will be a grandma soon." Her eyes shimmered.

My chin nearly hit the floor. I wasn't sure if I should laugh or cry. *Did I look pregnant? She didn't forget how old we are, right?*

Will's eyes widened and he looked at me apologetically as we each placed a hand on his parents' shoulders. Nolan swooped in and held a Christmas rose to their nostrils.

I did not know what I was expecting, but it was not this: thousands of images coupled with grief so intense, my knees nearly buckled. I wanted to rip my heart from my chest, the chasm too vast and wide. Guilt and anger were next, and I pushed my hand down as hard as I could on Lana's shoulder, preventing her from standing. Tears streamed down the Jamisons' cheeks, and slowly, guttural sobs ripped from Lana. Brantley moaned "Charlie" over and over again. My heart splintered with each plea.

After what seemed like hours, I went numb. I opened my eyes and dropped my hand. Lana and Brantley sat there, chests heaving, looking ten years older. I peered up at Will and he too looked ashen, like the living dead.

Nolan stood off in the far corner, a handkerchief in his hand wiping at his eyes.

"Abishai!" Lana screamed. "You promised!"

Will's arms cradled his mom. "It's OK. Please, trust us."

But this mama bear could not be consoled. Her eyes ignited bright green, the glow around her intensifying.

Shai peaked in from the adjoining room. "Sister, please. You do not want to scare him. I have kept my promise."

Lana's flames immediately extinguished. She slumped back into her chair, her hand clamped over her open mouth. Brantley still had not moved, a stone sculpture in Medusa's garden.

Nick and Shai came around the corner with Charlie between them.

Brantley bolted from his chair, knocking it back. It clattered to the floor with a loud bang, but he didn't notice. Or maybe he did and just didn't care. Lana tailed him, her hand still covering her mouth. Without hesitation, she flung her arms around Charlie. When Brantley wrapped his arms around the both of them, they all sank to the floor in a long overdue embrace. Lana held an arm out toward Will, beckoning him to join them.

Will ran over and kneeled down beside them, and Lana tugged him into the fold. Everyone else cleared the room, giving the family time to process the return of their son and brother.

Much time passed, and Nolan served us on TV trays in the family room.

"Liddy, my mom wants to see you." Will's voice was hoarse, and dried streaks of tears marked his face. I slowly rose, my body aching with the movements for some reason.

As I approached Will, he placed his hand on the small of my back to help guide me to the small study off the kitchen. Lana sat on one of the four tufted chairs that surrounded a round, wooden table. When my toes touched the carpet, Lana's head turned to me and she stood. She walked to me, her eyes shimmering with fresh tears, and gathered me in a strong embrace.

"I am so very happy to see you, dear."

I relaxed under her touch and lifted my arms to return the hug.

Lana pulled back. "Sit, sit. Both of you." We did as instructed. A second later, Will stood, pulling me with him. Then he sat in my chair and tugged me onto his lap.

Lana just smiled at us. "Seeing you together, in this way, makes my heart happy. A coupling like yours is rare and special. Though a little young yet, I cannot wait to have Lydia officially join our family."

I blushed at her statement. "Thank you."

"Lydia, you being here also means my failsafe worked."

"What do you mean, Mom?"

"Before we had Nick take our memories, I worked diligently to ensure Lydia was protected from Mara. I knew she had been approaching Lydia through dreams and I couldn't disconnect without securing Lydia's safety and our future."

Will and I continued to sit there, listening intently.

"I had shown Mara some gifting talents during our time at university, and I could not be sure she wouldn't figure out how to use them to harm someone in the abstract. So, I made a failsafe and left it in here."

Lana reached over the table and tapped my temple.

"My dreams," I whispered.

She nodded. "Yes, you were always protected in your dream state."

"The hooded figure. That was you?"

Lana smiled warmly. "Yes. Well, part of me anyway. William played a large role as well."

"I did?" Will asked, a crease deepening between his brows.

"Sweet dreams...ring a bell?"

Will and I looked at each other and then back to Lana. We nodded.

"I was the one to give William the idea to say that to you every night. Each time he did, it would reinforce my gifting armor over your subconscious. We've been linked this entire time. If Mara got too close, part of me and William would join and shield you."

Lana, a smart, beautiful woman made of long, lean lines and grace was a fierce warrior in sheep's clothing.

"Thank you," I whispered.

"My pleasure. Now, both of you head upstairs to bed. It's been a long evening and I think a little sleep could do us all some good."

As if on cue, I yawned.

Will and I were nearly to the staircase when Lana called out. "Oh, and one more thing. I know what it feels like once you have accepted your fated match. You both probably have it worse than the majority of us and will probably rest much better and efficiently if you did not part from each other when you retire for the evenings."

I could feel the heat creep from my chest to my neck and then my cheeks. I didn't dare look at Will.

"William, close your mouth, son." She patted under his chin with the back of her hand. "I am sure Nicholas has informed you that nothing serious can be done until the wedding night. You are a man and will honor that." She caressed his cheek. "Now, off to bed, both of you."

'Til Death Do Us Part

HE SUN PEEKED THROUGH THE PLANTATION SHUTTERS. Lana was right. Having Will by my side all night afforded me the best night's sleep I'd had since Will stayed with me in the hospital. I peered up at Will through my lashes. For the first time in weeks, his face looked completely peaceful. His jaw muscles were smooth, not pulsating, and his breaths were slow and deep. I pressed my ear to his chest and enjoyed the solid rhythm of his heart. The pad of my finger traced the beautiful heart shape of his lips, imprinting the details of his features in my memory.

Will's hand seized mine, and he kissed all five of my fingertips.

"Good morning," he breathed, his eyes still closed.

"And what a lovely morning indeed."

"How did you sleep?" he asked, snaking his arms around me.

"Pretty much the best night ever."

"I don't know how I'll sleep without you once we get back to Illinois."

Ugh. Will was right. His parents may have been cool with this sleeping arrangement, considering they knew what was truly going on, but mine definitely would not be.

"Let's not think about that right now," I muttered.

Voices sounded in the hall, and they were getting louder.

"Quick, pretend to be sleeping!" Will whispered. I quickly rolled onto my side and Will spooned me.

The door burst open.

"Will! Liddy! Up, now!" the voice boomed.

"Abishai, let them sleep!" Lana scolded.

The covers were yanked off of us. Cold air hit my legs and blew my hair from my face. I bolted upright.

"What's going on?" I asked, my voice shaky. Nick leaned against the door jamb, a bemused smile on his face.

"This!" Shai gestured between me and Will. "Do we want to let Mara know where you are? Endanger Charlie again?"

"Don't you dare guilt my son! This is my home and I encouraged them." Lana's eyes ignited a neon green.

"Whoa, Mom. It's OK." I could feel that Will was worried for Shai. Lana's eyes simmered, and she crossed her arms over her chest.

Shai gritted his teeth. "Why in Eira's name would you tempt them like this? Do you not recall how difficult it was for you and Brantley?"

"Like it was yesterday, actually."

"Well, it is at least a hundred times more difficult for them! We cannot afford for them to lose their self-control! Maybe they already did!"

"You have got to be joking. Can you not tell? They were suffering and needed sleep. The only comfort they would get is in each other. Besides, we would have known if they consummated their match."

"Alright, everybody out!" Will jumped from the bed, startling everyone.

"Will, you cannot—"

"Uncle, I love you, but I cannot sit here and allow you to order me and Liddy around, to yell at us like we are children."

Shai's neck reddened. A few agonizingly tense seconds passed, and then he relaxed.

Shai swiped his hand down his face. "I apologize. There's just so much riding—"

"And they are doing a fantastic job facing it all," Lana cut him off. She smiled at her brother, but I could see the warning behind her beautiful green eyes.

"How about we all meet downstairs for breakfast?" Nick piped up.

"Excellent. See you all down there," Will said. He shooed everyone out, then closed and locked the door behind them.

I started to get off the bed, but Will tackled me and we tumbled onto the mattress.

I giggled. "Will, what are you doing?"

"They ruined my morning. We need a do over."

After Will and I reenacted our wake up, the parts before we were barged in on, he left for his room and I got ready for the day, choosing a lavender sundress that hit just below my knees. Will waited for me at the top of the stairs and we walked to the kitchen together where Nick and Lana sat at the table, while Shai leaned against the counter.

"Good morning, son. You look well. How did you sleep?" She asked, acting as if she was seeing us for the first time.

Will pecked her cheek playing along. "Good morning to you, too. And I slept very well, thank you for the suggestion."

Lana nodded and gave Shai a smug *humph*. He rolled his eyes.

"So, what are the plans for the day?" I asked, curious to know what was going to happen now that the Jamisons' memories were restored.

"We will finish out the week here and then return to Illinois. From there, we will continue to work on the globital with Lana and Brantley, once they join us a few days later," Nick said.

"You can't come with us right away?" Will directed his question to his mom.

"Well, honey, we need some time as a family to reacclimate now that Charlie is back."

"Wait, so I'm staying back?"

"Only for a few days."

Will grabbed my hand and gave it a squeeze. He held it tight, not wanting to let it go. We'd not been apart for that long since his return to Illinois.

Lana's eyes flicked from Will, to me, then back to Will. "My William. I promise the days will go quickly. I understand it will be difficult for you and Lydia, but we need to do this... for Charlie."

Will still held my hand in his secure grip, his eyes sparkling with unshed tears. He blinked rapidly and they disappeared.

"It's alright. You spend as much time with her over the next few days as you need. Your father and I need to be alone with Charlie anyway."

Will nodded his head and hugged his mother.

"You should take Lydia to see your old school and maybe to some of the shops beach side," Lana suggested.

"I'd like that," I responded.

Will grinned. "And later, more surfing."

The rest of the week flew by. On my final night in Florida, I sat on the dock's edge, my feet dangling, as I watched the sunset. Will was still inside with his parents. Tomorrow, I would leave for Illinois without him and reality had set in. I thought of Pree and Justin and fear for their safety immediately gripped me. My blood ran cold and I trembled.

I don't know how long I sat there shivering when something soft and warm wrapped around my shoulders. Will sat next to me and rubbed his hands up and down my arms over the fleece blanket.

"What's upsetting you, Princess?"

"I'm worried about Pree and Justin. How could I be so selfish? Here I am with you at the beach, having fun, and they are prisoners!" A warm tear trickled down my cheek, quickly chilling from the soft breeze coming off the water.

Will gently moved me onto his lap, cradling me. "I'm sure our friends will be fine. They were not part of her plan."

"That's just it. If they aren't useful to her, will she just dispose of them?" I tilted my chin up to peer at Will. His jaw tightened and his eyes pierced the horizon.

"No."

"How can you be so sure?"

His lips twitched. "Because it's Pree. If anyone can get what they want, it's her."

I could feel his confidence as it pushed against the walls of my own inner storm, but I wasn't ready to let that in yet. He squeezed me tighter.

"I don't want to rush you, but we need to meet everyone on the back patio for dinner."

I sighed. "Let's go."

"We can wait a few minutes."

"No, it's OK. I would like my time with you alone tonight, before we are separated for a few days. The sooner dinner ends, the sooner you and I can hang."

Will stood, helped me up, and pulled me into a hug. When he released me, I slipped my hand in his, and he led me from the boat dock and down the long jetty back to his house.

"There they are." Lana beamed at us when we arrived, then turned back to the group. "Everyone please sit. Dinner is ready."

Alex joined us at the table tonight, and Charlie sat at the opposite end. Will smiled at his brother and slid into the seat next to him. This was the first time I'd gotten to see Charlie up close since arriving in Florida.

As if he sensed me staring, he lifted his chin and gazed into my eyes. Hues of orange and blue swirled in their depths, and I sucked in a breath. My chest tightened and my breathing turned shallow as my heart rate sped up. He continued to stare at me, unfazed.

"It was you," I whispered.

"Will, you may want to help your girlfriend," Alex drawled from across the table.

Will glanced at me, uncertainty clouding his face. "What's wrong?"

"I think she finally remembered who else has been helping Mara deliver her surprise envelopes," Alex said.

All at once, I felt everyone's eyes on me. Charlie blinked and turned his attention to his parents.

"I'm sorry, I didn't mean to make a fuss," I said, dropping my gaze to my hands.

"What is it, Liddy?" Nick asked, his voice quiet but full of concern.

"You may as well tell them," Charlie muttered.

A shiver crawled up my spine, goosebumps prickling every nerve ending. This jaded young man before me was distant...completely detached from reality.

"No."

"Tell them."

I chugged my water, everyone patiently waiting for me to speak. "Charlie came to my house, after..." I hesitated, biting my lip as I realized Will's parents had no idea about my attack. "After winter formal, and tried to deliver an envelope to me."

Will's eyes ignited and he turned his head, squeezing his eyes shut. He took a deep breath and let it out.

"Is this true, little brother?"

"Yes." That was it. No explanation or apology offered.

Will winced. "Why?"

"I made a choice."

Will growled, his eyes again sparking to life. Tears streamed down Lana's face.

I clutched Will's arm. "Stop. You have yet to meet Mara. He's been there with me...in my dreams. Believe me, whatever "choices" he had, I'm sure he was stuck between a rock and a hard place."

Will's eyes widened as the gravity of my words registered.

"Charlie," Brantley spoke up. "If you can, will you please tell us what happened?"

Charlie glanced at his dad. "One life for a hundreds of others. Would you not do the same?"

"No, I would never." Will slammed his fist on the table.

Everyone except Charlie jumped.

"Calm down!" Shai ordered.

"How—" Will's voice cracked— "how could you do that? To Liddy? You used to love her so much, and she definitely loves you."

Charlie shot to his feet, surprising all of us. "You think I don't love her? I did it *because* I love her!"

For the first time, I not only saw emotion in his odd, swirling eyes, but felt it as well. My heart squeezed.

Charlie made sure to meet everyone's gaze before staring down Will. "Do you have any idea what it has been like for me? To watch Mara torture Liddy over and over again? To watch her use kids, draining them of their innocence? Robbing them of their hope and joy?"

My throat constricted, dry and tight. I stood and walked over to Charlie. Opening my arms, I leaned in to hold him.

"No." He held up a hand and stepped back. "I don't want your pity."

"That's— that's not what I was doing," I stammered.

"I made a choice. Mara offered to let most of the kids go if I succeeded in bringing you to her. As a show of good faith, she released a handful from her lair before I was even transported to your house."

I covered my mouth with my hand. I could not imagine the horrors he'd witnessed.

"Obviously, I was unsuccessful, though if I'm being honest with myself, I didn't try that hard. I was hoping you wouldn't answer the door."

"And if she had?" Shai asked.

"Then Liddy would be dead, and hundreds of families would be restored." Charlie sat back down. I wanted to return to my seat, but my legs wouldn't move.

"What do you mean, you didn't try that hard?"

Charlie cast his face down. "I knew you were home. In fact, I knew you were on those stairs before you hid in your room. I could have easily broken the glass and let myself in. You were weak from the attack. It wouldn't have been difficult to hold you down until Mara came."

"But you didn't," I breathed.

He laughed, but it was without humor.

"And why didn't you?" It was Nick who spoke this time.

Charlie shrugged. "At first, whenever Liddy saw me, I was just a stranger to her. I knew she didn't recognize me. I thought that would make it easier to hand her over." Charlie's eyes glazed over. "But most recently, she looked at me like she was trying to place me. Like she recognized me, and suddenly I was no longer forgotten."

"You have never been forgotten," Will whispered. But

Charlie acted like he hadn't heard him.

"Why does she call you Jamie?" I asked.

He shrugged. "She didn't like Charlie, so she used a play on my last name." Charlie looked back to Nick. "To further answer your question, I guess, well... Liddy is so dang easy to love. She is part of what has kept me alive all these years. I'm sure Alex would say the same thing. Well, until Mara threatened his life."

The circles under Alex's eyes seemed to deepen as everyone turned their attention on him.

"I should have let her kill me," Alex whispered. "I was a coward."

"At least you can admit it," Will mumbled.

"William Lucas! Not another word," Lana chastised.

"I'm sorry, Liddy. I held off as long as I could. I saved your life once at the after party. I just wanted it all to end. I, too, could not stand seeing you tortured anymore. She promised me a painless and quick death for you."

"But if Alex failed? Let's just say there are worse things than death," Charlie added.

"How? How could you have known exactly where Liddy was in the house?" Will asked his brother.

Charlie flinched. "Mara has...*experimented* on me. I can find Liddy anywhere."

More than one person gasped at this revelation, but I didn't care. Faces of innocent children clouded my vision, their desperate voices pleading for my help, and all I could do was run from the witch. *I was the coward.*

My mouth went dry, but I forced myself to swallow. "If either of you told me, I would've gone with you willingly," I said, looking from Charlie to Alex.

Will jumped to his feet. "You don't mean that." His eyes were glassy, sorrow brimming them.

"But I do." I cupped his cheek and smiled faintly. "My life for hundreds, maybe thousands, of suffering children? For Pree and Justin? It's a no-brainer."

"William, take Liddy to her room and stay with her, *now* please," Brantley directed his son.

"No." I shrugged off Will's hands and sprinted over to Nick. "Please, let me fix this. So many are suffering, because of me! I cannot— I will not allow it!"

When Nick only stared back at me, his jaw twitching, I turned and pleaded with Shai. "Give her what she wants, but protect Will. You only need to keep him away from her." Hot tears washed my cheeks.

"If you die, I cannot live," Will said, his eyes nearly black.

Lana stood up. "Everyone, calm down!"

Nolan appeared at my elbow and assisted me to my seat. But before I could fully sit down, Will reached for me and pulled me into his lap. His arms wrapped securely around my waist, fearful that if he let go, I would disappear.

Once we were all seated, she continued. "Abishai, Nick... it appears we do not have a week to wait before enacting our plan. We will all be coming with you tomorrow morning."

"No, you need this time as a family," I protested.

"Liddy, dear, you *are* family," Brantley said, entwining his fingers with Lana's.

"He is right," Lana said. "This has all progressed a lot further than I imagined. Let's all eat to keep up our strength and spirits. Then we shall pack. Tomorrow when we land and get back to Abishai's, we inspect the globital and decide our next steps."

We ate in silence. Although Will placed me into my own chair so I could eat, his hand never left my thigh. Nolan walked by a few times, and each time his hand would momentarily rest on my shoulder to provide a dose of calm.

Exhaustion took me as I attempted to climb up the stairs to bed. Without saying a word, Will scooped me up in his arms, and I sighed contentedly at the contact. When he laid me back on the bed, I locked my hands around his neck, not wanting him to leave.

He laughed, but it was devoid of something. He grabbed my wrists and easily maneuvered his head out of my grip, placing my hands on my abdomen. His hands trailed down my legs to my feet. Carefully, he undid the buckles and removed my strappy sandals.

Will sat at the edge of the bed and his head slumped into his hands.

I slid to my knees and wrapped my arms around him.

"What is it?" I whispered in his ear.

"Promise me you will not offer yourself as a sacrifice."

I bit my lip. "I cannot make that promise."

Will turned and in one swift move, my hands were locked in his.

His red-rimmed eyes revealed that he'd been crying.

"I mean it, Liddy. This is a whole lot bigger than being devastated if something happened to you. Hell, just thinking about it nearly killed me tonight, but you must survive. You forget that we both are needed to defeat her. Without you, I am just an average Watcher who cannot save his people. But with you, together, we will have the strength to end this."

"I know, but—"

"There are no buts. I know your heart and how badly you want to save those kids. We risk a heck of a lot more if we save them now. But do not fret, we will save them together."

Will pulled me to him until our lips touched. His kiss, soft at first, grew more urgent as he deepened it. He broke away and moved a few pieces of hair behind my ear. Then he laid us down.

"Sweet dreams, Princess."

It's So Hard to Say Goodbye

WE ARRIVED AT PALWAUKEE AIRPORT just before lunch. A stretch limo greeted us and took us all to Shai's mansion.

Lana stared out the window transfixed, her hand tightly clutching Brantley's. *I wonder how she is really dealing with all of this.* Charlie sat on the other side of his dad, his eyes closed. I had the sudden urge to reach over and hold his hand. Charlie, the little boy once so full of life, still loved me enough not to condemn me to death. But I knew the guilt of saving my life instead of so many others was eating him up inside. I could feel it when he looked at me, the internal war he fought within himself. I slowly retracted my hand as I thought better of it.

Will sighed and nuzzled closer into my neck, his slow

breaths tickling the sensitive skin just below my ear. He hadn't left my side for a second since the events of last night's dinner.

I turned my gaze to Alex, who sat in between Nick and Shai, his head slumped back and chin down, his baseball hat set low over his eyes. Alex once chose me. Although I was still angry that Pree and Justin were gone, I could not blame him for choosing himself the second time. I so wished he didn't have to make the choice to begin with.

The chauffeur turned onto the long drive, and Will stirred.

"Finally," he mumbled before briefly kissing my neck. He attempted to stretch and laid an arm over my shoulder.

Lana turned to us and smiled. "Yes, it will be nice to get inside and get cleaned up."

The limo pulled up to the front steps. Nolan, who was seated next to Alex, moved first and opened the door. I swear he practically celebrated opening the door before the driver. One by one, we exited the limo, with Brantley being the last one out. Nolan had already made it up the steps and opened the door for us before returning to the trunk and retrieving our bags.

"Everyone, you have one hour to get cleaned up and eat something. We will meet in the training room," Lana announced. "Nolan, where shall we stay?"

"Lord and Madam Jamison, your room has always been kept ready for such a time as this."

My cheeks heated. *Would they be mad that I slept in their bed? Where was I going to stay?*

Nolan caught my eye. "Madam Lydia, you will be in Lord William's room."

Will's smile lit his entire face, but I couldn't help the

nerves that churned in my stomach, knowing what Shai thought about it. I turned to find him speaking in hushed tones to Nick just outside the front door. Will's parents were already halfway up the stairs, Alex and Charlie just behind them.

Nick stepped into the large atrium. "Lana, Brantley, I shall be back presently. I need to head to my place to get the globital and some other items."

"Of course, old man," Brantley hollered back.

"Who are you calling old? Technically you are older than me!"

"Maybe, but I don't look it!"

Nick belly laughed as he strode away.

Will grabbed my hand to lead me to his room, but I tugged it back.

"I need to talk to Nick."

He kissed the top of my head. "I'll wait right here."

"No, you're exhausted. Meet you in your room in ten?"

I could feel his uneasiness and I pushed all the reassuring energy I could into him. His shoulders relaxed and he smirked at me.

"OK. See you in ten, Princess."

I turned and ran. "Nick! Hold up!" I yelled when I made it to the front porch, finding Nick over by the fountain. He stopped and turned to face me.

"Is everything alright, dear?"

I placed my hands on my knees, panting. "Yes…"

He quirked a salt and pepper eyebrow at me.

"OK, no, it's not. Listen, you said before we left for Florida that I should be preparing to say goodbye to my friends and family."

Nick straightened and crossed his arms.

"I— I don't want to just say goodbye to them."

"Maybe not, sweet pea, but I promise it will make it easier on you. Trust me, you should say goodbye."

I shook my head. He was not understanding me. "No. I know it's selfish, but I'd like you to take their memories of me."

"And what good does that do?"

"It will save them from pain."

Nick scrutinized me, stroking his beard between his thumb and index finger. "Why do you think they would be in pain?"

"Because my gut is telling me there is a good chance that I'm not making it out of this alive."

Nick clucked his tongue. "Liddy, it will all work out."

I held my hand up to cut him off. "You cannot possibly know that. And while I appreciate your confidence, I want to be prepared."

Nick closed his eyes and gave me a curt nod.

I sighed in relief, turned, and headed toward the front door.

"And where are you going, dearie?"

"Uh, to the kitchen to grab some food, then to Will's room."

"Funny, and here I thought you were going to say your goodbyes."

"Right now?" I squeaked in surprise.

"No time like the present." Nick winked at me.

I sat in the passenger seat of Nick's Jeep, wringing my hands, and staring at my house.

"We don't have all day," Nick cautioned.

"I know, it's just. What am I supposed to say?"

"Whatever is on your heart. I will be right behind you to enact the enchantment."

So many thoughts tumbled through my mind, and I couldn't grab onto one. I didn't even know what excuse Will's uncle gave my parents for my sudden disappearance after the showcase.

The car door slammed and I jumped. Nick came around and whipped open the door. "You need to do this now. We still need to stop at my place."

Geesh. Nothing like a little tough love.

I walked to the front door and tried the brushed nickel handle. It was open. I ushered Nick inside, pointing at the living room for him to hide in. He dashed to the side and made himself invisible.

"Mom, Dad, I'm home!"

"Liddy, honey? You're back early!" Mom called out.

"We're in the family room," Dad replied.

My stomach rolled at the idea of never seeing my parents again. I clutched it, closed my eyes, and took a deep breath, trying to quell the nausea.

Mom and Dad were curled up on the loveseat, feet on the coffee table, watching a movie.

Dad clicked pause on the remote.

"How was Florida?" Dad smiled brightly at me.

"Looks like someone got some sun," Mom observed.

It just occurred to me that I had no idea— zero, zilch,

none— what Nolan or Shai had told my parents about my abrupt departure. I sat on the coffee table between their feet.

"How was it? Did you have fun?" Mom asked.

"I had a wonderful time. It was nice to see Mr. and Mrs. Jamison again, and the town they live in is so beautiful."

"How was the college tour?" Dad asked.

I paused, quickly trying to recall some facts about colleges in Florida I had looked into.

"It was great! I loved the campus, especially the Spanish architecture at Flagler."

"That's great, Honey, though I'm still rooting for a college closer to home."

"Mooom," I whined and then laughed. "I promise to look at some schools closer to home as well, OK?"

Mom sat straight up. "I would *love* that!"

"Don't get your hopes up, babe," Dad said as he squeezed her hand.

"Hey, I'm just happy she's giving them a chance."

"Well, I missed you guys. I'm exhausted and going to take a nap." I leaned in and gave them each a long, tight hug.

"Are you alright, Liddy?"

"I'm fine, why?"

"Normally you don't give me and your father hugs, not like that, anyway."

I gave them another hug. "Being away made me realize how much I'm going to miss you guys when I'm gone. I love yous."

"Way to make your mom cry," she said, sniffling.

Dad was quiet, but I caught him stealthily swiping a few tears.

I excused myself before my tears could fall, and when I reached my room, I found Nick sitting on my bed.

"It will all be OK, kid," he said quietly.

I closed the door and couldn't hold back the tears any longer. Nick stood held his arms out. I stepped into his embrace allowed him to comfort me. He let me sob into his shirt, not using any of his giftings to soften the harsh edges of this reality.

When I finally pulled away, he had a Christmas green handkerchief ready for me. I gladly took it and blotted under my eyes,

"Take only what you cannot live without. I will meet you in the car in ten minutes."

He closed the door behind him. I looked around my room. My heart gave an odd pang when I realized there wasn't really anything I absolutely had to take with me. I already wore the ring Will gave me at Christmas and Nolan had provided all of my necessities. I went to my picture organizer and quickly rifled through the photos. I chose one of my family and one of me with my best girlfriends. I placed them in my favorite book so they would not get bent.

I opened my CD player and took out the latest mixed CD Sara had made me. I glanced one last time at my bedroom and closed the door behind me. As I tiptoed down the stairs, I carefully placed the balls of my feet on the portion of each stair I knew would not creak.

A few minutes later, I was back in the Jeep, where Nick already sat waiting for me.

"Off to my place."

"Wait, I still need to say goodbye to my friends."

"I'm sorry kiddo, but we are out of time." Nick turned the

key in the ignition and maneuvered the stick into first gear.

"Can we at least drive by Sara's house? It's on the way."

"I suppose."

Nick knew exactly which house was hers, and he slowed just long enough for me to get one last good look at the blue house with the cherry-red door. More tears slipped down my cheek, but this time I felt a slight weight settle over my skin, warm and comforting, like a giant hug.

"Thanks, Nick."

He nodded in response.

Thanks to the Jeep, Nick was able to drive close to the entrance of his home. He hopped out and marched straight up to the gate. I followed closely on his heels.

When we entered the main living space, Nick froze, and I nearly crashed right into him. He held his hand up to stop me, his finger pressed to his lips, warning me not to make a sound.

My body tingled, my senses on high alert. Nick scanned the room, then took off for his office, his footsteps as quiet as a mouse and his bell-like melody silent. I stood stock-still. He emerged, his eyes lit to a dull blue, holding a small crystal orb in his hands.

He came to me, handed me the object, and proceeded to survey his home. A minute or two later he came back to me.

"Coast is clear."

"What was that about?" I asked, my body reeling from the pump of adrenaline.

"Something felt off in here. Normally the tree sings with my name or those who walk into my home. Sometimes it sings with the names of the most recent person she has taken."

"And it's silent now."

"Exactly."

"I didn't see you check that room," I said pointing to Arbolias Sang.

"I plan on it, but with the new fail safes I have in place to even enter the room, I am confident that no one is in there. Let me grab a few more things before I check it out, and then we need to get back to Shai's, pronto."

I went over to the red tufted couch and plopped down, studying the small crystal globe. Shai was right. It did resemble a giant marble with a swirly design inside.

Nick tinkered around in his office. Then he walked across the living room to his bedroom. Drawers glided on their slides and cabinets creaked open and closed. A few minutes later, Nick had a large leather satchel on his back.

I stood and followed behind him as he opened the door to Arbolias Sang.

As soon as he stepped inside, the tree began to chirp in a chorus of anxious voices.

"Nick! Nick! Nick!" It echoed over and over again.

I would recognize that voice anywhere.

"Hello? Earth to Nick!" The voice boomed.

"Pree?" I called out. Nick stood there, his eyebrows knitted together in confusion.

The message continued over and over again. Nick walked to the base of the tree, and I traipsed through the sandy earth after him. Scattered all around the base were folded pieces of paper with *Nick* scrawled across the front in Pree's handwriting.

Nick shrugged out of the leather sack on his back. "Liddy, if something happens to me when I open this, I want you to take my bag and drive straight to Shai's, am I clear?"

"But I can't drive stick!" I blurted.

"You'll figure it out."

"Nick, you can't—"

But he paid me no mind. He opened the note, and I threw my hands up in anticipation of the worst case scenario.

Nick huffed. "We've got to go, now!"

"Is that really from Pree?"

Nick placed his hand on my back and led me away from the tree. We careened out of the room, all the way back to the Jeep.

Once inside, Nick barked, "Buckle up!" He hit the gas and screeched out of the field, tearing up grass and flinging mud everywhere. My hand pressed against the window and dashboard so as not to fling about.

"Nick, you're freaking me out! What is going on?"

"The letter was from Pree. Clever girl was able to figure out a way to communicate with us."

He looked left, then right, then left again at the stop sign before peeling out of the parking lot onto Schoenbeck Road.

"Pree informed us that Mara herself is planning on crossing over into Mortalia. She no longer trusts her minions to do it."

"Hasn't she always come over?"

"Never. She has never crossed the portal barrier."

"What does this mean?"

Nick stepped on the gas at the yellow light and made a tight turn onto Hintz Road.

"It means we leave for Cristes...tonight."

No Sleeping Theory

NICK SWERVED AND YANKED ON THE PARKING BREAK, sending up a cloud of dust in Shai's driveway.

"Hurry!" he hollered as he opened the back passenger door and snatched up his bag.

I rushed up the stairs ahead of him and flung open the door. Nolan stood there, his eyes wide as the door missed cracking his face by less than an inch.

"Sorry, Nolan!" I cried as I raced to the center of the atrium floor. "Everyone, downstairs now, please!"

Nick was at the door giving instructions to Nolan. As Nick strode over to me, I watched Nolan lock the doors. He held up two fingers, tracing them, and a pink outline glowed brightly for a moment, then vanished.

Will burst through the kitchen, his sneakers squeaking on

the glossy wood floor.

"Liddy, what the heck! You said you were meeting me upstairs and you never showed!"

"I'm so sorry, but I have a good reason."

Will crossed his arms over his chest, clearly miffed and wanting an answer. I probably scared him, considering my meltdown yesterday.

"Good thing I could sense you were mostly OK. Otherwise, I might have believed you'd surrendered to Mara."

"What in Eira's name is all the commotion?" Lana ran down the stairs, Brantley and Shai trailing behind her.

"Where are Charlie and Alex?" Will asked.

"I will go get them," Nolan responded.

"Everyone will do what I say, when I say. Is that understood?" Nick ordered. Every adult's face paled.

"Wait a second, Nick. We get a say in the plans here," Shai retorted.

Nick's eyes flashed and I reflexively bent at my waist.

Shai's head flicked up and he scowled at Nick. "You would use your gifting to force us?"

"I am merely reminding you who I am in this moment. Currently, I am Prince of Cristes, not your friend or cousin. We do not have time for prideful requests and demands, Abishai."

Charlie and Alex walked into the atrium. Nick's gifting released its control, and we all stood straight again.

"Uh, what's going on?" Alex asked.

"Pree has sent us an urgent message." Nick rubbed his forehead, bracing himself everyone's reactions.

"Out with it!" Shai demanded.

Nick glared at Shai in warning but didn't remark on his impatience. "Mara plans on coming into Mortalia."

Charlie's head snapped up. Both he and Alex paled as if they might be sick.

"When?" Lana whispered.

"She may already be here. Pree sent the message that she was coming, and that we had to protect Liddy and Will." He handed the note to Lana. Brantley and Shai read over her shoulder.

"What does 'like yesterday' mean?" Brantley asked, pointing to part of the note.

"It means we should already be in Cristes," I responded.

Brantley took the note and pressed it between his hands. He focused his gaze on the note, and a teal glow scanned the paper.

"This note is a few days old. The author worked quickly and used some elemental magic. She took a huge risk."

What if Pree was caught? The intrusive thought struck me hard and I swayed on my feet. Will caught me at the elbow and clutched me to his chest.

Nick reached into the bag at his feet and procured the globital, holding it out for all to see.

"It's in worse shape than I thought," Lana huffed. "I don't think we can repair it in a day's time."

"Good because we have less than eighteen hours."

"Hand it to me," Brantley ordered. He grabbed the globital from Nick and made a beeline for the kitchen. I assumed he was headed to the apothecary lab.

"Lana, Nolan, you will both work with Brantley. Shai, you and I will need to create a list of the supplies we need.

Kids, your task will be to pack for all of us. But for now, Will and Liddy, to the library; Charlie and Alex, back to the media center. Wait in your location for further instruction."

Will and I retreated to the library. Once we were seated on the couch, I laid my head on his shoulder.

"There's never a moment's peace, is there?" Will laughed, but it was devoid of humor.

"I guess not. Why do you suppose Nick is keeping me from Charlie?"

Will's jaw tightened. "What makes you think that?"

"You know something."

"I don't know anything. Maybe I have my own theory, that's all."

"Which is?"

Will closed his eyes, resigning himself to the fact that I would not let it go until he answered me.

"I don't think Nick fully trusts him. You would make it easy for him to take you back to her."

I bit my lip. "Guilty."

An hour passed and then another. Neither Nick nor Shai came with updates. Nolan had come and gone with lunch, but he didn't speak. I grew bored and laid on the couch. My eyes grew heavy, and I let them close. Will's warm body wrapped around me, and I started to drift off.

"No! No sleeping!" A frantic voice pierced the room.

"Mom?" Will asked, his voice groggy.

I stirred. Strong hands gripped my shoulders. "Lydia! Wake up, please."

My eyes popped open, startled by the proximity of Lana's face mere inches from mine, her features wild.

"Mom, what's going on?"

"Both of you, please come downstairs."

Lana rushed out of the library and we raced after her.

The hidden door to the basement was already opened for us. When we arrived at the first landing, hushed voices streamed from the apothecary lab. We entered the lab where all of the adults, save for Nolan, were present.

"Mom, what was that about?" Will rubbed his sternum. "You have my heart racing faster than Tom Cruise in *Days of Thunder*."

The corners of her mouth dropped. "Mara could reach Liddy in her dreams. She cannot sleep now, especially when Mara could also be here in the present. She could call Liddy and her body would go to her."

I paled at the idea of being controlled by Mara again.

Will looked to me, then back to his mother. "Mara hasn't hijacked Liddy's dreams for a long while. And, she's never really gotten hurt in them before—" he winced— "at least not permanently."

"Well, not since the failsafe I conjured, anyway."

"Right, so I'm safe then," I said, not understanding her cause for alarm.

Lana leaned against a wall and dropped her head back and for the first time, she looked tired. "Except now, she has completely broken through. You are no longer protected while in Mortalia."

"How do you know, Mom?"

"Because, I can feel it. That protection orison was a part of me, and now I have that part back."

"Well, then, do the orison again."

Lana shook her head. "It's not that simple."

Tiny pricks of anxiety jabbed my stomach and at each new sensation, my stomach tied itself into another knot. Will squeezed my hand tighter, and the pricks sharpened into stabs.

I released his hand and took a deep breath. "Calm down, Will. I'm fine. I just won't sleep." I gave him what I hoped was a reassuring smile.

"She will only be able to stay awake for so long before sleep claims her. We will need to be in Cristes the next time she falls asleep," Brantley cautioned.

"So the globital is fixed?" I asked, looking over to the glass orb, which was centered on a table that Nick, Shai, Brantley, and Lana surrounded.

"Not yet," Shai answered.

"Let's not beat around the bush, shall we?" Nick said curtly. "We need to test some of your combined giftings as they are now, see if they can't help us to repair what has been fractured."

"And if they can't?" I asked.

"Then we take our chances and go anyway," he replied.

"There has to be another way," Shai pleaded. For the first time, I sensed fear roil off of him, a slight cloud outlining his body.

"Brother, we have discussed this," Lana said softly, placing her hand over his.

"Can we not just put a protection detail around Liddy when she sleeps until we are sure the globital is ready for use?" Will asked.

Nick shook his head. "No. Mara is far too powerful. We cannot risk it."

"What do you need us to do?" I asked.

Nick stepped around the table and stood before us.

"Remember when I said you two needed to keep things platonic? You know, making sure you didn't get too close?" Nick cocked a brow at us.

I could feel my face redden.

Will scoffed. "Dude, what the heck are you suggesting?"

Nick held his hands up, placatingly. "Relax, this isn't your wedding night. I am saying, you were told to be hands off because your giftings have no problem surging through one another and amplifying. I did not want you to be a lighthouse providing a direct path for Mara to your shores."

Lana stepped out next to Nick. "What Nick is saying is that we need you both to focus on combining the giftings that have manifested when we ask you to. We are hopeful that your giftings will be able to help us further repair our transport to Cristes."

"We cannot do this," Shai stated again, even more agitated. "We are asking them to become that beacon!"

Brantley cleared his throat, cutting through the tension in the air. "We have two options. We can risk alerting Mara to our whereabouts, fix the globital before she finds us, and get back to Cristes safely. Or, we risk traveling to Cristes as is."

"Or, we risk Mara knowing where we are, we are unsuccessful in fixing our portal, and still risk going to Cristes," Shai scoffed.

Lana turned to face her brother and clasped his hands with hers. "I know you are nervous. You placed a lot of blame on yourself when Charlie was taken. It was never your fault. We knew the risks. It was no one's fault but Mara's."

Will and I exchanged glances. I rested my forehead on his

chest, hoping he could sense what I was thinking. *If we have the chance to get everyone to Cristes safely, I say we take it.*

Will looped his arms around me. "We should at least try to fix the globital," he said.

Shai ran an exasperated hand down his face.

"But," Will added, "we should put a time limit on it. When do we need to leave for Cristes, no matter what?"

"Preferably before the sun fully sets," Nick said. "We do not want to give Mara the added advantage the cover of darkness brings."

I shivered involuntarily.

"Well, then there is no time to waste." Brantley clapped his hands. "William, Liddy, come join me over here, please."

"I have been working on a chemical and elemental compound utilizing the different Christmas roses and tinctures in Nolan's terrarium. My goal is to mimic the material of the outer shell so that once its center ignites, the centripetal force will be contained, providing a swift and safe passage."

I stared at him, trying to follow his explanation.

"I've made the compound many times before and it is reliable, especially for a one-time use. However, the globital is unique in that it is casted as one piece. Once broken, they are said to be irreparable. It does not like a foreign substance within its walls. The first goal is to help it stick to the surface."

"Like a band-aid," I offered.

He smiled at me. "Precisely. The second goal is to make sure the band-aid stays there once its inner bud is activated for travel. In other words, it needs to be able to withstand an abrupt and incredible amount of power."

"So, what do you need Liddy and I to do?" Will asked.

"Utilize your giftings together to try and force the shell to accept the compound."

"Great." Will's lips pursed. "And how do we do that exactly?"

"Well, son, that is for you to figure out."

"I'll be there to help," Nick said.

"And while the three of you are working with Brantley, Shai and I will be setting the muting wards," Lana said. "I know that this area is already well protected, but I want to try and further dampen the gifting Liddy and Will produce. We have no idea how powerful it is at this time."

My nerves woke, tiny leeches latching onto me. The fact that no one knew for certain if I was Will's whitelighter match gnawed at me.

"Can I please have a quick moment? Nature calls." I booked it out of the room, down the stairs, and to the training facility before anyone could respond. My hand found the slightly worn panel and I pressed lightly. The heavy door slid open and I made a beeline for the back end where the bathroom was.

I locked the door behind me, pressed my back against it, and slid down until my butt hit the floor.

A gentle knock rapped on the door a few minutes later. "Um, just a minute please!"

"Liddy, I can feel you are seconds away from a panic attack. Can I come in?"

I mean, it was sort of awesome that I had a boyfriend who knew exactly what I was feeling, but at the same time, it *so* wasn't. I got to my knees and unlocked the door, sliding over to the adjacent wall.

Will peered in. "Um, do you want to have this conversation on the bathroom floor?"

I shook my head, and he helped me stand, leading me out of the bathroom and sitting down with me on the weight bench.

"What if I'm the weak link?" I blurted out.

He rubbed his chin. "I don't understand."

"Will, no one who knew of Watchers knew what to look for when I was born. We all know that you were born with markings indicating that you had whitelighter potential. I am—" I shrugged— "A theory."

"And you are worried that the theory will be wrong."

"Exactly." I sighed. "All these sacrifices were made on my behalf. All this hope they have that I can fix everything with you. What if I am not your perfect match?" I gulped down the rising pressure. "What if I am a distraction that has stolen the time and energy to find your real match, and as a result, we lose everything?"

Will dove in and kissed me. There was no gentleness in this kiss, only fiery passion. He nipped at my bottom lip and seized the opportunity to capture my gasp with his mouth. When he pulled away, he slowly turned me to face the mirrors on the wall. We glowed brightly, me in lavender and him in aqua.

"This. This is how I know that you are everything they say you are, and so much more. I do not doubt for one second that our bond is unique, strong, and what Cristes needs. I choose to trust the people who love us. All we can do is try our best and believe in the best."

"Maybe we should, uh, warm up our giftings a little more

before we try to push them to their limits?" I smirked.

Will laughed, deep and robust. He spun me around, and slowly, ever so slowly, dipped down and brushed his lips against mine.

When we walked back into the terrarium, all the adults grinned and averted their eyes.

"What? Liddy had the great idea that we should warm up our giftings before using them in ways we haven't yet."

"Smart woman," Brantley said, peeking out from behind his beakers, test tubes, and scattered roses, a proud grin on his bright face. I blushed even more.

Lana clapped her hands twice. "Everyone, to the center of the room while Shai and I place the orison wards."

My eyes followed them as they walked in opposite directions. Each had their own shade of green that emanated from their palms.

"That should do it," Shai remarked.

"Then there is no time to waste," Nick said. "Brantley, how do you wish us to proceed?"

"When I place the compound on the edges of the break, you must act quickly to weld it to the shell, forcing the elements to accept each other so as not to reject it."

"Should we all hold hands or something?" Will asked, his voice hesitant.

"You and Liddy should, but let's have Nick on his own," Lana answered, coming up beside her husband, donning large black gloves that reached her elbows. Brantley wore similar gloves, although his were slimmer. They both pulled down holographic protective goggles over their eyes.

"On the count of three, Lana and I will place the

compound. Be ready for my command."

An azure light flickered to life in Nick's chest. The light traveled from his heart, through his veins and arteries. I had seen this once before.

"One..." Lana called out.

Will gave me a quick kiss and grabbed my hand.

"Two..."

I tapped into my gifting as I imagined what needed to be done. A little nudge at my core, and I knew Will's gifting wanted in, so I let it.

"Three!" Brantley and Lana worked like a well-oiled machine. She held the silver beaker in her hands as Brantley took a glass tapered dropper, dipped it into the beaker, and held it over the large fracture.

The initial gold liquid changed colors, swirling inside its glass case like a lava lamp. With careful precision and speed, Brantley decorated the entire outline of the break.

Just before he placed the last drop he said, "On the ready...now!"

The room lit up so brightly, my eyes reflexively closed to protect themselves. Still, shades of blue, purple and green danced before my eyelids. After a few minutes, my skin grew hot, and tiny beads of sweat collected along my hairline.

"That's it! Hold on just a little longer!" Brantley yelled, but his voice was muffled, as if I was within a cone of silence.

As the moments dragged, my core temperature went from hot to searing. My first sunburn of the lifeguarding season had nothing on the stinging rawness that lashed me. I whimpered just as I heard Will grunt.

"I can't hold much longer," Nick ground out.

"Brantley, they need to stop. Now!"

"Do not interrupt them, Shai. They are almost there!"

Suddenly, a grating sensation covering my skin sent me over the edge. I cried out as what felt like sandpaper scoured my body, and then I collapsed.

"Liddy! Liddy!"

"It's too hot, Will. It hurts...everything hurts."

"I've got you, Princess. I'm right here," Will said, as he started to lift me.

"Don't...touch...me.... please," I panted through the pain.

"I told you, Brantley. Lana, quick, get Nolan," Shai commanded as he kneeled next to me. Lana was a blur as she sped out of the room. Little pricks of cooling touched, then melted into my skin. But it wasn't enough. The fire was too intense and seeping deeper into my skin.

"This should help her some until I can get Nolan's help."

"What's wrong with her, Uncle?"

"I do not know. Normally, the light manifestation disappears when the Watcher orders it, too. These patches of neon purple and orange light all over her skin... I have not seen anything like it before."

"It burns," I cried out.

"Help her!" Will pleaded.

"She's been cursed," Brantley whispered.

Will's face paled. "What do you mean?"

"Mara...she must have done something to Liddy, something all of us missed..." Brantley frowned. "Manifesting when she joined powers with others."

"Well, fix it!" Will beseeched him.

He shook his head and looked away from his son. "We

can't... not here."

"Then where?" Shai asked.

"Cristes," Brantley whispered.

"Nolan!" Nick bellowed.

"Will, please hand me the Christmas roses from that shelf over there," Shai instructed.

Will left my side and I moaned. His absence only made the pain more unbearable.

"Thank you." Shai pruned a few petals from each rose, careful to pluck them so they would not tear. Each petal glowed a faint pink before he placed them on me. Like smears of aloe, they soothed the raw spots.

"Thank you," I sighed.

Thundering steps and a large commotion overhead seized all of our attention.

"Seal the door!" Lana screeched.

Nick and Shai's eyes met before they launched themselves out of the room.

"Son, grab Liddy...good. Sweetheart, hold onto the globital." He placed it on my stomach, took my hand, and laid it on top. "Go down to the training room. Now!"

"But Dad—"

Brantley didn't respond. He, too, was out the door and up the stairs. Will entered the hall and my blood ran cold.

"She's coming," I said. Fear gripped my body before it could even register in my brain. Uncontrollable shivers jostled me as adrenaline flooded my system.

"Stay with me, Liddy." Will spoke in my ear, waves of calm asking permission to soothe the shores of my nervous system.

I held my hand up, and Will maneuvered my body so that my palm pressed against the door's sensor without any extra effort from me. As soon as we passed over the threshold, the doors slid closed.

"I'll be right back. I need to go see what is happening," he said as he gently set me down on the nearest couch.

"Please don't leave me." I fisted his shirt in my hands, stalling him.

Will opened his mouth to speak, but before he uttered a single word, the door slid open and he threw his body over mine.

Pizza, Pizza

"**E**VERYONE IN, STAT!" Lana yelled.

Will whipped his head up. "Mom!" He scrambled off the couch and ran to her. "What is going on?"

I pushed myself up to sit and flung my arm over the edge of the couch.

Lana ushered in Nolan, the last of our small group, who hoisted an unconscious Alex over his shoulder.

The door slammed shut. Nolan laid Alex on the couch opposite me. Then all of the adults used their giftings to seal the doors.

Lana dusted her hands. "Well, son, when I went to grab Nolan, I came upon an altercation. Alex had taken it upon himself to order pizza. Instead of a delivery man, he was met with two of Mara's henchmen. We were able to subdue one of them, but the other got away."

"So what does this mean?" I asked, my voice shaking with both fear and pain.

"It means, we leave now," Nick interjected. "Shai, what is the best way to get to your cars?"

I hadn't noticed in the commotion of their entrance, but they all had slung a bag or two over their back and shoulders.

Lana noticed my gaze. "Lucky for us, Nolan and the boys had packed for everyone before the unfortunate mistake that one made," she said, pointing to Alex.

"Is he going to be, OK?" I asked.

"He will be fine. Just stunned. He should come to shortly," Nolan answered. "We will exit at the far end of this training facility. There is a trap door that leads through a short tunnel to the garage. We need to separate Lord William and Madam Lydia on the ride over for obvious reasons. You three—" he pointed to Shai, Charlie, and Nick— "will join Lord William in one vehicle. Everyone else will be with me in the other."

Nolan was usually so quiet; I was surprised he took the helm of our escape operation.

"We will take two different routes to Prince Nicholas's, though both travel times are within a minute of each other. We enter Hill House together and head straight for Arbolias Sang while Lord Abishai and Madam Lana reinforce its Orison shields."

My eyes went wide and found Will. He, too, had a shocked look on his face.

"Something I never told you both is that under the tree is a gateway where we will use the globital to transport back to Cristes," Nick explained.

"Speaking of the globital," Nolan cut in, "where are we with that?"

Brantley walked over to me, and I placed the device into his hands. I winced as the movement smarted. The colored patches marking my skin started glowing a little brighter, burning my skin once more.

Nolan eyed me for a moment before making a beeline to the kitchenette, while Brantley inspected the globital.

"Some of it mended; nearly sixty, maybe seventy percent of it, is my best guess. The other portion has a thin layer of protection, but that will not withstand the trip. We must prepare for the worst."

The couch cushion next to me sank a little and I turned to see who had sat down. Nolan held out a strip of cloth that shimmered like the opal stone in my ring. He took my arm and gingerly wrapped it around the neon splotches.

I sucked in a breath as the pressure on the stained skin increased. But then, three or four popping sounds later... relief.

"That was kind of gross, but thank you."

Nolan nodded. "I am not sure if it will keep them away indefinitely, but it should offer enough relief until we can get home."

Will stood by me watching as Nolan addressed the neon spots on my face, neck, and other arm. By the time he was done with his handiwork, I was mummified.

"Alright, everyone. We have the game plan. I'm sure Mara's henchman has relayed the message to her about our location. We need to head out now," Nick instructed.

"Unfortunately, that is all we have time for." Nolan said,

standing and plopping the remaining cloths into the bowl.

"Thank you. I feel much better." Uncertain of my tolerance to withstand the inevitable pain that walking would bring, given the raw skin and the chafing of my pants, toughing it out was the only option. Determined not to be the weakest link, I stood, biting back a scream, and reached for Will's steadying arm.

"You guys, Liddy can't walk in this condition." He gestured to my lower half. "She needs her legs and feet tended to."

"Son, we don't have time." Lana's eyes held a deep understanding of my pain, but she remained steadfast.

"In that case, I'll carry her to the car. Once inside, I'll apply whatever that salve is while we're on the way to Nick's."

"No!" Shai interjected "We cannot risk having you both in the same vehicle."

"Nolan and I will tend to her in the car," Lana offered.

"Fine." Will turned back to me. "I'm still carrying you though."

"That won't work either. You will not fit in the narrow tunnel," Nolan cautioned.

I shook my head at Will. "Thank you for offering, but I've got this."

"Liddy, seriously, what I feel is only a fragment of what you do and—"

"Do you think your girlfriend is a weakling who can't handle the hard stuff?" I playfully remarked, attempting to distract him. Lana mouthed *thank you* to me from behind Will.

He huffed. "Fine. But if you change your mind, I'm right here."

"I know." Then I quickly planted a peck on his cheek.

Just then, Alex popped his head up from where he laid on the couch opposite me. "Where am I?" he asked, his eyes wide and darting from side to side.

Shai gestured to the room. "We are in my basement. You woke up just in time, as we are exiting the premises."

"Where are we going?" Alex rubbed his forehead.

"To my place," Nick answered.

Alex gave him a glassy stare. "Dude, and where's that?"

A memory flitted to my mind, and I smiled. "A hobbit house inside the hill at Husky Park. And you'll need your magic to enter."

Everyone eyed me like I had lost my mind. "Pree," I explained, adding to Nick, "It's how she first described your place."

Nick chuckled, and a few others tittered along with him. But when Nick's laugh morphed into his contagious, full-on chortle, everyone couldn't help but join in, a release we all so badly needed. Once it died down, Nick wiped a tear from his eye.

He sighed, his expression sobering. "Let's go," he ordered.

Everyone followed Nolan to the back of the gym. He waved his hands over the floor in front of us, and a golden outline materialized. It was as if liquid gold had been poured into a corner, with the molten fluid spreading outward along the confines of the rectangular pattern. A handle appeared next; Nolan grabbed it and pulled.

The hatch opened with ease. Shai's eyes ignited, illuminating the dark tunnel below.

"I will go down first," Lana volunteered and no one objected.

We knew she was the most skilled warrior among us.

She hopped down the seven-foot drop without a sound.

"Shai, you're next. Then I'll hand you the globital and follow after," Brantley said.

Shai swooped down like Spider-Man. Brantley bent at the waist, his top half disappearing through the hole to hand off the device. Once it was safely in Shai's hands, he flipped his entire body into the hatch that was now glowing green.

"After you, Lord Charlie," Nolan beckoned, still holding the latch open.

Charlie looked to Will and I one last time before jumping down.

"Lord William, your turn."

Will brought me to his side in a protective stance. "No. I will go down just before Liddy."

"Of course." Nolan gave a curt nod. "Alexander, after you."

"Do you hear that?" Alex blanched.

"Alex, we don't have time for your jokes. Just get down there already," Will said impatiently.

A scratching sound scraped against the outside of the heavy metal doors. I locked eyes with Alex and he paled, his eyes beginning to swirl a muddy orange.

"He's not joking. She's here." My voice shook with each word.

"Critosi!" Nick hollered.

Alex remained rooted to the spot. Nick hoisted him up and lowered him into the hole.

This time, a piercing screech rang out, metal grating against metal.

"William, let's go!" Brantley commanded. Will obeyed,

leaping down.

A big bang erupted, and the ground rumbled beneath me; I fell to my knees.

"Liddy!" Will's voice echoed from below.

I whirled around and looked back at the door. It's center was bent inward, and a bright orange glow seeped through the cracks around the frame. Behind the door, I could hear the faint taunting call...

Lydiaaa...

Gruff hands snatched my waist, the pain so blinding I couldn't even scream as someone tossed me down the hole, into Will's waiting arms.

Nick landed with a soft *thud* next to us.

"Come on, man," he called up to Nolan.

Nolan was poised to jump when an ear-splitting *BOOM* shook the room. Small pieces of rock crumbled and skittered down the walls in the tunnel around us.

Nolan's face filled the hatch, resolute. Then he stood, bowed the traditional Cristes salute, and slammed the hatch's door shut.

Big Girls Don't Cry

"**N**OLAN!" NICK HOLLERED.

Pink flames licked where the hatch had been and then it went dark.

"No!" I cried.

"Anyone who does not start running will be dragged by me," Lana warned as she started moving.

The narrow tunnel was damp, and above, roots jutted out from the wooden surface at random intervals. The men had to duck their heads as they ran after Lana's green glow.

We hadn't gotten too far when we came across a large wall of dirt adorned with a silver outline of a Christmas rose. Nick shot a blast of gifting at it; the rose lit up, and the illusion of a dirt wall dissipated, revealing a short staircase. We said nothing as one by one, we climbed the steps and emptied into the large garage.

"We still take the cars as planned," Lana instructed. Shai tossed her a set of keys. She turned, raised her arms, and on the downswing, a blast of green concealed the staircase and door.

Will helped me into the back of the black Yukon.

"See you in just a few minutes," he said.

"I love you."

He kissed my cheek and darted off to the navy blue Bronco.

Brantley pressed the garage door button fastened on the passenger visor. The door bent and rose soundlessly. He only kept the fog lights on as he accelerated and steered down the long drive. Shai, driving the Bronco, trailed right behind us.

When we neared the gate, the pealing shriek of a malevolent witch racked my brain.

I held back tears, mourning Nolan. *How much more would this witch take from us?* My heart hurt, and my eyes stung as if they were poisoned by the tears that wanted to spill.

"Liddy, remove your pants, quickly," Lana instructed me.

"I'm fine." I pressed my palms into my eyes.

"I promised my son. Not to mention, we are going to need you in top shape if we are to make it to Cristes."

I unbuckled and shimmied out of my jeans, not stopping even as it felt like my skin was peeling off with them. Lana worked faster than Nolan would have, dressing multiple areas at once. I bit down on my lip, drawing blood as I stifled the scream brought on by the intense pressure that threatened to break my legs. I lifted my shirt so that she could tend to my abdomen.

"Almost there, ladies," Brantley called back to us.

Lana set the nearly empty bowl on the car's floor. "That will have to suffice. You can get dressed now."

As I pulled up my pants, they no longer felt like sandpaper grating over raw skin. I could withstand the feeling of clothes brushing against a sunburn.

We arrived at Nick's ahead of the others. Brantley drove along the forest line closest to the entrance. He parked the car, but we stayed put, holding our breath as we waited for the Bronco.

"They're almost here," I said aloud, a reassurance to myself as I sensed Will's presence. Sure enough, the Bronco pulled next to us, and we all jumped out at the same time.

Nick made a beeline for the grate, and it flung open behind him.

"I need you all to move!" he roared. When we all passed through, the iron bars swung shut as he muttered, "Slower than molasses, they all are."

Lana and Nick stayed behind to ward the entrance.

"Our giftings should keep it hidden from anyone who is looking for it, no matter the gifting or element used," Lana explained.

Nick brushed past all of us and stormed into his home, through the living room, and straight into Arbolias Sang.

Will held my hand as we ventured into the room, and my feet sank slightly into the pale pink sand. The thick, humid air enveloped me, giving the sensation that we were inside an actual cloud.

The incandescent tree continued to irradiate the space, its massive trunk still painted in bright shades of red, orange, and blue. I looked up, and a dense forest of branches were bent and woven together, creating a canopy.

Scores of glowing, amber envelopes fluttered in midair, acting as giant leaves filling out the branches on the massive tree. This time, no voices sang out to us as we approached.

Nick walked to the trunk and pressed on a knot in it, directly above where I had found Will unconscious just a few short months ago. My stomach cramped as I recalled how terrified I was, fearing he was dead.

Will squeezed my hand, reassuring me he was alive and well.

A few of the knots unfurled themselves, unveiling an oval-shaped door in the trunk.

"Before we enter, I feel compelled to share that this will be an unpleasant experience, especially if you have never been transported via gifting before." Nick looked pointedly at Will and me. "Brantley, can you please provide them with a brief summary of what to expect?"

"Of course. For only a few seconds, though to some it may feel much, *much* longer, you will essentially be freefalling through realms. Without a globital, you could become trapped there forever."

"What does our broken globital mean, then?" I asked. "Do we risk being trapped forever?"

"No, we are fortunate that it is mostly repaired and has not rejected the bond. However, if we are not within the protection of the dome as we exit the fall to Cristes, the force of the pathways is so strong, one could be sucked out, torn in half, or squashed to death."

"That sort of happened to you, right?" Will asked Nick.

"Not exactly. I never fully entered Cristes. I merely tossed the baskets of Christmas roses into their realm and returned straight home. Thus, I primarily stayed within the Mortalia pathway. Some of my organs, notably my lungs, were partially frozen and crushed. This was due to the large crack in the globital which allowed part of Cristes's realm to exert its force."

"We are aware that the fissure and hole are not complete," Shai spoke up. "The globital's inner core will expand to cover and protect us. If it shatters, we will be subject to the chaos of realm travel." He grimaced, his eyebrows squeezing together.

"How can we protect ourselves if the globital does fracture on entry into Cristes?" Will pressed.

"Well, there is truly nothing we can do," Nick stated bluntly. "Except to use our giftings in an attempt to counteract some of the force exerted on us. The tricky part will be protecting our non-Watcher friends as we work hard to safeguard ourselves."

"That is enough 'what if' explanations for now." Lana jumped in, briefly glaring at Nick. "Let's enter the tree and get started on our journey."

We crawled through the door, standing upon entry into the tree's hollowed center. Only about a foot of ground surrounded a gigantic black hole. One by one, we scooched around the strip of land, our backs pressed against the tree's smooth inner walls, until everyone was inside.

Nick peered into the gaping hole, then looked back up at each of us. "On the count of three, we all jump in together."

"Whoa, you expect us to just jump into a bottomless pit?"

Though he wasn't my favorite person in the world right now, I was relieved to see I wasn't the only one feeling scared.

"Yes," Nick answered.

"*On* three, or after?" Alex asked, rocking back on his heels.

Nick scowled at him. "After. Does everyone understand?" When no one spoke up, he carried on. "Good. Brantley will toss the globital into the air on 'two.' When we jump in, every Watcher will use their gifting to summon the globital's protection. It will feel a little tight, but stay calm."

"What about those of us who aren't Watchers?" Alex asked.

"You die," Nick deadpanned.

Alex looked expectantly at all of us. Only Shai wore a knowing smirk.

Alex tipped his head toward me. "He's joking, right?"

When I didn't answer, he turned to Nick. "You're joking, right?"

Nick ignored him. "Alright, everyone on the ready."

I glanced at the faces around me. Alex looked as if he'd be sick. Charlie stood between his parents, but he avoided all eye contact with everyone. Standing next to Will with Shai at his side, made me feel secure. Nick stood on my right, though he was positioned closer to Alex since he would be helping him with getting into Cristes.

"One..."

The adults readied themselves as first their eyes and then the rest of their bodies lit up. I quickly followed suit.

"Two..."

Brantley held the globital over the edge. He extended his arm downward, and with one fluid arc, he sent the globital soaring into the air.

I wanted to watch it, to see the globital in action. But before I could, Nick called out, "Three!"

And then I jumped. My stomach immediately sank, clenching as my body somersaulted into the black abyss. My hair whipped wildly around me, and as I tumbled down, down, down, the air grew colder and colder. My body, too tense to scream or flail, was like an anchor cast into the deepest, darkest ocean. I couldn't help but pray this would be over soon.

I heard and saw no one, all of our gifting's light had been snuffed out. *Did I jump correctly?* I finally remembered Nick's directive, to aim my powers at the globital to receive its protection and transport. My breath, coming in ragged gasps, felt like ice had crystallized my lungs, but I managed to dig deep and find the warm spark of my power, awaiting my command.

I threw it out once, like a lasso, and caught only emptiness. I swallowed the panic that threatened to constrict my throat and suffocate me. I tried again. This time, my illuminated rope wrapped around the smooth walls of the orb. The free fall stopped, and I became weightless, drifting in a sea of stars and diamond dust.

Everyone's eyes fell on me when I finally joined the group of invisible carriages. Will's slow smile and gesture of his hand over his heart conveyed his relief. His lips moved, but his voice was mute.

"I can't hear you. Can you hear me?" I cupped my ear then pointed to him, shaking my head.

Will shrugged, cupped his ear, and then shook his head. I reached for his hand, but it was as if we were in our own small bubbled made of glass. *Well, at least he was with Shai.*

Lana and Brantley sandwiched Charlie in an embrace.

Nick held Alex with one arm wrapped around his chest and a bored expression on his face. I surmised that they assumed these positions before calling upon their Watcher giftings. After the state in which we first found Nick this past February, I had anticipated a much more hazardous trip.

Time seemed to hold still in this beautiful place as we floated lazily along the trail of realms. The weight and warmth of the globital's protection cocooned me, and I finally relaxed.

But then my little chrysalis shook. I jerked my head around, but if the others sensed the vibrations, their faces didn't show it.

Probably just a little turbulence. As soon as the thought flitted by, another jolt of my glass enclosure shook me, and I hit my head. *Ouch!* My hand flew to my head where a large bump was already forming. Again, the disturbance came, harder and faster. The black, starlit sky faded into a hazy, glowing gray. More time passed, and the sky deepened to indigo, bleeding into shades of purple and magenta.

The temperature inside my cocoon dropped steadily. I glanced down at the encasement and noticed a few small fissures here and there. *Dang it.* I surveyed the others in my group, and from the clench of their jaws and widened eyes, I knew they were experiencing the same thing. And then, without further warning, our languid pace jumped into hyperdrive. The pressure thrust me forward and then jerked me back.

Spinning—so much spinning. I squeezed my eyes shut to ward off the inevitable puke-fest that would hit me if I dared to keep them open.

Spin. Spin. Flip. Flop. Spin. Drop. Drop.

The dizzying, erratic movements within the glass bubble stopped, but the its velocity only increased. I opened my eyes, marveling at the sight of a frozen tundra. *Wasn't Cristes supposed to be a tropical paradise?* I tried to shake my head, but the force of gravity was too strong. A more pressing threat grew nearer by the millisecond; our imminent landing. The gravitational force exerted on my body grew more and more painful as I plummeted to the ground and braced myself for a crash landing.

Trees and humongous chunks of ice exploded upon impact. Pain. Pain was everywhere, so sharp, I could barely breathe. I opened my eyes to what looked like a war zone. Dust eclipsed the air, and I could barely see two feet in front of me.

I hadn't realized I'd momentarily lost my hearing until the screams began. At first, they were distant. Then, as if someone slowly turned the dial up on a stereo, they grew louder. I tried to get up, but my legs would not move. I glanced down to see what had trapped my legs but there was nothing there. My jeans were shredded, and blood trickled from the tattered fabric scraps. I tried moving my legs again, but they would not obey my command. I flipped onto my stomach and began dragging myself by my arms across the frozen ground. I hissed. It was so cold, it stung my skin.

"Will! Will!" I cried out.

Lana let out a strangled cry. "He's over here!"

Faster, faster! I urged myself on. *Pull, drag, pull, drag.* Finally, I reached Lana and when I saw Will, I wanted to scream.

Blood, deep red and plentiful, surrounded his body.

"Liddy! Help me roll him off!" Lana pleaded.

I couldn't make sense of what she was saying.

Panic set in. "We can't move him! You'll kill him!"

"William will live. Now, help me move so I can save my brother!"

I looked, really looked this time, and just beneath Will was Shai, a perfect outline of his body pressed into the ground.

"Liddy, come on this side and we'll lift William. I need to help my brother!"

I began to army crawl and Lana gasped, "Your legs!"

Despite the pain, I bit my lip and kept moving. Something warm traveled over the top half of me, taking the bite out of the ice that had seared my skin and bones. I still felt nothing below my waist. Lana clamped her hand over her mouth.

"Lana!" Nick's voice echoed.

She held her wrist to the sky, and green sparks shot into the air like rockets. They exploded high over us and remained there, lighting the sky. A gust of wind rose up at the behest of a blue light, and the dust vanished. Nick came over to us, cradling his arm, Alex at his heels.

Tears streamed down Lana's cheeks, leaving trails along the glittering dust that painted her face. "Nick, Alex, help me move William."

They heaved and carefully placed Will on his back in a snowdrift. I watched in horror as Shai lay broken. Nick dropped to his knees at his cousin's side. He, too, lifted his wrist, and this time, sparks of royal blue replaced the green.

More of the scene revealed itself to me. Brantley held a shaking, inconsolable Charlie. I dragged myself to Will and placed my head on his chest, unable to look at Shai any longer. Will's breathing, deep and slow, let me know he was alive, and that kept me sane in the moment.

Thunder boomed in the distance. I tuned out Lana's cries and Nick's words, focusing solely on Will's breathing. More thunder clapped, closer this time. And closer. And closer.

My head grew heavy and slid off of Will's body. Warm, soft hands grasped my shoulders and gently laid me onto my back. Beautiful gray eyes stared down at me.

I furrowed my brows; she looked so familiar, and yet I could not place her.

"Hi," I said, my voice meek and froggy.

"Hello dear, I am Nicole. And who might you be?"

"I'm Liddy."

"Welcome to Cristes, Liddy. We've been waiting a very long time for you." She smiled and ran her hand softly down my face. Then everything went dark.

To be continued...

Acknowledgments

My village comes through again! Seriously, have I mentioned I have the best one ever?

My savior- You made a way and I am forever grateful. You have helped me to *get used to different*. I am beyond humbled by your grace and love.

My readers! Thank you for reading *The Witch and the Watcher*. Your time and feedback are invaluable to me. I am humbled that you have chosen to spend it on my story. Your reviews mean the world. I cannot wait to connect with you on lauradetering.com

To my CPs and Beta readers- Andrea, Luke, Sarah, and Rebecca- Thank you for taking the time. I appreciate you!

My editor, Erin- Thank you for helping to make my book baby shine. Your patience and dedication are so amazing. It has been such a pleasure getting to know you and I am so glad I now get to call you friend.

Julia- You inspire me to do my best. Thank you for making the inside of my book so pretty! Not only are you gifted, but I am beyond grateful to call you friend.

About the Author

I live in beautiful Florida with my college sweetheart and two daughters. When I'm not homeschooling my children, adulting, or writing, you can find me listening to audiobooks, chatting with friends, singing, crafting, and working on healing and training my brain and body.

In December 2017, I was struck with an invisible, neurological illness. MDDS and chronic VM have left me disabled. At times I've wanted to give up. However, my faith, coupled with the extraordinary people God has placed in my life, has given me the strength to keep going—to be a lamp for others who may find themselves alone in the dark.

Getting immersed in a good book that can inspire, offer hope, help the reader get lost in a new world, and expand the imagination has helped me through some seriously dark times and I can only hope my stories help you joyously escape as well.

lauradetering.com